M.S.

EX LIBRIS

(From the library of …)

Also by John Oehler

Tepui

Papyrus

Aphrodesia

EX LIBRIS

John Oehler

CreateSpace

This is a work of fiction. Names, characters, places, and incidents are the product of the author's imagination or are used fictitiously, and any resemblance to persons, living or dead, businesses, companies, or events is entirely coincidental.

Copyright © 2019 by John Oehler
All rights reserved

Cover design by Dorothy Oehler

ISBN - 9781689376655

PRINTED IN THE UNITED STATES OF AMERICA

Dedicated to my wife, Dorothy,

and

To the firefighters who saved Notre Dame.

The cover photo of this book shows a gargoyle atop Notre Dame cathedral. We chose it long before the horrific fire. To us, it symbolizes contemplation of difficult choices, which is a theme of the story. We were delighted to read that our chosen gargoyle survived the flames.

May the rebuilt cathedral be as glorious as its original architects intended.

ACKNOWLEDGMENTS

I am fortunate to have an insightful and ruthless group of critique partners. Their suggestions for this story ranged from "Delete comma" to "More feelings" to the ever-distressing "DIB—Do it better." In reprisal, I shall name names. Sarah Warburton, Rodney Walther, Chuck Brownman, Melissa Huckabay, Bill Stevenson, Heather Shelly, Chris Rogers, and Marcia Gerhardt.

I thank Chuck Brownman for suggesting the nature of the forbidden book that is central to this story.

I thank Rabbi Stephen Einstein for helping me with important aspects of the Pentateuch and related biblical texts. Errors in the story are, of course, mine.

Rick McLemore, now sadly deceased, helped me choreograph the hand-to-hand fight scenes.

I also thank Dorothy Stevenson, Rodney Walther, and Douglas Yazell who, as cold readers, gave me valuable suggestions for improving the "final" manuscript. And Beatrice Cartier-Yazell who helped me (successfully, I hope) with the proper use of *cher*, *chère*, etc. Again, remaining errors are mine.

Finally, and always, I could not do this without my wife, Dorothy, who married me 50+ years ago in Kathmandu, who tolerates my living in a fantasy world with my computer, and who remains the best thing that ever happened to me.

EX LIBRIS

Ex Libris
(From the library of ...)

Chapter 1

Under a moonless sky, Dan Lovel edged along a limestone outcrop until he reached the wrought-iron gate embedded in its side. Music and laughter drifted down from a party at the Mafioso's villa just up the hill. Pungent sage bushes covered the slope in between. He peered back along the pathway for any sign of the guard, then pulled the bolt cutters out of his knapsack. Only a padlocked chain secured the gate. He clamped the jaws of the cutter around one of the links. *Snap.*

Dan winced. The sound was louder than expected. He held his breath, listening for footsteps, a gun being cocked, any change in the sounds of revelry from the villa. One screw-up and a horde of armed Sicilians would descend on him like army ants on a bug.

Satisfied, at least for the moment, he creaked open the gate, slipped inside, and closed it behind him. The cave was pitch black. After several cautious steps, he caught his first confirming whiff. A sweeter, fruitier aroma than he should have smelled if the cave actually held aging wine of superior quality, instead of plonk being doctored for a major scam.

A few steps farther into the *grotta*, he switched on his flashlight. Small oak casks, stacked two high, lined either side. Walking between them, he estimated two hundred barrels. At the far end he found stronger evidence of fraud. Cardboard cartons of black licorice, mint leaves, and cheap chocolate for flavoring. A bottle of vanilla extract and a jar of plum purée, also for flavoring. A case of French Cahors for darkening the color, as it did legitimately in Bordeaux wines. Then the absolute clincher, a stack of labels bearing the Masseto name with characteristic red seal in the center.

The Mafia don hosting the party had to be either stupid, very well-connected, or extremely arrogant to run such a blatant operation on his own property.

A rough calculation told Dan he was looking at about thirty-six million dollars' worth of phony Masseto 1991. If you could find this stuff at all, real or fake, it would only be at wine auctions, where you'd pay seven hundred dollars or more for a single bottle, or in a few of the world's top restaurants, where you'd pay three times that amount.

His Robin Hood streak said, "Let the idiots with deep pockets delude themselves." But as a wine aficionado, he despised the thought of this crap hitting the market. Besides, his clients, three legitimate vintners in Tuscany whose wines had been counterfeited before, had paid for "destruction."

He checked his watch. Twenty-five minutes before the guard should come by on his next hourly round—if the guard stuck to schedule. Quickly Dan extracted two bricks of C-4 from his knapsack, placed one atop the barrels on each side of the cave, then inserted the detonators and set the timers to ten minutes. Cellphone detonation would be safer, but he couldn't trust the signal to reach this far back into a cave.

Leaving his knapsack to be destroyed with the wine, he returned to the iron gate. He was about to slip out when the crunching sound of nearby footsteps stopped him.

Nine years with the Diplomatic Security Service kicked in. He backed up to the side of the cave. As the chain previously securing the gate rattled and fell, he balled his fists. The gate squeaked open.

A single-barreled shotgun poked inside. Dan braced to strike. *C'mon, just two steps.* Precious seconds ticked away in Dan's head.

The guard's hand-held radio squawked.

Dan lunged, bashing the barrel upward and tackling the guy to the ground.

The shotgun boomed.

Dan wrenched it away and slammed his fist into the man's temple.

Another squawk on the radio, followed by someone speaking Italian.

Only four minutes left. Maybe less.

He dragged the unconscious guard outside and safely away from the entrance, then ran like hell.

He was almost to the Fiat he'd parked half a mile from the villa when he felt, more than heard, the concussion. Shouting erupted in the distance. Floodlights flashed on. As he climbed into his rental car, men came running down the road. Shotguns fired. Dan started the engine, glad to be too far away for the pellets to do any damage.

#

Two weeks after returning to his apartment in Washington, D.C., Dan was checking the mailboxes he rented at several UPS stores when he found a notice of a package awaiting his collection. He presented it to the proprietor, who brought out a heavy cardboard box sent from Tuscany.

Dan opened it at home to find a wooden box inside, cushioned in Bubble Wrap, and a note that read, *"Un bonus. Grazie."* A bonus was always appreciated. But when he pried it open, his jaw fell. Inside lay a wine lover's dream. Four bottles of genuine Masseto 1991.

Chapter 2

Three months later

Dan turned up the collar of his parka against a frigid December morning and walked past the concrete letters, five feet high, announcing ZOO. He saw no one else at this early hour, just thirty minutes after the eight o'clock opening, and was the happier for it. Generally speaking, he liked animals more than he liked most people, which was why he had specified Washington's National Zoo for the meeting that lay ahead.

Strolling along Olmsted Walk, one of the major pathways, he scanned the foliage on either side for anything suspicious and listened for sounds that might not belong to the resident creatures. Nothing unusual—until his ears picked up the rapid footfalls of rubber-soled shoes approaching from behind. He moved to the right, gripped the Walther PPQ in his pocket, and turned to see who was coming. A jogger in sweatshirt and track shorts. Asian female, late twenties or early thirties, five-foot-five, with black shoulder-length hair and a slightly pigeon-toed left foot.

She glanced at him once as she ran past.

Once was enough to confirm ID, if she was looking for him. But she kept on running and soon rounded the right turn at the far end of the path.

Near as Dan knew, he was not currently in anyone's crosshairs. But the jogger could be waiting for him around the turn, "tying her shoe" or concealed in the bushes. He moved to the left side of the path and walked around the curve without loosening his grip on the pistol. Only when he spotted her two hundred yards in the distance, still jogging, did he finally relax.

Turning full-circle, he saw no one else and continued past one of the elephant exhibits.

You chose this life, he reminded himself. And all choices had consequences. For the federal government, he had protected VIPs. Now independent, he retrieved stolen art and destroyed forgeries of all sorts. Both jobs were satisfying, but a consequence was that a lot of people wished him dead.

He reached the Great Ape House as an employee was unlocking its doors. Before entering, Dan looked around for Geoff Fairchild, his ex-boss who'd asked for this meeting. No one coming from either direction, which was fine. They weren't supposed to meet until nine-fifteen.

Grateful for a few minutes alone with these magnificent animals, Dan crossed the viewing area and perched beside one of the floor-to-ceiling glass windows. On the other side, several lowland gorillas preened each other or swung in rope hammocks or climbed around the habitat's artificial trees. The big silverback reclined in the background munching leaves, but an adolescent male bounded up to the window and sat to stare at Dan. When Dan pressed his palm to the glass, the gorilla did likewise. Its eyes looked human, inquisitive. A wave of sadness tightened Dan's throat. This animal's entire species was critically endangered. And in that moment, he gave silent thanks to Jean-Pierre.

In the nine years Dan had worked for the Diplomatic Security Service—five of them undercover—he had encountered a menagerie of characters who existed on the societal fringe, none more marginal than Jean-Pierre. The bald former sergeant in the French Foreign Legion now lived in Nairobi and spent his most fruitful hours killing poachers who preyed on elephants, rhinos, and other endangered animals. Legally, what he did was murder. But it was murder for a higher cause.

For the gorillas here at the zoo—even though they had no say in the matter—living in captivity was the tradeoff for not having to worry about hunters.

He felt, more than heard, the exhibit's door open.

"There you are," intoned the Bronx-accented voice of Geoff Fairchild. Always a snazzy dresser, he strode in wearing a smartly tailored wool-and-cashmere overcoat and a leathery "power" fragrance by Paco Rabanne. "Communing with your kin?"

"Just having a word with your mother," Dan replied. "She says you never call, never write."

Geoff cracked a grin that, thanks to Botox injections, didn't crinkle the skin around his eyes. "Pressures of work. You know how it goes."

"What I don't know is why we're having this meeting. Care to enlighten me?"

"Straight to the point, as always. I sure have missed you."

"I haven't missed you." That wasn't really true. Geoff had been his best friend, maybe his only friend. Over their years together in the DSS, they'd had big ups and downs but, in the end, Geoff had always been there when Dan needed a sympathetic ear.

"Sure you have," Geoff said. "Why else would you be here?" With another smile he pointed toward one of the benches in the middle of the viewing area. Over the years, his hair had grayed at the temples in a patrician sort of way that matched his self-assured carriage. After they'd seated themselves, Geoff said, "I heard a rumor. Seems, when Jesus was being crucified, one of your people stole the fourth nail, which was why they had to nail Jesus's feet with just one. Any truth to that?"

By "your people," Geoff obviously meant Gypsies. He enjoyed poking fun at Dan's ancestry, especially the notion that all Roma were thieves. The story about the nail was a fairytale told to children. Dan finished it for him. "Of course it's true. Jesus thanked the man and blessed our whole race for the kindness." Dan paused then added, "You can bow down, if you care to receive my benediction."

"No wonder I love you. You always find a way out."

"And now?"

Geoff looked around the room, where they were still the only visitors. "And now, I have a curious message to pass on. One of your old targets has requested your help."

Dan had always thought it bass-ackwards that the Service referred to people they protected as "targets." The rationale was that they were presumed to be targets of someone and were always treated as such. "I don't work for you anymore. Get one of your minions to handle it."

"Ah, if only I could. But she specifically asked for you."

She? Barely a handful of Dan's many targets had been female, mostly snotty wives of ambassadors or presidents. "No interest."

"Not even for Astrid Desmarais?"

Whoa. That was different. An image flashed into Dan's head—shoving the elegant Parisian behind a pillar at her hotel entrance as he fired three rounds into the chest of her would-be assassin. Her horrified face as he hustled her into the elevator and up to her room, then locked the door behind them.

Geoff's pleased expression suggested he was following Dan's thoughts. "You slept with her, didn't you? That night after you saved her life. C'mon, you can tell me."

Dan had *not* slept with her. Nor had the thought occurred to him. His job had been to protect her, and he'd spent the night sitting in an armchair in her room, pistol by his side, in case the dead man had cohorts. "My report was accurate."

Geoff shrugged. "If you say so."

What Dan said didn't really matter. DSS scuttlebutt was like the internet. Once an idea was out there, no matter how erroneous, it never went away. "What does she want?"

"So, you *are* interested."

"Just asking."

A banging noise made them both look toward the pane of another enclosure, where a female gorilla was playing with a plastic barrel, hurling it against the walls.

"Back to the matter at hand," Dan said.

"I don't really know what she wants. I'm a go-between here. Dot gov is not involved."

Yeah, sure. "Then why you?"

"She didn't know how to get in touch with you directly."

That was probably true. Given his former and current lines of work, Dan went to considerable length to maintain an anonymous existence—apartment, car, credit cards all in phony names. Jobs these days came to him by word of mouth via prior clients. "So once again, the matter at hand?"

"And once again, I don't know. I'm just doing you a favor."

"Wait." A change in air pressure told Dan the door had opened. "Someone's coming."

Three seconds later, two kids charged in with squeals of excitement, trailed by a woman pleading, "Not so loud."

As the kids, presumably brother and sister, ran to press their noses against one of the windows, Geoff said, "You knew they were coming before they arrived, didn't you? I swear, you have the sharpest senses of anyone I ever met."

"Inherited from my people," Dan quipped. "So, what's this favor you're doing me?"

"Ah, that. How about a vacation in the Cayman Islands?" Geoff handed over an envelope. "Ritz-Carlton, no less. Are you sure you didn't sleep with her?"

"I think I would have remembered." Dan opened the envelope to find a first-class ticket for two days from now, a reservation at the Ritz-Carlton, and a handwritten note saying, "Please meet me" above Astrid's signature and her own arrival time an hour and a half later. He frowned at Geoff. "Why?"

"No idea."

"Guess."

"Still no idea I'd bet on. But I expect you to enlighten me when you return."

Although Dan refrained from mentioning it, there was no return ticket.

#

In his Georgetown apartment, Dan lit the logs in the fireplace, then poured himself a cup of coffee and settled back on the leather couch to ponder the strangeness of this whole proposition.

The one-way ticket could have been an oversight, but he doubted it. Astrid was a details person, formerly a big shot in the French finance ministry and now a top executive at the World Bank. Maybe the length of their meeting was uncertain in her mind. But if so, she could have sent him an open-ended return. Or maybe she expected him to travel somewhere else from the Caymans and didn't yet want to reveal the destination. That would be strangest of all.

And why Grand Cayman Island? The World Bank was headquartered right here in Washington, D.C. There were any number of places they could meet. Possibilities? She had to go there on business, a private sit-down with a representative of some foreign country that had requested a World Bank loan. Or she was just taking a pre-Christmas vacation and thought he would appreciate getting together in the sun. The Caymans were definitely more pleasant this time of year than frigid, overcast Washington. But neither of those possibilities made much sense.

Most perplexing was why meet at all? He got up, poured himself another cup of coffee, and added a splash of Irish whiskey. He wasn't going anywhere today, so a little noontime alcohol wouldn't hurt.

As he sat again, he draped an arm over the back of the couch, half-expecting his Great Dane, Heidi, to nudge it with her cold nose, then lay her massive head on his shoulder. Man, he missed her. The most faithful female in his life. She would have enjoyed a taste of his Irish coffee as much as she did the splash of Masseto he had put in her bowl. But old age had taken her six weeks ago, and he wasn't sure he would ever get over the loss. Their loping runs in Rock Creek Park. Their walks through the Mall, her head at the height of his waist. Her slobbery kisses that kept his face "exfoliated."

He choked up at the memory of carrying her into the vet for her very last injection. It was the most recent time Geoff had been there to console him. Occasions like that cancelled out a lot of the despicable things Geoff had done before.

Dan blew out a long, miserable breath. Reminiscing about Heidi was not what he needed at the moment. What he needed was to focus on this strange request from Astrid and decide what to do about it.

Downing a slug of coffee, he pictured the lady—tall, slender, attractive in that way of French women who aged gracefully. He hadn't seen her, had barely even thought of her, for eight years. So, whatever the reason for her request, it had to be rooted in the harrowing episode outside her hotel. Or its aftermath.

He replayed his mental videotape.

She had held a senior finance position in the French government and was in New York for a UN conference. He'd accompanied her for three days without incident. But on that scorching afternoon in mid-July, when they climbed out of the Town Car in front of her hotel, he noticed a man in a heavy jacket. During a heat wave? Dan zeroed in on the guy's face. Hatred in the eyes, a gold hoop earring, the distinctive Basque nose bump. The man shoved his way to the front of the thin crowd. He pulled a pistol from his jacket pocket, a French MAB, .25 caliber. The barrel came up, but Dan's came up faster.

It turned out the dead man was a member of the Basque separatist group, ETA, and was wanted in both France and Spain for three assassinations of government officials.

In her hotel room that night, Astrid had drunk half a bottle of Pernod while huddled on the bed, her back to the headboard, her knees drawn up, the bedspread wrapped around her as she gushed out her life history. Finally, frayed nerves drained her, and she fell asleep.

The next morning, Dan and two security men from the French embassy escorted her onto an Air France flight back to Paris, on which the Frenchmen accompanied her.

And that was it, aside from a letter she sent one week later thanking him profusely.

So why contact him now, after all this time?

Then there was Geoff Fairchild, with his "Dot gov is not involved." If that were true, he could have placed Astrid's envelope in another one and mailed it to Dan's apartment. Geoff was one of the few people who knew the address. So, an ulterior motive? Dan wouldn't put it past the guy who, despite abundant evidence to the contrary, fancied himself a master manipulator. In reality, Geoff's goal in life was higher status—a seat at more exclusive tables, a bigger slurp from the government trough. To that end, he more than once had concocted dramatic schemes that jeopardized agents in the field. Those failures in judgment, later artfully concealed, had been a major factor in Dan's decision to leave the Service.

On the other hand, Dan saw no way that conveying an invitation from Astrid could possibly benefit Geoff's ambitions. So why had he done it? What was in it for him?

The whole thing set off alarm bells. Dan took another swallow of his Irish coffee. If it weren't for the fact that he liked and respected Astrid, he would have run her envelope through the shredder.

But the sheer weirdness intrigued him. And if he wanted to get answers, there was only one way to get them.

Chapter 3

Unfortunately, Astrid had sent the plane ticket in Dan's real name, which obliged him to use his personal passport. It made him feel exposed, traceable. As always, however, he carried two other passports, both non-American. An advantage of having a dark complexion and black hair was that he could pass for a wide range of ethnicities. That was one reason the DSS had tapped him to work undercover.

After clearing Immigration at the airport on Grand Cayman, he walked out into hot, thick air and chose the shabbiest taxi in the queue, a Mazda sedan with rust showing through its latest paint job. When the driver climbed out, Dan instantly liked him, a lanky islander in shorts and T-shirt, with a gap in his grin where an incisor was missing.

"I take your bag, sir?"

"Thanks, but no need."

Suddenly the cabby from the head of the queue stomped back to them, protesting that Dan should go with him.

"I know this man," Dan lied. "We are old friends."

"I know him also." The second driver shot a threatening glare at the man Dan had chosen.

Was it the lost fare or a more nefarious motive that drove this guy? It wouldn't be the first time an adversary had tried to kidnap him via a taxi driver. To test him, Dan peeled off two twenty-dollar bills and handed them over as a gesture of apology. Then he pointed at a man and woman pushing two cartsful of luggage toward the fellow's cab. "Don't let them get away."

As the cabby he'd mollified dashed off to intercept the new arrivals, Dan's driver said, "Thank you. He is a bully."

"Will you be okay later?"

"I think no problem. My brother is more bigger than him."

Now headed north up Seven Mile Beach, Dan gazed out at the occasional views of sugary sand and a pale blue sea, views that flashed past between more beachfront hotels than he remembered. The one time he'd been here before, years ago and with his then-girlfriend, they had come for the scuba diving. Grand Cayman was as famous for it as for its secret bank accounts. Twice in his DSS career, he had nailed crooks with money-laundering accounts in similar offshore havens.

With the A/C wheezing ineffectively, Dan rolled down his window. The air smelled like hot cement, thanks to the limestone bedrock. Standing water flanked the road in several places, a consequence of the whole island being basically flat. Clumps of scrub trees along the roadside testified to the nutrient-poor soil.

Only luxury hotels could afford to maintain plantings of the exotic trees and big-flowered bushes tourists associated with a tropical paradise. They were islands within the island.

His taxi turned into the curving, palm-lined driveway of the queen bee among these artificial paradises, the Ritz-Carlton. Stopping under the entrance portico, the driver announced, "We are here, sir." Dan tipped him well and took his business card. He liked the man and his infectious grin.

Inside, he was directed to a private check-in desk where it took barely three minutes to register. *Kinda cool.* As Dan thanked the lady, a middle-aged white man wearing a dark suit and a British tie—stripes down to the right—introduced himself in a BBC accent as Dan's personal assistant, on call at any hour. He escorted Dan to a private elevator that took them to the seventh floor and Dan's two-bedroom suite, where "kinda cool" became "wow."

The place was twice the size of his apartment and way more luxurious. An ocean-view terrace, a full kitchen, a dining table that sat eight, a curved bar with four upholstered stools, and a master bath apparently intended for parties. Not to mention the iced champagne and a bowl of fresh fruit waiting for him on a coffee table.

Why such luxury? Three possibilities came to mind. As a major force in global finance, Astrid Desmarais had become accustomed to plush accommodation and felt it would be stingy to put him up in anything less. Or she was trying to impress him for reasons unknown. Or, least likely, she thought she was saddling him with a debt of gratitude he could only repay by agreeing to do something she had in mind.

None made much sense. In actuality, he would have preferred a smaller room.

Especially now, as he began checking the place with an HP calculator that had been modified to detect electronic bugs. It took twenty full minutes, due to the size of the suite and the number of furnishings. Thankfully, neither the suite nor the verandah produced a response.

Reassured, he changed into cotton slacks and a short-sleeved shirt, then took the elevator down to the lobby to nurse a gin and tonic while waiting for Astrid.

She had been Madame Desmarais until the assassination attempt. In her room afterwards, she had insisted he call her Astrid. He liked that name, and the woman.

Shortly before one-thirty, she walked through the front doors looking as elegant as ever. Her short hair, now generously streaked with silver, seemed to enhance her dignity. He was about to rise and greet her when, close behind Astrid, came a second woman. Early thirties, chin-length auburn hair, and facial features that unmistakably proclaimed "daughter." A warning pulsed through him, the kind he got whenever there was an unforeseen development.

The younger woman followed Astrid to the private check-in desk, her stride as athletic and confident as her mother's. Unlike her mother, she had a three-inch scar on her left triceps and trailed a faint scent of Ma Griffe, one of the few floral fragrances he liked.

When a man in suit and tie, a portlier version of Dan's personal assistant, came forward to take the women's bags, Dan got up. "Astrid."

"Dan!" She smiled broadly and planted an air kiss on each of his cheeks. "I'm so happy to see you. Thank you for coming." She drew the other woman forward. "I'd like you to meet my daughter, Martine. Martine, this is Mr. Lovel."

Martine shook hands with him. But her smile was forced. Either she didn't want to be here, or she regarded meeting him as an obligation to get out of the way, like a person of zero interest she might meet at a party.

Fine with him. To Astrid he said, "Thank you for the flight and the fantastic room. Both of them were huge surprises."

"It was the least I could do to thank you for that … trouble in New York."

The look in her eyes seemed sincere. But the "trouble" was eight years ago, so there was clearly another reason. One he was sure he'd soon find out, as they agreed to meet in thirty minutes for a late lunch at the poolside lounge.

He waited for the elevator doors to close behind the two women, then found the lounge, a place called Bar Jack, located between the pool and the beach. He strolled around, conducting a recon before securing a pair of umbrella-shaded loveseats with a coffee table between them and the beach just feet away. Not his kind of beach, with its waiter-tended chaise lounges lined up in rows. But if you came here to be pampered, you were going to get your wish.

Astrid arrived right on time, gliding up to him in a sleeveless, white, short-skirted sundress that highlighted the fitness of her arms and calves. He recalled from her old DSS file that she had been a candidate for France's Olympic gymnastics team about forty years ago. Obviously, she'd stayed in shape.

He stood until she'd seated herself, then he looked for Martine.

"She sends her regrets," Astrid explained, evidently sensing his thoughts. "She's exhausted after flying from Paris."

Secretly relieved that this first substantive meeting would be with Astrid only, he sat in the loveseat opposite her. When she turned her head to look at the sea, her face struck him as a mature version of Vermeer's *Girl with the Pearl Earring*. It suggested a quiet, unself-conscious poise that had not been evident in her hotel room after the assassination attempt.

"So," he said, "you're both here on vacation?"

"In part."

"What's the other part?"

"You don't waste time," she replied with one of those faintly seductive smiles only a Frenchwoman could bestow.

A waiter fronted up with menus. After a quick perusal, they ordered two of the bar's signature piña coladas, plus a spinach salad for her and a mahi-mahi sandwich for him. When the waiter left, Dan said, "We can chat for a while first, if you prefer."

"No. I'm not comfortable with small talk, and you deserve an explanation." She leaned forward. "I have a favor to ask you. It's somewhat dangerous, and you can refuse, of course."

Warning flags flew up again. A favor was one thing. "Dangerous" was quite another. Still, she had piqued his curiosity. "I can't refuse an offer I haven't heard."

Their drinks arrived, and they each took a sip through their straws. Creamy, and not too much rum.

She looked around, plainly not realizing that his eyes and ears were constantly on the lookout for eavesdroppers or anything else irregular. "There are some books in a monastery in Prague. If you can recover them, it would help to rectify many wrongs."

Straight out of left field. Astrid wanted books? "By recover, I assume you mean steal."

"That's an ugly word."

Their waiter approached, plates in hand. Dan waited for him to leave. "What's so important about these books? And why me?"

"You, because I trust you." The faint smile returned briefly before her expression again became serious. "The books go back to Napoleon. You know about the Napoleonic Wars?"

"Early eighteen hundreds. He conquered a number of countries."

"And plundered them all." She shook her head. "Not plundered exactly. He extracted tribute, in the form of artworks. He had a man named Denon travelling with him who supervised a group called the Commission of Arts and Sciences. They chose the art to be confiscated and taken back to Paris."

Astrid took another sip of her drink but left her salad untouched. "Napoleon wanted to expand the collections in the Louvre, to make the Louvre an expression of France's greatness. His greatness."

"It's a world-class museum," Dan acknowledged neutrally.

"Founded in theft!"

Her raised voice surprised him. This clearly was a matter that touched her deeply. "Isn't that the way of many museums? I mean, the Elgin Marbles are Greek, for instance, looted from the Parthenon. But they're on display in the British Museum."

"The Louvre is worse." Fire lit her eyes. "Much worse. Napoleon's greed is the backbone of its fame."

He thought a moment. "You said, 'rectify many wrongs.' Are you suggesting that the Louvre should return the artworks Napoleon confiscated?"

"Every one of them. What he did was a crime, a black spot on France's reputation. It must be redressed."

Dan took a bite of his sandwich and chewed slowly, intrigued at how impassioned she seemed about stolen art, a subject that happened to be dear to him, also. A coincidence?

Apparently calmer now, she forked in a bite of her salad.

Dan set down his sandwich. "What's the connection between Napoleon and these books? Were they part of the tribute someone paid him?"

"Much more important." Again, she looked around. Then she lowered her voice. "They are a catalogue of everything in the Louvre, as of eighteen-eleven. Originally there were many copies, four volumes each. But nearly all were destroyed by Napoleon because they showed that he had … I suppose we must say 'plundered,' all of the most important pieces during his military campaigns."

"And public knowledge of this would have been an embarrassment to him?"

"A very large embarrassment." She pushed aside the straw in her glass and took a long drink of the piña colada. "They made the emperor seem like a common thief."

"But this monastery in Prague has a copy."

"One of only two that survive. Napoleon's wife, Josephine,

visited the monastery in eighteen-twelve and gave them a set, among several other gifts."

"Why would she do that if the other copies were being destroyed?"

"It was before that decision was made."

So, Josephine was not acting against the emperor's will. "Where's the other set?"

"The Louvre keeps it in an underground vault."

That was the age-old problem with destroying evidence—you could rarely destroy it all.

A breeze wafted the unappetizing odor of coconut-scented sunblock from guests lying around the pool. Seeing Astrid had little interest in her salad, and not being terribly hungry himself, he asked, "Would you care to go for a walk on the beach?"

"That would be lovely."

He recalled now how uneasy she was around groups of people. He'd had to hustle to keep up with her each time she left the UN building and ploughed through reporters to reach her car. It must take a lot of internal strength, he mused, to cope with meeting dignitaries in her World Bank position.

Astrid signed the check on their way out, then removed her sandals and carried them as they strolled past three rows of chaise lounges where the hotel's guests glistened in the sauna-like air. Dan's cotton shirt was already sticking to him. Turning left toward an unoccupied stretch of seashore, he walked on the sand in his deck shoes while she splashed along through ankle-deep water. "Your next question," she said, "is what will I do with the books."

"It's kind of obvious. They contain a complete record of everything Napoleon stole."

"Exactly. With them, the artworks can be identified and returned to their rightful owners." She stopped and faced him. "Your grandparents would approve."

Grandparents? He thought back to that long night in her hotel room when she'd droned on about her background before asking him about his. Apparently, his mental videotape had failed to record his response. "What do my grandparents have to do with anything?"

"You told me they were art dealers in Berlin and lost everything to the Nazis, because your grandfather had epilepsy."

"I told you that?" Astrid must have been persuasive in drawing him out. Hardly anyone knew that much about his family. "What else did I say?"

"You don't remember?"

Maybe it was the stress of having just shot a man to death. It was, after all, his first kill. But his memory was patchy, at best. "Not as well as you seem to."

"You said that during the T-Four atrocity, your grandparents sent their son to Madrid with as many of their best pieces as he could carry. He married a Gypsy woman. They sold off the artworks and tried to use the money to help your grandmother escape. But it was too late. Then came the purges under Franco." She paused. "You really don't remember telling me this?"

Bits and pieces came back to him, which made him wonder why in the world he'd been so open with a woman he barely knew.

"You're a private man," she said, reaching to squeeze his hand. "But that was an extraordinary day. I think we both said more than we intended."

Fuzzy images on his mental videotape began to sharpen. In her hotel room that night, while he sat in the armchair and Astrid huddled on the bed, she had spilled her guts then grilled him like an Inquisitor about his background. He was well-trained in resisting interrogation, but she was his "target," not his adversary. With soft light from the table lamp illuminating her profile, he had indeed mentioned Hitler's T-4 operation against people deemed "mentally unfit." His epileptic grandfather was hauled off and sent to a gas chamber the next day. His grandmother, a Sephardic Jew, simply "disappeared," supposedly after Hermann Goering walked into their gallery and liked what he saw. As to the son and his Gypsy wife—Dan's parents—they ultimately fled Spain and settled in New York, then Seattle, where Dan was born.

Despite the heat, he shuddered at his weakness. At least he had confided in someone he trusted. But never again would he let his guard down that far. It was an invitation to find frailties that could be exploited.

Which, it occurred to him, Astrid might be doing right now. He resumed walking with her along the water's edge. "Do you think that helping you return stolen art to its rightful owners would be some sort of surrogate for returning confiscated art to my grandparents?"

"Would it?"

Suspicion confirmed. He bit his cheek and smacked himself mentally for not anticipating this turn of events. He had never known his grandparents, had seen only one photo of them, and would not be swayed by appeals to the injustices they'd suffered.

Astrid stopped again and turned to him. "Dan, I need your help. Please."

Don't be a sucker, he told himself. But her pleading eyes and tone of voice tugged at his conscience. In spite of her tactics, her goal was ... noble.

He glanced up and down the beach. Two kids splashing in the water about a hundred feet ahead. No one in the other direction, except on lounge chairs. Guardedly he said, "Four books. That's all you want?"

"There might be a fifth one." For an instant, her eyes bored into his. "If you can find it."

Never mind the eyes. Just get the job straight. "Okay, five books."

"Yes, that's all I'm asking."

On the possibility—possibility only—that he might accept, he switched from what to how. "Do you know where they're kept in this monastery?"

"In a small locked room behind an iron grate in the library. It's where they store the volumes they consider to be forbidden."

"Forbidden meaning …?"

"Alchemy, heresy, anything not doctrinal. Apparently, the friars chose to seal them up, rather than destroy them. For centuries, only the abbot has possessed the key."

A screenful of question marks scrolled through his head. Buying time to sort them out, he took off his deck shoes, rolled up his pant legs, and shuffled through the warm, lapping water on the seaward side of her. First question. "You know this how?"

"Empress Josephine's gifts are no secret. Nor is the locked collection of forbidden books."

"Why not just ask for them to be returned?"

"I have. I sent several formal requests. But the abbot refused. He wouldn't even give permission to examine them in his library." A sheen of perspiration highlighted her collarbones. "He said they are 'prohibited,' and underlined it three times."

"Perceived duty versus reason."

"A medieval duty that has no place in modern times."

Dan reflected a moment on whether he would steal back art that had been confiscated from his grandparents. The answer was yes. But in this case … "Let's say I could get them for you. Do you honestly think the Louvre would be willing to part with the looted pieces?"

"The atmosphere in France has become, as you would say, 'politically correct.' If the Louvre refuses to do it quietly, public disclosure will force them."

The sun was halfway through its downward arc, shining straight into her face. He took a step to his left to shade her with his body and caught the same scent of her skin that he'd smelled in her hotel room. An apprehensive female scent that must intoxicate her lovers.

Pushing it out of his mind, he said, "The danger you mentioned is getting caught in the monastery?"

"That, yes. But there is also something else." She stepped closer, almost uncomfortably close. "As in your country, France has a powerful, xenophobic, right wing. If they knew you were bringing the catalogues back to Paris, and especially if they knew why, they would do everything possible to stop you. In their view, your intent would be to rob the nation and disperse its treasures into the Third World."

An unwelcome twist. "I assume they'd be armed."

She lowered her eyes, then raised them again. "Dan, you don't have to do this. But if anyone can, I believe it's you."

Oh, nicely played. *It's okay, Dan, if you're a coward. Crush my heart. I'll understand.*

No, that was being too harsh on her. Stripped of emotion, all she'd done was inform him that it could be a two-pronged problem, stealing the books and maybe needing to elude a bunch of armed zealots. Unless ... "Do these 'patriots' know about the mission you're proposing? About me?"

"I don't see how they could." She backed up a step, putting a bit more breathing space between them. "But their networks are tuned to detecting all sorts of plots, real and imagined. I just wanted you to know."

Okay, so a lethal threat from the French right wing was a possibility but not a probability. He'd dealt with worse odds. The key was to anticipate and avoid. And he could now anticipate. "I'll take that risk, *if* I take the job. But I need to do a lot of research first on the monastery."

Her face brightened. "You don't. Martine has been there and studied it thoroughly."

Oh? That explained her daughter's presence here. But it didn't help. "Telling me what she saw is not enough. I need to—"

"She will do more than tell you. She will show you."

"What?"

"Martine is going with you."

Chapter 4

Feeling dirty, Astrid returned to her suite, found Martine asleep in the second bedroom and, with shaking hands, poured herself half a glass of Pernod. She added water, turning the liqueur white, and carried her drink out onto the verandah. A shower might have been better, but it wouldn't wash away her sense of griminess. She'd been less than honest with Dan.

She took a long swallow of her Pernod, savoring the strong anise flavor that soothed her more than the gently lapping waves below. Yes, the Louvre volumes were very important. But recovering the fifth book, the one she'd been careful to bring up offhandedly, was absolutely crucial. If it fell into the wrong hands, it could mean global financial meltdown, if not all-out war.

Of course, Christophe didn't think so. He thought it was all a joke. No wonder French intelligence, and specifically the Direction Générale de la Sécurité Extérieure, had failed to anticipate so many terrorist attacks, failed to foresee fateful regime changes. They acquired data but could not extrapolate it beyond the ends of their noses, unless it was economic data. At that, they excelled, which was how she first met Christophe.

As if she needed a reminder, the sparkling blue sea mimicked his eyes. It was his eyes, more than his smile or the way his fingertips caressed her, that had lured her into his bed—and kept her coming back for five passionate months before they agreed to part and merely remain friends.

In truth, she didn't mind leaving him. It was always best to kiss goodbye before the bickering started, then the shouting. One look at the finger where her wedding ring once glittered confirmed it. In fact, for long stretches of her life she had lived contentedly alone.

Still, she enjoyed her dinners with Christophe whenever she returned to Paris. Knowing she hated crowds, he always chose small neighborhood restaurants where they could speak freely about the secret things they'd each learned since their last tête-à-tête. Which countries were in a precarious financial situation, which extremist groups were gaining ground. More often, they shared humorous tidbits like the kitschy excesses or minor embarrassments of odious despots. Entertaining but inconsequential things.

Until the last time, when he'd unwittingly stunned her.

She could see them now. In a working-class bistro with superb cassoulet and a vin ordinaire that took some getting used to, Christophe mentioned an interview on Italian television with a Vatican librarian. One particular segment of the interview, barely two minutes long, amused him to the extent that he brought along a transcript to share the fun.

But as she read it, a cold claw gripped her.

"Are you okay?" he asked.

"This is horrifying."

"It's a stupid old book. The only thing horrifying is how much blood religious nuts would shed to get their hands on it." He tipped back the rest of his wine. "I say, let them kill each other."

What he failed to grasp was that, if the book came to light, "killing each other" could escalate into war between Arab states and Israel. And if Israel's survival became threatened, it could mean a nuclear war that sucked in the world's superpowers. Wheels had spun in her head, gears turning like the insides of a slot machine, offering almost no chance of coming up winner.

Christophe reached across the table to place a hand on hers. "*Ma chérie*, I'm sorry if I upset you."

She needed to think, to ponder the ramifications that obviously hadn't occurred to him and his DGSE colleagues. She held up the transcript. "May I keep this?"

"Why? It's nothing important."

"I just find it curious," she lied.

With a shrug he replied, "If you like."

As Christophe had done in the bistro, Astrid now polished off her drink. She was about to pour another when Martine came out, rubbing her eyes.

"How did your meeting go with … Don?"

"Dan," Astrid corrected. "He agreed to consider it. I don't think he likes the idea of you going with him."

"He'll have to adjust. He'd never find the books on his own."

That attitude had to go. They needed Dan, and whatever hardheaded arrogance Martine felt or wanted to project had no place in the negotiations. "Be nice to him tonight."

She cocked an eyebrow. "Nice, meaning …?"

"Polite." *And get rid of the innuendo.* Martine was a so-called modern girl, an occasionally unsettling consequence of her father's genes. "You're intelligent, you speak English better than I do. You've been there. Just don't give him any reason to reject this mission." Astrid glanced at her watch. "We'll meet for dinner in two hours."

"Two hours? That's barbaric. It's not even six o'clock yet."

"It's what he asked for."

She rolled her eyes. "He 'd better be worth it."

When Martine left to take a bath, Astrid stretched out on one of the couches. Dan *would* be worth it. Not only was he quick as lightning, but he was also smart, fearless, and more observant of details than any other person she knew. He had even spotted the Basque nose of her would-be assassin in New York.

Most important, in the event of trouble, she felt certain he would do everything to protect her only child.

But he was also secretive, or had become so. No amount of effort had turned up any trace of him when she'd tried to approach him directly about the books. Closing her eyes, she felt a moment of pride at her solution. As with deadlocks in financial negotiations, she had appealed to higher authority, in this case one Geoffrey Fairchild. Now a deputy director of the Diplomatic Security Service, he was the man who had originally introduced her to Dan with, "You can count on him to ensure your safety."

That time, Fairchild had been all smiles and warm handshakes. This time, when she'd asked how to find Dan, he'd hedged his answer by proposing a lunch meeting at one of Washington's more exclusive clubs. Was there a problem, she'd wondered, or was it simply a case of not divulging anything about a government agent over the phone?

She smiled now at her first impression of that meeting. In a private room at the club, Fairchild ordered champagne and recommended the foie gras to start, a rather obvious attempt to impress.

Then his tradecraft revealed itself. Over main courses, he skillfully probed deeper into her reasons for wanting to meet Dan. She played along, trying not to reveal more than was absolutely necessary. But Fairchild was good. He knew he had the advantage and seemed to relish bending her to his will. Only when she capitulated, told him about the Italian TV interview, and finally showed him the transcript, did he stop devouring his lobster.

He spent a minute in silent contemplation, then lifted the champagne out of its ice bucket and, when she covered her flute with her hand, emptied the bottle into his own glass. "Dan left us several years ago. He now works freelance. Quite lucratively, I gather." This last comment was delivered with a hint of envy. "He's in the business of retrieving stolen art and destroying counterfeits."

At last, some information. Information that raised her hopes. "Then maybe he would be interested."

"It's possible." Fairchild jammed the champagne bottle, neck-first, back into the ice bucket. "But he's half-Jewish. So, I wouldn't divulge the nature of that book."

This comment, delivered with authority, was the reason she'd been circumspect with Dan this afternoon. The mission was too important to risk hesitation for religious reasons.

"I also think it best," Fairchild had added, "that Dan not know we have discussed this. I'll do what I can to recruit him for you, but since leaving us he's become rather antagonistic toward the Service. I'm sure you've had similar experiences with employees who left the World Bank."

She had not. But then the World Bank was not a clandestine organization. Probably Christophe would have agreed with Fairchild. Which was good enough for her.

Despite her continuing discomfort at having been less than open with Dan, what mattered now was that Fairchild's plan had worked. Dan was here and willing to listen.

"Daydreaming?" Martine asked. She stood there with wet hair and a towel wrapped around her. "The sun's down. An evening with your Sir Galahad awaits. Shouldn't you be getting ready?"

#

Annoyed at Astrid's insistence that her daughter accompany him—"guide" him, for God's sake—Dan had spent two hours on a computer in the hotel's nearly-vacant Club Lounge, chewing on an unlit cigar and memorizing everything he could find about the monastery and the city of Prague.

No way would he walk into a situation without foreknowledge of what to expect, what to do if something went wrong, and how to get out.

Plus, he always worked alone. Having to worry about another person could jeopardize them both. Especially if that person had no helpful skills, which described Martine perfectly.

He'd checked her out on three of the professional investigator sites he subscribed to. Aside from no criminal record, the results were uninspiring. Martine, a thirty-three-year-old childless divorcée with degrees in ancient languages from Oxford and Yale, was currently employed in the Middle East Antiquities Department of the Louvre. In other words, an academic with no discernible experience in undercover activities. *Guide him? Not going to happen.*

The whole proposition grated on his better judgment. Only his respect for Astrid, and admittedly the thought of his ancestors nodding their approval, had kept him from refusing her outright. Instead, he had promised his decision in the morning, after tonight's dinner. He anticipated there'd be a falling out between himself and Astrid—a scene that hurt just to think about—followed by his catching the next flight back to Washington.

Unless he could convince Astrid that Martine should stay home.

He tossed his gnawed cigar into a wastebasket and went back to his suite. Thanks to the one request he'd given his "personal assistant," the slacks Dan had worn on the beach now hung freshly pressed in a closet. Ice in the champagne bucket had been replaced. The sheers had been drawn across the sliding glass doors to his verandah, presumably to diffuse the glare of the setting sun, which had now sunk below the horizon.

He showered, then spread out naked on his bed. Dinner would be early, a concession Astrid had made so he and Martine could talk as long as necessary. She'd suggested one of the hotel's restaurants, a five-star place called Blue.

No. *Let's throw a monkey wrench into the works.* Dan sat up, thinking an unexpected or uncertain situation might fluster Martine and convince Astrid that her daughter would be more of a burden to him than an asset. Local food and local transport might fit the bill.

From the drawer in his bedside table he pulled out a phonebook. Last time he'd been here, his favorite dish had been sea turtle. He found the restaurant where he and his girlfriend had eaten, called them, and learned they still served turtle steaks. He made a reservation for three people an hour from now. Then he dug out the business card from his taxi driver, Billy.

"Thirty minutes?" Billy said. "Yes, I take you."

Dan dressed and went downstairs. When Astrid and Martine showed up, both decked out in form-fitting evening gowns, he said, "Change of plans."

Chapter 5

Pleased with the wary surprise he'd generated, Dan escorted Astrid and Martine out the front doors of their hotel to where Billy, in cargo shorts and a Led Zeppelin T-shirt, stood grinning beside his well-worn Mazda.

"Ladies, you are welcome," Billy enthused and opened the rear door. "Please."

Astrid shot Dan a look. Martine smiled faintly.

Hoping the two elegantly dressed women noticed the dent in the rear quarter panel, Dan climbed into the front passenger seat. Over his shoulder, he said, "I think you'll like this restaurant. They have great turtle steaks."

"Sea turtles are endangered," Astrid told him as Billy's cab rattled off into the night. "It's illegal to hunt them."

"To hunt, yes. But not to farm. There's a sea turtle farm right here on the island. Correct, Billy? There's a sea turtle farm?"

"Yes, sir. But is close now."

"Never mind."

Astrid let out a typically French puff, as if there were no difference between hunting and farming. Martine stared out her window.

The restaurant, a clapboard place on a back street in George Town, was jammed with locals who could have been Billy's kin. Aside from a foursome of obvious tourists sporting sunburned faces and bright new running shoes, Dan, Astrid, and Martine were the only foreigners. Definitely they were the most over-dressed.

"It smells delicious," Martine said.

So far, he was batting zero in his attempt to fluster her. But the evening was young, and she was right about the smells. As a middle-aged woman led them to the only vacant table, Dan picked out aromas of chowder, fried seafood, braised meat, and curry.

A waitress about eighteen years old brought them menus.

Astrid asked for the wine list.

"I'm sorry, but we don't serve alcohol. We have lemonade or iced tea."

"Iced tea," Martine told her without missing a beat.

Astrid shot Dan a harsh glance before following suit.

Dan made it three, and the waitress left. Turning to Martine, he said without preamble, "You work in the Louvre. So, why would you want to divest the museum of some of its most important pieces?"

"The Louvre has four hundred thousand pieces," she replied, apparently unfazed at the abruptness of his question. "Ninety percent of them are stored in the basement. It will still be a great museum if some are returned."

Thinking Astrid must have prepped her about his tendency to come straight to the point, Dan pressed on. "Your mother said many of the best works were looted."

"Not Mona Lisa. Not Venus de Milo or Winged Victory." Martine spoke the names as though they were personal friends, rather than saying *the* Mona Lisa or *the* Venus. "Tourists will keep flooding in. The endowment fund will remain in place. The museum will continue to prosper and will probably benefit from the publicity of doing what is morally correct."

That settled the question of whether mother and daughter were on the same page.

The waitress set down their iced teas. There were two cubes per glass, a slight improvement on the one-cube British concession to American taste. "Are you ready to order?"

Inspecting his menu, Dan suggested to Astrid, "If you're opposed to turtle, how about the curried goat or braised cow's feet?"

She played it safe with lobster tail.

Martine surprised him by ordering turtle steak. "Let's see if it's as good as you say."

A challenge? Although he would never say so, Dan liked that. He ordered the same, then resumed questioning Martine. "These books you're interested in. If there's a set stored in the basement of the Louvre, why not use those?"

As though only an idiot would ask such a thing, she said, "You think the museum would comply?"

"With public pressure, if you inform the press."

"How can there be public pressure without evidence?" She lowered her voice, seemingly aware that other diners had turned their heads at her outburst. "The museum will say, 'There are no such books.' Then what?"

Finally, a crack in her armor. But all it revealed was a passion for the goal. "Maybe you could approach the government."

"The Louvre is effectively independent, a power unto itself." Martine's face reddened with exasperation or anger, he wasn't sure which. "Do you think we have not considered every alternative?"

"Or," Astrid added, "that I would ask for your help if we had not exhausted all other options?"

Silently conceding the point, he switched subjects. "What about this monastery? I've seen photos of it on the internet. The grating that safeguards their forbidden books is high up on a wall in the library. It looks inaccessible without a ladder."

"The internet is not reliable," Martine told him in a condescending tone. "I should think you would know that."

Dammit, his attempt to get under her skin was not going well. So far, he'd only managed to annoy her. Now she was annoying him. "What have I failed to learn from the internet?"

"Undoubtedly many things. In this case, the fact that there's a hidden stairway, behind a bookcase."

That was news. "How do you know?"

"Proper research." She paused, evidently to enjoy her little zinger. "Plus, I have been there. I climbed the stairs and saw the locked door to the room. The grate in the library is decorative. It does not open."

"The monks let you go up there?"

"Friars, not monks. And of course they didn't. Only the abbot is allowed to do that."

"So, you ... what?" This was becoming interesting.

"I hid in a janitor closet until the monastery closed to visitors. When the time came for the friars to have dinner, I went into the library and found the handle that releases the bookcase."

Gutsy. "And to get out? If the monastery was closed?"

"The doors to the library open from the inside." With a touché smile, she repeated, "Proper research."

Dan sat back in his chair and reappraised her. Her tone was justified. It took nerve to do what she had done, not counting her pre-work. And her information was valuable, so far as it went.

"What about you?" Martine asked. "Are you married?"

Huh? What difference did that make? "No."

"Girlfriend?"

Astrid scowled at her.

But Dan played along, curious to see where this was going. "Not at the moment."

"Why not? Are you difficult to get along with? Or maybe gay?"

"Martine!" Astrid scolded.

Dan smiled at her. Apparently, Astrid didn't recognize what Dan now did, that Martine was merely giving him tit for tat with potentially flustering questions straight out of the blue. "Not gay, and between girlfriends."

"Is that like 'between jobs'?"

"Sort of." In fact, he was pretty sure it was his long absences, due to work, that girlfriends couldn't handle. Never mind that he tried hard to make up for it when he returned. Too often they'd given up by then.

Fortunately, the waitress arrived with their meals before Martine could grill him further.

When they'd taken a few bites, Martine passed a forkful of her turtle steak to Astrid. "You must taste this."

Astrid tried it reluctantly, and her eyebrows rose.

Dan knew exactly why. The flavor resembled the finest crown of rib eye you had ever eaten, but better. No wonder Spanish sailors in the nineteenth century called these islands the Tortugas, the turtles, and had mercilessly hunted the easygoing reptiles for their meat. He almost felt bad for eating one now, but it pleased him to know that farming had reduced pressure on the wild populations and allowed them to rebound.

They ate in silence for a while, Dan grateful for an end to Martine's pointless questions and now trying to picture himself repeating her discovery of the locked door. "Back to the monastery, what kind of lock was it on the door you found."

"An old iron one. The kind that takes a ... skeleton key? I think that's the right word."

"I get the idea." A simple warded lock, with one or more internal obstructions that could be bypassed fairly easily. Standard lock picks, like the ones he always carried, wouldn't work. But something as simple as a nail file or screwdriver should. "Okay, let's assume we get the books and can successfully take them back to a hotel, or somewhere else in Prague. They're antiquities. How do we get them out of the country?"

Martine clanked her fork down. "If I had all the answers, I wouldn't need you."

At that moment, it occurred to Dan that he'd said "we." Twice. Well, "we" remained to be seen.

Astrid broke in with, "I could arrange UN passports for the two of you. Then you could pass through Customs unhindered."

"Sorry," he said, "but that's not true." From his DSS days, he knew a lot about passports, including, in the UN case, the two forms of UNLPs. "It's not a real passport. It's a *laissez-passer*. It might gain you some courtesies, but avoiding Customs is not one of them."

Astrid narrowed her eyes. "Are you sure?"

"Positive."

"Then you should contemplate this problem," Martine told him. "We must return the books to France."

#

When Billy had dropped off his three sated passengers at their hotel, Astrid touched Dan's arm. "Have you decided?"

"I'd still like to wait until morning."

She pursed her lips. "Okay. Then we will see you at breakfast."

Upstairs, Dan changed into swim trunks and grabbed a towel. A nighttime swim would help him organize his thoughts.

The moonlit beach was deserted. Music and laughter around the hotel's pool intruded on his solitude but disappeared the moment he dived into the sea. He swam hard for about fifty strokes, then flipped onto his back and gazed at the stars. After catching his breath, he jackknifed and headed toward the bottom where dark ridges of coral alternated with white stretches of sand.

Roughly twenty feet down, he stopped as a great gray shape winged its way under him. A manta ray. Dan kicked just enough to maintain his depth as he cupped his hands around his eyes and forehead and exhaled a stream of bubbles through his nose. It was a trick he'd discovered entirely on his own, a way to make a temporary facemask by trapping air under his eyes. The manta came into clear focus. Harmless, it "flew" gracefully and slowly just ten feet below him, its wings wider than his arm span, its huge mouth open to scoop in the plankton it lived on. What a treat to see such a magnificent creature in the wild. He could have watched it for hours, except he had run out of breath.

He shot to the surface, sucked in several lungfuls of air, and headed down again. The manta was gone. Recalling something he'd noticed on his previous visit, Dan shook his hand back and forth. The water around it blossomed with the pale blue glow of phosphorescent algae. This truly was a diver's paradise.

But he had a decision to make.

Once more on the surface, he treaded water. What to do about Astrid's request? He accepted the morality of what she wanted. But the main consideration was the fact that he didn't want to be stuck with the added baggage of her daughter.

Granted, Martine's knowledge would probably be an asset. But she could also be a liability. If things went south, what then? Say someone caught them in the monastery. Or no one caught them, but Customs at the airport arrested them for trying to smuggle out antiquities?

He rolled over and swam a slow backstroke toward shore. Arrest could land them in prison. He'd seen east-bloc prisons.

Squalid, filthy conditions with no blankets and barely any food unless relatives provided it.

The obvious solution was avoid getting caught. *Genius.* The solution always was not to get caught.

As the poolside music came back to his ears, he flipped onto his stomach. And stopped.

On the beach, thirty feet ahead, Martine dropped a towel in the sand and fiddled with the top of a very small bikini. Apparently not seeing him, she looked around, then reached behind and took off the top.

Nice.

Although it was illegal to go topless in the Caymans, he doubted anyone tried to enforce the law along this stretch of high-end hotels. Still, he didn't want to embarrass her by making himself known while she stood there bare-breasted. So, what to do now?

She solved the problem by waving to him and calling out, "How's the water?"

Taken aback, he managed, "Great. Same temperature as the air."

She waded in and swam to his side, where they treaded water together. "Thanks for suggesting the turtle steak."

"I'm glad you enjoyed it."

"How soon can we leave?"

Dan pushed back a stroke. "I haven't yet decided if *we* are going anywhere."

"Am I the problem?"

"Frankly, yes."

She ducked under the water and resurfaced, sweeping her hair back with both hands. "If I thought you could do it without me, I'd stay behind. But there won't be much time in that room, and someone needs to identify which books are the ones we want."

"That won't be obvious?"

"No one has seen them in two hundred years. I'll probably have to look through dozens of volumes to find the right ones. Maybe hundreds."

Not necessarily. He reckoned the four or five books they were looking for would stand out due to similar covers. Plus, inscriptions on the front pages, if not the spines, would surely include the word, "Louvre."

As to her other point, "Why won't there be much time?"

"Because friars sometimes use the library after hours, and the movable bookcase only latches from the outside. Unlatched, it stays partly open. A friar could notice that and raise the alarm."

Great. Hundreds of books, plus a short time fuse.

"Besides," she said, "if something unexpected happens, two heads are better than one."

"Until an emergency arises. Then having to look after a second person endangers both."

She moved back a foot or so and shoved water in his face. "I don't need you to look after me."

Caught off guard, he wiped saltwater from his eyes but refrained from giving her a shot in return. This wasn't a playful issue.

"I can take care of myself," she said. I have a P-five rank in Krav Maga. Do you know what that means?"

It meant practitioner level 5, one step below graduate in the Israeli art of street fighting. There were also five levels of graduate and five of expert. Though Dan's training in Krav was limited—two courses from military specialists—he figured he could probably qualify for P-4.

To assess whether she really knew her stuff, he said, "Suppose a mugger comes up and tries to choke you."

"Simple. Two-handed pluck and a knee to the groin, then a palm-strike to the chin."

"If that didn't take him down?"

"Continue kneeing him while driving him backwards, then an elbow to the throat as I push him away and a final kick to the groin."

Impressive. "Pluck" was Krav-speak for a two-handed outward strike to break the assailant's grip on your throat. Invariably it was accompanied by a simultaneous counterattack. The first two rules of Krav were "Don't get hurt," hence the pluck, and "Counterattack as soon as possible," hence the simultaneous groin strike. Krav loved groin strikes, whether to a man or a woman.

But perfecting moves like these in class said little about a person's ability to use them in a real situation. They had to become second nature, something you did almost without thinking.

Inching closer to him, she asked, "Do you really think there'll be any need for physical violence?"

"I don't know." He lay back in the water and gazed at the star-strewn sky. His inclination now was that having her with him might be more beneficial than detrimental.

One of her breasts brushed his arm.

He righted himself and glided away with a few fanning motions of his hands underwater. He loved women as much as any straight guy did, but sexual innuendo—if that's what she intended—would have no influence on this decision. To make that point, he returned to her last question. "Speaking of violence, how did you get the scar on your left arm?"

A momentary squint told him she hadn't expected that. But she answered matter-of-factly. "I got mugged two blocks from Yale. When I resisted, the bastard slashed me. That's when I took up Krav."

He pictured the terrifying situation of a young woman being accosted at knifepoint. But Martine had not withdrawn into the dark realm of gloom. She'd taken steps to ensure she could combat any similar event in the future. He liked that. And he was starting to like her.

"Dan," she said, her expression deadly serious, "recovering these books is very important. It's the right thing to do."

"Stealing from a house of God?" He wasn't religious, but most French people were Catholics, and he wanted her to consider that point. "Would you return them to the monastery after they served their purpose?"

She stared at him as though considering that question for the first time. "I suppose we could."

Her comment hinted at a willingness to adapt, or at least consider alternatives. But his question was hypothetical, like the attacks against her in Krav class. In a real emergency, would she take orders or stand there protesting?

He still had a lot to think about, and out here treading water beside her was not the place to do it. "I'll see you in the morning."

#

In the master bedroom of her suite, Astrid lay wide awake atop the sheets. Not only was it too early to take her usual sleeping pill, but the guilt that gnawed at her would have counteracted it anyway. Although she'd mentioned the French right wing to Dan, she had withheld the greater danger. A danger that, if it came to fruition, imperiled both him and her daughter.

Nothing was worth losing either of them. But if "religious nuts," as Christophe had called them, ever got hold of the fifth book, the whole world could be plunged into crisis.

By "nuts," he'd meant fundamentalists of all sorts, Muslims, Christians, Jews. Jerusalem, sacred to all three of the Abrahamic faiths, was a match just waiting to be struck. The greater Middle East was a tinderbox atop huge reserves of oil and wealth. The whole precarious region was "armed to the teeth," as Americans said. And those arms included missiles equipped with nuclear warheads.

Only a stalemate akin to the old concept of "mutually assured destruction" kept the so-called peace. It had worked for years. The world had become accustomed to it. Superpowers sustained it. But an unforeseen spark, like that fifth book, could ignite a conflagration that wiped out everything.

Struggling to cope with an incipient migraine, she got up and walked out onto the bedroom's verandah. Small waves washed up on the beach below. A light breeze caressed her naked body but did nothing to calm her. If only she could think of a way to destroy that book without endangering Martine and Dan.

But she'd racked her brain and come up with no reliable alternative. Nor could she afford to tell either of them how important it was. Geoff Fairchild's admonition prevented her from revealing it to Dan. Martine, in her hardheadedness, would have said, "Fuck it," and simply left the book in the monastery. For the sake of the world, Astrid could not afford that risk.

She needed to throw the book into her own fireplace and watch it burn.

Chapter 6

Having satisfied himself that working with Martine would be more beneficial than not, Dan joined her and Astrid for breakfast and gave them the news they both wanted.

Astrid clasped his hand with, "Thank you. You're doing the right thing."

Martine smiled victoriously.

Broaching the next subject, the uncomfortable one in this case, he said, "The job will need financing, as I'm sure you know. Beyond expenses, I'm accustomed to receiving compensation for my time and effort. It's how I make my living."

"I understand," Astrid said. "I'll pay for your airfare and hotel and give you a credit card for other expenses. What is your day rate?"

He told her.

Martine arched her eyebrows. "Are you worth it?"

But Astrid seemed to take it in stride. "Assuming five days to acquire the books, take them to Paris, and return to Washington, is half now and half upon conclusion acceptable?"

"Fine." He wrote a bank account number on his napkin and passed it to Astrid. Five days should be plenty, even if there were complications.

#

Dan flew back to Washington to repack, then caught a flight to Paris, where he met up with Martine in the departure lounge for Air France's nonstop service to Prague. She looked good, her auburn hair shiny, her subtle makeup emphasizing her brown eyes. He was pleased to see they'd dressed similarly, with practicality in mind. Jeans, sweaters, and waist-length leather jackets, although her jeans were tighter, nicely showing off her long legs.

In Prague, as they wheeled their suitcases out of the airport into a light snowfall, Dan geared up mentally for operations in "enemy territory."

An elderly couple and a young family of three were climbing into cabs at the taxi rank. He and Martine joined the short line of waiting travelers. When they reached the front. he waved for the people behind him to go ahead as he pretended to look for something in his bag. After two more cabs had departed, he stepped up to the next one and said, "Grand Bohemia Hotel."

When they had climbed into the rear seat, Martine asked, "Why didn't you take the first one?"

"Habit."

Their taxi was immaculate inside, a far cry from Billy's Mazda on Grand Cayman or anything Dan had seen in D.C. Once beyond the airport, it took them through snow-dusted farmland on the left and an assortment of blocky Soviet-era buildings on the right. Gradually the farmland gave way to suburbia, complete with KFCs, while more modern apartment and office buildings replaced most of the Russian concrete blocks.

Everything suburban vanished when they crossed the Vltava river into the old part of town. Prague had not been bombed during World War Two—thankfully, Dan thought, as they negotiated narrow streets between majestic stone buildings enhanced with domes and spires and grand balconies supported by neoclassical statues of male and female figures. Shops at ground level advertised Rolex, Cartier, Chanel, and Bulgari. Welcome to capitalism.

Their hotel occupied a corner on one of those narrow streets, where it intersected an even narrower lane. Dan paid the driver then followed Martine through the rotating glass-and-brass door. The lobby was as grand as the establishment's name, with marble floors, oriental carpets, and tall windows framed by brocade drapes. A middle-aged couple sipped afternoon tea in one of the seating arrangements near the windows.

At the front desk, an impeccably dressed young man with close-cropped hair confirmed Dan and Martine's reservations. But as soon as the man read off their room numbers, Dan shook his head and requested a change.

"Why?" Martine asked. "We haven't even seen them yet."

"Humor me." To the fellow behind the counter, he said, "Something on a higher floor, if you can."

After consulting his computer, the man, who wore a tiny gold crucifix pinned through his lapel, offered two "Junior Suites" on the seventh floor.

"We'll take them. And could we arrange a hotel taxi for fifteen minutes from now?

"Certainly, sir. Where would you like to go?"

"Just around town." Although their cab from the airport was fine, Dan had read that hotel cabs were safer. He completed the formalities, took the two keycards, and handed one to Martine.

In the elevator riding up, she said, "Another habit? You don't take the first taxi or the first room?"

"Not if I can help it." In fact, he was always leery of arrangements made by other people. While he trusted Astrid, any pre-arrangement carried the risk that someone with foreknowledge could set up surveillance gear, or worse. The quick-switch had saved his butt three times in the past. "Think of it this way," he added with a smile. "We got suites for only thirty euros more than the rooms your mother booked. What's not to like?"

On the seventh floor, they wheeled their bags to her door, the first on the right. "I'll be ready in a few minutes," she said.

"Meet you downstairs."

His room was adjacent to hers. Half of the ceiling sloped upward at an angle from windows that looked out onto red-tiled rooftops from which the light snow had melted. The slope obviously corresponded to the hotel's roofline and meant there were no rooms directly above. Excellent. Aside from electronic devices in a room itself, listening through adjacent walls or the ceiling were the most common surveillance techniques. Probably his caution was unnecessary in this hotel, but better to find out early than too late.

After a quick examination of the room with his HP "calculator" revealed no bugs, he left his bag unopened and descended the stairwell to check it out. He found unlocked access to the other floors. A further plus.

On the ground floor, a doorway near the check-in counter led to a small bar ringed by booths and tables around the walls. The tables, to his surprise, sported ashtrays and boxes of matches, something you rarely saw these days, even in Europe. The breakfast/dining room on the other side of check-in was as elegant as the lobby, with tables spaced well-apart, crisp linens, flowers in vases, and a glittering chandelier.

Astrid had definitely chosen well when she picked this place. And it was only a five-minute walk from Old Town Square. With luck, the book snatch would go smoothly, and he and Martine could stay here another day or two, enjoying the Christmas festivities in the square and taking in some of the concerts for which Prague was famous.

"*There* you are," Martine said.

He turned to see her dressed as before but with a knapsack hanging from her shoulders. "You have everything?"

She pointed at her watch. "The library closes at five o'clock and doesn't admit anyone after four."

Their hotel cab, a black Mercedes, took them back over the Vltava river, then zigzagged uphill through a forested area into a well-kept town dominated by three- to four-story stone buildings with shops at street level and what were probably offices or apartments above. Dan concentrated on the main street and its crossroads, comparing them in his mind to maps and photos he'd studied on the internet. If necessary, these would be their primary escape route.

The driver pulled off the main street into a broad forecourt and, after confirming they didn't need him to wait, bid them goodbye outside the monastery's gates.

"Are you nervous?" he asked her as the taxi disappeared.

"A little."

"Good. Nerves keep us on our toes."

The monastery's entrance, a tall arched gateway flanked by Corinthian-style pillars and topped with statues, was the only visible portal through twelve-foot-high walls obviously intended to thwart invaders from an earlier age. The buildings within the grounds were more austere, like white, two-story dormitories with red-tiled roofs.

As Dan and Martine made their way toward the library, he recalled Google Earth images that showed the monastic complex to be much bigger than it appeared from here. There was even a hotel and restaurant. The hotel was good news. It meant the iron gates at the entrance had to stay open fairly late, if not all night.

In the foyer to the library, they paid their entrance fee and nodded when the cashier pointed to a wooden sign that announced in several languages, "Closing 17:00 hours."

They walked through a door into a long gallery lined with display cases and glass-fronted cabinets. "This is the only room," Martine said, "where visitors are allowed."

"We better take it slowly, then. We have an hour and ten minutes to kill."

"Don't worry. There's a lot of interesting stuff in here."

Maybe, but what interested him at the moment were the three other visitors, all down near the far end of the gallery—an Asian man photographing displays with his cellphone, and a portly couple peering through a large open doorway into what Dan's memorized floor plan told him was the library. All three of them needed watching, especially the guy taking pictures.

There was also a well-dressed, gray-haired woman he took to be a docent and who now approached them. "English?" she asked through lips overly glossed with red. To Dan's "Yes," she offered her services if there was anything he or Martine needed explained.

He thanked her and turned Martine toward a large glass case that displayed a variety of "natural wonders," basically a Renaissance cabinet of curiosities. Prominently featured were a narwhal tusk and two three-foot-long bacula, penis bones that probably came from walruses. As they pretended to study the exhibit, he whispered, "Where's this janitor's closet?"

"At the other end, near the library."

He saw it now, artfully designed to be unobtrusive within the dark, wood-paneled wall.

They ambled from one display to the next. More cabinets of curiosities, showing mostly dried-out sea creatures, including stingrays, octopuses, crabs, a small shark, and fronds of seaweed, as well as turtle shells and an array of seashells.

"Collections like these," Martine said, "were the precursors of our natural history museums."

Then came cases of old books. She stopped him at one of them, where each book had a chain through the binding. "The chains were to keep friars from stealing them."

All very interesting, but with the docent standing against one wall, he was unsure to get into the janitor's closet. He was about to ask Martine how she'd managed to evade the docent when a mild commotion made him look back toward the foyer.

He retraced his steps and saw a group of ten people arguing with the woman at the ticket counter.

"Just the library," a man pleaded in an American accent. "I promise we'll be out in thirty minutes."

The docent touched Dan's shoulder in a polite gesture to move aside, then walked past him into the fray. More words and pointing at watches. "Twenty minutes, tops," the American man offered. Finally, wallets came out, and the woman at the counter started spooling off tickets.

"Quick." Dan grabbed Martine's hand and hustled her down to the library's entrance.

In no time, they were surrounded by the Americans, who'd been herded by the docent in an evident effort to ensure they remained this side of the library's rope barrier and didn't overstay their time.

The portly couple who'd been there before were now leaving. The Asian man frowned at the new crowd and apparently gave up on photographing the library.

"Damn," Martine said. "There are too many people."

"Sometimes a crowd is good." Dan inched Martine out of the gathering and toward the door of the janitor's closet. "Just stand here," he said and knelt behind her, lock picks in hand. With a well-oiled click, the door opened.

He waited until he was sure all the tourists were fully engaged in the docent's lecture, then he drew Martine into the closet and quietly closed the door behind them.

"That took balls," she whispered in the darkness.

His pocket Maglite revealed mops, buckets, and a shelf of cleansers and polish that smelled like an institutional corridor after the custodians had buffed it. There was precious little room to sit. "The monks eat at six, right?"

"They're not monks. They're friars. Monks don't leave a monastery, friars do."

Hair-splitting, he thought, until it occurred to him that friars could conceivably chase them. Something to consider, although he doubted it would come to that.

He aimed his light at a small patch of open floor behind the buckets and mops. "You can sit there."

"I've been here before," she reminded him in a tone that said, "Proper research."

When she had squeezed past him, he turned off his light and hunkered down beside the door, listening to the Americans outside "ooh" and "ah" and say, "Look at that." The docent's voice attempted to explain what they were seeing but did not, thank goodness, inquire about the younger couple who'd been there a few minutes before.

Dan shut his eyes and concentrated on the view of the library he'd had just moments to absorb. A barrier of twisted rope, like you'd find outside a popular nightspot, barred the entrance. Beyond it, two floors of bookshelves ran along either side and across the far end. A row of six old globes stood like regimental soldiers down the center. The vaulted ceiling was luxuriously ornate and painted with religious scenes framed in plaster ovals.

Everything confirmed the photos he'd seen on the internet, including the ten-foot-wide iron grate in the middle of the second-floor bookshelves at the far end and a quarter-round bookcase in each of the far corners.

One of the Americans said, "Thank you." It was followed by more thanks and the sound of footsteps receding. Then silence.

Now more waiting.

That was always the hardest part, champing at the bit but being held back by the starting gate. The great danger was that waiting too long could dull the reflexes when you needed them most. Even worse was waiting in cramped quarters, in the dark. To counteract the effect, he flexed his muscles, starting with his toes and working his way up to shoulder lifts. On top of that, he did breathing exercises—in through the nose, hold it, out through the mouth.

Above the odors of cleanser and floor polish, he smelled Martine's perspiration, a sharp, feminine scent he would find enticing under other circumstances. But these circumstances weren't "other."

After what seemed an interminable half hour, he switched on his light to see Martine huddled in a corner, the knapsack in her lap. "You okay?"

"What time is it?" she whispered.

His internal clock told him a little past five-thirty. But he checked his watch. "Five-forty."

"Let's go."

"How long did you wait before?"

"Until about quarter to six."

"Let's wait." What if one of the friars had the job of checking on the visitor area before their dinner at six?

It was no use telling her to relax. She'd done this before and no doubt had found her own ways to cope.

Finally, his watch showed 6:05. Getting to his feet, he said, "Stand up and stretch your muscles to get the blood flowing."

"It's about time."

He cracked open the door and peered around. The corridor was dark, except for a few nightlights, and as quiet as a morgue. "Let's go."

They stepped over the rope barrier to the library and headed for the bookcase in the far-right corner. Martine shifted two books, then reached behind them. He heard the scraping sound of a heavy latch being released. The bookcase rotated outward about six inches. When she pulled it open a little wider, he squeezed through into pitch black.

As he turned on his Maglite, she reminded him, "It can only be closed from the outside."

He ran the beam of his light over the inside of the bookcase but saw no handle or knob or anything they could fasten a rope to or even grasp. So, she was right about that. Next thing: "You said there were stairs leading to a basement. Where are they?"

"Around that corner."

He turned toward the corner to his right and saw them. He would have liked to confirm the outside door down there, but she was probably right about that, also. "Okay."

Martine led the way up a stone staircase that ended on a small landing in front of a heavy wooden door with an ancient iron lock plate. Kneeling to inspect it, he said, "Give me the Swiss Army knife."

In less than a minute, the door swung open to reveal a cramped, dusty room surrounded by bookcases, except in front of the ornamental grating and the door itself.

This was it, the monastery's so-called forbidden books. There might not be thousands of them, but there were definitely hundreds.

Using her cellphone light, Martine started scanning the volumes.

They comprised a real hodgepodge. All sizes from slightly larger than a cigarette pack to bigger than a coffee-table art book. Some thick, some thin, most bound in leather like the books on display in the gallery. A few had no covers, just a bunch of pages stitched along one edge with twine or leather cord. On an upper shelf lay a stack of rolled-up scrolls. The room smelled of dry rot and mouse droppings.

"Here." She pulled down four books bound in cream-colored vellum, each half again as large as a ream of printer paper. Black script on the spines read, "Louvre."

"Okay, let's go," he said.

"No. We have to get the other one."

Astrid had only said there *might* be a fifth book. But mentioning that to Martine would be fruitless. She was already rummaging through the shelves.

Antsy about the open bookcase downstairs, Dan inched his way to the grating and knelt to peer through it into the library. Nothing, so far. "Hurry up."

When he looked back, she was pulling out books and tossing them aside, with no apparent regard to the fact that a heap of scattered books would be a sure-fire sign of pillage.

"Dammit, Martine."

"The friars are still eating." She pulled out more volumes, glanced inside, and dropped them. Then she let out a muffled squeal. "This is it."

"Great. Let's go."

"Moshe," she said, her fingertip planted on a page.

"What's Moshe?"

"Just a minute."

The volume she held was about the size and thickness of a National Geographic magazine. It had leather covers front and back but nothing to protect the spine edge where five loops of coarse twine pierced the covers and pages and held the whole thing together. Rather precariously, he thought.

Wondering what could be so important about such a thin book, Dan looked out the grate again. And froze.

A friar in white robes stood at the library's entrance.

As Dan watched, all his senses on high alert, the friar moved aside one of the posts that supported the rope barrier and advanced toward the partially open bookcase. Halfway there, he stopped.

"Shit," Dan whispered. "We've been made."

"Made?"

The friar turned and dashed out.

Dan whirled on her. "Pack it up. Now. They know we're here."

Chapter 7

No time to clean up the mess or relock the door. The instant Martine had jammed the last of the five books into her knapsack, Dan rushed her down the stairs and around the corner to the next flight of steps. "Stay close."

They descended into a basement that smelled of musty stone and old wood. The beam of his flashlight picked out three broken chairs, a damaged statue of some saint, dusty crates, and walls made of roughly hewn rock.

Dead ahead, four stone steps led up to another door—a duplicate, essentially, of the one guarding the forbidden books. But the iron lock on this one would not yield to his Swiss Army knife, neither to the blade nor to the can-opener attachment. He peered inside with his flashlight. Rusty.

Muffled voices came from the landing above.

His heart thumped harder. "Look for some place to hide."

As she threaded her way between the crates, he gambled on the knife's saw. Something gave. He jiggled the saw blade back and forth and applied torque. A slight movement.

"Martine, come back." He applied more torque, so much that he feared the attachment would snap off.

A shout came from the top of the basement stairs.

With a clack, the lock released.

As footfalls descended behind them, Dan grabbed her hand and ran her up the steps into frigid night air. Run now, or try to relock the door? "Head for the gate. I'll catch up with you."

"What are you doing?"

"Just go. And stay close to the building." He pushed the door closed and shoved the saw blade back into the lock. With its seal of rust broken, the mechanism turned more easily this time.

The latch rattled. Pounding and hollering came from inside.

Dan figured he had just bought a five-minute lead. In a sprint, he caught up with Martine at the corner of the building. The monastery's gates stood four hundred feet to their left, over open ground. No cover. "We run for the gates."

Halfway there, she stopped to switch the heavy knapsack to her other shoulder.

"I've got it," he said, taking the pack from her hands. "Go!"

In the forecourt just outside the gates, he slipped into a shadowed area on one side and turned to look back. Nobody coming. He was about to congratulate himself for relocking that door when a man in a white habit charged out of the library's public entrance.

The friar looked left and right. He yelled something. Three more friars joined him. They split into pairs, one pair heading toward the hotel while the other came straight for the gates.

Dan hustled Martine out of the forecourt to the main street, where they turned left and kept to the left side until he found a recessed doorway they could duck into. Cautiously, he peeked back along the storefronts.

Two friars emerged onto the street. After looking in both directions, they dashed back into the monastery's grounds.

Dan told her what he'd seen. "They could be summoning reinforcements. And they know what we look like, at least from behind."

"How could they?"

"Our flashlights were on when they came down the stairs."

"*Merde*. We need to call a cab."

"Not until we get farther away." *And maybe not then.* It all depended on what the friars did. He hated having to wait and see, but all he and Martine needed to do was stay one step ahead. "Come on."

They stuck to this side of the street. Traffic had thinned. Shops were closing for the night. Small-town business hours, he thought, as a glance at his watch showed 6:58. Few pedestrians, unfortunately. In this situation, he would have preferred a crowd.

They'd fast-walked maybe fifty yards, Dan checking over his shoulder every five or six paces, when he spotted headlights coming out of the monastery's entrance. Two white vans. One turned right, one left. He rushed her to the next side street. "Behind that parked car."

The car faced the main street. They bent over its trunk and peered through the rear window and windshield. A van crawled past their view. When it was gone, Dan crept back to the main street. One block to his right, a friar walked slowly along the storefronts they'd passed just a minute ago. Two blocks to his left, the van stopped and deposited a friar on the far side of the main street.

These guys weren't giving up.

He dashed back to Martine, said, "This way," and set off in a jog down the dimly lit road. When his internal timer told him the first friar was about to reach their side street, he turned onto an even narrower road and stopped to peek around the corner.

The friar came their way for one block, ventured a short distance in each direction along the intersecting road, and turned back.

Dan set down the pack to give his shoulders a break. "These books better be worth it."

"They are," she said firmly.

But the "it" part of "worth it" wasn't over. They still had to get to their hotel. And that was only the first leg of returning the books to Paris. The goal is noble, he reminded himself. Wrongs will be righted. He sure hoped so. God only knew what kind of hornet's nest he and Martine had just cracked open.

"We can forget calling a cab," he said. "The main street is swarming with friars, and these side roads don't even have names, at least that I've seen."

"Then we have to keep walking." Yellowish light from a bulb over a doorway illuminated her resolute face. "Or hide out here."

With adrenaline still coursing through him, he much preferred moving to staying put. "This road parallels the main street. Let's follow it for a mile or two, then head back into town. The friars may have given up by then."

But Dan's memorization of the town's layout had not extended this far south of the main drag. "Do you know this area?"

"No."

"Then we wing it."

The road they followed wound between other, equally twisted roads. They'd plunged into a dark warren of warehouses, apartment buildings, and occasional shuttered shops that sold things like tires and paint. Only his navigation by the moon kept them oriented on a generally westbound course.

At one crossroad, he heard the heavy beat of punk rock. A bar or club. Briefly he wondered how residents in nearby apartment buildings could stand the noise. But that wasn't his problem.

Ten minutes later, he and Martine reached a T-intersection he couldn't picture on his internal map. Town, however, lay to the north. He was about to head that way when headlights rounded the corner and came toward them. One of the white vans cruised past. It screeched to a halt and reversed.

"Run," Dan yelled, turning back into the maze behind them. They zigged and zagged, left here, right there. Headlights caught them. When he glanced back, Martine was a racing silhouette in their glare. "Faster," he shouted.

They sprinted through three more turns. Then Dan stopped, waited for her to catch up, and knocked over a metal trash can into the road. After two more random turns, they ended up on a road where he again heard the thump of punk rock drums.

"There," she panted. "Maybe we can hide inside."

They followed the sound to an unmarked door. Opening it, Dan found a short passageway and another door, this one with a hand-written sign that read "Krak."

They stepped through into something akin to a rave. *A crowd, at last.*

The place stank of spilled beer. Under flashing lights, four maniacs on stage beat the hell out of their instruments: two guitars, a drum kit, and a giant double bass that a tattooed guy held in his arms and played like a Stratocaster. All were amplified full-blast through an assortment of tortured speakers that buzzed with the base notes.

Twenty feet from the stage, a bar ran along the opposite wall. Rough wooden tables left barely enough space for the pierced and tattooed goths who gyrated wildly in what he took to be their individual versions of the Tarantella, the dance of death. The couples on the floor included a pair of women who looked stoned and unable to keep their hands off each other.

Martine balked. "Bad idea."

"No, it's perfect. I don't think the friars would endanger their souls by venturing into this portal to Hell." He gestured toward the far end of the bar, where two stools were unoccupied. Pointing to a door behind the bar, he said, "If anything happens, that's where we go. It's probably an office with a separate exit."

"Probably?"

Based on his knowledge of bars, "Almost certainly." If not, a door closer to the stage had a sign above it with the universal man and woman symbols for Restrooms. *Just use your elbow to bash out the window.* A similar escape route had worked for him once before.

The wiry bartender, decked out in eyebrow rings, a green Mohawk, and a sleeve of tattoos down one arm, sidled up to them.

Dan ordered two beers. Prague, he'd read, was famous for its pilsner.

"What now?" Martine asked anxiously.

"We wait."

"What? I can't hear you."

"Wait! Until this place closes if necessary."

"I'll be deaf by then."

He waved toward the restroom. "You can probably find some toilet paper in there to stuff in your ears." When she got up, he added, "I'd be grateful for some, also."

No sooner had she left than the bartender deposited two half-pint pilsner glasses in front of Dan, each capped by an overly generous head of foam.

Martine returned, her lips curled in a sneer of disgust. "That place is filthy. The toilet is clogged. There's water all over the floor. And there's no damned toilet paper. The men's room is even worse."

Well, it had been worth a shot.

With a triple crash of cymbals, the current "song" ended. Fortunately, so did the set. The leather-clad guitarists racked their instruments. The bare-chested drummer stood from his stool. The burly bass player, in jeans and a wife-beater, laid his instrument on the floor. As all four vacated the stage and bellied up to the bar, a wasted-looking guy at one of the tables applauded enthusiastically. No one else seemed to notice.

Grateful for the quiet, Dan slung the knapsack off his shoulders onto his lap. "We should drink our beers slowly. We want to be alert when we leave this place."

"We can call a cab now."

"What address do you suggest?"

"We could give them the name. Or the GPS location."

"Go ahead and try." The name wouldn't work. It was an underground club. But GPS might, if a taxi driver was willing to track down a fare in this part of town.

After five minutes of frowning, she jammed her cellphone back in her pocket. "Dammit, Dan. You were supposed to handle any problems."

#

Half an hour into the next set, Dan left to scout out the "friar patrol." He wended his way to the T-intersection where they'd first been spotted. From there, he moved cautiously up to the main street where he lurked in shadows until he was satisfied the friars had given up or gone elsewhere.

At last. Although he wasn't religious, there was something disconcerting about being chased by men of God.

Okay, time to scoot. But not in a taxi. Who knew whether the holy men had contacted cab companies? Across the street and down one block stood a bus stop. He strolled to it as casually as he dared. Comparing the route numbers to bus maps on his cellphone, he chose route 119.

Back inside Krak, he found Martine fending off a fat creep in a studded leather vest that "manfully" displayed his hairy shoulders and gut. Dan was about to step in when Martine knocked aside the guy's outstretched hand and delivered a palm strike to the chin that laid out her admirer in a puddle of spilled beer.

Grinning, Dan walked up to her. "You're no fun at a party."

"Up yours. Let's get out of here."

"My thought precisely."

The band never missed a beat. The dancers kept dancing. Freaks at the tables nodded or simply stargazed into space as Dan and Martine walked out. Just another night at Krak, he supposed. Good riddance.

They walked to the bus stop where he checked his watch.

"A bus?" she said.

"In five minutes, if they run on time." He explained his reasoning about the possibility that the friars could have notified taxi companies.

Martine rolled her eyes. "You're paranoid."

The bus arrived early. Only two other passengers were on board, a plump woman with two plastic shopping bags and an old man whose head lolled to one side in obvious slumber. Dan gestured to a pair of seats adjacent to the rear exit, where they could skip out fast if necessary.

Thankfully, it was not necessary. He spotted no friars and no white vans.

After two transfers to buses on other route numbers, both of which took them through boring suburbs, they disembarked a hundred yards from their hotel.

Martine's mood had improved with each mile from the monastery, and Dan's stomach was rumbling. Glad to be "home," he said, "Let's find somewhere to eat. There's a Christmas market in Old Town Square."

"I know a better place." At the corner where their hotel was located, she pointed in the opposite direction of the lane leading to the square. "It's for locals."

True to her words, the place was called Lokal and greeted them with succulent aromas of sausages and roast pork. A row of tables ran down each side of the long, narrow room. The walls showcased an interesting variety of graffiti. He especially liked a large, white-painted diagram showing the flow of liquid from five beer mugs to a urinal, then through an underground aquifer to a water well and back to the beer mugs. If there had been a caption, it could have read, "We recycle."

A slender, twenty-something waitress wearing black slacks, black shirt, and a ring in her upper lip, seated them. After a few words, she returned with menus in English. So, Dan thought, not entirely for locals, although the other patrons, half of them smoking, seemed definitely to fit that description.

Martine ordered a glass of Pinot Noir, from a Czech vineyard called Lebkowiez, then pork neck with a cucumber and sour cream salad. Having liked the beer at Krak, Dan ordered a pint of pilsner, followed by bean soup with sausage, and beef cheeks with pickles.

When their waitress left, Dan excused himself to use the bathroom.

"Take a look at the women's while you're at it," Martine suggested.

He entered the men's room to find the walls plastered with photos of bare-breasted women and flashy sport cars. When he finished, he knocked on the ladies' room, got no reply, and opened the door to see exactly what he now expected—magazine pictures of soccer stars and scantily clad muscle men.

"Well?" she asked when he returned to their table.

"A far cry, I imagine, from the ladies' room at Krak."

"Don't spoil my appetite."

Their meals came with a basket of crusty brown bread and a bowl of shredded cheese. Everything was delicious. Hearty, filling, and perfect for a cold winter night, especially after heisting a bunch of books from a monastery and getting chased by angry friars.

Which brought him back to an unnerving realization he'd had, first at the T-intersection when the white van spotted them and then at the bus stop. "Between the time we left the monastery and the time we caught that first bus, did you hear any sirens?"

"No," she said as though wondering why he'd asked.

"Neither did I. And it's a little unsettling."

"Why?"

"Because it suggests to me that the friars don't want the police involved. They plan to handle this themselves."

"What can they do?"

"I'm not sure. And that bothers me."

#

After sharing a dessert the menu described as "hazelnut crust topped with whipped chocolate," they returned to their hotel, where a woman now stood behind the check-in counter. Dan smiled at her and continued with Martine to the elevator. On the seventh floor, they agreed to meet for coffee in the morning. He waited in the hall while she unlocked her door and stepped inside—then gasped.

"Dan!"

He pushed through to see her suitcase open on the floor, her clothes scattered. Bedspread, blankets, sheets, all thrown in a corner. Drawers pulled out, the mattress diagonal on the bed.

"Wait here." It could be a chance burglary, but he doubted it. Tensed to strike, he unlocked his own door and kicked it open with his boot in case someone waited inside. There was nobody, but the place looked like a tornado had blown through.

Struggling to control the alarm bells clanging in his head, he ran back to Martine. "We need to find another hotel. Grab whatever toiletries you need, a change of underwear, your passport, anything you *must* have, and shove them in your pockets or the knapsack. Everything else stays here."

"But—"

"We have to move fast. I'll be back in one minute."

In his room again, he snatched up the bare minimum of essentials. His iPad was missing, along with the calculator that detected electronic bugs. He hated to lose either, but there was no time for remorse. After patting an inside jacket pocket to confirm his passports were there, he stuffed the remaining pockets with a toothbrush, toothpaste, socks, and underpants.

Shutting his door, he went back to her room.

"It doesn't all fit," she said.

"Then it stays. We can buy things later."

"Why can't we take our suitcases?"

"A, they'll slow us down. And B, I don't want the hotel to know we've left until the housekeeper shows up tomorrow morning."

Apparently accepting that, she zipped up her jacket.

Dan shouldered the knapsack and headed for the stairwell. Three floors down, it struck him. The gold-crucifix lapel pin. "That son of a bitch."

"Who?"

"The guy who checked us in. I'll bet a kidney he has ties to the monastery."

"He did this?"

"More likely, someone called him, and we matched the descriptions of the people they were looking for."

In the lobby, Dan risked a minute of escape time to ask the girl behind the counter, "The fellow who was here this afternoon, is he still here?"

"I'm afraid not. He had to leave early."

"How early?"

"About an hour ago. But I can assist you."

"Never mind. I just wanted to thank him for some help he gave us." And break his knees if I see him again.

With a deep breath to settle himself, Dan walked with Martine to the revolving door. In front of it, he stopped. "Oh, crap."

"What?"

"The hotel took copies of our passports." He looked back at the front desk, where the woman was now speaking on her phone. She wasn't wearing a gold crucifix, at least visibly. But that didn't alter the main fact. "Anybody with an 'in' can search the hotel's records."

"Then we really do need to move fast."

Outside, another light snow fell, big flakes that disappeared almost on contact. To their right ran the major street where they could certainly find a cab, but where an unwelcome white van might also cruise by. Taking Martine's elbow, he went the opposite direction.

A brisk five-minute "stroll" past shops displaying women's clothing and Czech glassware brought them to the festivities in Old Town Square. At least a thousand people milled around booths purveying gingerbread, smoked pork, candies, toys, beer, mulled wine. Toward one side rose a gloriously decorated Christmas tree larger than any he'd seen outside of Rockefeller Plaza. Musicians played. Puppeteers danced marionettes over the cobblestones. Children laughed. Ornate old buildings around the square blazed under floodlights.

In normal conditions, he and Martine could have had a good time here. Not now.

Having glanced back frequently to be sure no one was following them, he led her through the crowd to the other side of the square and down a lane to where his memorized map said they should find another main street. When he saw it, he stopped to consult his phone. "There's a two-star hotel just a mile away."

Fifteen minutes later, they got out of a taxi in the middle of a street that showed no signs of life.

"Where's the hotel?" Martine asked.

"A block from here. I gave the driver a false address."

"Do you really think—"

"I don't know. But I prefer not to chance it. We've committed a crime in a foreign country. Against an obviously powerful religious organization that might not give up until they've captured us." He peered up and down the dark street. "Our goals now are a safe place to sleep and time to figure out our options."

At the address he'd found on his phone, they entered a bathroom-sized lobby with a counter on one side, a rack of tourist brochures on the other, and a bare wooden staircase at the far end. The place smelled like wet wool. The owner must have bribed someone to get his two-star rating.

"It's a dump," Martine said.

"Exactly."

Chapter 8

Dan "showered" under a lukewarm trickle, then turned down the bed to discover sheets that, judging from the pale stains, hadn't been laundered anytime recently. *Lovely.* Not only a dump, but a place where most customers probably paid by the hour. That explained why the bored old man at the front desk hadn't asked for their passports or questioned their lack of luggage.

Thinking back to the Indonesian cathouse that had once sheltered him for two days, he turned the pillowcases inside out, laid the bedspread bottom-side-up over the sheets, and tucked in the blanket on top. In jeans and T-shirt, he slid in between the relatively unsoiled sides of the blanket and bedspread, then turned off the table lamp.

The question now was, should they risk the airport? The books in Martine's knapsack might pass through x-ray without raising any suspicions. But if a security person did decide to check, the books could be viewed as antiques that required an export license. He might be able to bribe a local bookseller into giving them a phony sales receipt. But there was a chance the friars had alerted bookshops, maybe even the police. Slim though that chance seemed, the consequences of getting caught were not worth it.

Frenzied knocking pounded his door. "Dan. Open up."

Alarmed, he tossed aside the blanket and switched on the light.

No sooner had he turned the handle than Martine charged inside. "I can't sleep in that room. It's full of cockroaches."

"Just squash them with a shoe." He'd done that to one on his bathroom floor.

"I can't get near them. They're horrible." She shot a panicky glance at the door as if expecting a horde to be hot on her trail. "One ran over my face in my apartment in New Haven. I almost threw up. We had to have the place fumigated."

He had no love for roaches, either, despite the fact that they were supposedly clean.

"Are there any in here?" she asked.

"One, but I killed it."

She winced. "We have to go somewhere else."

"It's too late to find another place, and we have to get up early."

The firmness of his statement seemed to take her aback. Well, too bad. She had informed him just hours ago—unnecessarily—that he was supposed to handle problems. Moving again was a problem best handled by avoiding it.

In a guilty tone, she offered, "We could switch rooms."

"Not if yours is as bad as you say." The thought of roaches crawling over his face was as repulsive to him as to her.

"Then I'm staying here with you. No, wait." Frowning, she checked his bathroom and under the bed. "Okay."

"I'm not sleeping on the floor." The threadbare carpet was more stained than the sheet.

She pulled off her jacket, crawled onto his bed, and ran her hand down the middle. "Your side, my side. Got it?"

He was about to tell her not to flatter herself when he noticed a roach on the ceiling. Instantly he switched off the light. Please, he prayed silently, do not fall and land on her.

#

Dan's mental alarm clock woke him at 5:30. Martine lay in a fetal position, facing away from him on the double bed. He had confined himself to eighteen inches of mattress, lest their bodies inadvertently touch and provoke an outburst. All he wanted now was to conclude this job and get back to D.C.

Nudging her shoulder, he said, "Time to get up."

"Huh?"

"I'm going downstairs to find a taxi."

The taxi arrived in fifteen minutes, by which time Martine had made herself presentable, her preparations including a dab of Ma Griffe. He liked the fragrance and had once given it in bath-oil form to a girlfriend. The name, translated variously as "My Claw" or "My Scratch" or "My Signature." The first seemed appropriate for what lay ahead, clawing their way out of this mess.

"Airport?" the driver asked.

Martine whispered to Dan, "That's not a good idea."

"I agree," he said, glad they were on the same wavelength. "We're better off going overland."

"By train."

"At least partway." When they'd climbed into the cab, he told the driver, "Take us to an internet café."

"Only one is open now. More after eight o'clock."

"The open one." They had a couple of hours before sunrise, and pre-dawn darkness was his favorite time to work.

As the cab pulled away, Martine said, "Why not use your phone?"

"I need a real computer." Before falling asleep on their cramped bed last night, Dan had recalled stories of Gypsy persecution in the Czech Republic and wondered if a surviving community might help a brother in need. It was a long shot, but better than trying to cross the border on their own. And a helluva lot better than gambling against Security at the airport.

Their driver let them off at a storefront with "All Night Internet" emblazoned in red neon across the window. Inside, two young men and an older fellow sat at computers lined up along one wall.

Dan paid the sleepy-eyed attendant at the desk for one hour. In half that time, he found several Roma communities, one of which stood out. It lay within a town called Usti nad Labem, just twelve miles from the German border. Better yet, in 1999 a wall had been built in that town to isolate Romani from the rest of the inhabitants. Under international pressure, the wall was torn down that same year. But given the long memories of Roma people, feelings of injustice and outrage likely still ran high.

"Look here," he said to Martine, who'd been pacing behind him like a caged tigress. He pointed at the map on his screen. "This town, Usti something-or-other, is close to the border and on a direct route to Dresden."

"Can we get there by train?"

After a few more minutes, with Martine peering over his shoulder and Dan inhaling her perfume, the screen showed that trains ran almost every hour from Prague to Usti nad Labem.

"Let's do it," she said.

He double-deleted his search history and walked with her outside to catch another cab.

Prague's main train station, on the eastern side of Old Town, greeted travelers with a three-story, arched entry flanked by ornate, dome-topped towers. "Ornate" also described the interior, where arched windows, statues carved in high relief, and paintings that looked like coats of arms drew the eye upward to a magnificent rotunda that would have done justice to an Italian cathedral. Only the standard European blue-and-white directional signs marred the religious atmosphere.

That, and two clean-cut men in black business suits and close-cropped hair who loitered near the ticket counters.

"Shit."

"What's wrong?" Martine asked.

"We have company." He thought a moment. "Okay, listen closely. We need to split up. Behind us, near the entrance, there's a busker playing a violin. Just this side of him is a small coffee shop. Walk over there and get something to drink. Wait fifteen minutes, then go through to the platforms, those big doors there in front of us. I'll be waiting for you."

"What are you going to do?"

"Buy our tickets." Taking her knapsack, he ambled toward a tourist shop, where he purchased an "I-heart-Prague" sweatshirt and paid extra for a large shopping bag. With an effort, he worked the knapsack full of heavy books into the bag. Then he covered it with his jacket and pulled on the sweatshirt over his sweater.

The bag's corded handles cut into his fingers as he swung it nonchalantly while walking up to the ticket counter. One of the men in black suits eyed him. Pretending not to notice, Dan bought two tickets for the 8:38 train.

As he strolled casually toward the platforms, the man came up to him and said, "Excuse me. Are you Mister Lovel?"

Dan flipped up his palms to signify he didn't understand. But he understood completely the gold crucifix pinned through the fellow's lapel. Minions of the friars must be staking out all avenues of escape.

Shifting to French, the man said, *"Monsieur Lovel?"*

Dan shrugged. He could easily take down both him and his buddy, who now approached from behind. But crippling two people in a crowded station would surely bring the cops.

"*Señor,*" the fellow tried in Spanish.

Time to change gears. With a seductive smile, Dan stepped closer and murmured, "*¿El lavabo?*" The lavatory? Then he reached out to touch the fellow's crotch.

The man shrank back, clearly horrified at Dan's homosexual suggestion. "No!"

"*¿Estás seguro? Te puedo hacer feliz.*" Are you sure? I can make you happy.

Crossing himself, the guy backed up three more steps and barked something at his colleague.

Dan looked at the other guy, shook his head, and muttered, "*Eres feo.*" You're ugly. Then he walked away, his hips sashaying.

At the entrance to the platforms, he looked back to see the guys in suits arguing with one another. Relieved, he handed one ticket to the collector and stepped just inside to wait for Martine.

When she showed up, a few minutes later, Dan gave her ticket to the collector.

As they hurried toward their train she asked, "Do you think those men were from the monastery?"

"They're wearing the same gold-crucifix lapel pins as that receptionist who ratted us out at our hotel."

"Oh, Lord."

"With any luck, we've ditched them." But there was no guarantee.

#

After boarding their train with only minutes to spare, they made their way to a First-Class car, where they took two seats at the rear.

"First class?" Martine said.

"Your mother's paying. Besides, it's a lot cheaper than air fare."

She tilted her head as though agreeing he was probably right. "This place we're going, Usti …"

"Usti nad Labem." He pronounced it Oosti na Blabem, the closest he could get to what the lady at the ticket counter had said. "But Usti is fine."

"I found this in a rack of pamphlets." She held up a brochure displaying routes of the main Czech train lines, called Transit Corridors. "Our train goes all the way to the border. That would be simpler."

"I'm not so sure. I'd rather get out of this country without passing through any checkpoints, by car or train. Especially if those errand boys tell their masters what happened, and maybe what train we boarded, and maybe their masters—who undoubtedly have connections to the monastery—also have connections in the government."

"That's a lot of maybes."

"It's the way I think."

A steward rolled a refreshment trolley down their aisle. They bought coffee and croissants. Outside their window, Czech farmland rolled by, pastoral scenes straight out of a tourist book, broken only by occasional stops in towns you'd never think about twice.

Dan, however, did think twice. At each station, he scanned the platform for anybody even remotely suspicious. No one caught his attention, and no one entered their carriage.

After polishing off her croissant, Martine again held up the brochure with the train routes. "After Usti, there are three other stops that are closer to the border."

"But I think we can get help in Usti. There's a Roma community." Silently, he recalled what he'd learned on the internet that morning about the infamous wall down Matiční Street. "I'm guessing they have no love for the authorities and won't mind telling us how to evade them."

"What's Roma?"

"Gypsies."

"What? I'm not going near any Gypsies." She spat out the last word the way a racist in the States might say, "nigras."

Dan's stomach tightened. *Settle down, son.* Prejudice sprang from ignorance and unfamiliarity. To nip this in the bud, he said, "You're sitting next to one now."

Her mouth fell open. With a look of revulsion, as though he might infect her with some disease, she pushed herself away as far as she could go in her window seat, and sat there, eyes straight ahead, her jaw muscles working.

As his blood pressure rose, he contemplated getting off at the next station and letting her fend for herself. See how far that got her. Hell, if it weren't for him, she could already be in jail. Or worse.

The insults and jeers and fights he'd suffered as a kid, just because he was half-Gypsy, came tumbling back into his mind. They'd strengthened him but also made him feel ashamed. His Jewish father said he had to fight back, like the Israelis, and enrolled him in karate school. His mother told him he should be proud. "Look at Yul Brynner and Pablo Picasso. Even Elvis Presley. They all have Gypsy blood." Yul Brynner struck a chord. *The Magnificent Seven* had been one of Dan's favorite movies as a kid and, at that moment, Brynner became his role model. Soft-voiced but confident and tough.

In college, students who learned of Dan's ancestry either didn't care or thought it was cool. Since then, a few might joke about it in good humor, the way Geoff Fairchild had done at the zoo, but no one had insulted him personally.

Until now.

Why, he wondered, should Martine be so prejudiced, especially considering that she was well-educated? Speaking to her profile, he asked, "What do you have against Gypsies?"

Silence.

"Look," he said, "you can act like a petulant child or tell me what's bothering you."

"Screw you."

"So, the former."

She whipped her head around to face him. "Don't you read the news? They're a plague. All over Europe and especially in France. With their filthy camps and their children stealing everything in sight? A band of the grimy little shits yanked my purse right off my arm, just outside the Louvre."

"That justifies the French police bulldozing their encampments? They're refugees, for Christ's sake. I don't see you bulldozing other refugee communities. In case you haven't noticed, you're *building* encampments for the Kurds and Afghans."

She chewed her lower lip, then muttered, "Kurds and Afghans don't steal."

Exasperated, Dan stood from his seat. No sense pointing out that street urchins, regardless of background, had always been a problem in major cities. Or wasting his breath on a lecture about Gypsy persecution over the past thousand years, including half a million of them murdered in Nazi concentration camps. Or informing her that, where Gypsies had been allowed to settle, they'd adapted to the local culture, established successful businesses, and been accepted as a colorful part of the community.

He stomped into the connecting area between their carriage and the one behind. The clacking of wheels on rails and the whoosh of outside air helped drown out the sound of her voice still squawking in his ears. After looking fore and aft to make sure no conductor was coming, he lit up a cigar.

From its very start in the Caymans, this whole job had been a bad idea. He had let himself be swayed by the morality of the mission and Astrid's appeal to righting the injustices his grandparents had suffered. Hell, he'd never even met his grandparents.

Astrid had played him. And she obviously hadn't told her daughter about Dan's ethnicity. Did she know of Martine's prejudice and hope the issue wouldn't come up? It didn't matter. The issue *had* come up, revealing an ugliness he never expected.

So, now what?

Sucking in a lungful of the rich smoke, he reminded himself that emotions cloud judgment. If he were ruthlessly logical, Martine's disclosure of her racism was the only thing that had changed. The mission, bad idea or not, was something he had accepted. And never before had he failed in a mission. Plus, the goal of returning looted artworks to their rightful owners was still worthy.

Granted, continuing to babysit someone who despised him would grate worse than chewing a mouthful of aluminum foil. But the main part of his mission was to keep her safe. He couldn't just leave her in the lurch.

On the other hand, maybe she would leave *him*. No. Despite her bigotry, she wasn't stupid enough to think she could make it to France alone.

Man, he yearned to let her try.

But he'd give her the option. One more racist comment, and she was on her own. If, by some miracle, she managed to keep her trap shut, then he'd deliver her to Paris. His parting words would be, "Au revoir, sweetheart. And remember, you were rescued by a Gypsy."

Chapter 9

As their train pulled into the station in Usti nad Labem, Dan told Martine, "You can come with me or not. I don't care."

"That's a cruel thing to say. What choice do I have?"

"Plenty." He stood and pointed north. "The border's twelve miles that way. Stay on the train, take a taxi or bus, hitch a ride. Or go back to Prague and catch a flight."

"You pompous bastard."

The train halted outside a three-story yellow terminal building with no frills and equally little charm. From tall erector-set poles, power cables connected by black insulators crisscrossed the tracks.

Dan pulled off his Prague sweatshirt and dropped it on his seat. "If you come with me, I don't want to hear another word about Gypsies. Do you understand?"

"You're the one who started it."

That was playing loose with the truth. He slipped on his jacket, handed her the knapsack, and left the large shopping bag beside the sweatshirt. "Follow me or don't."

As expected, she did. What he did not expect was to suddenly feel guilty about his ultimatum. She was a novice at crossing borders illegally—or at least he assumed she was—and part of the job he'd accepted was to protect her. He wasn't about to apologize, but he could be a bit more civil.

They walked out of the station into a bright crisp day, marred only by the smells of diesel exhaust and what Dan assumed to be a nearby petrochemical plant. At the taxi rank, there were only two cabs. Deciding on the first one for a change, he told the driver, "Matiční Street," then held the door for Martine, a gesture that raised her eyebrows.

Their driver sped them along a highway adjacent to the Elbe River, a dark green watercourse on their right with a sprinkling of barges and a couple of graceful bridges. Forested hills to their left lent a woodsy scent to the cold air streaming in through Dan's partially open window. Low mountains capped by snow glinted on the horizon.

That scenic setting changed when they angled away from the river. A wooded hill on their left turned out to be only half-wooded. As they passed it, he saw that the other half had been gouged out into white terraces of raw rock. Limestone mining for cement, he guessed. Dead ahead, soulless concrete buildings obscured the mountains. They entered an industrial area with rows of tank cars on one side and semis backed up to loading docks on the other. The air coming in brought odors of heavy-duty grease and more diesel exhaust, realities of an emerging economy.

A few hundred feet past the last loading dock, their driver stopped at an intersection where red street signs identified the cross road as Matiční Street. It ran left and right for a block in each direction. Unpainted, two-story, concrete cubes on one side of the street faced skeletal trees and tall weeds on the other.

"Lovely," Martine uttered in a tone that could wilt cactus.

He let it slide but decided he had to stow her someplace before knocking on any doors. Roma were sensitive to attitudes, and hers would scuttle his efforts to find help.

"Café?" he asked the driver, a twenty-something kid with oiled black hair and a silver stud in one ear.

"By train station."

Dan handed him a hundred euros and said, "You take her to café. Stay with her. Two hours."

"What?" she blurted.

"Two hours, then you bring her back here. Okay?"

"Yes, sir."

Martine snatched up the knapsack and grabbed her door handle. "I'm not going."

"Listen to me! You don't know the first thing about Gypsies. If we want their help, I have to do this myself."

She stared at him venomously. Then the venom appeared to drain. Slowly, she released the door handle.

Relieved, he tried to sweeten the pot with more reasoning. "By the time you get back, I should know whether they'll help us or not. If they won't, we'll decide together on an alternative. In the meantime, go get some lunch. And pay for the driver's meal, also."

When at last she sat back in her seat, Dan climbed out of the taxi and walked away. As soon as it drove off, he stopped and rubbed his palms on his jeans. This would not be easy. The Roma would be wary, maybe hostile. He was an outsider in their community but had to forge a bond of brotherhood, especially since he'd be asking for a favor. Although it nettled him, he would have to act submissive. Only if he failed miserably would he revert to Plan B, where he and Martine settled on some other escape route.

Positive he would be interrogated about his background—provided he managed to reach a leader—he foraged through his mother's stories as he approached the first door.

The woman who answered, a Slavic-looking dumpling complete with apron and babushka, claimed to speak no English and shut the door in his face. At the second, third, and fourth doors, he received basically the same reaction, always from matronly women. Then it struck him. At this time of day, their husbands would be working.

He was about to try the next door when four young men came around the corner of the house and spread out like a barricade. All were about Dan's height, had ear-length black hair, and wore threatening scowls. Three had wide moustaches. The clean-shaven one was shirtless in the cold and smacked a length of pipe into one palm like a cop with a billy club.

Dan struggled to remain calm, loose-limbed. If things went sideways, the guy with the pipe would go down first.

Do not let that happen, he told himself. They're just protecting their persecuted community. You'd do the same.

Suddenly his sixth sense flashed a warning. He looked behind and saw five other young men advancing from the direction he'd just come. Sweat ran down his sides. It was nine to one now, and they had the home field advantage.

Turning his back to the house so he could keep an eye on both groups, he wiped his palms again, then raised them the way a bank customer would if facing armed gunmen. "Does anybody speak English?"

After a long silence, punctuated by a tightening circle of glowering men, a mustachioed fellow with a broken front tooth said, "Who are you? What you want here?"

At last. Dan puffed out his chest in a gesture of pride. "I am Jardani Camlo, a Rom from America."

"Rom?" The guy squinted at him suspiciously, his broken tooth now obscured by an uncertain frown.

"From the Camlo people. You know the Camlo?"

The circle of menacing faces closed in a step. One of the five who'd approached from the main street produced a double-edged knife. No telling what other weapons they might have.

Dan took deep breaths through his nose. This was bad. If push came to shove, he might still get out alive, but being so tightly surrounded, he would never get out uninjured. He needed to reach someone in authority.

Racking his brain for words he had learned from his mother, he finally recalled the term for leader. "If you do not know the Camlo people, your *bulibasha* does. Tell him I am here. The police are looking for me. I need his help."

More silence. Then the English speaker addressed the others, probably translating Dan's request. Several shook their heads. One frisked him, inexpertly, to which Dan submitted with clenched teeth. After more chatter, another guy knocked on the door behind Dan. Dan heard the door open, then a few curt words before the door closed again. He guessed the guy was making a phone call. *Progress, I hope.*

When the man returned, an argument erupted with his cohorts. Shouts, balled fists. Fortunately, the fellow who'd gone inside prevailed. With grumbles, the whole group marched Dan between two of the houses, then through a wooden gate and into the densely treed backyard of a house on the next street.

As they approached the rear of the house, a thin, bearded man in his middle fifties stepped out. He wore heavy black trousers and a gray sweater with a loop of wool dangling from one sleeve where he'd evidently snagged it. Unmarried, Dan figured, since an attentive wife would have hooked the loop into the inside of the sweater.

In a tone not of recognition, but of wary curiosity, the man said, "Jardani Camlo?"

"Yes, sir."

"What is your American name?"

"Dan Lovel."

The man seemed to mull this a moment. Below the left ear of his weather-beaten face, he had a knife scar that he absently rubbed with his forefinger. "Why Lovel?"

Glad he'd prepared, Dan replied, "Camlo means lovely. When some of my people were given land by Lord Lovel in England, we adopted his name." He considered adding that it was fairly common for Roma to adopt the names, languages, even religions of countries where they settled. But he didn't want to insult a man who was apparently a *bulibasha* and would know those things as well as Dan's mother did.

"Camlo people have dark skin." The man stepped closer, peering at Dan's face as if assessing whether his complexion was real or possibly sprayed on by Czech authorities attempting to plant a mole. At last, he dismissed the vigilantes and said, "Come inside."

With a silent exhalation of relief, Dan stepped into the house and halted, his mind swirling in a storm of déjà vu. His mother's "sanctuary room" had looked just like this.

Well, not exactly. Hers was smaller, a single bedroom of their house in Seattle. But she'd decorated it like this, as a retreat from the pressures of life in America, a return to the culture of her forebears. Ali Baba's cave, he had always thought as a child.

And here it was for real. A couch, two armchairs, and a table, all covered with tasseled carpets depicting red roses and swirling vines on green, blue, and orange backgrounds. More tassels hung from a long shelf on one wall. Above the shelf ran a row of bath towel-sized tapestries, again with roses on variously colored backgrounds, then an arrangement of decorative plates and, unlike in his mother's room, a framed print of the Madonna and Child.

Dan felt almost overwhelmed by the psychedelic onslaught. And pained that his mother could not be here with him.

"Are you okay?" the elder asked.

"Your house reminds me of my mother."

The man cocked his head. "And your father?"

"He's Jewish. His tastes are more spartan."

A slight smile curled the man's lips. "Like yours, I think."

Dan nodded and now noticed the blue and white porcelain stove that stood on claw-footed legs in a corner, giving warmth and accentuating the aromas of wool, incense, and tobacco smoke.

When his host led him to a couch, Dan also noticed a bulge in the small of the man's back, under the sweater. A pistol. "I didn't catch your name," Dan said.

From an ornately carved wooden cabinet, the fellow withdrew two shot glasses and a bottle of clear liquid. "You like Slivovitz?"

"Love it." Not really. To him, the plum brandy tasted like moonshine and not far off its Chinese cousin, Maotai.

After filling the glasses, the man handed one to Dan. *"Bahkt tu kel."*

Thanks to his mother, Dan knew the toast meant, "To your good luck and health," or something like that. He repeated it and knocked back the liquor in one godawful swallow. At least that part of the traditional greeting was over.

Wrong.

The man refilled their glasses, then seated himself in an armchair. "I am Besnik Lom. You know the Lom people?"

Dan shook his head, embarrassed that he hadn't paid closer attention to his mother's teachings. But there were lots of Roma clans, and only a few she had told him about stuck in his mind—Ursari, the Balkan bear trainers; Djambas, Macedonian horse trainers and acrobats; Mango, because he liked the fruit.

"From Armenia," Lom said. "Some call us Bosha." He lifted his glass and, this time, took just a sip.

Dan reluctantly followed suit, steeling himself against the smell that made him think of vomit.

With a penetrating gaze, Lom asked, "Why is the police looking for you?"

Initially caught off guard by the adroit change of subjects, Dan snapped back to the reason he was here. "I'm not actually certain about the police. But there is another group, with strong ties to the Czech authorities. And they are definitely searching for us."

"Us?"

"I'm traveling with a *gadji*," the Romani word for female outsider.

Lom looked perplexed, then irked, as though this were information his men should have brought him. "Where is this *gadji*?"

"In a restaurant near the train station. A taxi should bring her here in about an hour. To the intersection up there with Matiční Street."

"And then?"

"Then I hope you will welcome her, as you have welcomed me. And help us cross into Germany."

Poker-faced, Lom said, "Tell me about this group that searches for you."

Dan leveled with him, to an extent. The Louvre books, their value for righting many wrongs. But in case Besnik Lom was a devout Catholic, as the painting of Mary and Jesus could signify, he mentioned only a "library" and that his pursuers were powerful fanatics.

"These books are so important?"

Dan wondered if the man ever spoke in anything other than questions, but replied, "I believe they are. That is why we have stolen them."

With a tilt of his head, Lom conceded, "Stealing is sometimes necessary."

Twenty more minutes of interview passed, along with two more glasses of Slivovitz, to which Dan's nose mercifully was becoming inured. Then someone knocked on the door. Lom answered it and returned. "You said one hour. Your *gadji* is at the corner now."

#

To avoid crossing backyards again, Dan left through Lom's front door and hurried to the corner. One block to his left, Martine stood beside the taxi, looking around. He was about to walk out and greet her when he spotted a police car approaching from behind the cab. He ducked back and watched as the car cruised by slowly. A block farther on, it stopped at the curb.

Reigning in an impulse to dash to Martine and rush her into the wooded grassland across from the houses on Matiční Street, he forced himself to keep watch on the police car. If it made a U-turn, he would snatch her and run. If it stayed put, there might be a better way.

The car remained parked, which could only mean the cops were surveilling Martine via their rear-view mirrors.

He sprinted back to Lom's house, where he summarized the situation and his plan to get out of it.

"A distraction?" Lom furrowed his brow in unconcealed irritation, as if to say, *In my house barely an hour, and already you're a pain in the ass.* Then he turned on his heel and, after a brief phone call, returned. "In a few minutes you will have it."

Dan went out the back door this time and retraced the route that had first brought him to Lom's house. He hoped he could somehow return the favor to Lom, but that would have to wait. He charged across Matiční Street and through the wooded grassland on the other side until he reached the intersection with the main road.

Now only forty feet from her, he called, "Martine! Turn around and face the opposite side of the road. No! Don't look at me. Turn around."

Obviously perplexed, she finally complied.

"Now dismiss the cab and walk across to the other side of the main road. Then stand there."

Her taxi drove off. With the knapsack on her shoulders, she crossed the street.

Dan hustled to the corner house on his side and peered around at the police car. Suddenly chaos erupted two blocks beyond the cops. Yelling, young men "brawling," bottles breaking.

The police car's lights flashed into action. Its siren wailed. With a squeal of tires, it shot off toward the melee.

"Martine," Dan shouted, "run back here. Now!"

The "brawling" men scattered in all directions.

Looking scared to death, Martine jogged up to him. "What's happening?"

"I'll tell you in a minute." He pulled the heavy knapsack off her shoulders and slung it onto his, then grabbed her hand. "This way."

He took her back the way he had just come, between the houses, through the gate, into Lom's tree-shaded backyard, where the man motioned them to get inside.

"Your men will be okay?" Dan asked.

"Do not worry." Lom shut the door. "You will pay them for their effort."

Fair enough, he thought and introduced Martine, who was still panting.

To his relief, she shook hands with no hint of revulsion. But as she looked around at Lom's colorful—some would say gaudy—furnishings, her face registered the same mixture of surprise and curiosity that Alice must have felt when she stumbled into Wonderland.

Before she could say something awkward, Dan suggested this might be a good time for a drink.

"Some Slivovitz?" Lom asked her.

"What's that?"

With second thoughts, Dan said, "An acquired taste. Perhaps, sir, you have something else?"

"Only whisky."

Dan nodded. "That would be great."

It turned out to be a pretty decent Scotch. As Martine sipped hers slowly, Dan told her they'd been followed or tracked. "It was my fault," he admitted. "The sweatshirt and shopping bag I left on the train. It would have been a fairly simple matter to figure out where we disembarked and contact the local cab companies and the cops. I should have known better."

"We learn from our mistakes," Lom said sagely. "But now you have brought the police to our doors. They will be … ugly to us. You must leave tonight."

Chapter 10

After refilling their glasses, Lom produced a detailed map of Usti nad Labem and the surrounding area. He pointed out several routes into Germany, describing the pros and cons of each. None was what Dan would call convenient.

The best of a bad lot was Road 2488. He traced it with his finger from where it passed under the main highway to where it ended in rural countryside at the edge of a forest. From there they'd have to go on foot, but not far. A stream within the forest marked the German border, and fifty feet beyond the stream lay a road called Nasenbach Strasse. A mile of walking along that road should bring them back to the main highway, well past the checkpoints.

Dan tapped the spot where Road 2488 stopped. "This one."

"You have a good eye," Lom said.

"What about the stream?"

"The water comes to here." He touched his waist. "We have done many times."

Of course, you have. "What do you think?" Dan asked Martine.

"The books cannot get wet. We'll have to hold them over our heads."

"I'll do that."

"Fine," she said and stood from the couch. "Let's go."

"No, no." Lom held up his hand in a "stop" gesture. "You go at night. Now is too dangerous."

Glancing at her watch, she protested, "That's an hour or two from now. What if the police car comes back?"

"Men are watching," Lom assured her. "Also, you must eat first. It will be cold tonight. There is no food on the German side before many kilometers."

"Thank you, sir." Dan welcomed the thought of dinner. He hadn't consumed anything but railway coffee and a croissant all day, plus more alcohol than was wise on an empty stomach.

Lom excused himself. A few minutes after he returned, delectable aromas of sautéing onions and garlic wafted out of a kitchen Dan couldn't see.

Seated again, Lom gestured toward the knapsack, which rested on the floral carpet beside Martine's feet. "These so-important books, you will show me?"

Martine hesitated, but Dan said, "Sure," and pulled out one of the thick Louvre volumes. It was the least they could do for the man who was helping them escape.

As Lom placed the book on the coffee table and opened it, Dan realized that he, himself, had never actually looked inside. He'd imagined written descriptions of the Louvre's treasures but now saw that each page Lom turned also contained three or four finely drawn etchings, so detailed they might have been produced by a medical illustrator. "Have you looked at these?" he asked Martine.

"Not really. There hasn't been time." She came closer, peered at the open page, and started turning more. "This is a work of art in its own right."

Briefly, Dan wished he had similar drawings of the art looted from his grandparents.

To Lom he said, "Many of these statues and paintings were stolen from famous places two hundred years ago."

With a shrug, Lom replied, "And …?"

"Sometimes things that were stolen should be returned."

Lom balked. "You are embarrassed by our reputation? Those were old days. It is not so true today."

"Roma did not steal them. The emperor of France did."

"Oh." Lom cracked a smile. "That is different."

#

As dusk fell, a young woman poked her head in and said something in a language Dan didn't understand.

"My daughter, Florika," Lom announced as she retreated. "It is time to eat."

Dan couldn't have been more thankful. The aromas were driving his stomach crazy.

They adjourned to a room just large enough to contain a small table painted turquoise and four straight-backed wooden chairs. Through a curtain separating them from the kitchen, Dan glimpsed a cast-iron stove topped with steaming pots and backed by a bright red wall with open shelves that held cups, glasses, and plates.

Florika, whom Dan guessed to be in her early twenties, placed bowls of soup before them. She wore a light blue blouse and a dark blue, ankle-length skirt with deep pleats and an orange sash tied around the waist. Straight black hair cascaded over her ample chest. But her face, with its hooded eyes and dour mouth, resembled a death mask, which probably explained why she still lived at home. That she was cooking added weight to Dan's previous deduction that Lom's wife had passed away.

The soup, consisting of eggs and cheese in a chicken broth, smelled heavenly and tasted even better. Next came mutton, cooked in red wine and black olives, with mushrooms and steamed cabbage on the side. Dan wondered now if Lom didn't keep his daughter here for her culinary talent.

"Delicious," Martine proclaimed as Florika cleared their plates. "Thank you very much."

Lom translated, and his daughter smiled.

Only out of deference to their host did Dan refrain from drawing Martine's attention to the fact that she'd been dining among "uncivilized filth."

No. That was the wrong attitude. Maybe getting to know, traditional Roma, real Roma, would grind down her bigotry more effectively than he ever could. Certainly her contented face, as she brushed auburn hair from her eyes, suggested progress. Go with it, he thought. Don't screw things up.

Florika returned with small bowls of what looked like berries in heavy cream. But before she could set them down, loud rapping sounded at the door.

Lom answered it, spoke rapidly to someone, and returned with urgency in his eyes. "Men are coming."

Dan pushed back from the table. "Police?"

"One police, but he is gone. Now other men. *Gadjo.* Eight of them. They are working in twos on each street. They demand to go inside one house, then come out and demand to go in the next." From under his sweater, Lom drew the pistol he'd been concealing, a Czech CZ-75 semiautomatic. "Come. You must hide."

"No way," Dan said. "Do you have another gun?"

Martine got up and planted herself in front of Lom. "Two more guns."

Lom's dark eyes flicked between them. "I have an old German one."

"If it works," Dan said, "I'll use it."

Looking doubtful, Lom left the room.

Martine whipped around to face Dan. "Do women not count? I can shoot."

"Maybe you can," he allowed, "but I'm qualified as 'expert' with both sidearms and long guns." When that seemed to sink in, he added, "As to your question, in this society women do count. But historically they use knives."

Martine winced, which brought to mind the knife scar on her arm. Then her expression hardened. "They will not get these books."

"I'll make sure of it."

Her eyes bored into his. "If you fail, I will not."

When Lom returned, he unwrapped a polishing cloth from a handgun-shaped object to reveal a Luger "Black Widow," a Nazi pistol worth about two thousand dollars in the U.S. "I have never shooted it."

Dan had never even held one. Feeling privileged, he ejected the clip, checked that it was full, then pulled up and back several times on the knee joint of the toggle lock to open and close the slide. Lom might not have shot it, but he'd kept it clean and lubricated.

Uncertain whether Lom planned to take up a post outside or stay in here, Dan told him, "Martine is highly skilled in hand-to-hand combat. She'll make sure nothing happens to Florika."

"I do not think the men will come this far. Soon we will throw Molotov cocktails."

"Excellent. Just in case, though, I'm going to stand guard out front."

"Jardani, these men are dangerous."

"So am I."

#

Dan slipped out of Lom's front door into the cold night air and immediately spotted a pair of goons in black leather jackets and buzz cuts barging into a house two buildings away. He dashed across the road, hid behind a tree, and sighted down the pistol. True to tale, pointing a Luger felt like pointing your finger. Aside from the tapered barrel, all of its weight rested in or above his palm.

No sooner did the two thugs come out than shattering bottles and flaming gasoline exploded around them. Yellow-orange fire roiled into the air. Lom's forces kicking some ass.

The thugs ducked, then ran and started shooting into the darkness. At the same time, gunfire erupted on neighboring streets, probably similar attacks to the one Dan had just witnessed.

Closer at hand, the men across from him crouched low and fired again. If they had actual targets in sight, Dan couldn't see them. But no way would he let them shoot up a residential neighborhood, especially this one. He drew a bead on the goon to the left and was about to squeeze the trigger, when the one on the right jerked backwards and crumpled.

Christ, someone was firing back at these guys.

He peered into the darkness but saw no one. From his right he heard a *pffft*. The second man spun around and collapsed.

Both of them howled in pain.

Dan flattened himself on the ground, his pulse hammering. Based on the sound, whoever dropped those two had done it with a silenced rifle. A professional firearm. The Roma here must be better equipped than he'd imagined.

Grateful for the help, he tuned out the *pop pop* of pistol fire on adjacent streets and strained his eyes and ears for any sign of this mysterious benefactor, a sniper skilled enough to "decommission" without killing.

Sirens blared.

With little time left before cops swarmed all over the place, he sprinted to the side of Lom's house, then slipped around to the rear door. He knocked and, to avoid alarming Lom who could be waiting inside, called out, "It's me, Jardani."

Lom opened the door. "Come quickly."

Martine stood in the entrance to the dining room, her feet slightly apart, arms at her sides in what Dan recognized as a Krav stance. Ready for any assailant. "You're okay?" she asked.

"Fine. You?"

Looking relieved but edgy, she stepped forward. "Thank God, the shooting has died down."

"Probably due to more Molotov cocktails," Dan thought out loud. He was about to hand Lom the Luger when a soft knock came to the back door. Dan whipped around and aimed at the door.

"Not to worry," Lom told him and admitted a clean-shaven young man wearing black trousers and a black turtleneck. "Jardani, this is Yoska. He will take you to the border. You must leave now."

Relaxing his grip, Dan lowered the pistol. "You'll be all right? The police are coming." He would stay, if necessary.

"Do not worry for me."

Envious of the elder's confidence, Dan held out the Luger. "I didn't need it. Your man with the rifle is a good shot."

"Rifle?"

"The one with the silencer. He dropped both of the bad guys coming down your street. Don't worry, they're just wounded."

Lom furrowed his brow. "We have no rifles."

A shiver of alarm ran up Dan's spine. If the sniper wasn't a Rom, then who was he?

"Did you see this person?" Lom asked.

"No. But whoever it was only targeted the bad guys."

"I will ask. Now you must go." Lom embraced him. "Be safe, *bar*."

Dan recognized the word for brother. "Thank you, *bar*."

Shouldering her knapsack, Martine came forward and extended her hand to Lom. "I thank you, also."

Lom shook it. "I do not say so to many *gadji*. But I will say to you. You are welcome."

A flush of gratitude coursed through Dan's body. Surely tonight had converted Martine, or at least opened her mind.

But as he and she followed Yoska out the back door, Dan felt an ominous presence lurking over them—a sniper who could be a guardian angel, or an enemy who'd missed his chance to fire a bullet into Dan's head.

#

Yoska guided them through backyards down to the house farthest from the main street. There he pulled a drop cloth off an elderly Toyota Camry that fired up at the first turn of the key. Dan offered Martine the front passenger seat, but she shook her head and climbed into the back.

As they drove along an unpaved route out of the neighborhood, she said, "I was really scared."

"Anyone who wasn't scared was a fool." Even Lom, who apparently had stayed inside and would have shot an intruder before Martine had to act, certainly feared for his daughter's safety. "Just so you know, I'm glad you and I are together in this."

Leaning forward she handed him a five-inch paring knife. "Sorry, I forgot I had this. It's from Florika's kitchen. I hid it in my hip pocket in case Krav wasn't enough."

Could she possibly know what it was like to stab someone? Dan sure-as-hell hoped not. He had done it only once and would never forget the awful sensation of a blade penetrating skin and muscle, then an internal organ.

Thankfully, Martine hadn't suffered that experience tonight.

Dan tapped Yoska's arm, placed the knife on the center console, and said, "For Lom. Yes? Lom."

Yoska glanced at it, then nodded and returned his eyes to the road. So far, the somber-eyed kid hadn't spoken a word. He drove at safe speeds, both hands on the wheel, along rural roads with hardly any other traffic. The perfect wheelman.

Beside him, Dan thought back over the past several hours, his first experience with a real Roma community. He had not exactly been accepted. Nor, of course, had Martine. But Lom had taken them in, fed them, and gone to exceptional lengths to help them escape. At his direction, many others had also helped.

Supremely thankful, Dan nevertheless felt guilty as sin. Because of him, the whole community had suffered, and would probably suffer more in the coming days. Yet none of them complained, at least that he had seen. They rose to the challenge and worked together. Dan, accustomed to working alone, couldn't help admiring that camaraderie. It made him wish he'd known his mother's people.

Maybe one day he could track them down and meet them.

Yoska turned onto a route sign-posted 2488. In the moonlight, farmland and forest slipped by, punctuated by occasional habitations. After twenty minutes or so, they passed under a major motorway, Czech Route 8 by Dan's reckoning, which became a German autobahn barely half a mile from here.

After passing more farmland, Yoska switched off the headlights and coasted to a stop. Just ahead of them, the pavement ended and forest began. Yoska pointed at the trees, made walking motions with his fingers, and pointed again.

"*Nais tuk,*" Dan said, finally recalling the Romani words for thank you. Too bad he couldn't remember them at Lom's house. And too bad he hadn't paid closer attention to what his mother tried to teach him.

Concentrate. They had a border to cross.

He climbed out, opened the rear door for Martine, and stood back as the Toyota made a U-turn and disappeared, its lights still off.

And there they were. Dead of night, middle of winter. Silence. Not even the chirping of insects. Ideal conditions for hearing anyone who might pursue them. He would have preferred a crescent moon to the full one that shone down on them like a floodlight. But at least there was no snow on the ground to record their tracks.

Which reminded him, "By the way, both of the men who were shot back there had buzz cut hair. Just like our original desk clerk at the hotel and the two assholes who were watching for us at the train station in Prague. I'll bet anything the wounded thugs are tied to the monastery."

She blew out a long, slow breath. "I had no idea they were so powerful. Or so brutal." She paused then asked, "What about the person who shot them?"

"I wish I knew. But right now, our immediate concern is getting out of this country."

He walked with her a few paces into the woods. "Before we go farther, put all your valuables in the knapsack. Phone, passport, money, anything you don't want to get wet." When they'd done that, he fastened the pack's straps. "Stay close behind me and try not to step on any twigs."

Moving cautiously under a canopy of branches that blocked out most of the moonlight, Dan thanked his Gypsy genes for the gift of good night vision. Especially when, after a minute or two of searching, he noticed a broken branch within the undergrowth, a sign someone had come this way before. He pushed past it to a pathway narrower than a game trail.

In ten more minutes, they came to the "river," which looked more like a Louisiana bayou than any channel where the water actually flowed. "I'm going to take off my boots and socks. You don't have to, but it'll be no fun tramping along the road on the other side in wet footwear."

"I'll do what you do."

They sat on the bank, stuffed their socks into their boots, then tied the laces together and hung the boots around their necks. "I assume it's a muddy bottom," he said. "But just in case, shuffle your feet forward before taking a step."

He waded in. *Kee-rist.* The water was freezing. It's winter, idiot, just three days before Christmas. Steeling himself, he inched across, saying "branch" every time he encountered one. No sharp rocks, thank goodness.

By the time he trudged up the other bank, his toes were numb. He turned to give Martine a hand, but she scrambled up without his assistance and didn't even mention the frigid water. Tougher than she looks, he thought.

After using the elastic ankles of their socks to dry their feet, they re-donned their walking gear and continued along a twisting trail even less visible than the one on the Czech side.

"I don't know how you can see," she whispered.

"Just stick close." The trail forked. No broken branches to point the way. Summoning his internal compass, Dan went left. At the next fork, he veered right. Their supposed fifty feet of forest seemed more like several hundred.

Finally they emerged onto a dirt road that had to be Nasenbach Strasse. Dan moved aside to let Martine stand next to him. "Welcome to Germany."

"We did it." She turned his head with both hands and kissed him on the lips. "You're amazing."

"For a Gypsy?"

With a smile, she said, "Maybe even for a regular person."

Chapter 11

"We still have serious problems," Dan said as he and Martine headed north along Nasenbach Strasse, a moonlit swath through dense forest.

"But we've escaped the bad guys, as you called them."

"Maybe, maybe not. We don't know how far the monastery's influence extends. If they've involved the Vatican, it's all of Europe and the U.S."

"That's farfetched, don't you think? Why would the Vat—"

"Shhh." Dan tugged her arm to stop her. The sound he'd heard came again, like the footsteps of a dog on fallen leaves. Clenching her wrist, he stayed perfectly still. They were in the middle of the road. No weapons, no cover. Fully illuminated by the floodlight moon.

Thirty feet ahead, a massive boar with six-inch tusks emerged from the woods. It stopped and swung its head toward them. In a rage, a boar could chase down a man and gore his guts out.

Martine pulled her wrist free and clamped his hand in a death grip.

His brain flashed back to an old codger in Texas who'd hunted feral pigs all his life. "If you're caught without a rifle, get your ass up the nearest tree." Dan scanned the nearest trees. No low branches. Trunks too wide to shimmy up. He would have to confront the boar, use his jacket like a matador's cape, and tell Martine to drop the knapsack and run. Lousy plan, but the only one he could think of.

The boar peered at them with fierce, beady eyes. Its snout quivered, processing their scent. It advanced one step. Dan braced to yank Martine out of its path. But after a heart-stopping moment, the beast apparently decided they were neither food nor enemy and trotted across into the forest on the other side.

"*Mon Dieu,*" Martine breathed. "He could have killed us both."

Dan willed his muscles to uncoil. As his tension subsided, he tried unsuccessfully to dispel images of tusks ripping flesh.

"Come on." Martine pushed his shoulder. "Let's get out of here before it comes back."

At a brisk clip, they reached the spot where the animal had disappeared. Without breaking stride, Dan peered into the forest and strained his ears for any hint of the beast. Nothing. After another thirty feet, he began to relax. "I think we're safe now."

Martine looked behind them, then slowed her pace a little.

To help calm her, he reverted to their previous discussion of other problems. "About the Vatican, I have no idea if or why they might become involved. But it's something we can't discount."

"Forget the Vatican." She glanced back again before seeming to accept that they really were out of danger. "A lot of Napoleon's loot came from there. They'd want it back. So, if they even know what we've done, which I doubt, they should be on our side."

"But that other book, the thin one. What's it about?"

"I'm not sure. It mentions Moses, Moshe in ancient Hebrew. But that was the only word I could identify quickly. I don't know the language very well."

"If it's an old religious text, like the Dead Sea Scrolls, that could explain why the friars, or even the Vatican, would want it back."

"I think it's more likely to be secular. Perhaps a commentary on some aspect of the Pentateuch, the five books of Moses. There's a huge body of Jewish commentary on the Old Testament."

Dan's father had mentioned this. The Mishna, or something like that. A waste of brainpower, in his dad's view. "If that's all it is, then why would your mother want it?"

"I don't know. But there's a man at the Louvre who should be able to tell us."

"We have to get there first." And they were still a thousand kilometers away.

Above them, heavy clouds moved in. Tiny snowflakes started falling, drifting through the air like lazy gnats. Not enough to visibly dampen the road, but possibly a harbinger of more. He picked up the pace. According to his watch and the map he'd memorized, "We should reach the main highway in about twenty minutes. Close to midnight. Then we'll flag down a ride."

"We'd better hope we get one fast, before any border guards come by. They might change shifts at midnight."

"Good point." This close to the border the two of them might look suspicious. On top of that, hitchhiking was illegal on German autobahns. He rubbed his face. The fatigue he'd been fighting seemed to settle on him more heavily. At least, both of them were thinking. "If we have to, we can sleep in the forest until morning. Scrape out a hollow in the ground, then line it with leaves, crawl in, and pull more leaves in on top of us."

She peered at him. "You've done that before, haven't you?"

"Once. I don't recommend it."

"Good, because spending a night in the forest with wild animals is not going to happen." She looked back again. "I'd rather poke a stick in my eye. Or take my chances with the police."

"You could show some leg," he quipped. "It might catch us a driver before any cops come by."

"In this weather? My jeans are wet. My legs are frozen. They're probably covered with enough goose bumps to look like a plucked chicken."

"I was joking."

"Uh huh. On a serious note, you mentioned we still have problems. More than just the Vatican?"

"Definitely." As Nasenbach Strasse curved to the left, he said, "One of them is that, when your mother reserved our hotel rooms in Prague, she used our real names. Plus, they copied our passports. So, anyone looking for us—"

"Knows who we are. But we're no longer in the Czech Republic."

"If the monastery's reach extends beyond—"

"You don't really think that, do you?"

"I think, just like in Prague, our main restriction here is that we shouldn't try to fly on any commercial airline. I'll rent a car using my Spanish ID, and we'll drive into France at some rural crossing. I don't care how extensive a network 'they' might have, they can't possibly cover every route across a border that's open to EU citizens."

"You have Spanish ID?"

"And Canadian. Passport, driver's license, credit cards. You only have your real passport, right?" When she didn't answer, he said, "Which is why we need to do it my way."

"You do think ahead," she allowed. "No wonder my mother speaks highly of you."

Nice to hear, but those were totally different circumstances. Saving Astrid's life had been a quick, almost reflexive action. This situation with Martine required navigating a far more complex decision tree, one limb of which was that, if people were trying to find them and they had Martine's real name, then they probably knew her address in Paris. Fortunately, he would have time to mull that one before they reached the French capital.

She turned up her collar. "Here's something that's been bothering me. You said you didn't know who shot those men outside Lom's house. Do you have any ideas?"

"Only two. Both are even less plausible than any involvement of the Vatican."

"Tell me," she said. "Any ideas better than none."

"Best case is somebody with a grudge against the authorities saw an opportunity and took it."

"A huge coincidence, wouldn't you say?"

"Which is why I don't believe it."

"What's the other?"

"The only alternative I can imagine is that the sniper, or whoever he works for, is someone who wants us to succeed and is willing to shoot people to ensure it."

She halted. "How would that be possible? Nobody knows but the friars. And their thugs."

"That's what we think. But is it true?"

#

By the time they reached the highway, snow was falling in earnest. Dan now figured it could actually benefit them, that drivers might have sympathy for a couple with snow-dusted shoulders.

If any drivers came by.

He and Martine waited five minutes before the first truck roared past, kicking up a storm of wet in its wake.

Martine lowered the arm she'd held out.

"Patience," he said, thinking the more pathetic they looked, the better.

Two cars whizzed by, then another truck. Then no one. How much traffic could you expect between the Czech Republic and Germany at this time of night?

Dan zipped the front of his jacket all the way to the top.

With hunched shoulders, Martine jounced on her toes. "I think part of our problem is we're wearing black, so we're hard to see. If you can find a fallen branch, we could wave it to attract attention."

He doubted that would work. But they had to do something soon. He retraced his steps and hunted around in the woods until he found a three-foot branch that still had plenty of pine needles on it. With numb fingers and the guilty certainty that Martine was freezing her butt off, he carried the branch back and ... *I'll be damned.*

Martine stood beside the open passenger door of a big semi.

Perplexed but relieved, he dropped the branch and jogged up to her.

In the cab, a kindly looking fellow with bratwurst-sized fingers and a Santa Clause beard peered at him. The kindly expression vanished.

"Please," Martine said in German, clearly aware that having Dan beside her severely downgraded the driver's aspirations.

In a resigned tone, Santa asked, *"Wo gehen Sie?"* Where are you going?

"Leipzig," Dan replied.

"Einsteigen." Get in.

As Dan gave her a hand up, he said sotto voce, "I'm impressed."

She arched her eyebrows like Groucho Marx. "Your idea. But no leg needed. All it took was a damsel in distress."

And the penny dropped. That's why she'd sent him into the forest, not for some stupid branch but so she could be there by herself. A woman alone, attracting the attention of a trucker who surely saw her as an opportunity.

When they'd seated themselves and shut the door, he said, "What would you have done if I hadn't come back right away?"

"Left without you."

"I have the books."

"Okay, I would have waited. But I hope you now appreciate that you need me as much as I need you."

Playfully, he replied, "We hold these truths to be self-evident."

Santa turned down the volume on his CD player and informed them in German that he was going through Dresden and Leipzig on his way to Hanover.

Dan thanked him again and said Leipzig would be fine.

As the man put his truck in gear, Martine whispered, "Why Leipzig? No one goes there."

"That's why. And by the way, most of my German either comes from the gutter or pertains to clandestine stuff. Can you handle the conversation?"

"If I have to."

Dan winked. "I'm sure he'd rather talk to you, anyway."

"You'll pay for this," she mouthed. Then she dished out a load of hogwash to the driver about a camping vacation they had to cut short because someone had stolen their sleeping bags.

Santa nodded as if to say you couldn't trust anyone these days. His cab felt almost too warm. His stereo emitted the dissonant noise of what Dan now recognized as a Bartok string quartet. Who listened to that crap by choice?

Having apparently exhausted her topics of conversation, or her willingness to pursue them, Martine squirmed out of her jacket and folded it in her lap. Before they'd travelled ten more kilometers, she fell asleep, her head on Dan's shoulder.

A few minutes later, the rig skirted Dresden and turned northwesterly toward Leipzig. Snow flurries blew across the road. Santa turned on his wipers.

Using his cellphone, Dan checked driving times and train schedules. They should reach Leipzig in an hour and a half. The first train to Paris left four hours after that, at 6:31 in the morning. Then he kicked himself mentally. A sophisticated pursuer could identify their location from the phone's GPS. That anyone might be doing so was a long shot. Nevertheless, he switched off Location Services, as well as the entire device. So far as he knew, only NSA and a few of its counterparts in other countries could track a turned-off cellphone. At the first opportunity, he would buy a couple of burners.

After digging out Martine's phone from one of her jacket pockets, he shut it down also. Then he unzipped his own jacket and settled back in the seat.

A kilometer or so later, Santa cocked his head toward Martine's chest. *"Nizza titten."*

Uh-oh. How to respond to "nice tits" without challenging the guy, maybe angering him and losing their ride? Dan rapidly trawled through the spy-speak he'd learned and came up with the words for false and double. *"Sie sind falsch."* He made an up-down slicing gesture over his chest. *"Doppelte Mastektomie."*

The effect was that Santa winced, muttered, *"Scheisse,"* and returned his eyes to the road. The other effect was that Dan stayed wide awake all the way to Leipzig.

#

ALERT Both Signals Lost.
Last location Route 4, west of Dresden.
Average speed 80 km/h. Vehicle unknown.
Next likely destination is Leipzig, air or train. Probably train. All haste.

The trucker, less amiable than he'd been initially, let them off in a warehouse district. As the rig pulled away, Dan and Martine hustled to the nearest protected doorway. Bitter wind whipped snow flurries into a riot under yellow halogen lamps. Luckily, the cab's heater had dried their jeans.

Leaving the GPS on his phone turned off, Dan called for a taxi, and named the two warehouses whose signs he could make out through wind-lashed snow that was now turning to sleet and pelting their building with the rattle of a million BBs.

The taxi dispatcher squawked something Dan couldn't catch. He handed the phone to Martine.

"He needs a better location," she said.

"Damn. Give me your phone." Their need to get out of this cold dwarfed the slim chance that anyone was monitoring their movements. As she kept the dispatcher online with Dan's phone, he activated her GPS, pulled up Google Maps, and showed her the screen.

After some back-and-forth, she ended the call. "Okay, the taxi can find us."

#

Leipzig confirmed. Her phone. Signal lost again.

#

A quarter of an hour crept by, during which Dan listened for the crunch of tires on ice while he and Martine huddled in the recessed doorway. He filled part of the time telling her why he had turned off both of their phones, an explanation that made her roll her eyes. The rest of the time, they just shivered.

Finally, he heard what he'd been waiting for and stepped out to wave down the taxi, a Mercedes diesel, like nearly all cabs in Germany.

The driver, Mohamet Addi according to the ID on his dashboard, seemed grateful for a fare at this hour and in this weather. He drove them at a safe speed and without comment to Hauptbahnhof Leipzig, the central railway station.

Dan tipped him well.

As he and Martine climbed out, she surprised him with, "Would you mind if I called you Jardani?"

Aside from his mother and Lom, nobody called him that. But it was his real name. Did her request signal an end to her racism regarding Gypsies? If so, he was game. "Go ahead."

"It's kind of long, though, compared to Dan."

"I'll answer to either." With a lightness to his step, he walked with her through two sets of doors into the station.

The place was spotless. You could have performed open-heart surgery on the shiny floor. It was also deserted, except for a person in a black hoodie dozing on one of the benches with a hard-shelled roller bag under his feet and, at the far end of the hall, a stoop-shouldered man slowly pushing a floor buffer.

Three tiers of shops ran around the walls, a sign of resurgent capitalism after the Soviet era. All the shops were dark except for a coffee bar on the ground floor. It looked unattended. But when Dan and Martine fronted up, a middle-aged Sikh materialized, his beard trimmed, his turban perfectly wrapped, and a kara—the traditional steel bracelet—on his right wrist.

Savoring the rich aroma of freshly ground coffee, Dam ordered two lattes, then turned to Martine. "Is that okay with you?"

"Extra espresso für mich, bitte," she told the Sikh.

"For me, also," Dan said. An added jolt of caffeine would serve him well.

When he'd paid for their coffees, he walked with her to a bench on the opposite side of the hall from the guy with the roller bag. "Here's what I'm thinking. We buy tickets to Saarbrücken but get off at the stop before, in Mannheim."

"Why?"

"In case someone, somehow learns our supposed destination is farther down the line."

"My mother said I was not to use the word 'paranoid' in your presence. But—"

"You already have." He gave her a Jack Nicholson crazy look, then turned serious again. "So I rent a car in Mannheim, with my Spanish ID, and we drive south into France. In Saverne, we catch a high-speed train to Paris."

She shook her head slowly in wry amusement. "My very own hero."

#

On the train to Saarbrücken, Dan checked out the passengers in only five of the carriages before he felt himself crashing and went back to his seat to catch some shut-eye. He hadn't slept since that fleabag in Prague, and the chances of anyone following them at this stage were roughly nil.

Crossing into France in a rental car from Mannheim went off without a hitch, as did catching the TGV—the high-speed train—in Saverne. They'd just settled in their seats when Martine said, "If anyone is after us and they know my name, they might also know where I live."

So much for waiting to broach that subject. It had slithered in and out of Dan's head ever since leaving the Czech Republic. "Where else can you stay?"

"I or we?"

"You, mostly. I can find a place. But I think it would be better if we stayed together until this is over."

Martine slumped in her seat, looking suddenly spent. "When will that be?"

"I presume when you deliver the books to ... where?"

"I'm supposed to take them to my mother's house in Rueil-Malmaison, just west of Paris. But if someone knows where I live, they could also know where she lives."

Glad his caution was catching on, he said, "Do you have a friend you trust?"

Her eyes de-focused, a sign of inward concentration, as she evidently leafed through possibilities and discarded them. Surely, she had one good friend.

"Paulette," she said.

"Tell me about her."

"She has a large flat, actually a house, on Rue Saint-Jacques in the Fifth Arrondissement. Do you know Paris?"

"I know where Rue Saint-Jacques is." An old Roman road that ran south from Notre Dame, up a hill past the Sorbonne and the Panthéon, and out into the suburbs. "How do you and Paulette know each other?"

"A support group for divorcées. That was several years ago, but we have remained friends. She's an artist."

"How often do you see her?"

"Once or twice a month. We meet for lunch."

So, no familial connection to Martine, a house close to the central city, and a neighborhood in the Latin Quarter where they could probably blend in.

"Sounds good," he said. Plus, they were almost certainly out-of-range for anyone in the Czech Republic or Germany who might have been tracking them. "Okay, call her and let's see what she says."

#

*Active again. TGV Saverne to Paris.
Arriving Gare de l'Est at 14:20.*

Chapter 12

In the cavernous main hall of Gare de l'Est, Paris's terminal for rail traffic to and from the eastern regions of France, Dan took Martine's hand and waded into the swarm of people.

"The exit's that way," she said.

"I want to get some burner phones first."

"There." She pointed to a concession stand that sold snacks and tobacco products.

On a wall behind the African attendant, an array of prepaid phones hung in plastic-sealed packages. Dan bought four for local use, plus an international SIM card "in case." Handing two of the phones to Martine, he said, "One call, then throw it away and use the other. If we need more, we'll buy them somewhere else."

"I thought you couldn't trace one of these."

"Not as well as with a regular phone, but you can still triangulate from the cell towers that—" *What the hell?*

Through a momentary break in the crowd, he glimpsed a black roller bag, stationary among the scurrying legs. Samsonite, hard-shell, shiny new. The woman clutching its handle wore a black headscarf and quickly turned away. As she disappeared into the mob, he told Martine, "I'll be back in a minute," and took off after her.

To no avail. The woman was not at a ticket window or any of the concession stands, and not outside near the taxi rank. Maybe in one of the restrooms? He could ask Martine to go check, but by the time he explained what to look for and why, the mystery woman would surely have vanished again. She was good. Too good.

Rejoining Martine, he said, "We could have trouble."

"What kind of—"

"I'll tell you as soon as we're out of here." He steered her through the crowd and out of the station, where he broke habit for the second time in two days by grabbing the first taxi in line. "Châtelet–Les Halles," he told the driver. *"Rapidement."*

"Dammit, Dan." In the back seat next to him, Martine glared. "I'm getting tired of this cloak-and-dagger stuff."

As the cab pulled away, he twisted to scan the station exits behind them. No woman in a black headscarf. Maybe he was being overly cautious. But caution and instinct had saved him too many times to ignore them now. "I'm almost certain I just saw the same person who appeared to be dozing in Leipzig train station last night."

"You're crazy. There's no way to know that. We couldn't even see his face."

"Her suitcase was identical. Black, hard-sided."

"Black suitcases are everywhere. Thousands of travelers have them. Millions."

"It was an American bag. Samsonite." He held on as their cab swerved around a red Citroën and plunged into holiday traffic. "What are the chances we'd see one in Leipzig, a shiny new one, then an identical new one here?"

"You said 'her.' The person in Leipzig was a man."

"We assumed that. But I think we were wrong." Although he'd barely seen the woman's face when he spotted her twenty minutes ago, he had an impression she might be Asian. What that meant, if anything, he had no idea. In any case, their objective was the home of Martine's friend—by a route that would be difficult to track.

"Would you just stop?" Martine said. "No one could have followed us from Leipzig. We took a train, then a car, then another train."

"I know, but—"

"But what?"

"Let me think a minute." Dan shut his mind to the outside world. Say it was the same woman and she was following them. What was her motive? If it was to "interfere" with them, she'd had ample opportunity already but for some reason had chosen not to. Assuming she wasn't a whack job with a stalking fetish, the only other motives he could imagine were to follow them for someone else or to protect them. Safeguarding from a distance wasn't unheard of. He'd had to do it with two of his DSS "targets."

Uh-oh. His body tensed. The sniper?

"What's wrong?" Martine asked.

He barely heard her, barely felt the cab rock as it veered around another car. His mind replayed the scene in front of Lom's house. The buzz-cut guys falling to the silenced shots of a professional rifle. But no shots fired at *him* when he dashed across the street to Lom's back yard. And Lom had said the sniper wasn't any of his men. So, an outsider. Which made no sense, unless the motive was some altruistic goal of protecting the Romani—or protecting Martine and himself.

"Would you like to let me in on what you're doing?" she said in obvious exasperation.

"I'm trying to figure out something."

"More of your conspiracy shit?"

"Please, just give me a moment." Pursuing the protection motive, he started at the beginning. The only danger they'd been in came from friars or from goons associated with the monastery. That risk, probably but not certainly, ended at the Czech border.

As to who might pursue them for that or any other reason, connecting the woman with the suitcase to the sniper in Usti beggared belief. As Martine had said, there were too many gaps in between. No one had followed them from Usti to the German border, he was positive of that. No one could know which semi driver would pick them up on the autobahn. They couldn't have been followed from the border to Leipzig.

Besides, the person apparently dozing in Leipzig train station had arrived there before them.

On the other hand, a hard-shelled roller bag was ideal for transporting a sniper rifle that had been broken down.

He was going in circles.

Blaring horns yanked his attention to the road. A stalled van forced cars behind it to thread into adjacent lanes.

"You're wasting your time," Martine told him.

"Until we reach Châtelet–Les Halles, I have time to waste."

She turned her face to the window.

Dan returned to motive. Aside from protection, which still seemed farfetched, why else would anyone follow them? The only thing that made them different from any other "couple," that might make them worth following beyond the Czech Republic, was that they'd stolen some books and still had them. Could the sniper be after the books?

He shook his head. If she wanted them, there'd been any number of occasions when she could have acted, not least of which was the empty train station in Leipzig.

Still, when he considered everything, the books were the only explanation that made sense.

But it didn't answer the question of why. The monetary value of the books couldn't be worth the sniper's efforts. There was, however, a political value. Maybe he'd been too hasty in dismissing the French right wing. Astrid had mentioned them specifically, said they had extensive networks and could react violently to anyone attempting to "rob" the nation of its treasures. If those were the people behind the sniper, then by arriving in Paris, he and Martine were playing straight into their hands.

A shiver swept over his back. Experience had taught him that fanatics on the far right were much more dangerous than those on the far left. The best thing he and Martine could do was get rid of those books, ASAP.

Their cab angled to a halt at Châtelet–Les Halles, jolting Dan back to the present.

"Are you done fantasizing?" Martine asked.

"I'll tell you inside."

He'd chosen Châtelet–Les Halles because it was the busiest train station in Paris and the perfect place to elude a pursuer. Still, as they made their way toward the ticket counters, he studied the throng around them. So far, so good. Satisfied for the moment, he said, "There's a possibility that the woman I saw in Gare de l'Est was the sniper in Usti."

"What!" Martine stopped and gave him a fed-up look. "First, he, or she, was in Leipzig. Now he, she … or it … was in Usti? You're worse than paranoid, you're delusional."

"Look, I'm only trying—"

"No. You look. I'm finished with all this running and hiding and constant looking over our shoulders. I'm back in Paris. I have the books. You've done what my mother asked you to do. Thank you, but you can go home now."

Dan bit his cheek. The scurrying crowd disappeared from his vision. Not only did her words sting like salt in a wound, but he also feared she was wrong. Shoving all that aside, he laid out the facts. "Yes, we're in Paris, but I think the sniper is, also. I think she's trailing us, maybe trailing you specifically because you have the books. We don't know her objective, but if it's the books she wants, then you're in real danger. Especially if she's working for the French right wing."

"You're trying to scare me."

"You should be scared." He paused then said, "Look, I know you're upset with me, and I apologize. But, believe it or not, I care about you. I want you to succeed, and I don't think you will if I go home."

Crap. His last words sounded patronizing, even to him.

For a long moment she stared at him, her brow furrowed. "You really are worried, aren't you."

"Deeply."

She exhaled a long breath. "Okay, one more day. Until the books are in a safe place."

A small victory, but the most important one. He headed for a Metro map on one of the walls to refresh his memory of stops near Rue Saint-Jacques.

"RER B," Martine said, referring to one of the long-distance commuter trains. "It stops at Jardin du Luxembourg, which is close to Paulette's house."

Less familiar with the RER network than the Metro, Dan thanked her, bought a *carnet* of ten tickets, and reached to take the knapsack from her shoulders.

She pushed his hand away. "I can carry it."

#

From Luxembourg station, adjacent to the famous formal gardens and the palace where the French senate met, they hiked uphill along narrow streets with closed doors set into four- and five-story stone buildings. Some of the buildings might still house old money, but most had been converted into apartment blocks. All looked cheerless under the overcast sky.

The scene changed at Rue Saint-Jacques. Locals bustled along the sidewalks. Shops on both sides beckoned with windows bearing wreaths and framed in colorful holiday lights. The street itself, only one lane wide here, was jammed with traffic.

"I should call Paulette again to let her know we're almost there." Martine pulled out her phone, then looked at him and switched to one of the burners. After pressing numbers, she shook her head and said, "Voice mail."

"I'll get rid of it for you." Dan held out his hand. They hadn't been followed from Luxembourg station. He was sure of that. And he wanted to keep it that way. He took out the SIM card, broke it in two, and dropped the halves in separate waste bins on the sidewalk. "What now? Do you want something to eat?"

"I want a bath. My clothes are sticking to my body. I stink. You don't smell so great, either."

Thanks for calling that to my attention. He'd been wearing the same clothes since departing Washington for Prague and knew exactly how rank he smelled.

She walked him three blocks along Rue Saint-Jacques, past a wine store, a cheese shop with at least a hundred varieties in wheels and wedges and ash-covered pucks, a Tibetan restaurant whose aromas of meaty broth made his mouth water, a chocolate shop he didn't dare venture into, a butcher with delectable-looking cuts in a glass-fronted case.

Martine might want a bath. He wanted food.

She stopped at a pair of tall wooden doors, clearly doors meant for horse-drawn carriages in the past. Typical of most inner-city areas, the buildings here were contiguous. They might have different façades facing the street, but there was not an inch of open space between them.

Martine punched a four-digit code into the adjacent metal panel. A buzz sounded, and she pushed open the left-hand door.

The entryway took them beneath the second floor of a rectangular U-shaped building that enclosed an open-air courtyard paved with cobblestones. Once home to some wealthy family, the four-story mansion was now divided into apartments. Two bicycles and three motorbikes were parked against the white-painted walls. Flowers, dead or dormant for the winter, stuck out like black chicken's feet from several window boxes overhead.

At the far end of the U, a wrought iron gate and eight-foot-high hedges barred access to a more modern, two-story construction with floor-to-ceiling windows on both levels. From the gate, he could see a living room and an array of large abstract paintings.

After unlocking the gate with another code, Martine ushered him across a wood-planked patio to a glass door that yielded to yet another four-digit code.

The Parisian penchant for security suited Dan just fine.

Inside, the abstract paintings he had glimpsed from the gate seemed to explode in a riot of color. Cobalt blues, blood reds, black, white, slashes of purple and chrome yellow, all strewn across canvases that were four by six feet, seven by ten feet. Dan loved the vibrancy and bold strokes.

"Those are Paulette's work," Martine said.

At one end of the room, a work in progress rested across two easels centered on a big tarp that protected the hardwood floor—or almost protected it. Paint spatters on the polished oak suggested this woman could get pretty enthusiastic when the spirit moved her. A strong smell of oil paint suggested the muse had inspired her quite recently.

Martine slung down her knapsack on a black leather couch

fronted by a chrome-and-glass coffee table. "I'm going upstairs to soak in the tub."

When she'd left, Dan checked out the rest of the ground floor. Several of Paulette's completed paintings leaned against a long wall opposite the front windows. The wall was faced with horizontal slats of polished wood in various natural hues. The stairs protruded from it like piano keys on end. Nice architecture.

A door beyond the work in progress opened to a bedroom and bath that looked unused. At the other end of the living room, next to the kitchen entry, stood a seven-foot-tall bookcase filled with a couple hundred books in colorful covers.

The kitchen itself gleamed with stainless steel appliances, either rarely used or spotlessly maintained. The refrigerator contained quince jam, grapefruit juice, milk, and half a round of Camembert. Nothing that required preparation. He pictured the artist as a skinny woman with studs in her eyebrows, tattoos on her neck, and stringy black hair that hung halfway down her back. A neo-hippie more obsessed with her creations than her diet.

Off the kitchen lay a laundry room with a small washer and dryer. No door to the outside. In fact, there were no exterior doors at all, except the glass one in front. Fine, in the sense that nobody could enter without being seen. But by the same token, the only escape route was plainly visible.

A shudder rippled across his chest. His first impression of security had been perilously wrong. The floor-to-ceiling windows offered zero privacy, except from ground level where the hedges grew intertwined with the wrought iron fence. Anyone at the gate, or in a courtyard apartment from the second floor up, could see inside and draw a clear bead with a half-decent rifle. If they needed to get out and made it past the gate, they still had to run across the courtyard, like a ducks in a shooting gallery, to reach the big wooden doors that opened onto Rue Saint-Jacques.

That meant that the security of Paulette's residence, if challenged by a determined assailant, relied entirely on the code buttons next to the sidewalk. Anyone out there could simply follow a resident inside.

In reality, this beautiful home, which had to be worth two or three million euros, was a fishbowl protected by nothing.

He flexed his hands, scratching the palms as a futile surrogate for the pistol grips he wished they held. Much as he liked this place, they could only stay here one night. Anything beyond that would be at a hotel.

"It's all yours now," Martine called from upstairs.

Dan climbed the steps, thick mahogany planks that jutted out three feet into midair with only a wound-wire cable covered in clear plastic serving as a handrail.

She stood at the top with a white towel wrapped around her and a bundle of clothes in her arms. "I tried to leave you some hot water."

"Thanks," he said. "Out of curiosity, did Paulette's art pay for this place?"

"Her ex did. She got it in the divorce settlement."

Good lawyer. "Any idea when she'll be back?"

"Before nightfall, I imagine."

So, no rush. He headed for the open door of the bathroom, where steam still fogged a couple of the mirrors and a lemony scent of soap perfumed the air.

The hot water ran out before he finished his shower. But he didn't care. It felt good to be clean again.

He cinched a towel around his waist, then gathered his grimy clothing and headed downstairs, hoping Martine hadn't yet started the washing machine. He found her in the kitchen with— *Oops.* Dan cinched his towel tighter. "Sorry. I didn't realize —"

"Dan, this is Paulette."

The woman had short blond hair and wore black slacks, a white dress shirt, and very dark glasses. Definitely not the neo-hippie he'd imagined.

On the countertop beside her sat a saddlebag-sized purse, a bottle of rosé, and ... a collapsible white cane with a hand strap and a red tip.

My God, she's blind.

Instantly admiring her, a sightless person who could create such beautiful paintings, he reached to shake her extended hand and noticed she wore a large, steel-gray wristwatch. *"Enchanté,"* he said, glad to think she wasn't completely blind. "I hope you don't mind our staying here. You have a beautiful home."

She smiled and replied in a soft lilt, "I am happy you like it. Martine says you have been living in lorries and trains. It sounds romantic. Like 'On the Road.' You have read Jack Kerouac?" She pronounced Jack as Jacques.

"Years ago. Our trip from Prague was not so ... entertaining."

"Quel dommage." What a pity. "Perhaps some wine will help. I brought a bottle."

Dan imagined a matchmaker's twinkle in the eyes behind those opaque glasses, a hint that wine could make things more "romantic." He glanced at Martine, who was tightening the towel under her arms. More romantic was not likely.

"You will pour?" Paulette asked him.

"Avec plaisir." As the two women adjourned to the couch in the living room, he felt honored—or at least accepted, to the extent that Paulette apparently had no qualms about his rummaging through her cabinets to find wine glasses. The bottle had a screw cap, the most popular solution to the worldwide shortage of cork. For Paulette personally, screw caps would also mean a welcome solution to fussing with a sharp-ended corkscrew or with a cork that fell apart in the bottle when she tried to pull it.

Her blindness also explained the lack of food that required preparation. As did her short hair, which would only have taken a few strokes of a brush to make presentable.

He liked her. Not only was she pleasant and thoughtful, but she had also developed practical ways to cope with a disability that would have plunged him into a bottomless pit.

After handing out the wine glasses, he said, "Excuse me a moment," and returned to the kitchen to pull on his T-shirt and dirty jeans. Martine might feel comfortable sitting around in just a towel. He did not, especially with another woman he barely knew, blind though she might be.

Barefoot but clothed, he took a seat in the black leather chair at one end of the coffee table and toasted, "Santé."

"You're a little late," Martine told him. "We've already started."

"Story of my life." He listened to a few minutes of catching up between the two women, then said, "Paulette, I have to ask you—"

"How does a blind person paint?" She cracked a playful smile. "With brushes, of course."

"Touché."

Her smile broadened. Then turning more serious, she swept her hand to indicate the works arrayed against the wall in front of them. "Paintings like these, I make for therapy. After the accident, my *psychiatre* ... you understand?"

"Yes."

"She told me Beethoven made symphonies after he was deaf. She said, 'Do big and bold.' So I tried it."

"You were a painter before the accident?"

"*Oui*, but much smaller. In this new size, it is easier for me now. I see it in my head, and I paint it."

Martine, whose towel had loosened and enticingly slipped partway down her breast, nudged Paulette. "And sometimes you paint the floor."

"Oh, no. I have done it again?" Paulette turned her head toward the work in progress. "It is good René does not see it. Or perhaps better if he does."

"Better," Martine said. "René is a *connard*," which Dan figured meant something like shithead.

"But he gave me this." Paulette swept her hand again, this time indicating the whole house.

"No, he didn't. The judge did." Martine looked at Dan. "Because they'd lived here for three years before the car accident, and she could find her way around. René would have taken it from her if he could."

Oh, the joys of divorce. Still, Dan was glad that Paulette had come out of it well and charged ahead. "Do you have many customers for your art?"

"Ça alors." She tilted her face toward the ceiling, a gesture he took to mean, "More than I can handle." Then she pointed again toward the finished works along the wall. "Two of these are sold already. The gallery wants more."

"A blessing and a curse," Dan offered.

When Paulette seemed not to understand, Martine translated.

Paulette nodded. *"Exactement."* With another smile, she held out her glass in Dan's direction. "There is more wine?"

He took the glass from her, refilled it, and gave it back, noticing now that her watch had no hands. "I can't help but wonder about your wristwatch."

"This? It is a Bradley." She touched its face. "The time now is eighteen-ten."

Meaning six-ten in the evening, as his own watch confirmed. "You didn't look at it."

"I cannot see," she replied, as if he were thick.

Martine grinned. "Show it to him." When Paulette removed it from her wrist, Martine pointed out two small ball bearings. "This one on the face tells the minutes. This one on the side rotates around to show the hour. She just has to feel for their positions."

Taking back her watch, Paulette asked him, "You know of Bradley Snyder?"

"The Olympic swimmer? Yes." Paralympics, actually. He was blind. "Is this his design?"

"I do not think so. Only it is named for him."

"Very cool." Maybe blindness—something he'd feared worse than death ever since a hunting accident cost a childhood friend both eyes—wasn't so bad after all. Maybe with the right mental attitude and some clever gear, you could cope with anything.

Buoyed by the thought, he settled back in his chair, only to be startled by the wheezy pop-popping of a motor scooter engine. Surely a resident, but just in case, "While you ladies talk, I'm going to step outside for a minute."

Praying he hadn't brought danger to Paulette's threshold, he closed the door behind him and moved silently to the side of the wrought-iron gate. Just beyond it, a girl wearing a parka with the hood up hurried toward one of the four sets of stairs that led to upper-floor apartments. Another hidden face? His muscles tensed, until he noticed two baguettes protruding from the canvas satchel in her left hand. Two implied a roommate. There was no way any pursuer could have planned that far in advance. He relaxed, then started shivering. Winter darkness had descended, along with winter chill.

#

Lost them at Chatelet. Now staking out girls apartment.
No lights on so far
-
If no activity by morning, move surveillance to the Louvre.

Chapter 13

Dan crawled out from under the covers in the ground-floor guestroom. The patch of sky visible through his window glowed grayish-orange from city lights reflecting off the overcast. His watch showed 5:20, three hours before sunrise on this Christmas Eve. Despite his earlier qualms about security, he'd slept more soundly and for more unbroken hours than at any other time since leaving Washington.

While scrubbing his face in the adjacent bathroom, he recalled Paulette's whispered suggestion last evening that he share the extra upstairs room with Martine. *Dream on.* Today they'd take the books to the Louvre before depositing them at her mother's house. Then it would be mission accomplished and time for him to go home.

At least his clothes would be fresh for the return flight. Halfway through helping the women consume the rosé—on a stomach still deprived of food—he had reverted to wrapping the towel around his waist and had tossed his things into the washer with Martine's. By the end of the bottle, their clothing had gone into the dryer.

With the towel again tied around him, he headed for the laundry room. At the kitchen he stopped. Paulette was pouring hot water from a kettle into a French press. She wore a white silk camisole that ended at mid-hip and did nothing to conceal the blond thatch of pubic hair below.

"Good morning," she said, turning to face him.

"Good morning." *And wow.* Her casual stance told him she was comfortable with her nudity, and his seeing it. Her smile, besides suggesting she could imagine the effect she was having on him, also drew his attention to her eyes. He hadn't really thought about them before but would have guessed they were white, as though covered by cataracts. Instead, they were blue and appeared to be normal, except that they were "looking" a spot just above his head.

Say something, idiot. "I didn't realize you were up."

"Day or night is the same for me. If you prefer, I will go and put on my glasses."

"No need." Clearly, she'd realized he was staring at her eyes.

"You thought they are white?"

"I suppose so."

Another smile hinted that she enjoyed his surprise, or maybe that she just enjoyed toying with him. "Coffee will be ready in five minutes. You drink coffee, yes?"

"Yes, please. After I've collected my clothing."

"In there." She pointed toward the laundry room. "I folded them for you."

He dressed in front of the dryer, then said, "I saw a razor in your shower last night. Do you mind if I use it?"

"There are new ones in the top drawer by my sink."

"Thank you." He climbed the stairs and found the razors. On the way back down, he encountered Paulette coming up. Positive she knew he was there, he stepped toward the cable handrail to let her pass.

As she came beside him, she felt for his hand and squeezed it. "You are a good man. Martine is fortunate."

That caught him off guard. Had Paulette taken advantage of their scantily clad encounter in the kitchen to test him? Feeling awkward, he replied, "I don't believe she thinks so."

"She will." Paulette pecked him on the cheek and continued upstairs.

#

When Dan finished shaving, he found Martine and Paulette, both dressed in jeans and sweaters, sipping café au lait on the couch. They drank, as French workmen did, from what he regarded as small, deep soup bowls. A third bowl rested on the coffee table in front of the chair where he'd sat last night.

"Sleep well?" he asked Martine.

"Like a baby."

Paulette shook her head, as though she knew better. "One only sleeps like a baby after making love."

"Paulette!" Martine scolded with a look of embarrassment.

Smiling inwardly at the perseverance of their resident matchmaker, Dan took his seat and sampled the brew. Delicious. Also delicious was a whiff of the Ma Griffe that Martine had rescued from her plundered hotel room in Prague and evidently dabbed on this morning.

But he still hadn't eaten more than a few bites of Camembert since who knew when. After finishing his coffee, he said, "Can I take you ladies to breakfast? I'm famished."

"Take Martine." Paulette ran a finger over her watch. "There is a place that will open at six-thirty. Le Soufflot, by the Panthéon."

"Come and join us," he said. A hot breakfast was the least he could do to thank her for putting them up.

"No, you go. I have a painting to finish."

Twenty minutes later, Dan sat with Martine at a table about the size of a bathmat. Martine, who'd brought her knapsack full of books, ordered yogurt and fruit. He went for a ham-and-cheese omelet with pommes frites on the side and two glasses of orange juice. As they waited, nursing lattes, he said, "We need to find a hotel for tonight."

"Why?"

"Because Paulette's house isn't safe. It's like a goldfish bowl. Anyone can see in."

"Oh, come on. This is getting ridiculous."

"I don't think so. And I'd rather not endanger her with our presence."

Martine shook her head slowly, as if to say his paranoia never ceased. "Move if you want, but I'm staying."

He perked up, not at what she'd just said but at what she didn't say—she did not reiterate that his job would be done today and that he should go home. More time together would suit him just fine. And if she wasn't moving, then neither was he. If the sniper did manage to track her down, he needed to be there. Speaking of which … he glanced out the window, saw no parked cars, no pedestrians, and no other sign of anyone observing them.

Their meals arrived. Between enthusiastic bites, Dan asked, "When does the Louvre open?"

"Nine o'clock. But we can go there anytime. I have a cardkey. And the man I want to see will already be there by now."

"You mentioned this man before, back in Germany."

"His name is Bernard Leroux. He's been with the Louvre forever, and he's an expert when it comes to ancient Middle Eastern languages. Unfortunately, nobody appreciates him."

"Why not?" Dan said and forked some French fries into his mouth.

"Because Europeans no longer care about those languages, until something like the Dead Sea Scrolls or the Rosetta Stone pops up. So, he sits in an old office in the basement and pursues his passion alone."

"You said he can figure out what the small book is. Did your mother ask you to have him do that?"

"No. That's my idea. She told me the book was important, but she wouldn't say why. I don't like doing something without knowing the reason."

"Same here." Dan polished off the last of his orange juice.

After he'd paid their bill, they made their way down narrow streets to Boulevard Saint-Michel, where they caught a cab to the Louvre, Martine specifying, "Porte des Lions." They arrived a few minutes before 7:30. The Seine was still black. Sunrise had not yet touched the Eiffel Tower. The porte, flanked by a pair of arrogant-looking bronze lions weathered to green, was an arched passageway that ran about fifty feet through one of the museum's two long arms into the interior courtyard. Based on a map of the museum he'd seen, Dan reckoned they were far removed from the areas that held the main tourist attractions.

Martine led him halfway through the passage, to a heavy wooden door that she opened by inserting a cardkey into a panel at the side. They stepped into the dimly lit interior where she stood aside, waited for the door to automatically swing closed, then nudged it until the electronic lock clicked.

Having to push on an exterior door to help it close illustrated how hard it was to modernize a five-hundred-year-old palace, he thought as he followed her down a flight of stone stairs to a basement. The musty odor reminded him uncomfortably of the monastery's basement in Prague.

"This way," Martine said and set off along a corridor illuminated by fluorescent tubes.

"You know my French isn't very good," Dan reminded her.

"Don't worry. Monsieur Leroux speaks eleven languages and reads about thirty."

Okay, that was impressive.

She stopped at an unmarked door, knocked twice, and entered a room that stank of cigarette and marijuana smoke and looked like a used-book shop after an earthquake.

A throwback to the Seventies turned in his chair. "Martine! *C'est bon de te voir.*" It's good to see you. True to his name, Bernard "The Red" had once had copper-colored hair, strands of which still highlighted his now-rosy-white mane. It hung to his earlobes in unruly waves and matched an equally unruly beard. He hoisted his bulk to embrace her. *"Ça va bien?"*

"Very well, thank you. I'd like you to meet my friend, Dan Lovel. Or Jardani, as some people call him."

"Jardani? A common Arab name, but you don't have Arab features. A Gypsy?" Leroux held out a hand with nicotine-stained fingers. "I have not met many Gypsies. Welcome."

Dan shook hands, thinking it strange that Martine, who hadn't used his real name since Leipzig, did so with this man. "Thank you, sir."

"Which family?" Leroux asked.

"Camlo."

"I thought so. Because of your darker skin."

Surprised that he would make that connection, Dan made one of his own. "And your hair is red, or used to be. Celtic ancestry?"

"Good for you." With a grin, Leroux turned to Martine. "I like him. Both of you, please, take a seat." He quickly removed stacks of books and papers from the two guest chairs. "Can I get you some coffee? It's terrible here, made by a machine. But it's hot."

"We just ate," Martine said, opening her knapsack. "I have some books I want to show you."

"I love books." He winked at Dan through thick, rimless glasses. "As you can probably tell from the way I have 'decorated' my little lair."

As Dan glanced around, Martine got straight to the point. One by one she extracted the four-volume inventory. "First—"

"*Mon Dieu.* Where did you get these?" Leroux snatched one from her and fanned through the pages. "The museum. *Ils chieraient dans leur pantalon.*" To Dan he said, "They would shit in their pants."

"We removed them from a monastery in Prague," Martine told him, seemingly unconcerned that he learn the truth.

Dan wished she'd been more circumspect, at least at first. But this was her gig.

Leroux's eyes widened. "These are the ones Josephine gave? That's wonderful. What are you going to do with them?" He paused, then smiled impishly. "Slay the emperor?"

Dan couldn't care less about Napoleon's reputation, but he shared Leroux's evident disrespect for idol worship. It warped history and nurtured extremists. So far, this man was batting a thousand on Dan's scorecard.

Martine took back the volume, then handed Leroux the small, thin book. "What about this?"

He took it delicately and turned it over in his big hands. Muttering something unintelligible, he caressed the five loops of coarse twine that bound the covers together.

Dan half-expected him to cradle the book the way Koko the gorilla had done with the pet kitten her keepers gave her.

Finally, Leroux opened it and peered at the first page. His brow furrowed. "Hmm?" He pulled a magnifying glass from his desk drawer and studied the page again. "Oh, my God."

Alarmed at the reaction, Dan leaned forward, watching the man's stubby finger drift over the text and his ruddy complexion pale.

"This also came from the monastery?" Leroux asked.

"Their collection of so-called forbidden books."

"I should think so. If this is real, and if it is what I fear it is, this book is very dangerous."

Dan sat up straight in his chair. All his training with informants and captives told him Leroux was speaking the truth, at least as he saw it. Steady breathing, no loss of eye contact, no inadvertent touching of the nose or throat.

"Why is it dangerous?" Martine asked, giving voice to his own question.

"It could bring war to the Middle East. Maybe beyond."

Dan sat back. "The Middle East is always at war. It's a fact of life everyone has learned to live with."

"Not like this." Leroux pointed at the open page.

"Not like what?" Dan said. "What is it? If it's what you fear."

Leroux took off his glasses and rubbed the bridge of his nose. "I would need to study it carefully to be sure. But it appears to be a text that would fit between Deuteronomy and Joshua in the Old Testament. You are familiar with the Old Testament?"

"Sort of," Dan replied.

Martine pulled a sour face. "We had to study it in school."

"I will refresh your memory." Leroux put on his glasses again. "The first five books are called the Pentateuch, or the Five Books of Moses. They comprise the Jewish Torah and end with Deuteronomy, where Moses dies without setting foot in the Promised Land. Leadership of the Hebrews then passes to Joshua, who leads them in their conquest of Canaan. Traditionally, this begins the fulfilment of God's promises in Genesis that the Holy Land shall belong to the Jews."

"But," Dan prompted, sensing a twist.

"Very roughly translated, this passage says the spirit of Moses appeared to Joshua in a dream." Leroux moved his finger farther down the page. "And here it says that God is angry ... no, the word is closer to 'furious.' He is furious with the Hebrews for their drunkenness and continuing worship of graven images."

So what? "God was frequently angry with the Jews."

"Not like this," Leroux told him. He turned the page. "If I am correct, it says here that the Hebrews are no longer God's chosen people. They might occupy the Promised Land, but it will never be theirs."

"Then it has to be a fake." Everything Dan had learned from his father ran counter to what Leroux had just said.

"A fake, perhaps. But if it is actually part of the Torah—"

"It isn't."

"Young man, certainty is the roadblock to knowledge."

"You said you weren't even sure it was real."

"True." Leroux nodded solemnly. "But I must tell you there have long been rumors of a text like this. Most biblical scholars discount them. Those who do believe refer to it as the Sixth Book of Moses."

Chapter 14

Gazing out at Washington's night skyline, a once-enchanting view that had gone stale over the four years she had lived in this condo, Astrid gnawed a hangnail. Her manicurist would "read her the riot act," as Americans said, but she couldn't help it. Something was wrong.

She checked her phone again for messages from Martine. Nothing since, "We landed in Prague." That was three days ago.

Every time Astrid tried to call, Martine's cellphone rolled to voicemail. The landline in her apartment went to an answering machine with a recorded message that Astrid was beginning to hate. She'd also tried the landline at her own house in Rueil-Malmaison, only to hear an endless series of rings.

Had Martine and Dan run into problems at the monastery? Or while trying to leave the country? Even if there *had* been problems, Martine should have been able to dash off a text, if only to type, "Help."

Despite having turned up the temperature, Astrid shivered. If things had gone according to plan, Martine and Dan should have obtained the books and been back in Paris the next day. If they'd failed to obtain them but were otherwise safe, Martine definitely would have called.

"*Merde.*"

Outside Astrid's windows, most of Dupont Circle was dark, its high-flying residents presumably tucked into their beds at—she looked at her watch—two-twenty in the morning. The workday for senior functionaries in Washington began well before sunrise.

Her own work had been piling up in her office. She'd hardly slept in two days.

Plopping down on one of her couches, she cursed her decision to send her only child on such an undertaking, never mind that Dan was supposed to protect her. Given the nature of the books, he could well face forces too powerful for even him to handle. French nationalists bent on destroying the Louvre volumes. Religious zealots willing to use obscene violence to get their hands on the Moses book.

She bit again at the irritating hangnail. So many agendas. So many fanatical groups, any one of which could mount an overwhelming attack. *If* they knew what Martine was doing.

But that didn't seem possible.

Unable to just lie there on a couch, Astrid got up and poured herself another Pernod and water. She'd been very careful to reveal the mission to only a handful of people, all of whom she trusted. And she'd given Martine explicit instructions to call at least once a day.

Even if something had happened to Martine's phone—she had lost or damaged it—she could have used Dan's. He probably had several, considering how cautious he was, how prepared for any eventuality. Besides, there were public phones, for God's sake.

"*Merde. Merde!*"

Her hand shook so badly she had to set down her drink. Bracing herself against the credenza, she peered at the framed montage of her favorite photos. Martine building a sandcastle at the beach. Martine smiling bashfully in her first school uniform. Martine, barely pubescent, her jaw set as she struggled to master the kayak. Martine grinning in cap and gown upon graduation from Oxford. Martine looking radiant in one half of a wedding photo, Édouard's half having long ago been sliced off and thrown out.

My little girl. She could be irksome as the devil. Annoying, exasperating, even infuriating. But deep inside, they loved each other. Astrid would do anything in the world to keep her safe.

She racked her brain yet again for an explanation of why Martine had neither called nor answered. Any explanation that didn't involve capture or injury. Yet again, nothing came to her.

She bit her lip. If one more day went by with no news, she would have to take drastic action.

#

"Now what?" Dan asked. "Carbon-fourteen dating, analysis of the ink and paper?"

Leroux shook his head. "The age of the paper or ink will tell us nothing. There are no original texts from the Old Testament. All are supposed copies of older texts. This one could date from pre-Christian times or much later. The book's binding suggests the fourth or fifth century."

"Then how can you know if it's real?"

"If by 'real' you mean ancient, then the best way is linguistic analysis." Leroux gave him a smile that hinted at devilish satisfaction. "A field in which I happen to be rather skilled."

If not rather modest. Dan looked at Martine, who seemed willing to let him carry this ball. "Is there another meaning for real?"

"Authoritative, by which I mean considered to be sacred, divinely inspired."

"Aren't all books in the Bible regarded as sacred?"

"You are a man of many questions, Jardani Camlo."

And diminishing patience. "Are you a man of many answers?"

Leroux rummaged through several cigarette packets on his desktop until he found one that wasn't empty. After lighting up, he said, "If you give me a few hours, I will give you some answers."

#

After checking into a hotel, for the sole purpose of stashing her suitcase, Jade had spent the whole damn night pretending to be asleep in a recessed doorway across the street from the girl's apartment. Girl. Despite their similar ages, Jade couldn't help thinking of the French woman as an innocent with no practical experience in the adult world. Whatever. Political correctness wasn't her strong suit.

She cursed herself again for neglecting to swipe a blanket from her room to sit on in the doorway. She'd stayed there until the first hint of daybreak, then walked half an hour to the museum. Her ass still felt frozen, even after another half hour spent completing her recon around the museum's exterior.

All for nothing. Surveilling the Louvre, as Control had instructed, was impossible. The place was almost half a mile long. Maps posted outside the various entrances confirmed her impression that the building resembled a pair of tongs—its handle to the east, its long pincers opening to the west. A street, with a roundabout in the middle called Place du Carrousel, crossed through the pincers about midway along their length. Halfway between that and the handle rose the big glass pyramid that was the museum's main entrance, but only one of many.

An employee like the girl could probably get in through any one of the other entries. No way could Jade watch all of them. Frustrated, and dog-tired after almost no sleep last night, she concluded there was only one thing she could do. She pulled the phone from her pocket.

Louvre has too many entrances to cover. Returning now to watch her apartment

NO!!! Find her office and grab the book.

How in hell was she supposed to do that? She wanted to type, "Do it yourself asshole." But he held the purse strings.

#

A dizzying swarm of uncertainties swirled through Dan's head. Unwilling to sit there twiddling his thumbs, he got up from his chair. If the book was fake, they could throw it away. No problem. But if it was genuine, there was a lot more he needed to know.

"Maybe we'll get some coffee, after all," he said to Leroux. "Where's that machine?"

"Down the hall." Leroux waved a hand over his shoulder as he bent to study the slender volume he had laid open on his desk.

"Do you want some?"

The man's only response was to stub out his cigarette in an ashtray that already overflowed.

Dan motioned for Martine to follow him out the door. After closing it behind them, he said, "Should Leroux be smoking around an old book that's potentially valuable? Even if he's careful about fire, the smoke could discolor it."

"I've asked him that twice before, because all the books in his office are valuable. His response is that centuries of exposure to smoke from candles and oil lamps hasn't damaged them. That's the short version. You don't want to hear the long one."

"And the museum's okay with this?"

"I doubt any member of the staff has been down here in years, except janitors and the occasional guard making rounds."

Accepting her assurance, Dan switched to his main reason for bringing her out here. "Do you have a computer in your office?"

"Of course. Why?"

"I'd like to use it."

"Why?" she repeated, her brow now furrowed.

Dan lowered his voice. "I want to see what we can find out independently."

"You don't trust Leroux?"

"No, I think he's fine. But I also think we'd be wise to gather some information ourselves, before deciding what to do. Especially if he's right that the book could escalate tensions in the Middle East."

"He said 'war.'"

"That's what I mean."

Martine glanced down pensively, then nodded.

As she led him up the stairwell and along a corridor on the ground floor, Dan sorted through his objectives and laid them out for her in approximate order. Assuming it was real, would a biblical text specifically denying Jewish claims to the Holy Land have any real impact, beyond inciting Islamic extremists to shout even louder? What were the views of those other scholars who believed such a text existed? Which groups, religious or otherwise, might benefit from having the book? Would they use violence to obtain it? Much closer to home, was this book the reason they were being pursued by the sniper from Usti?

Martine stopped. "You mentioned before that she might be after it."

"I don't really know. She might want the inventory books. But I think she wants something."

Martine shut her eyes a moment. "What have we gotten ourselves into?"

"That's what we need to find out."

Halfway down the corridor, she opened her office. It was the same size as Leroux's but way less cluttered. Her bookshelves were maybe a third full. Her desktop had a single stack of papers, barely an inch high. The two wooden guest chairs, which he figured must be standard issue, stood empty against one wall. Best of all, she had a window. It looked out onto formal gardens within the Louvre's courtyard, where pale gray light foretold a cheerless morning.

She logged onto the computer, then stood from her chair. "All yours."

Trying to blot out the seductive fragrance of Ma Griffe that hung like a cloud over the space she'd just vacated, Dan ran a Google search on "Sixth Book of Moses." The top hit was a Wikipedia entry titled "Sixth and Seventh Books of Moses," which described texts from the 18th or 19th centuries that supposedly revealed magical incantations for invoking miracles portrayed in the Bible. The page also noted an Eighth Book, a Greek papyrus from the 4th century, with more magic. Other websites spoke of love spells and summoning demonic powers.

"This is all bullshit," he muttered to Martine, who was peering over his shoulder and replenishing the aroma of Ma Griffe. "If biblical scholars ever crack jokes, these would be what they laugh over."

"Go to the next page."

He did. Then to the page after that. "Nothing useful."

"I suspect that small circle of scholars Leroux mentioned doesn't publish their speculations. I certainly wouldn't. I'd wait until I had proof, or something close to proof."

"So, no easy way to check on whatever Leroux tells us. Assuming the book's authentic, let's see what impact it might have on Israel." His next search turned up a ruling by an Israeli court that biblical texts had no bearing on Israeli law. *Glad to see it.* Real or not, the book wouldn't matter much to the Jewish state—although if real, it would probably have considerable value as a historical document. An image popped into Dan's head: Talmudic experts in wide-brimmed hats and flowing beards arguing over each dissected word. His father would have shaken his head in disgust at the thought of so much brainpower "wasted on trivialities."

"What about Muslim extremists?" Martine asked.

"No need to look that up. Most of the powerful ones are state-sponsored, principally by Iran, Syria, and Saudi Arabia." He thought a moment. "Damn. Do you think those countries could use the book to justify a coordinated assault?"

"No. America would never allow that."

"I'm not so sure." Biting his lip, Dan wondered if the U.S. would actually go to war to prevent an invasion of Israel. "Thanks to oil, Saudi is a major ally in the Middle East. Syria is known to have chemical weapons. Iran very likely has nuclear weapons, at least small ones, possibly purchased from Pakistan. If the U.S. engaged them in an all-out shitfest, it could be catastrophic."

Then a more chilling thought struck him. "Even giving Israel our blessing to use their nuclear arsenal could literally blow up in everyone's faces. And if push came to shove, Israel wouldn't wait for our consent."

"I think you're overreacting. You've forgotten diplomacy."

"You've forgotten about speed. Without really good intelligence, a major Islamic attack and Israeli retaliation could catch Washington completely off guard."

That seemed to give her pause. "My mother says the French intelligence services have failed to anticipate several *coups d'état*."

Wishing he could be prouder of the much-touted agencies in his own country, Dan swiveled to face her. "The whole alphabet soup of U.S. intelligence services is not much better. We'd be lucky to get a heads-up five minutes before incoming missiles bombarded the Iron Dome and four minutes before Israel started pushing launch buttons."

She let out a long, slow breath. Then her tone brightened. "But *you* could tell Washington."

"I don't work for them anymore, and even if I did, they wouldn't believe me. They'd nod and thank me, then write me off as yet another nutcase with a conspiracy theory."

"So, what are we going to do?"

His immediate thought was: destroy the book. But maybe he'd been letting his imagination run away with him. What if Islamic states viewed it with a yawn, the way Israel probably would? The idea of destroying knowledge soured Dan's gut.

But there were other groups who weren't countries and who might not yawn. They likely mattered less, but it always paid to know your potential adversaries, powerful or not. He stretched to relieve the tension in his shoulders and turned back to the computer. "We aren't finished gathering information."

Recalling comments his father had made, Dan typed "Jews against Israel." His search brought up several sites dedicated to Jewish groups who condemned Israel as a secular, materialistic state. They believed the truly devout should immerse themselves in the Torah and remain in exile until the Holy One redeems them.

"These people exist?" Martine asked, again reading over his shoulder.

"Apparently so. Harmless splinter groups, I suspect, like snake cults in Christianity. Which reminds me, we need to check out Christians, too." His search turned up a load of sites claiming the Israeli state was a prerequisite to the Second Coming, when Jews would be converted to Christianity. Pointing at one of the entries, he said, "Fat chance of that."

"Perhaps," Martine allowed. "But it's potentially important. Evangelical Christians are a powerful force in American politics. Especially now that your government has swung to the right. If a Bible text told them Jews have no claim to the Holy Land, that they don't even belong there, then Christian support could vanish. Along with American government support."

"I don't believe that. We support Israel because it's the right thing to do. The Holocaust proved that. Plus, they're the only democracy in the Middle East."

"France supports them for the same reasons."

Off and on, Dan thought, although he wasn't about to quibble.

"But there's a delicate balance," she insisted. "Even a splinter group, as you call them, could tip it."

Dan doubted that. Nevertheless, he ran a quick search that revealed Christian groups who supported Palestinians in their "holy war" against Israel. While their support appeared to consist mainly of money and encouragement, two sites did mention arms shipments.

"See?" Martine said triumphantly.

Dan shook his head. "We're getting off-track. A book like this might bolster their opinions, but so what?"

"How about the Vatican? You mentioned, way back in that forest when we first crossed into Germany, that if the book was an old biblical text, the Vatican might want it left where it was. Maybe they don't want it revealed."

"Tough luck for them. They have no say in the matter."

"Unless ..." She paused a moment. "Is it possible they sent the sniper?"

"What?"

"They're the ones with the Assassini."

Dan swiveled again to face her. "You've been reading too many novels. The Vatican's guilty of a lot of things, despicable things, but I don't think employing a band of killers is one of them. At least not these days."

Looking offended, she said, "Then who *is* she?"

The big question. "A hired gun. As to who she works for, we've come up with several possibilities. My best guess is some Muslim group, most likely Iranian. They're the main backers of terrorism against Israel."

Martine's face paled.

As well it should. Iranians could be fanatical opponents. "But that assumes she's after the Moses book. If it's the inventory she wants, then we're probably looking at the French right wing."

"Jesus, Dan. We're back to square one."

"Not really. We've eliminated a lot of possibilities and clarified others." He switched off Martine's computer. "As to the sniper and us personally, the main thing we need to do is stay vigilant."

"That's not very consoling." Although Martine was clearly trying to remain composed, fear showed in her eyes. Good. At least she now believed that the sniper's threat was real. That was half the battle.

The other half was cooperation. "Look, we've worked well together so far. We should keep that up. Picture this. Female, your height, athletic build, maybe Asian, maybe a scarf or hoodie partially concealing her head. Maybe, but probably not, wheeling a black roller bag. If you see her, or even think you see her, don't stare. Just steer me into the nearest shop or side street. I'll take it from there."

"Meaning what?"

"Depends on the situation. Best case, we let her follow us to an out-of-the-way spot, where I disable her. She answers our questions, and we leave her there."

"Disable her?"

"Believe me, she'll be grateful. Worst case is, I kill her."
"No. The worst case is, she kills *you*."

Chapter 15

The only entrance with any activity was the main one, in the glass pyramid, outside of which a long line of tourists bundled in heavy coats waited for the museum to open. Jade hated long lines. But if that wasn't bad enough, this one waited under the alternately bored and suspicious eyes of eight soldiers with automatic rifles who milled around in camo gear and black berets. Soldiers out here guaranteed metal detectors inside, which meant she would have to get rid of her pistol and switchblade.

There had to be a better way.

To avoid looking conspicuous, she walked to the rear of the line and hunched her shoulders against the cold. Employees wouldn't wait out here and might not have to pass through metal detectors. If she was quick and convincing, she could follow one inside. But there were three other public entrances, as well as unmarked doors that employees might be able to use.

Wait a second. She'd noticed two entrances that took cardkeys, one in the Richelieu passageway on the north side and one in the passageway of Porte des Lions on the south. She flipped a coin in her head. It came up tails. Porte des Lions.

A few minutes later, she stood next to one of the green lions flanking the street side of the passage. A woman ambled past, walking a cute little dog that reminded Jade of Pom Pom, the cuddly Shih Tzu her parents had given her when she was twelve and her ambition in life was to become a nurse. She shook off the memory. What kind of nurse went to pieces when her dog was diagnosed with cancer? One who hadn't learned her lesson, that caring was a slippery slope to heartbreak.

After the woman and her dog, no one approached from either direction. Maybe employees didn't show up until nine. Or maybe today, being Christmas Eve, was a holiday for most of them.

By ten after nine, she was ready to kill anyone who looked at her sideways. One couple speaking German had walked through the passageway into the museum's courtyard. An old man with a gift-wrapped package in one hand and a cane in the other had hobbled by. This was not the solution.

With the same reluctance a mother must feel upon laying her infant on the church steps, Jade stashed her knife, gun, and silencer behind one of the lions, then strode back to join the line that was now inching into the pyramid.

A broad spiral staircase inside led down to a ticketing area half the size of a football field. Sure enough, at the bottom of the stairs she had to put her jacket on the conveyor belt of an x-ray machine, then pass through a metal detector.

As if that wasn't enough security, four pairs of black-clad policemen wearing baseball caps and sidearms circulated through the crowd. In case you were stupid, the backs of their jackets proclaimed "POLICE" in letters six inches high.

She smiled inwardly. Start a commotion in one area—by dropping a thumb-drive incendiary device in some woman's purse, for instance—and the cops would all dash there, leaving the objective area unwatched. She had done that once in an airport departure lounge. The resulting mayhem allowed her to slip in behind her target and garrote him where he sat.

Refocusing on the present, she surveyed the rest of the playing field. Ticket machines ran along one wall. Ticket holders dutifully lined up at the wide corridors that led off in four directions toward the exhibits. On a wall beside each corridor, so-called universal symbols with red slash marks through them informed visitors that food, beverages, running, coughing without covering your mouth, and the use of cellphones or cameras were all forbidden. For the hell of it, she coughed out loud. None of the cops even looked at her.

Enough fun. She headed for the Information counter and asked one of the women, "Can you tell me where to find Martine Desmarais's office? She's an employee."

"We cannot give that information."

Oh? How about if I reach across the counter and rip out your esophagus? But instead, Jade smiled affably and said, "I'm a reporter from the New York Times. I'd like to interview her for a story. Can you at least call her?"

"Is she expecting you?"

"Look, I travelled a long way to get here. Can you just call?" *Before I gouge out your eyes.*

After more cajoling, the useless female finally phoned someone who apparently had a modicum of authority. With a sour expression, the woman hung up and said, "Your name, please?"

"Emily Grant."

"One moment." Sourpuss typed on her keyboard, picked up a telephone handset, and pressed some numbers.

#

Dan and Martine were about to leave her office when the phone buzzed twice, then twice again.

"That's an internal ring," she said and went back to her desk.

"Probably Leroux," Dan thought out loud.

"No." She pointed at the phone's display screen. "It's Reception."

"Why would they call you?"

"I don't know. Maybe Paulette called the museum. Or my mother. Damn, I was supposed to phone my mother at least once a day." Martine snatched up the handset. *"Allô?"*
After a short pause, *"Oui, c'est moi."*

Coming to her side, Dan leaned his ear close to Martine's but could hardly understand anything the woman on the other end said.

Martine pressed the handset to her chest and looked at Dan with a rattled expression. "A reporter named Emily Grant wants to see me. She says she's from the New York Times."

Dan tensed. "Why would the Times want to interview you?"

"No idea."

"Ask Reception to describe the woman."

Martine spoke into the phone, and her face turned ashen. Covering the mouthpiece she said, "Maybe your paranoia is wearing off on me, but I think it's the sniper."

"Tell me."

"Asian, slender, pushy."

Pushy meant nothing for a reporter. But slender and Asian meant a lot. Martine's conclusion that Emily Grant could be their sniper rang too true for comfort. *Turn danger into opportunity.* "Say you'll meet her in Reception in twenty minutes."

"Are you insane?"

"If it's the sniper, I want to meet her. Or at least see her."

"But …"

"Please, just do it."

With obvious reluctance, Martine complied.

When she'd hung up, Dan said, "I assume we're in a part of the museum that's off-limits to visitors. If I go out, can you get me back in?"

"Not without a special pass, after a written request and a background check."

That figured, given the recent bombings and shootings in Paris. "Is there a place where we can look into Reception without actually entering it?"

She thought a moment. "One of the security doors has a small window."

"Good enough. Let's go."

#

Screw twenty minutes. That was too long for comfort. She would wait fifteen, tops.

"Emily," a name Jade had chosen on the spur of the moment, turned away from the counter and walked into the Louvre's bookshop to think. The reporter ploy seemed to have worked. But something didn't smell right. Was it this Dan Lovel character? If the girl was here, he probably was, also. The two of them had been inseparable. Plus, while on the phone, the cretin at Information had looked Jade over and said something like "Asiatic." That and the twenty-minute wait suggested Lovel might be planning something.

For sure, he had spotted her in Gare de l'Est, or at least looked at her suspiciously. She wasn't sure why. No way could he know she had been tailing them. She'd taken care to conceal her face and change clothing twice. But his eyes had revealed recognition.

If Control—the grandiose name her client chose for himself—hadn't insisted that she covertly ensure the girl and her books arrived safely in Paris, she would have removed Lovel from the equation a long time ago. There were any number of nonlethal ways. But the girl was apparently too incompetent to make it here without him.

Moving to a position near the front of the shop where she could observe the Information desk, Jade pulled down a glossy volume of the museum's Egyptian collection and absently thumbed through it.

Lovel was the one she had to be careful about. According to the guy's dossier, he'd done some impressive things. A regular Jason Bourne in some instances. And if it hadn't been for Control's text messages, guiding her, Lovel would have lost her in Germany. Taking him out would be a shame. But she would do it in an instant to secure that book and the second half of her fee.

Jade ground her teeth. Maybe she was being paranoid. Say there was no plot against her. The girl was here alone and had simply been curious about the "reporter." Then the problem was different. Her dossier contained only one page, nothing remarkable except for two college degrees. How to convince a woman that intelligent to take her back to her office for an interview?

Five minutes left. Jade re-shelved the Egypt book and dug her nails into her hands. She'd never even been to college. High school, U.S. Army, Ranger training but not allowed into combat, the pricks. Well, she'd shown them. Working for hire, she pulled down buckets more money than any of them would ever see.

She loved the work. The satisfying kick when she pulled the trigger. The feel of flesh yielding to her blade. The faint crack when she twisted a head and snapped the neck.

All of which did her no damn good when it came to sweet-talking her way into the girl's office. Maybe if she hadn't spent a sleepless night shivering in that doorway, she might have come up with a better plan. But it was too late now. She glanced at her watch.

One minute. Time to abort.

#

Despite his best efforts, Dan couldn't calm Martine's nerves. As they rushed along the corridors, she kept peppering him with "what if" questions. Telling her, "Don't worry. I just want to see her," did nothing to alleviate her anxiety.

Finally, in an area of glass-walled offices, they came to a steel door with a narrow, vertical window at one side. "Here," she said.

Dan peered through the window at a crowd of tourists. To his left, two couples stood at the Information counter. No single people. He shifted his attention to the spiral staircase where new arrivals were descending beneath the glass pyramid. Again, no singles. Then he noticed the distant figure of a woman near the top of the escalator that took visitors back outside. Straight, black hair hung to her shoulders. His heart rate jumped.

"I think I've spotted her," he said to Martine. "Can I borrow your cardkey?"

"Dan, if you get caught, we'll both be in big trouble. I could lose my job."

"I'll be careful, I promise." *Just give it to me, dammit.* "In the meantime, you could go back and check on Leroux. See what he's found so far. I'll join you as soon as I can."

After what seemed like endless hesitation, while his quarry reached the top of the escalator, Martine finally relented.

Dan grabbed the card, pushed open the steel door, and strode to the escalator as fast as he could without drawing attention. He took the moving stairs two steps at a time. Outside, he scanned the huge courtyard for anyone leaving, then walked along the line of waiting tourists in case she was trying to conceal herself in plain sight. No luck.

And no sign of alarm among the armed soldiers keeping an eye on the growing crowd. They definitely would have chased down anyone running away.

Visually he searched farther afield. Acres of open space, couples and families and backpackers trickling in from various directions. To the west, the two long arms of the museum were interrupted by a street with a roundabout where tour buses were disgorging passengers. Beyond that lay more open space, then the Tuileries Gardens, another vast expanse.

Dammit. He'd been so close.

After a final perusal of the courtyard, he clutched Martine's cardkey in his pocket and headed for the door they'd entered in the Porte des Lions.

#

As nonchalantly as possible, Jade loitered near the lion where she had stashed her weapons, waiting for a half-decent break in the pedestrian traffic that had surfaced like ants in the past hour.

The past useless hour.

No, not completely useless. She had learned the girl was here, which surely meant the book was, too. Old book, museum. It made sense. Except the museum was huge and the girl's office could be anywhere. On top of that, there was the potential complication of having to deal with Lovel.

A break in foot traffic at last. Two Middle Easterners had just turned into the passageway. The next pedestrians were forty feet away. Quickly she reached behind the lion and retrieved her pistol, silencer, and switchblade. As she did, she heard footsteps enter the passage from the courtyard side. She peeked around the corner and froze.

Lovel was walking toward her.

Ducking back, she fought down an adrenaline rush. Had he somehow spotted her? The fact that the girl wasn't with him suggested it was a possibility.

Jade screwed the silencer onto her pistol. She had no desire to kill him. Control hadn't paid for that. Besides, it wasn't necessary. One bullet to the knee would incapacitate him and remove him from her concerns just as effectively as a bullet to the head. Pressing her back to the wall beside the lion, she waited for him to emerge from the passageway.

But the footsteps halted. Had he sensed her presence?

She heard the click of an electronic lock. Very cautiously, she peered again around the corner. Just in time to see Lovel push open the wooden door and disappear inside.

Fuck. She'd missed a chance.

Then something tugged at her awareness—or rather, the absence of something did. She had heard the door click open, but not click shut.

Chapter 16

It wasn't Martine's fault, Dan told himself as he descended the stairs and headed for Leroux's basement office. As much as he might want to blame her for the sniper's escape, the logical side of his brain said, "You should have anticipated her reluctance to give you the cardkey." But he hadn't even foreseen a need to ask her for it, and that was *his* fault.

One thing was chillingly indisputable—whatever distance they'd previously put between themselves and their pursuer had now closed to a few feet, and fewer minutes.

#

Jade hustled to the wooden door and found it not quite seated in the jamb. Luck was with her, after all. Placing her toe against the bottom of the door to prevent belated closure, she listened at the barely visible opening. No sounds inside. With glances at each entrance to the passageway, she withdrew the silenced pistol from her waistband, then inched open the door until she could make out a dimly lit landing. Still no sounds.

But could Lovel be waiting behind the door?

She gripped the pistol, stepped inside, and spun around to look at what turned out to be vacant space. In fact, no one was in sight. So far, so good.

In case the electronic lock was monitored somewhere, she eased the door closed. *Click.*

After shoving the pistol into the back of her waistband, she surveyed her surroundings more thoroughly. To the left, a flight of stone stairs ran down to what was probably a storage basement. Ahead, a hallway lined with smaller doors led off in two directions. The doors up here would be for offices, one of them almost certainly the girl's. But in which direction? Her mental coin toss had proved lucky before, so she tossed it again. Heads. Left.

Ambling casually down one side of the hall, she paused at each door to listen. If anyone was inside, they weren't making noise. She reached what had looked like the end of the hallway, only to find a short jog that led to a continuation, and more doors.

Crap. This could take all day. She hadn't yet checked the other side of this corridor, let alone the corridor that ran off in the other direction from the vestibule.

Patience, she admonished herself. The book was here somewhere.

#

In Leroux's office, Dan shook his head at Martine to indicate he hadn't found the sniper, then asked what they'd learned so far from the book. A lot, he suspected, based on the excitement in Leroux's eyes and the semicircle of other books, presumably reference materials, that now lay open on the man's desk.

"Please sit," Leroux said. When they had, he picked up his notes. "As I was telling Martine, this book you have 'found' is very important."

"In what way?" Dan asked, hoping the importance lay in some esoteric nuance of biblical scholarship.

"It strikes at the heart of Israel's legitimacy, the very basis of its existence."

A cold knot swelled in Dan's stomach. He would burn the book himself if Leroux was right. And if it was real. Two huge "ifs," both of which needed proof, or at least a believable explanation. He glanced at Martine, whose uneasy expression mirrored his own concern.

In a forced tone of neutrality, he said to Leroux, "What makes you think so?"

"Not think. Know." Leroux paused, clearly to let his expertise in the matter sink in. "How I know is through a more careful reading of the text so far. Which, I assure you, is no simple matter. It is written in ancient Hebrew—what Isaiah called 'the language of Canaan'—before vowel signs had been developed. The writer or writers presuppose that readers will understand the words, but there are cases in which meaning depends on vowel choice and context."

"So, you could be wrong?"

"No, Jardani. I am not wrong. If you'll settle down, I will explain."

"Okay, I'm listening." Especially for the slightest flaw in the man's logic.

"First, I confirm what I said before. Moses appears to Joshua in a dream or vision, which would qualify this as a Sixth Book of Moses."

"*Would* qualify?" Dan said. "It sounds like there's a catch."

Leroux held up a hand. "Allow me to continue." He looked from Dan to Martine and back. "Secondly it says that, on the eve of their conquest of the Holy Land, the Hebrews celebrated with what we can only call a drunken orgy, including crying out in ecstasy to other gods."

Didn't sound like any Jews Dan ever knew.

"That night, Moses tells Joshua that God is enraged with the Hebrews for breaking His covenant more perversely than ever before. Moses declares forty days of penance but says, despite their penance, the Lord will never totally forgive them. He will continue to guide them, and they may *possess* the land, but they will never own it." Leroux looked at them over his glasses. "This is a crucial distinction."

"Then the book is bogus," Dan blurted, his irritation rising. "Israel is the Jewish homeland."

"That is the crux," Leroux told him. "But listen to this. Moses says The Lord's wrath is so great that He will remind them of it constantly. He will send other nations against them. There will be rebellions and conquests. They will become slaves of foreigners and will be taken forcibly, in chains, from the land. Their great works will be destroyed, their fields and orchards and livestock will be laid waste. To quote again, 'You shall know no peace, such have you offended the Lord.'"

"It's bullshit." Dan sprang from his chair and thrust out his hand. "Give me the book."

"Wait." Martine clamped Dan's arm. To Leroux, she said, "Are you sure this book is real?"

"Ah, the biggest question of all. Was your text inspired by God?" Leroux grinned. "We must admit it appears to foretell the destruction of the Temple, the Babylonian captivity, and all the wars the modern state has had to fight."

"That's what I mean," she said. "Do you believe anyone can predict the future?"

"What I personally believe does not matter."

"You're right about that." Dan wrenched his arm from Martine's grasp. "But you surely have some opinion on the subject."

Maddeningly, Leroux took time to shake the one cigarette pack remaining on his desk. When nothing came out, he opened a drawer, withdrew a joint, and lit up.

He obviously enjoyed this bit of theater, a captive audience urging him to continue. Dan figured it was the most attention the old scholar had received in decades.

"There are," Leroux admitted through the earthy smell of his smoke, "some inconsistencies with the next book in the Bible, Joshua." From his cluttered desktop, he picked up a well-worn volume inscribed in Hebrew on the cover. Opening it to a dog-eared page, he said, "This is God speaking," and read, " 'Moses my servant is dead; now therefore arise, go over this Jordan, thou and all this people, unto the land which I do give to them, even to the children of Israel.' And three verses later, 'There shall not any man be able to stand before thee all the days of thy life: as I was with Moses, so I will be with thee; I will not fail thee, nor forsake thee.' "

"Then this supposed Sixth Book is a sham."

"Not so fast, Jardani Camlo." Leroux took a long drag, held it in until there was almost no smoke to exhale, then leaned back in his chair. "One could argue that 'all the days of your life' means all the days of Joshua's life. So, giving them the land does not mean it's theirs forever."

About to have a fit, Dan demanded, "Has anyone ever argued that?"

"The Haggadah, a text recited during Passover. I have heard it mentions this question. But I don't know that for a fact."

"Then why are you bringing it up now?"

A twinkle lit the man's eyes. "To give you a taste of how scholars might address the problems your book presents."

"I don't need a taste. I just need—"

Clutching Dan's arm again, Martine addressed Leroux in a conciliatory tone. "Have you formed *any* opinions about the validity of the book? Its so-called authority?"

"They are forming," he replied with a nod of appreciation. "The consensus among Old Testament specialists is that the Pentateuch, or rather one version of it, was first written down in the sixth or seventh century BCE, probably during the Babylonian captivity."

Dan winced inside at the prospect of another lecture. But the issue was too important not to hear the man out.

"It was later revised," Leroux said, "and expanded and merged with the stories kept by those Jews who were not taken captive. So what we have today is a hybrid document. That's why Genesis has two versions of the flood, for instance."

"I've read about that," Martine said. "One with two of each animal, and the other with seven. And Noah sends out a dove in one version but a raven in the other."

Leroux nodded again. "Precisely."

Dan hadn't heard of this and didn't need to learn about it now, not with Israel's status in question and the sniper prowling around too close for comfort. But he could finally see where Leroux was going. "You're saying that maybe this book was excluded during the rewrite?"

"Possibly. It would certainly have done the Hebrews no good to include it. A similar thing happened when the New Testament was first compiled. Four gospels were chosen while several less 'miraculous' gospels were left out. And in your book, there *are* some words that would suggest a later date than the Babylonian captivity."

"Good enough for me," Dan concluded. "With all the inconsistencies, no one would regard it as genuine."

"Jardani, you are missing the point. The key thing is what we can learn about the Pentateuch from completing my translation. Remember, these are the foundation stories of the Jews. Who they are, where they came from, how they received their laws, the achievements and ordeals of their ancestors. All religions have such stories, whether written or oral."

"No. The point is whether this book could be used to incite a major war in the Middle East."

"On that question the answer is yes. Unless…" Leroux's eyes drilled into Dan's. "… I find something contradictory in the remaining pages."

"You haven't finished?" Martine asked.

"Six pages so far. There are five more."

Six pages? Dan wanted to call it quits. But Leroux might find more evidence that the book was phony. "How long will this take?"

Leroux looked at his watch, then dropped the miniscule butt of his joint in the overflowing ashtray and stood. "Tomorrow afternoon, if the gods are with me."

"You're leaving?" Martine jumped to her feet. "How can you leave now, if the book is so significant?"

"Alas, I must. My sister is preparing a Christmas Eve supper, and I have not yet bought her a gift. But I will be back here tomorrow." His expression turned wistful. "Where else can an old man go?"

Dan might have felt sorry for him if he didn't want to chain the guy to his desk until he finished. Swallowing his frustration, he switched to practical matters and turned to Martine. "Do we take the book or leave it?"

"It'll be safe here." Then, as if she'd had second thoughts, she asked Leroux, "You will lock your door, yes?"

"Of course."

"Then we'll leave it."

Dan bit his cheek at her decision. But this *was* a part of the museum the sniper could never reach.

#

Having listened in mounting frustration at every door in the hallway that ran left from the entryway landing, Jade was partway down the hallway that ran right when voices sounded behind her. She spun around but saw no one. Backing to the wall, she palmed her switchblade. The voices, a man's and a woman's, came from the landing. She tested the door handle next to her, found it unlocked, and slipped into a dark office, leaving the door cracked just enough to peek out.

After fifteen long seconds, she exhaled. Whoever they were—and her instinct told her it was Lovel and the girl—they were not coming into this corridor. They must be leaving the museum. With the book.

Jade moved to the landing. Nobody. But a hint of perfume that hadn't been there before lingered in the air. Cautiously she opened the big wooden door. Again seeing no one, she opened it wider and looked both directions along the passageway. Were they ghosts?

In case she needed to get back in, she laid her knife on the ground to stop the door from closing completely, then hurried to the passage's street entrance and peeked around the corner. There. Lovel and the girl, striding along the sidewalk. The girl carried a knapsack in one hand, but she carried it lightly, its canvas sides limp. Lovel carried nothing. So where was the book? They'd surely brought it here. Why else would they spend the whole morning at the girl's workplace?

Wait. They'd come up from the basement. Maybe that's where her office was.

Jade returned to the door, retrieved her knife, and stepped inside. Cautiously she descended stone stairs into a dank corridor. She smiled at the thought that the chick with two college degrees probably wasn't important enough to rate a room with windows.

Beside the point, Jade told herself. Find her office.

But how? They obviously weren't inside, which meant listening for sounds wouldn't help. Then it struck her. That perfume she'd smelled on the landing and again in the outdoor passageway. There were hints of it here, also. It had to be the girl's.

Slowly, so as not to stir the air and disperse the scent, Jade worked her way down the corridor until she could no longer smell the fragrance. She retraced her steps, sniffing at each door. Here.

She tried the handle on her right. Locked. The one on her left turned. She inched open the door to see an old man with reddish-gray hair standing at a desk against the far wall.

Wrong office.

But as she was about to step back, he opened the bottom desk drawer and carefully laid inside what appeared to be a very old book.

Jade's pulse quickened. Maybe it was the one she wanted, maybe not. His whole damn office was full of books. But when he shut the drawer and inserted a key in its lock, she knew this book was special. Plus, the smell of the girl's perfume was much stronger here. She definitely had been in this room.

With no idea who the codger was, Jade stole up behind him and threw her arms around his neck in a jiu-jitsu choke that cut off flow in his carotid arteries. He grabbed at her wrists and struggled briefly before collapsing at her feet.

In twenty seconds, he would regain consciousness. Jade snatched up the key that had fallen from his hand, opened the drawer, pulled out the book, and quickly flipped through its thick pages. Weird writing. Maybe Greek or Hebrew. How was she supposed to know? She couldn't even read the Japanese characters her parents had tried to teach her. But this had to be what Control wanted.

The old man moaned. Before he could fully come to, she tucked the book under her jacket and dashed out the door.

Twenty minutes later, she'd crossed a bridge over the river and found a café called Le Fregate. After ordering a ham-and-mushroom omelet, her first solid food today, she texted Control.

Got it

EXCELLENT!! I'll be there tomorrow. Where are you staying?

No need to know. Will tell you where to meet

Jade turned off her phone. For any face-to-face meeting with a client, she always set the ground rules. No way would she trust someone criminal enough to hire her.

Relaxed at last, she wolfed down her omelet and the fries that came with it. This had been a weird assignment, her first to involve no killing. Nevertheless, it had tested her skills. Now all she had to do was deliver the book, collect her payment, chuck her weapons into the river, and fly home. Maybe a week in Cancun or the Bahamas. No. Given her fee, this time she'd try Tahiti. She pictured big Tahitian guys, big where it counted. Oh, yeah.

#

After sitting in offices all morning, it felt good to walk. Dan relished not only the exercise and chilly air, but even more so Martine strolling beside him along the Seine. As Pont Neuf came into view, he said, "How about we walk all the way to Paulette's house?"

"Oh, hell." She stopped. "I almost forgot again. I have to call my mother. She hasn't heard from me since … since Prague, I think." She pulled out her personal phone and switched it on. "Fourteen messages? She's going to kill me."

"Turn it off," he said. "Use this." He inserted the international SIM card into one of his prepaid phones, then handed her the phone and walked on a little farther to give her some privacy. A stone balustrade separated their sidewalk from the Seine, twenty feet below. At river level ran another sidewalk, the cobblestone one you always saw in nighttime photos of lovers lost in each other's eyes. He pictured Martine and himself walking there but suspected it would never happen.

"Well, that was fun." She came up to him with a look of exasperation.

Jarred from his thoughts, Dan said, "I gather you got through?"

"First she was relieved. Then she was angry." Martine shook her head. "Does a mother ever stop treating her daughter like a child?"

"I doubt it. My mother still thinks of me as her little boy."

"Sometimes I ... Oh, never mind."

"Did she have anything interesting to say?"

"Only if you're interested in fits."

"Tell me," he said, wondering why Astrid would throw a fit.

A gust of wind whipped Martine's auburn hair. "After scolding me for not calling, she asked if we'd taken the books to her house, 'as instructed.' When I said we were having the small one translated by a man at the museum, she blew her top. We had no right, it was too dangerous, blah, blah, blah. I told her we'd gone through hell to get it and, by God, I was going to find out what it said."

So, Astrid knew what was in the Moses book. "Did you tell her we've already learned the gist of the text?"

"I could hardly get a word in ... sideway. She instructed me to get it back and take it to her house immediately and stay there with it. She'll be here as soon as she can get away."

"What did you say?"

"I hung up."

Dan thought a moment. "Did she ask about the Louvre volumes?"

"No."

In the Caymans, Astrid had mentioned the "small book" only as an aside. If it was her true objective, which now seemed to be the case, then she was one devious woman. Convinced of it, he said, "This isn't just a mother-daughter thing. She deceived us both. It was the Moses book she really wanted when she sent us to Prague. The Louvre books were a cover. She used them to lure you in with the promise of righting wrongs Napoleon perpetrated. And she played the same card with me."

"The Nazis looting your grandparents' art? She told me about that."

"Not just looting their art, but killing them."

Martine's eyes widened. "I didn't know about that. I'm sorry."

"It doesn't matter anymore." *Unless I ever get my hands on a surviving Nazi.* "As to the present, how you and she deal with her deception is your business. For my part, I'll never trust her again."

Martine rolled in her lips then said, "I don't blame you. I'm not sure I can either."

"What does matter is what we do with that book."

"If she thought it was dangerous when she sent us, then she already had some idea of what it contained."

Same conclusion he had reached. Good that they were on the same wavelength.

Martine brushed a fall of wind-blown hair out of her face. "She knows, or believes, the contents could escalate conflict in the Middle East."

Suddenly a corollary possibility popped into his head. Astrid was a big shot at the World Bank. "Large-scale war could crash financial institutions in the region. The resulting chaos might even spread to Europe and the U.S."

"Christ. That kind of thinking would be just like her. And it would explain why she wants us to take it to her house. She plans to destroy it."

"It might also be why the sniper has been trailing us. She wants it for a client who either plans to destroy it or worse, much worse, intends to use it to start a war." He studied the sidewalks on either side of the street. No sign of a woman with straight black hair, let alone an Asian one. But she was out there, somewhere.

"How are we going to handle this?" Martine said.

"We'll know better tomorrow, after Leroux finishes his translation."

"I hope so."

As they continued walking, he said, "Give me the phone, please." He took out the SIM card, broke it in two, then tossed one half over the balustrade and dropped the other in a tree well. "We'll get another card if you need it."

"I won't."

Fine with him. Despite the uncertainties they faced, strolling with her along the Seine on a chilly afternoon lifted his spirits.

At Pont-Neuf, she stopped. "I hate this bridge."

And there go the lifted spirits.

"It's the oldest bridge in Paris," she said. "But look at it now."

Thousands of padlocks, tens of thousands, encrusted the metal fencework that bordered the railings. Like barnacles on the pilings of a wooden pier. It had been several years since Dan was last in Paris, and this sight was new to him.

"They're called love locks," she told him disdainfully. "People put them there as a sign of their love for each other. They add so much weight to the bridge that workmen have to cut them off, almost daily, and haul them away. They're like graffiti."

Dan kind of liked the idea, symbols of love in the City of Love. But he kept his silence.

At her insistence, they continued to Pont Notre-Dame, which crossed to Île de la Cité, the island in the Seine where the Parisii tribe first established a stronghold during Roman times and gave the modern city its name. More engaging in Dan's view was the island's breathtaking triumph of Gothic faith, Cathedral Notre Dame.

Another short bridge brought them to Rue Saint-Jacques, which they followed uphill into the Latin Quarter. The cold breeze stiffened. The temperature dropped. He and Martine turned up their collars. By the time they reached the Sorbonne, snow flurries danced around them, the flakes melting on their faces.

At the top of the hill, Martine paused again. "We should get Paulette something for Christmas. And to thank her for letting us stay with her."

Dan glanced at the shops, their holiday lights shining festively in the falling snow. "You know her better than I do."

"She loves wine. Let's buy her a good Bordeaux. There's a wine shop just up there."

They purchased an outrageously expensive 1990 Cheval Blanc, then walked two blocks farther and proceeded through the various keypads until they reached Paulette's house, where the artist, clearly visible through the windows, was slashing paint on canvas as if fighting off an attacker. "We can't interrupt her," Dan said. "She's in the zone."

"You like her work?"

"I like it a lot. It's a treat to see her creating."

After a few more minutes, Paulette stood back from her canvas. Martine knocked and stepped inside. "It's us."

"Oh." Paulette felt her Bradley watch. "I expected you later."

"We brought you something." Martine held out the bottle. "*Joyeux Noël.*"

#

Exhausted after no sleep last night, Jade stretched out on the bed in her hotel room.

When she woke, it was dark outside her window. She stripped, showered with one of those idiotic handheld sprayers, and dressed again. Dinnertime. Could she find a decent cheeseburger? Probably not, but a steak would do nicely.

She opened the armoire that passed for a closet and placed the book at the back of the top shelf under a spare blanket. A worthless hiding place, but chances were zero that anyone would come looking.

Outdoors on the sidewalk, snowflakes swarmed like mayflies. Fuck snow. Give her sand and sea and a tall drink with an umbrella, hold the umbrella.

Soon.

Looking both directions along the street, she spotted a restaurant two blocks away and strolled toward it. Her mind conjured images of a sizzling steak and well-hung Tahitians, her consciousness barely registering the stocky figure who crossed to her side of the road a few doors behind her.

Chapter 17

Jade came to with a splitting headache, her cheek pressed to frigid pavement. *What the hell?*

When she tried to rise, her hands wouldn't move. They were tied behind her back, and a weight held her down.

"Snap out of it," a man's voice snarled. "I don't have all night."

A small part of Jade's recovering awareness detected a British accent. The greater part suddenly realized she'd been struck in the head, laid facedown in a filthy alley, and pinned there by some asshole who was sitting on her lower back and had no idea what deep shit he was in.

She struggled to turn over, but her wrists were cinched tight. Bound with a plastic lock band, judging from the sharp edges. *Fuck.* This was no simple mugging. To make matters worse, he'd taken off her jacket. It lay in a heap, four feet away, her weapons on the ground beside it.

Shivering in the cold, she said, "What do you want?"

"The book. Where is it?"

The book? Was this Control? It didn't make sense. She was supposed to give him the book tomorrow. A simple exchange for the second half of her fee. No need to get violent, unless he was trying to cheat her out of her money.

Or maybe this creep wasn't Control. Now fully alert, she tested him with, "It's where I told you in my last text."

"Tell me again."

So, he *didn't* know. This was not Control. It was someone else, and he was in for a world of hurt. But to gain an advantage, she had to first turn onto her back. "It's in my hotel room."

"What room number?"

"I don't remember. It's on my key."

Something very sharp pressed into the skin at the top of her neck. "Don't move." His weight shifted from the small of her back to the tops of her thighs. He patted the hip pockets of her jeans.

"In my front pocket."

His weight lifted. He rolled her over, revealing a middle-aged face with five o'clock shadow and a steady hand that held a stiletto. Instead of straddling her again, he spread her legs as if that would disadvantage her and knelt between them.

With a surge of relief, she now knew this asshole was a lightweight. Stiletto or not, no one even half-skilled in martial arts would kneel *between* her legs. As he fished in her front jeans pockets, she raised her hips and grasped him in a triangle choke, one leg over his shoulder and behind his neck, locking the ankle under her other knee, capturing his neck as well as the arm that was under her knee, and squeezing with all her might.

His free hand, the one without the stiletto, grabbed at her uselessly. In seconds he collapsed.

She kept squeezing, cutting off the blood flow to his head and crushing his windpipe into the captured arm to choke out his ability to breathe. "Die, motherfucker."

A few moments later, he did.

Best defense any woman could use against a would-be rapist, but apparently he'd never learned that.

As her heart rate settled, Jade squirmed out from under him, rolled into a ball on her back, and worked her bound wrists under her butt and over her feet. With her hands now in front of her, it was a simple matter to retrieve the fallen knife and slice through the thick lock band.

A quick inventory of her body revealed no injuries other than the very tender goose egg on the crown of her head. That was the good news. The bad news was that she now had a body to deal with. And a lot of questions that needed answering.

While putting on her jacket and adding the stiletto to her arsenal, she surveyed the surroundings. A narrow alley, dark except at each end, where light from the streets illuminated the first few feet. She and the corpse were about a third of the way in from one end. Aside from the spot where they'd struggled, a few inches of snow coated the pavement. There were two trashcans in the alley, beside two closed doors. No windows at this level or overhead. No voices.

Gripping the body by its ankles, she dragged it to the nearest trashcan. The trail it left in the snow was a giveaway, but she couldn't help it. Quickly she searched the creep's pockets and found a wallet and cellphone. Anyone who carried ID on a job was definitely a lightweight. Or in this guy's case, since he looked to be in his fifties, past his prime. Either way, he'd screwed up big time. *And for fumbling your mission, you'll be found like this.* She propped him against the brick wall in the pose of a passed-out drunk.

In his wallet, she found some money and several plastic cards. But it was too dark to read the cards. She would have to wait to find who he was. It was time to scoot.

Which direction?

If Asshole had a partner, that person would no doubt be on watch close to the alley entrance where she'd been attacked. Figuring that to be the nearer entrance, she headed for the far one. *Heroics only when necessary.*

The street where she emerged was brighter than the one in front of her hotel. Christmas lights surrounded the windows of shops now closed. Illuminated signs marked several restaurants still open. A few cars drove past. On the sidewalks, she saw only three men, one woman, and one couple, all hustling along with upturned collars. No potential partner loitering.

Maybe she was being paranoid, but the throbbing pain in the back of her head justified extra caution.

The alley continued on the other side of the street. Holding the pistol against her thigh, Jade dashed across and entered it. After three paces, she spun around. No one heading her way. She pocketed the pistol and palmed the stiletto, in case.

The alley ended at a bar. A few losers—Who else spent Christmas Eve in a bar?—nursed drinks inside. Nobody on the sidewalks. The street itself was cheerless, its storefronts either dark or dangling token strands of red and green bulbs. She felt comfortable here.

A drink would go down well right now. She'd hardly touched alcohol since getting off the plane in Prague. She glanced again into the bar. One bartender, six patrons, all men, most with potbellies. A woman alone would attract too much attention. Screw it.

But she did need food. A block to her left a lighted sign announced Gyros Kebabs. Good enough.

The place smelled of Mediterranean spices. It had three tables inside but no customers. With gestures she ordered a gyro sandwich to go. The sullen young man behind the counter shaved slices of meat off the upright rotisserie onto a round piece of pita bread. As he did, she checked her assailant's phone. A burner. Nothing on it except a single text message received. It named her hotel and gave the address.

Son of a bitch.

No wonder he hadn't asked which hotel she was staying in. He already knew. And that's where he'd been waiting for her.

A sudden chill of realization swept over her. Control sent this creep. It had to be. Only Control knew she had the book. The text was in Control's style, fully punctuated the way old people did. But how had he known where— "Shit!"

The young man behind the counter turned to look at her.

"It's nothing," she said with a dismissive flick of her hand.

But it wasn't nothing. She'd been a fucking moron. Control was tracking her through the GPS in her phone. That's how he knew where she was staying. She should have realized he could do that when he kept telling her where Lovel and the girl were. How could she have been so damned naive?

"Madame?" The fellow making her sandwich had now wrapped it in brown paper and was handing it over the counter.

She held up one finger in a gesture meaning "Wait," then pulled out her phone and turned it completely off. Control's deceit changed everything. No one betrayed her and lived.

After paying for the sandwich, she took it outside. Snowflakes still swirled in the air. The only pedestrians were a man and woman one block away.

She devoured half of her meal, barely tasting it. The second half she ate more slowly as she circled back to her hotel. Control was as good as dead. But who was he?

In her room, a place the size of a monk's cell, she sat on the narrow bed and emptied the wallet, hoping for clues. A British driver's license in the name of Colin Ross, Orkney Street, Durham. Three credit cards on British banks, a loyalty card for a pharmacy and another for a supermarket. A restaurant receipt and hotel bill from London, neither one particularly expensive. Cash in the amount of seventy British pounds and two hundred euros. No hint of Control's identity.

Wait.

Control had communicated with this guy, and with her, by text. Texts were sent via phone numbers. She rechecked the dead man's phone. No number shown for the text he'd received. She reactivated her own phone, quickly ran through Control's messages, and found the same thing. No number. Why hadn't she noticed that before?

Again, she turned her phone fully off. She was about to do the same with her assailant's when it struck her that leaving it on might trick Control into thinking the dead man was in her room, mission accomplished. *Dream on, motherfucker. You're in for more agony than you ever thought possible.*

But how was she going to find him? He obviously didn't intend to meet her. He'd sent his hatchet man to do that. The hatchet man would deliver the book. If fury hadn't driven her to kill the creep immediately, she could have questioned him and found out where the handover was supposed to take place. That was two screw-ups in one night, not detecting his approach and not keeping him alive long enough to talk.

She shut her eyes. *Get your act together.*

After a minute of re-centering—slow breaths in through the nose, slower breaths out through the mouth—her path forward clarified. She switched off the dead man's phone. He'd "been here" long enough. Let Control wonder what limpdick was up to. Next on her agenda was finding another hotel. No easy task at eleven o'clock on Christmas Eve.

From the top shelf of her armoire, she retrieved the hard-won book. She was about to place it in her suitcase, next to her disassembled rifle, when she noticed the three dossiers Control had sent her. Lovel, the girl, and the girl's mother. Lovel's was the thickest, five pages. In contrast, the mother's was a page and a half, the girl's only one. If thickness was any measure, Control knew Lovel best. Jade reread his dossier. More details than were necessary for a job in which she only had to track him. Details of Lovel's training and past work as an agent of the Diplomatic Security Service, a cautionary statement about his ability to hear and see things other people missed, his "uncanny" sixth sense.

That was it. Control knew Lovel personally. He had to if he could provide such depth of background. And that meant Lovel must know him.

Lovel was the key to finding Control.

She dropped the folders in her suitcase. Somehow, she had to extract Control's identity and location from the man who'd been her nemesis for the past four days. She doubted capture and threats would work. Lovel was a pro.

But there might be a better way.

#

If Dan had been a Catholic, the music could not have stirred him more. As he made his way out of Notre Dame, Martine on one side of him and Paulette on the other, the choir's voices still sang in his ears, lingering like the heavy aroma of incense hanging in the air.

Paulette, apparently a "lapsed Catholic" like Martine, had encouraged them to leave right after the white-clad priests paraded up the cathedral's long central aisle. The first priest had swung a smoking censer forward and back. The second held high a golden crucifix on a staff. The third brandished an open Bible held equally high, as though to expel the devil. Two dozen others followed. A pageant of holy men about to celebrate Midnight Mass, a ceremony in which Paulette and Martine evidently had no interest. Nor did he. The preceding hour of choral music was why they'd come.

Outside, under a light snowfall, Dan said to Paulette, "That was absolutely beautiful. Thank you for suggesting it."

"Thank you for bringing that lovely wine."

He squeezed Martine's hand in a gesture meant to convey his gratitude for her having chosen it.

After giving him an appreciative smile, she said, "Paulette, should we find a taxi, or would you rather walk?"

"Let's walk."

As Paulette swept her cane side-to-side over the cobblestones, Dan thought back to the earlier parts of this wonderful evening.

It began in Paulette's living room with slowly consuming the truly superb wine. While sitting on the couch, he'd asked her if her latest painting was finished.

"Almost."

Martine, evidently reading his mind again, had placed a hand on Paulette's. "Finish it now. He would love to watch you."

Paulette had looked doubtful but, after a few more words of encouragement, walked to her easel and selected a brush. "I think some royal purple." She dipped the brush in a can of paint, then touched the bottom two corners of the canvas, evidently for orientation, and slashed the brush down the right-hand side. After dipping the brush again, she slapped a blotch just above the centerline, a third of the way in from the left.

She'd been about to dab another blotch when Dan said, "No."

Paulette turned to him. "Is too much?"

"I'm no expert, but I think it's perfect just the way it is."

She dropped the brush into a can of solvent. "Then it is finished."

He recalled now how uncertain he'd felt about giving advice. She was the artist. But she'd accepted his suggestion. Cool.

She was also the one who had recommended dinner at a restaurant called Le Petit Châtelet, just across a strip of river from

Notre Dame. During their meal, Martine had told Paulette about the Moses book. He'd balked at first, but decided Paulette was no risk and did deserve an explanation of what they were up to.

Paulette surprised him with, "I hope it is false. The world does not need more religious wars."

After dinner, they'd made the short trek to the cathedral. Then came the music. Now a bracing walk back.

Refocusing on the present, he noticed a vendor selling roasted chestnuts fresh off the brazier. They smelled like Christmas. He bought three paper-wrapped packets, gave one to Martine, and handed the other to Paulette before realizing she could hardly hold the packet and her cane *and* feed herself. "Sorry," he said. "I keep forgetting you're blind."

"I am glad." Her face lit up in a big smile. "Also, I can eat and walk at the same time." With that, she used her cane hand to open a chestnut and place it in her mouth while continuing toward the short bridge that crossed to the bottom of the hill where Rue Saint Jacques began.

Their climb up the grade progressed mostly in silence, except for the munching of chestnuts and the scrape of Paulette's cane on the sidewalk before her. A comfortable, companionable silence, as though words weren't needed. They walked along the walls of the Sorbonne, through the intersection where the Panthéon was lit up on their left and the Eiffel Tower shone like a Christmas tree in the distance to their right, then past the closed but still festively lighted shops of Paulette's immediate neighborhood.

While she pressed buttons on the code pad next to the sidewalk door, Dan perused the street. Not a soul in either direction, let alone anyone resembling the sniper.

In the welcoming warmth of Paulette's house, Martine walked over to the recently finished painting. "I think Dan was right. The painting is perfect, as is."

"Perhaps he should do the next one," Paulette said playfully. "Yes, Dan?"

"When Hell freezes over."

Martine spoke in French, presumably translating the expression.

Paulette laughed. "Must I wait so long?"

"Maybe longer." He pecked her on the cheek. When Martine yawned, he said, "We should get some sleep. We have a big day tomorrow."

"You will spend Christmas with that book?" Paulette asked. "How ... *morne*."

"Dreary," Martine translated.

Worse than dreary. Ever since Martine's call to her mother, Dan had been nagged by an ominous sense of trouble on the horizon. Although he'd successfully banished those thoughts during most of the evening, stored them away in one of many mental compartments, they now reemerged.

Like a bad moon rising.

Chapter 18

Jade solved the problem of finding another hotel by moving upmarket. Posh places had staff on duty throughout the night, every night, including the wee hours of Christmas morning. This one was only a ten-minute walk from the museum and, being part of an American chain, its bed was big and comfortable, the bathroom sparkling. After filling the tub with hot water and some bath oil that came with the room's amenities, she submerged her body, closed her eyes, and reviewed her next moves.

No one survived in this business without backup plans. During the cab ride from her old hotel to this one, she'd considered several and discarded all but two.

The first involved Lovel. She would offer him a swap, the book she had stolen for Control's name and location. Win-win. And if he refused or tried something "brave," she would simply threaten his girlfriend's life. The biggest stumbling block was not knowing where they were staying. But they had to return to the museum, because they'd left their precious book with the old geezer. Probably they would come back tomorrow, not today on Christmas. But she couldn't be sure. Which meant she'd have to freeze her butt off again, staking out the entrance they'd used. At the thought of that, she sat up and turned on the hot water tap to refresh the warmth of her bath.

After swishing the water to circulate its heat, she leaned back again. In her second plan, she would use herself as bait to lure Control into the open. She preferred it by a mile, because it did not include Lovel, and the fewer people involved, the better. But it was far less certain. How street savvy was Control? Would he take the bait?

To double her chances, she decided to pursue both plans. Finding Lovel would have to wait until morning. But luring Control could begin right now. All she needed was yet another hotel.

She toweled off, dressed, and went back downstairs. The sidewalk glistened. After two steps, she realized why. It was icing over. She stepped off the curb and made her way along the more roughly textured pavement of the street. At another hotel, four doors down, she walked in and rapped on the counter. A young man with black hair that was well-oiled and combed straight back came through a door behind the counter. In fairly short order, one of her fake passports had been copied and the corresponding credit card had been approved.

As she walked toward the elevator, he said, "No luggage?"

"The airline lost my suitcase. It's supposed to be here tomorrow."

He nodded knowingly. *"Bonne nuit, madame. Et joyeux noel"*

Her room here was less upscale than the one where she was actually staying. Smaller, only a double bed, a window that looked out at another building, a bathroom with a tiny shower stall and one of those hand-held nozzles. But it didn't matter. She would only be here for twenty minutes.

If Control had been tracking her phone, he was surely tracking the dead man's also. She was counting on it. Make Control think she was staying at this place, then wait for him to come find her. She might not know what he looked like, but from the café across the street she would definitely spot anyone asking questions at the front desk or hanging around for no good reason. The thought sent a sweet thrill through her body.

True, only idiots became emotionally involved in killing their targets. But Control's sending a has-been to take her out showed a lack of respect for her skills, an insult almost as infuriating as the act itself. He'd pay for that. Big time.

Although torture wasn't her thing, she wanted this bastard screaming in pain, begging her to just kill him, before she finally obliged.

Fired by the imagery, Jade propped a pillow against the headboard, settled back, and used the dead man's phone to text:

She killed me

\#

Geoff Fairchild stared at the message. Was Colin screwing around? If so, Geoff was in no mood for it.

For the past two days he had holed up in DSS's safe house in Paris, monitoring Jade's and Colin's movements, planning the op, directing the op. A cakewalk for an old hand like Colin. Take her down, wring the book's location out of her, then eliminate her, grab her phone and the book, and bring them both to him. How hard could that be? She was just a girl, for God's sake.

And it appeared to have gone perfectly. He'd watched their two signals converge. After a quarter of an hour, the signals moved on, together. Then Jade's went dead and Colin's continued to her hotel, where it stayed for another thirty minutes before inexplicably switching off.

Geoff had downed two bourbons while peering at the inactive computer screen and racking his brain about what Colin could be up to, where he was.

At last, the screen had shown him at a hotel near the Louvre. And now this?

Geoff stabbed the keyboard:

Explain yourself.

-

I died in an alley near her hotel

-

Stop fucking with me.

-

Never dream of it

Jade? It couldn't be.

Who is this?

-

Your worst nightmare asshole

Son of a bitch. It *was* Jade. Bile welled up from Geoff's stomach and stung his throat. He doused the burn with another slug of bourbon.

Somehow Jade had gotten hold of Colin's phone. Which could only mean she'd disabled him, if not actually killed him like she said. What had gone wrong? Before retiring and moving back to his native England, Colin had been one of Geoff's best foreign agents. Tested and proven. Zero failures. He'd been the perfect choice for permanently erasing all knowledge of how the book would come into Geoff's hands. No evidence, no trail.

Now this. Steadying himself, Geoff willed the text messages into better focus. Had he underestimated Jade? No. Her reputation was first-class, but Colin was almost as good as Dan. The guy must have screwed up. Or Jade got lucky.

Btw the book will now cost you an extra million dollars non negotiable

Bullshit. Geoff slammed his palm on the desktop. She didn't make the rules. He did. He owned her. He was her Control, the man *she* worked for.

Knock it off. We have a deal.
-

Had a deal til you sent that dickhead to kill me. Now we have a different deal.
One million in my account PLUS the second half of my fee.
Then I hand over the book.
Take it or leave it

Screw her. One million bucks was nothing compared to the book's value, but it was far more than he could afford before selling the book. He was drowning in debt. The book was his salvation. He had already set up an auction on the Dark Web and attracted five interested parties with the information Astrid Desmarais gave him at lunch that afternoon in D.C. Quick as a fox, he'd seen the book's potential. And the fulfillment of his dreams. Now this Jap whore threatened everything.

He'd take her out himself.

We need to meet.
-

Money first

No way. Geoff stood and worked the knots from his shoulders. The bitch was going down. He'd been a field agent. He had the skills.

Although he'd seen her only once, surreptitiously at the Washington zoo as she jogged past before his meeting with Dan, his eye for faces was unerring. He'd spot her again in a New York second.

As to weapons, the safe house had a small armory, including switchblade combat knives. He'd gut her like a deer and let her watch while he did it.

Too bad he couldn't take his time with her. He had to snatch the book from her room ASAP. Four of his potential buyers had demanded photos of it before they would bid a dime.

So set the trap.

I'll deposit the money when I see you.
Meet me at the Holocaust Memorial behind Notre Dame. 0800 hours.

-

No. I say where and when. Tell you tomorrow

Her green dot on his screen went dark.

Damn. By "tomorrow" did she mean today? It was now 2:10 in the morning. She could mean "after daybreak." Or possibly the day after Christmas. Probably she meant *this* morning. There was no reason to wait longer.

In any case, it didn't matter. He knew where she was. Not the room number, but the hotel. All he had to do was wait there, in the lobby or across the street. She'd never see it coming.

#

Still fully awake, Bernard Leroux punched his pillow and flopped back down. He'd been a horrible guest at his sister's tonight, mouthing praise for her coq au vin and feigning attention to her attempts at conversation, while totally preoccupied with his miraculous good fortune.

"What is wrong with you?" she'd asked.

To which he could only apologize and claim a problem in his research.

Now, with only a few hours left before daybreak, he gave up trying to sleep. He was too excited. The opportunity he'd been given was a godsend beyond measure.

He padded into his kitchen and set a kettle to boil. Who would have guessed that being strangled at your own desk could prove to be such a stroke of luck? He touched his neck, then sat at the wooden table and lit a cigarette. Thanks to inheriting strong genes from Celtic warriors, he had recovered quickly, in time to see the strangler leaving his office—with a book in her hand.

The kettle whistled. He scooped three measures of coffee into his press, poured in water, and set the plunger. To fortify himself for meeting today with Martine and her impatient Gypsy, he stubbed out the cigarette and lit a joint. Cannabis and coffee. They took him back to the glory days of flower power and "chicks for free."

With fond memories merging into a blur, he plunged the coffee, poured himself a large mugful, and sat again to relive the events in his office. Panic at first, gut-wrenching fear that the woman had stolen the only known copy of the Sixth Book. Struggling to his feet, lurching to his door, only to find the corridor empty. Anguish so debilitating he could still feel its remnants in the pit of his stomach. Then back to his desk, and Hallelujah! The Sixth Book still rested at the bottom of the drawer, beneath the texts he'd been using for reference. A quick inventory revealed the attacker had made off with a 5th Century volume of dissertations by Talmudic scholars.

And that realization was when inspiration struck. The Sixth Book of Moses, as fabled and sought after as the Grail itself, was now *his*.

All he had to do was play his cards right. He'd been attacked. The Sixth Book was missing. Martine and Jardani would be furious. But they could not dispute him. They weren't there.

The idea had been a stroke of genius, aptly befitting his long-ignored intellect and accomplishments. He swallowed a mouthful of coffee, then pinched out the last of his joint and lit another. After several months, during which Martine and Jardani would lick their wounds and go on with their lives, he would publish his discovery of the book, along with his translation and interpretation of its significance. Accolades would pour in. His status among biblical experts would soar.

It was only right that such an earth-shattering document be kept in the hands of one who could fully appreciate it. And that he, Monsieur le Docteur Bernard Leroux, should finally bask in the acclaim he deserved.

#

Christmas morning dawned with a hard freeze that coated the sidewalks in a thin layer of ice, treacherous even in boots. Dan and Martine opted for calling a taxi from Paulette's house. At the Louvre, Dan tipped their driver generously. It was Christmas, after all.

Leroux had anticipated finishing his translation by this afternoon. But Dan's impatience had irked Martine to the point that she finally agreed to come here earlier.

They picked their way past the two green lions into the covered passageway, where the pavement was ice-free. Once they were inside the building, Martine turned to him. "You like her like that, don't you."

Huh? Then it dawned on him. Suppressing a smile, he said, "Like who, and like what?"

"Don't play dumb with me. Paulette naked."

Their hostess had joined them for coffee this morning, clad the same way she'd been when he encountered her in the kitchen the morning before. "I like any woman naked. But she wasn't. She was wearing a camisole."

"Which hid nothing."

"I guess I didn't notice."

Martine rolled her eyes and headed down the stairs. At Leroux's door she knocked.

He opened it with a look of anguish, one hand covering half his face. "Something terrible has happened," he bleated. "Your book is gone."

"What!" Dan shoved past him into the office, scanned the man's desk, and whipped around. Outrage flared inside him. With barely controlled fury, he growled, "What the fuck happened?"

Leroux shrank visibly.

Martine rushed to the desk and started rummaging through all the books and papers. Then she pulled open the desk drawers. "It must be here someplace."

Leroux's bloodshot eyes peered pleadingly at Dan. "A woman stole it. Right after you left yesterday."

How was that possible? Dan grabbed the man's shoulders, marched him to his chair, and sat him down hard. Towering over him, he commanded, "Start at the beginning. Tell us everything. Every single detail."

The words came in short eruptions, Leroux wringing his hands, speaking to the floor. In essence, he'd been "strangled" from behind. When he came to, a woman he only saw from the back was leaving his office with the book in her hand. When Leroux searched for her, she was gone. He confirmed it was the Moses book by checking the desk drawer where he'd just locked it up. The key, he speculated, must have dropped from his hand when he passed out. To Dan's question about the woman's appearance, he answered that she had straight black hair. That was all he saw.

"The sniper," Martine breathed.

Leroux's head jerked up. "Sniper?"

"You're lucky to be alive." She leaned over and wrapped a consoling arm around the man's shoulder.

Luck had nothing to do with it. The sniper was a pro. She would only kill when necessary. She'd demonstrated that in Usti when she merely wounded those two goons.

Martine straightened from comforting Leroux. "Dan, we have to find her. She tried to contact me here just yesterday, for that supposed interview. Maybe if I make myself more accessible, she'll try again."

"I doubt it. We now know for sure that what she wanted was the book. Yesterday you were her best chance of getting it. Today—"

"Then what's a better idea?"

"I don't have one, dammit." He checked himself. "Sorry. I'm just frustrated. And angry." Taking deep breaths, he paced to the door and back. "Let's start with what we do know. The main thing is, she's working on contract. I'm sure of it. She stole the book for whoever hired her. Why her client wants it is unclear. We ran through a bunch of possibilities yesterday in your office."

"Jews, Muslims, Christians. My guess would be Muslim. But … Oh, no. The Middle East. Do you think she's left the country?"

"I doubt it." On that question he was relatively certain. "I'd bet anything she and her client are here in Paris."

Leroux's face paled. "She's still here? How can you know that?"

"She's been following us since Prague," Dan told him. "She had several opportunities along the way to incapacitate us and take the book. But she waited until now. To me, that says the handover will take place here."

"That narrows things," Martine allowed. "But 'here' is still a city of two million people."

Chapter 19

You fool. You old fool. From a bookshelf at head height, Leroux dug out the bottle of Armagnac he kept behind a three-volume set of treatises on the Ionian Enlightenment. Despite the early hour, he needed a drink. And another joint. Filling his coffee mug halfway with the liquor, he inhaled the rich fragrances of prunes and walnuts, then lit up and sank into his chair. He'd almost lost control of his bowel when Martine said, "sniper," and Jardani confirmed it.

Thank God, they had finally left.

What was he going to do? The sniper woman must have been after the Sixth Book. Martine and Jardani certainly thought so. Her arrival coincided with theirs. Nothing else in his office, out of all these hundreds of volumes, was a fraction as valuable. That had to be what she wanted.

If she found out—no, *when* she found out—that she had taken the wrong book, she would be back. He hoisted himself from the chair and locked his door. It was three inches thick and solid oak, built in the days when royalty lived in the Louvre and his office was one of a hundred-odd storerooms in the palace basements.

In his chair again, he took a drag from his joint and a large sip of Armagnac. Then a terrifying insight bit into his stomach like the fangs of a demon. His office might serve as a safe haven, but it could equally be a prison cell. Like medieval castles that were too strong to be breached but where those behind the walls could be starved sinto surrender.

He wiped perspiration from his face. If the sniper woman came back today, he would call Security. They were always on duty, even when the museum was closed, as it was on this miserable Christmas morning. But he couldn't stay here forever.

Where could he go? Not his apartment. The museum knew where he lived, and if the sniper could gain access to this restricted area, she could probably hack into the employee database. Or simply find his home number online and track it to his address.

He sucked down the last of his joint, chasing it with another gulp of Armagnac. It was so eerily quiet in here. Normally, he relished the silence. But now it seemed ominous, as though the sniper were listening outside his door.

And he had to urinate. The curse of an old man's bladder. Last night in his sister's apartment, he'd had to excuse himself three— Wait. His sister's apartment. The museum didn't have her address. She was a widow who'd taken her husband's name, totally different from the surname they were born with. No one would find him there. Brilliant.

If she would have him.

He picked up his phone but stopped punching buttons halfway through her number. If he called her from here, it might leave a record.

The discomfort in his bladder grew more intense. To take his mind off it, he stood and paced. *Whore of Babylon, thy name is Old Age.*

Forget calling. Élise would take him in. She might even be happy to have a man around the house after six years alone. Or was it five? Never mind. With luck, she'd still be in a good mood from the Margaux he'd brought her last night and his effusive compliments on her mediocre coq au vin. She would welcome his offer to stay with her a while. Her deceased husband's office would make a good bedroom for him. Certainly, the old train engineer had no further use for it.

That was the solution.

He unlocked his door. Bless all the gods, the corridor was vacant. With a nearly bursting bladder, he dashed to the lavatory.

#

Jade could hardly believe her luck. She'd been lurking out here barely twenty minutes in a frigid breeze when Lovel and his girlfriend exited the museum through the same door they'd used yesterday. Both of them looked despondent, no doubt at the news that their precious book was missing. Neither noticed her peering with one eye around the corner where the passageway entered the museum's courtyard. *Advantage: me.*

Apparently deciding not to risk the icy sidewalks, they made their way to the curb and looked right, the direction from which traffic would come on the one-way street. If there *were* any traffic. From Jade's narrow vantage point, cars came by at about one every thirty seconds.

Finally, Lovel raised his arm. A cab pulled up in front of them. They climbed in, and it left.

Jade hustled to the curb. Two cars approached in the distance, one with a taxi sign on top. She hailed it, hopped in the back, and pointed at Lovel's cab, which was turning onto a bridge. "Follow that taxi."

The driver said something in French.

"There!" She pointed again. "Taxi. Go fast."

He hit the gas. Soon, they were only fifty feet behind Lovel.

"Slow now," she said.

Her driver flipped his palm up. "Fast? Slow?"

"Slow." Was the guy stupid? "Fifty meters."

He frowned at her in the mirror.

In ten more seconds, she'd rip his ass out of the seat and drive herself. Pointing, she hissed, "Him, us. Fifty meters."

Her driver muttered something and dropped back.

They climbed a long hill, Lovel now a hundred and fifty feet in front of them. At the top, their road narrowed and became one-way. Closed shops lined both sides. In the middle of a block, Lovel's car halted.

"Slow," she told the driver and slumped low in her seat, out of sight. After a few tense seconds, she peeked out the rear window. The girl was pushing open a wooden door even larger than the one at the museum. "Stop here!"

#

The door to the sidewalk clacked shut, leaving Dan and Martine in the short dark walkway that led onto the building's cobblestone courtyard. Halfway through the passage, on their left, lay an even darker alcove lined along one side with large trash bins. The sight of them fit perfectly with Dan's foul mood. Cold garbage.

All their efforts—from escaping those crazed monks in Prague, to surviving the gunfire and Molotov cocktails in Usti, to freezing their asses off in Germany—all of it to bring five stolen books to Paris just so that Asian woman could grab the most important one. He clamped his jaw so tight his teeth hurt. They should never have left it with Leroux.

"Are you coming?" Martine stood a few paces into the courtyard, her miserable expression made even grimmer by the gray light of the bleakest Christmas on record.

He caught up with her, and they were walking together toward Paulette's house at the far end when a mental alert interrupted his frustration. He stopped and looked back at the door to the sidewalk. "That taxi that went by when we were getting out of ours. Its roof light wasn't illuminated."

"That means it's engaged."

"But there was no passenger in it. At least, I didn't see anyone."

She shrugged. "Maybe it was going to pick up somebody who booked by phone."

Maybe, but his sixth sense told him to check it out. "Go on. I'll be there in a minute."

"Suit yourself."

He returned to the sidewalk door and cracked it open a hair. *Son of a bitch!*

An Asian woman was jogging across to this side of the street.

Adrenaline tightened every muscle in his body. It had to be the sniper. Easing the door closed, he flash-assessed the situation. Without doubt, she had seen where he and Martine entered. She couldn't get past the combination code, unless a resident happened to arrive while she was waiting. So they were safe for now. But equally, he couldn't let slip this opportunity to grab her. Almost certainly she was armed. He was not. He did, however, have the advantage of surprise. Was that enough?

He inched open the door again.

She was scrutinizing the combination pad. And evidently heard him. She turned toward the sound.

Dan pulled the door open and charged. Her eyes popped. Her hands went out defensively. Grasping one of her arms, he took a step past her, planted his foot, and twisted her sideways and back over his leg. As she hit the ground, he followed on top of her, crushing one knee into her sternum and seizing her neck with both hands. "Why are you following us?"

She winced with pain, but an instant later slipped her hips out to the side, tucked her free leg, and kicked him in the face.

Dan almost blacked out. In the second it took him to regain his faculties, she was on him, straddling his stomach, one hand on his throat, the other cocked back to strike.

He gripped the choking arm in both hands, yanked it down to his chest, and simultaneously arched his back and rolled over the captured arm, coming up on top of her, belly-to-belly. But he wanted her face-down.

Before she could react, he pushed one of her knees to the pavement, shoveled his free hand under the opposite thigh, and rolled her again, flattening her on her stomach. Straddling her back now, he cinched a forearm across her chin.

"Move one muscle, and I'll break your jaw." To prove it, he rotated his forearm slightly.

A grunt of pain escaped her throat.

Dan kept up the pressure. The whole fight had taken only seconds, but his chest heaved from the exertion. "Why have you been following us?" he repeated.

"To keep you safe."

"Bullshit." He gave her chin another slight twist.

She cried out. Her body twitched beneath him. When he released the pressure, she panted, "You and your girlfriend would have been killed in that Gypsy ghetto if it wasn't for me."

If she thought that, she didn't know him very well. "Say I believe you, which I don't. Why do you care what happens to us?"

"Let go of me."

Soon he would have to. Or get her out of sight. They'd been out here on the sidewalk almost a minute already. A car or pedestrian could materialize any time. Quickly he searched her left jacket pocket and came up with a silencer and a switchblade. Holding both in his left hand, he pushed the button that flicked open the knife, then pressed its point to the corner of her eye. "We're going inside. Try something stupid, and I'll blind you."

He rose from her back, grabbed her collar, and hoisted her to her feet. As he did, a car breezed past. The moment it was gone, he jammed her cheek against the door and extracted a Glock .40 caliber from her right jacket pocket. With her face turned to the right so she couldn't see the combination code, he punched the buttons.

Inside, he pressed the knifepoint under her chin, collar-walked her to the room with the trash bins, and shoved her toward the back wall. "Sit! On the ground. Legs straight out in front of you. Hands on top of your head."

"Afraid of me?" she asked in a taunting tone.

Not afraid, but definitely wary. She'd almost got the best of him out there.

When she'd lowered herself to the ground, he screwed the silencer into the pistol and pocketed the switchblade. Aiming the pistol at her chest, he said, "I'll ask you for the last time. Why follow us to Paris?"

"I thought you were supposed to be smart."

Any other captive would be cringing. "Enlighten me."

She gave him a reptilian smile. "To make sure you and your book got here safely."

"What book?" he demanded, to see if she knew what she had.

"Lovel." She shook her head slowly, as though he were the dumb kid in class. "Are you really that clueless?"

She knew his name? "Why do you want it?"

"My arms are getting tired like this."

"And I'm getting tired of your cat-and-mouse bullshit."

After a visible exhalation, she said, "I'm no threat to you."

"Oh?" Dan rubbed his jaw, which still ached from the kick she'd delivered.

"Hey, you're the one who attacked *me*."

He pointed the pistol at her face. "Answer my questions. Now."

#

Jade doubted Lovel would injure her. But he looked furious, as if any moment he could snap. Time to stop goading him in hopes of a slip. "I don't want the damned book. My client does."

His unchanged expression suggested he'd already guessed that.

"My butt's freezing," she said. "Can I get up?"

"Who's your client?"

We reach the bottom line. "I don't know. But I think you do."

Lovel's brow furrowed. For a pro, he was pretty easy to read. Maybe she'd overestimated him. Or maybe he wanted her to think that.

In either case, he asked the expected question. "How should *I* know?"

"Because he obviously knows *you*." She told him about the dossier and how Control had double-crossed her and tried to have her killed. "I want that son of a bitch. Just read the file, tell me who wrote it, and the book is yours. Plus, I'm out of your life forever."

Lovel stared at her with a mixture of surprise and suspicion.

Jade grinned inside. The tables had turned. Now she had *him*. "Do we have a deal?"

#

Dan's peripheral vision caught Martine striding across the courtyard. To the sniper, he said, "Stay where you are and don't utter a sound. I see you move, there's a bullet in your knee."

From the darkness at the back of the trash room, she gave him a look that as much as said, "I don't think so."

He popped a silenced round through a wrinkle in the denim of her jeans, half an inch from her knee.

She jerked. "Bastard!"

"Shut up." He jammed the pistol into the back of his waistband, turned toward Martine, and intercepted her about ten steps from the trash room.

"What are you doing out here?" she asked.

"Thinking about the book and how we might track down the woman who took it."

"I hope you're making better progress than I am."

"I'm working on it." *Please get out of here.*

"Well, come inside. Paulette just opened a bottle of champagne."

"I'll be there in a minute."

"That's what you always say. And a minute turns into half an hour."

"One minute. I promise."

With a glance skyward, she headed back across the courtyard.

When Martine had passed through the wrought iron gate to Paulette's house, he pulled out the pistol again and rushed back to the trash room.

The sniper was standing now, rubbing the outside of her knee. "You cocksucker."

Maybe he had shot a tad closer than half an inch. Still, nothing debilitating. "Put a Band-Aid on it."

"Go fuck yourself. This didn't have to happen."

"How do I know you have the book?"

She squared her shoulders. "You'll see when I bring it to you."

That assumed he would let her go. But he had little other choice. To recover the book, he'd do almost anything. And the sooner, the better. He did, however, want time to prepare in his mind for all the possible ways another meeting with her could go down. "Tonight, seven o'clock."

She stepped toward him. "I'm gonna trust you on this. The book for Control's name."

"Deal." Maybe the best deal he'd ever made. If it worked.

Moving closer, she held out her hand. "Give me back my gun."

"No chance."

"Never mind." Her lips drew back into another irksome smile. "I have more."

"Leave them at home. I'm gonna search you."

"What a guy."

Her arrogance had returned, the slight grazing from his bullet evidently no longer bothering her. As she walked past him toward the exterior door, he said, "What's your name? If we're going to get social, I should know."

"We're not getting social."

But the more he knew about her, the better. "Say I want to hire you, sometime."

She turned to face him. "I doubt a hotshot like you would ever stoop to that."

"What do you know about me? Or think you know?"

"You'll see when we make the exchange."

Man, it would be easy to hate this woman, but her unnerving confidence and demonstrated skill forced him to respect her. "There are times when I could use a partner. But not one whose name I don't know."

She tilted her head to one side, possibly considering. "Call me Jade."

"Jade. And how do I contact you?"

"If you're as good as you think you are, you'll figure it out."

Chapter 20

When Dan walked in, Paulette rose from her chair and held out a flute of champagne. "I think you need this. Martine told me about your book. I am sorry."

"Thank you." After a grateful swallow, he dropped the news. "I might be able to get it back."

Martine's glass stopped halfway to her lips. "How?"

Leaving out the fight on the sidewalk and his grazing Jade's knee with a bullet, he told them he'd found her outside, she'd offered to trade the book for information she thought he had, and they'd agreed to meet at seven tonight to make the exchange.

"That's fantastic." Martine leapt to her feet. Then a worried expression darkened her face. "Do you trust her?"

"No." He took a seat on the couch. "At least not completely. There's a very real chance that things could go wrong."

"Like she sets an ambush for you?" Martine asked.

"Possibly, but I'll be prepared for that. It's more likely that she doesn't bring the book. Or doesn't like the information I give her."

Martine glanced down, evidently processing these possibilities. Then her eyes fixed on his. "She could bring a different book. Thinking she can fool us."

That was something he hadn't considered. Despite having seen the original, he might not be able to tell it from a similarly old book. Jade could pull a switch. She gets her information *and* keeps the book. He wouldn't put it past her.

"We must examine it first," Martine insisted.

"She is right." Paulette sat up straighter and raised an index finger, as though to drive home a lesson. "It is like art. A qualified appraiser must inspect it."

Dan bit the inside of his cheek. It would have to be Martine. Only she and Leroux were qualified to determine the book's authenticity, and he wasn't about to drag Leroux any further into this. Much as he hated to expose Martine to potential violence, she could keep a cool head in a difficult situation. If push came to shove, he hoped that would be enough. "Martine, are you willing to come with me?"

"I intend to."

Her presence would add a degree of risk he needed to minimize. "But you wait inside the door to the sidewalk until I've frisked her. No. On second thought, I'll bring her inside to you. In case she plans an ambush or tries to pull some other trick."

"This woman," Paulette asked, "is so … *sournois?*"

"Devious," Martine translated.

Dan nodded. "And dangerous."

With a gesture toward the top of the stairs, Paulette said, "I have a small pistol. You can take it."

A blind woman with a pistol? Well, her hearing was good enough that she could probably fire it accurately, more or less. Certainly close enough to scare off an intruder.

"My husband left it here," she added.

"Thanks, but I don't need it." Might as well tell them now, so Martine wouldn't be surprised if he had to use one of Jade's weapons. "I have a gun I took from her. And a knife."

"You *what?*" Martine gaped at him.

"We had a small confrontation."

With a withering glare that clearly accused him of not being completely open with her, Martine demanded, "What is this information she wants from you?"

"She—the name she's using is Jade—was hired by someone anonymous. She wants to know who he is. She has some documents he sent her and thinks that, if I read the documents, I'll be able to tell her who sent them."

"After following us for days and choking Leroux to steal the book, she's willing to trade it for a name?"

"That's what she says."

"It doesn't make sense."

"It does to her." And knowing Jade's motive, he believed her. He'd seen it in her eyes, heard it in her tone of voice. Raw hatred for the man who'd betrayed her and a fierce determination to exact revenge. It was never a good idea to let feelings drive your mission. But truth be told, in her place he would probably do the same.

"What if you can't give her a name?"

"Then things could get ugly."

#

This wasn't going quite as Leroux had hoped. Grasping his sister's hands, he said, "Please. It will only take about a week for the painters to finish my apartment."

"You have lived there for … twenty-five years? And *now* you decide to paint?" She shook her head, strands of gray hair dangling from the bun on top. "Why didn't you say something last night?"

"I forgot. We were having such a nice time. Your coq au vin was delicious. I couldn't eat enough."

Her eyes lit up. "It was good, wasn't it?"

"So, you'll let me stay for a while?"

She waddled over to the big armchair that faced her television and lowered herself into the well-worn cushions. "I have only one bathroom."

"Our whole family shared one bathroom when we were growing up."

"The couch is too short for you to sleep on."

"I could sleep on the floor in Dominic's old office."

She bestowed on him the same frown she had perfected as a child when making him grovel for a chocolate.

"I will clean the dishes," he offered. "And I'll bring more of that Margaux you liked."

After a long pause, clearly intended to impart the enormity of her sacrifice, she said, "You may not smoke cannabis in my house. I will not allow it."

"I promise." *To open the office window when I do.*

She laid down a few more rules, including no snoring, as if he could help that. When he'd agreed to everything, she flicked her hand toward the door of her dead husband's office.

More relieved than she could ever imagine, he pecked her on the cheek. Safe at last.

In Dominic's precious sanctuary, with its photos of trains on the walls and its stupid toy engines on the desk, Bernard unpacked his shoulder bag. He stacked two changes of shirts, underwear, and socks on a wooden chair in the corner. Now for a place to hide the book.

In the DSS safe house, Geoff bounced on the balls of his feet, barely able to contain his excitement. There it was on his screen, a promise by someone named Adar to beat any other bid by one million dollars. The only proviso was that Adar wanted to personally inspect the book first. He would be in Paris tomorrow.

For a moment, Geoff considered rejecting the offer and demanding a higher price. But that could scuttle the deal. Thinking better a bird in the hand, he typed, "Where would you like to meet?"

"Le Meurice."

One of the finest hotels in Paris. The kind of place he would soon be able to afford. Geoff was about to ask what time when it struck him that there could be a hitch with Jade. Plus, he had to make sure this "Adar" understood exactly who was in charge. Pumped with confidence, he typed, "Lobby. Ten PM."

"No. Ten AM. I have other business later."

Damn. That severely shortened the timeframe. But for a million-buck bonus, he'd make it work. "How will I recognize you?"

"I will be in a corner with coffee and two cups."

One man, two cups. Good enough. Geoff signed off and poured himself a congratulatory shot of bourbon. In seventeen hours, he'd hook Adar like a bass. One million over anyone else's bid. He knocked back the shot.

The only snag was that, to meet Adar in the morning, he had to get the book tonight. But that shouldn't be a problem. He was planning to stake out her hotel, anyway. *So do it now.*

After arming himself with a combat switchblade and an Uzi, he went down to the basement garage where the Service's black Mercedes "taxi" stood in one of the parking slots like a warhorse awaiting its rider. Its big engine kicked over on his first push of the Start button.

Fifteen minutes later, as darkness fell on the almost-empty streets, he parked three doors down from Jade's hotel. Soon she'd come in from wherever she might be, or maybe go out for dinner. If neither, he could use his DSS badge to extract her room number from the person at the check-in counter. The French, plagued with recent terrorist attacks, always caved to a shiny gold badge.

Half an hour passed with no activity, except an old woman walking her dog. The dog squatted and crapped. The woman left its deposit where it lay.

The hands on Geoff's Rolex crept past 6:35. He yawned. This was exhausting. How did anyone on a nighttime stakeout manage to stay awake? In TV programs, cops usually did it in pairs, eating junk food, nursing coffee in take-out cups, chatting about their personal lives. In reality—

Hang on. What was this?

#

Dan declined another glass of champagne. When Martine followed suit and excused herself to use the bathroom, Paulette said as a statement, "You do these dangerous things because you love her."

Oh, boy, the matchmaker in action again. "No. I like her a lot, but I don't love her."

"Then why do you take such risks? What is the benefit for you?"

"If we can avert a war in the Middle East, it benefits everyone."

"What benefits everyone?" Martine asked as she returned to the living room.

"Preventing a second Holocaust. I lost grandparents in the first one, and I'll do damn-near anything to prevent a second."

Paulette looked shocked.

"Six million Jews live in Israel today," Dan said. "Does that number ring a bell? And the Germans killed two hundred thousand Gypsies."

"One of his parents is Jewish," Martine explained to Paulette. "The other is Gypsy."

"*Mon Dieu.* I am so sorry." She started to stand.

"Don't get up." He didn't need sympathetic arms wrapped around him. He needed that book. And in the ten minutes between now and his meeting with Jade, he needed to calm down.

As a precaution, he told Paulette to turn off all her lights. It would make no difference to her but would keep her out of sight in the event things got out of hand. "Martine, it's time."

As the two of them crossed the courtyard, she said, "Don't worry about me. I can take care of myself."

Against Jade, he wasn't so sure. But if he played his cards right, he'd never have to find out. He gave her his Maglite. "I'll stand between you and her. If the book's genuine, say so, and I'll look at her file. If not, hand it to me, and I'll give it back to her."

They reached the sidewalk door with a few minutes to spare. Inching it open, he peered outside. No Jade. *She'll be here.* Probably approaching from the other side of the street, as she'd done before. Habits die hard.

He pictured her jogging across the road. "Wait a second."

"What?" Martine whispered in a tone of alarm.

Jade jogged with a slight inward turn of her left foot, a pigeon-toe. Where had he seen the exact same thing? Recently. "Oh, no." *The zoo.*

"Dammit, Dan. Don't pull this on me again, with you expecting me to stay silent while you disappear into your own thoughts."

"I think I've seen her before. Back in Washington."

"How could that be?"

"Very good question." He'd been heading for that meeting with Geoff Fairchild when a slightly pigeon-toed Asian woman jogged past. She'd looked at him and kept going. He recalled thinking it was just a glance but enough to fix his face in her memory.

"Dan?"

Jade at the zoo changed everything. No one knew he would be there, except Geoff. And the jogger had come by before his meeting with Geoff in the Great Ape House even started. *Jesus God in Heaven. Was Geoff her Control?*

Martine slugged him in the shoulder. "I'm tired of your crap. Level with me."

"I don't even want to level with myself." Dan felt like he was drowning, like he couldn't get enough air. He and Geoff were friends. For nine years, Geoff had been his colleague then his boss. They'd remained friends after Dan left the DSS. He was the only person who knew where Dan lived. He was the one who'd been there for him when Heidi, his beloved Great Dane, had to be put down. Hell, he was probably the best friend Dan had. "Maybe I'm wrong."

"About seeing her before?"

"Yeah." He sucked in a breath. How could Geoff hire someone to trail him? There'd been nothing to trail, even after their meeting. Geoff had presented him with air tickets to the Caymans but could have no idea whether Dan would go. No, the wily bastard knew how much he respected Astrid. He *knew* Dan would go. But Geoff couldn't possibly know the assignment. Unless he and Astrid were somehow in this together. No way. "This is fucked up," he muttered. "Seriously fucked up."

Martine jabbed him with his Maglite. "Tell me now, or you can take this and do the exchange by yourself."

Dan struggled to separate conjecture from evidence. But evidence included the file, the "dossier" Jade had called it, that allegedly contained a lot more information about him than she needed. Dan had gone to great lengths to erase any publicly available information about himself. His work came through word of mouth. But the Diplomatic Security Service kept untouchable records of everything he'd ever done in their employment. And Geoff Fairchild knew even more. The personal stuff.

"I'm not wrong." With deeper sorrow than he had felt since losing Heidi, Dan gave in to evidence. "Jade's client. I'm ninety-five percent sure I know who he is."

"Who?"

"The guy I used to work for." Dan swallowed against a lump in his throat. "A guy I thought was my friend."

"Why would a friend of yours send someone to steal the book? Why not just ask you for it?"

"I don't know. But I intend to find out."

Chapter 21

Dan's watch showed 6:59. "It's time," he told Martine. "I'll bring her in as soon as it's safe."

He stepped out onto the sidewalk, leaving the heavy door not quite closed. No traffic, no pedestrians, barely any sounds other than the indistinct hum of a city in near-hibernation. The brightest lights came through windows of a coin-op laundromat one door up the road. He strode ten paces, saw nobody waiting inside for a washing machine or dryer to finish its cycle, and walked back to stand in front of the door. The situation was about as good as he could want for a covert meeting on a city street.

A cab pulled up across the way.

With one hand gripping the silenced pistol behind his back, he watched Jade get out on the opposite sidewalk and survey the terrain in both directions, using the cab as a shield between herself and him. In terms of caution, she and he were equally matched. He liked that. Pro-to-pro was infinitely better than pro versus unpredictable amateur.

Apparently satisfied, she reached back into the cab, then shut its rear door. The cab drove to the next street corner and parked.

Good tactic, having it wait for her.

After glancing again in both directions, she crossed the street, her right hand in her jacket pocket and her left holding a book. But instead of heading straight to Dan, she stopped in the darkness just his side of the laundromat windows.

He put his free hand on the door. "Come with me."

"No. We'll do it here. And you're not going to frisk me."

An exchange on the sidewalk? Sensing a possible ambush, Dan brought the pistol to the side of his leg and quickly restudied every doorway and intersection as far as he could see.

"I'm not pulling a fast one," she said. "But I'm also not going to do this on your turf. It's out here or nowhere."

He was tempted to tell her she needed him more than he needed her. But the opposite was true. On the plus side, the laundromat offered better light for examining the book than his Maglite would. "Take off your jacket. Lay it on the sidewalk and turn around."

She grinned. "Still don't trust me?"

"Do you trust *me*?"

"Lovel, you're one for the textbooks."

"The longer we wait," he said, shoving the pistol into his hip pocket, "the greater chance someone will come by."

Her expression sobered. "If I do it, you do it."

"You first."

Keeping her eyes on him, she shrugged out of her jacket, laid it on the ground, and set the book on top. Then she quickly turned full-circle. "Now you."

Dan relaxed a little. Having seen no weapon tucked into her waistband or hip pocket, he felt fairly comfortable shedding his own jacket.

"Turn around," she told him.

He did. "Happy now?"

As she bent to retrieve the book, she said, "The dossier is in my jacket."

"I don't need it."

Abruptly she straightened. "Don't be a shithead. No name, no book."

"I've figured out who your Control is."

She eyed him suspiciously. "How?"

"From things you already said."

"Tell me," she demanded, her fists clenched.

"After we've examined the book."

"We?"

"I brought someone who can verify whether the book you brought is the one we want."

"That old fart from the museum?"

"Someone else."

Jade's face brightened with understanding. "Your girlfriend. Well, bring her on."

"Back away five steps from your jacket." She'd said she had other weapons, and one or more could be in her jacket.

"Christ, Lovel. You really are afraid of me."

"Back up."

With a smirk, she complied.

Dan inched open the big door and stepped inside. "Okay," he said to Martine. "We're set. All you have to do is—"

Automatic gunfire rattled outside. It sounded like an Uzi.

Instantly he shoved Martine back and slammed the door behind them. *What the hell?* He yanked the pistol from his hip pocket. Listening at the door, he heard nothing. He opened it a crack and crouched to peer out.

Jade was down. A lean, dark figure snatched up the book and jumped into the driver's seat of a black Mercedes taxi. Dan thrust his pistol through the opening. But another burst of automatic fire sent a *thunk-thunk-thunk* of bullets into the door above his head. He flattened himself on the ground.

Tires screeched. Dan looked to see to see the taxi speed away, heading the wrong way on the one-way street.

He sprang to his feet and dashed out to Jade. Blood spread from a hole in her shirt, just below her left collarbone. And from another in her side. But she still had a pulse. He repocketed the pistol and pressed hard on both wounds to staunch the flow. The cab she had come in was his surest bet of getting her to a hospital fast. But it was gone.

"Martine! Call nine-one-one."

#

Only later at the hospital did Dan learn that the French emergency number was 211. In any case, Martine had called it.

She stood with him now, staring in through the window of a recovery room. Jade lay inside, wires from a heart monitor taped to her chest, an IV drip in the back of her hand. She'd spent almost three hours in surgery.

With a glance at her watch, Martine said, "There's nothing we can do here."

"I know."

"Then why are we staying? It's eleven o'clock."

"I just feel ..." What? A weird camaraderie with Jade, the fellow freelancer? Yeah, a little. But what he couldn't suppress was the horrific truth that, had he drawn Martine out to the sidewalk thirty seconds earlier, it could be her in that hospital bed—if not a morgue.

She touched his arm. "You're worried about her. I get that. What I don't get is why. For days you thought she was trying to kill us."

"I was wrong." During the hours he and Martine had waited on hard plastic chairs, sipping god-awful machine coffee, he'd explained Jade's mission as best he understood it. "Her job was to protect the book until it reached Paris, then snatch it. The only person she wants to kill is the man who hired her."

"Sorry to sound harsh, but that's *her* problem. Ours is recovering the book."

As if he weren't aware of that. You didn't spend hours in a hospital merely waiting for news about someone whose condition you could not possibly influence, or shuddering at how you'd feel if that person were Martine. You analyzed the events that had brought you here. Drew your best conclusions. Figured out what to do next. "We find Geoff, we find the book."

"Who's Geoff?"

"The guy I told you about, my former boss in the Diplomatic Security Service. Jade felt certain her Control hired the man who tried to kill her yesterday. And I'm almost positive her Control is Geoff Fairchild. Those pages you retrieved from her jacket will tell me for sure."

"I should have brought them with us."

"Never mind. We were occupied with Jade. I'll read them when we get back. But even without them, I'm willing to bet almost anything that Geoff is the bastard behind the shooting tonight. He might even be the one who pulled the trigger. I'm equally sure he now has the book."

"What if you're wrong?"

At the moment, he had only one answer. "Then we're screwed."

#

Delighted with a good night's work, Geoff kicked back, his feet on the coffee table, a tumbler of bourbon and ice sweating condensation in his hand. *You still have what it takes.* Anyone who imagined deskwork might have dulled his edge was dead wrong.

He knocked back a mouthful. *Daring, man. Straight out of a Bruce Willis movie.* Jade, for all her vaunted talent, obviously didn't expect a car to come from the wrong direction on a one-way street, never noticed him coast up behind her until it was too late. Then she'd been dumb enough to whip around and present him a frontal target. Three-shot burst, and she'd dropped like a sack of shit.

Then five seconds, eight seconds tops, to jump out, grab the book, and roar off. Willis himself couldn't have done it better.

The only glitch had been that slightly open door. Someone had been crouching behind it, he was sure. Someone who'd left his or her jacket on the sidewalk near Jade's. A weird thing to do, especially on a cold night. But it didn't matter. His second burst of fire had relieved that person of any inclination to interfere.

Bottom line: Mission accomplished, no collateral damage. The perfect op.

And all it took was the sharpness to capitalize on an opportunity. Most of the kindergartners coming into the Service would have sat there wetting their pants with indecision, uncertain whether their stakeout had paid off, torn between what they thought they knew and indications to the contrary. Not him. When a cab pulled up to a hotel several doors down from Jade's, he'd gone on full alert. When a woman whose face he couldn't see clearly came out with what looked like a book, it had instantly brought to mind the classic two-hotel ploy. Make contact from one, stay in the other.

Jade, honey, you were so naive. You never should have screwed with an old dog who knows all the tricks.

Geoff knocked back another congratulatory mouthful of bourbon. It burned going down. Burned in a good way.

His only regret was not having time to prolong that bitch's death. But when an unexpected opportunity fell in your lap, you damn-well took advantage of it. That was the difference experience made. It gave you the confidence to change course in midstream.

Thanks to his quick thinking and flexibility, he now had the book that guaranteed him a gold-plated future. It lay there next to his feet on the coffee table. Old Testament stuff about Moses and the Jews and Israel. Stuff that could be "catastrophic," Astrid Desmarais had said.   Catastrophe in the Middle East was fine with him. The whole region was a pain in everyone's ass. Let it go up in flames. Besides, for the cool-headed, catastrophe presented opportunities to capitalize on other people's fears and needs. Exactly what *he* was doing with the person who called himself Adar. Geoff nudged the book with his heel. All yours, Adar, for a million over the highest bid.

Geoff's heartbeat quickened at the thought, a bit of residual adrenaline he welcomed. No more Washington, with its stupid rules and meetings and idiotic forms for everything from gassing up a car to blowing your nose. No more fudging expense accounts. No more Nag-Hag. She could have the house *and* its mortgage. Next stop, Ibiza, queen of Spain's three Mediterranean islands. White sand, nude beaches, a paradise where no one pestered rich foreigners with unwanted questions.

Which reminded him of the one question he still couldn't answer—that person behind the door. Obviously, it was someone Jade had met. A friend? Or sexual liaison? Maybe. Or possibly …

Geoff rose unsteadily from the armchair. He felt a bit too foggy to analyze it now. But not too foggy to know that he had to tie up loose ends. Whoever had been hiding behind that door was a witness.

Witnesses had to die.

#

It was just after midnight when Dan and Martine approached Paulette's house. More lights than usual glowed in the apartment windows surrounding the central courtyard, especially those at the front where residents presumably had heard the gunshots. No doubt the police had knocked on doors to find out what, if anything, people had seen, and tenants were still agitated about the whole bizarre affair. *Merry Christmas.*

The cops were gone now. From the sidewalk in front, you'd never know they had been here, with their flashing lights and squawking radios and crime-scene tape. The only remaining signs of a brazen shooting were three splintered holes in the entrance door where forensic people had dug out the bullets that narrowly missed Dan's head. Plus a ragged dimple he'd noticed, as the police surely had, in the stone wall just this side of the laundromat windows—a pit left by the one round that hadn't struck Jade in the initial three-shot burst.

"She's asleep," Martine whispered.

Dan looked through the front windows and saw Paulette slumbering in the black leather chair. A single light burned in her living room, probably left on for their benefit. "I doubt we'll get past her," he said. "Her hearing's too good."

Sure enough, the moment Martine opened the door, Paulette sat upright.

"It's us," Martine announced.

Paulette, in a thick terrycloth bathrobe but without her dark glasses, rubbed her face then touched her watch. "So late." She adjusted her position in the chair. "The woman. Is ... *est-elle bien?*"

"She's badly injured," Martine said, slumping down on the couch. "But still alive."

"C'est un soulagement."

"Yes, a relief." Martine yawned. "Sorry, but I'm exhausted."

"Go to bed," Paulette said. "I shall go also. We are all *fatigué.*"

As Martine pushed herself up from the couch, Dan touched her shoulder. "Before you go, I want to thank you."

"For what?"

"For taking charge out there when I couldn't. Hiding my gun and knife, emptying Jade's pockets, handling the cops when they descended like locusts in riot gear." Not to mention helping him beforehand to put his jacket back on while he kept pressure on Jade's wounds and folding Jade's jacket under her head. "Thanks to you, we looked like good Samaritans."

She smiled at him. "Didn't think I could do it?"

"I'm very glad you did."

"Well, sleep on that thought."

"Soon. But first there're some other things I need to think about." Things that required solitude to unravel.

As the women climbed the stairs, Dan picked up the thin sheaf of stapled pages lying on the coffee table—the so-called dossier. He read it all, grinding his teeth as his anger rose with each sentence. Jade and he were both right. There was far more information about him than she could possibly need, and far more than anyone other than Geoff could possibly know. "You son of a bitch."

He took the pages outside and used his lighter to set them on fire. As they burned, he carried them to the hedge at the front of Paulette's deck, where he let the ashes fall harmlessly into the soil.

Dan now felt positive that Geoff himself had gunned down Jade, just as he'd done that unarmed woman in Madrid seven years ago. Also with an Uzi, Geoff's favorite weapon. Officially, the woman pulled a pistol, but Dan had been Geoff's backup and knew the pistol part was bull. Geoff had panicked.

Lying for him had tortured Dan's conscience and strained their friendship. But this act tonight kicked him in the balls.

Why did Geoff want that book? How did he even know about it? Would the bastard have shot *him* if he'd been out there?

Dan reached into an inside jacket pocket and extracted the small watertight case that had originally protected three Cuban cigars. It now held only one. The Cohiba had survived a lot of hardship on this mission but lit up perfectly, engulfing him in a cloud of soothingly aromatic smoke.

A few snowflakes drifted through the dead-calm air. Around the courtyard, all but two of the previously lighted windows were now dark, as bleak and joyless as he felt inside.

He crossed the deck and reclined on a patio lounge, ignoring the dampness of melted snow as he pieced together relevant information. Geoff, in his field days, had worked several times in Paris. DSS maintained a safe house here. Dan had never used it, but he'd seen the address on internal documents. Something sort of Jewish, like David or temple. With three numbers in sequence. 123? No, *almost* in sequence. 132.

That was it. 132 Rue du Temple.

Grateful for mental recall that still worked at this hour, he pulled out his phone and, leaving Location Services switched off, used a map application to identify the building and fix it in his mind.

Geoff might not be staying there, but in his place Dan definitely would. DSS safe houses came with surveillance gear, high-speed internet, weapons, and always a car. What better car in Paris than one disguised as a taxi?

No, there was no "might" about it. Geoff *would* be there. Probably with a bottle of the best bourbon he could find in Paris. Geoff, the bourbon connoisseur, the guy who needed exactly three glasses before he started boasting about how inventive he'd been in the field, how many women he'd conquered, how James Bond could have been patterned after him. The closet drunk who'd been Dan's bosom buddy.

A sour taste rose in Dan's throat. He couldn't count how many times he'd listened to Geoff's shit.

Worse, he'd been passively complicit in supporting whatever off-the-record activities kept Geoff in his high-flying lifestyle. He knew the man's salary. No way could it cover payments on his big house in Maryland, the Cadillac Escalade, the designer clothes. Yet Dan had refrained from asking too many questions.

Was I so in need of a friend?

No longer. If Geoff was willing to kill for the Sixth Book of Moses, there could be only one reason. Money.

Standing, Dan relit his Cohiba. This time, the rich smoke did nothing to soothe him. He could not separate Geoff from the likes of a murderous double agent or some rich kid who ran off to join ISIS. Any government official who double-crossed a colleague was equally a traitor—on a more personal level. And "personal" was the part that burned in Dan's belly.

Especially when it coincided with acquiring a book that could rain hellfire on Israel. Did Geoff even know this? Did he give a damn? Obviously, he knew something, or he never would have hired Jade to snatch it. Most likely Geoff planned to sell it to some client with deep pockets.

Well, tough luck, pal. If you wanted to get rich working for the government, you should have run for elective office.

With a waft of warm air, the door behind him slid open. "You are troubled," Paulette said.

He turned to see her, barefoot but with her hand clutching the bathrobe to her neck. So much for solitude. "You'll freeze out here."

"I will not stay long." She came to stand beside him, her unseeing eyes seeming to gaze at the heavens as if seeking spiritual guidance. "I like the smell of your cigar. It is *masculin*. But you will be ... without value, if you do not sleep. Especially to Martine."

"I was thinking about someone else."

"The one who shot that woman? It is a man, yes? Always it is a man."

"Not always, but yes."

"So you will find him. And then?"

"We'll see."

"Ah, the answer *ambigu*." She reached for his shoulder and squeezed it. "Men think it makes them mysterious. Yes?"

"You really will freeze out here."

"Do not worry for me. Worry for Martine. She is good for you. Yet you resist her."

"Me? She's the one who's not interested." *So please drop it.*

Instead, Paulette puffed out one of those dismissive breaths typical of the French. "Men are more blind than I am."

"I'm not blind," he insisted. "She and I make a good team." There were colleagues, and there were partners. Colleagues helped. Partners had your back. Martine tonight had become the latter.

Of course, that was not what Paulette meant. But he had no intention of entertaining further discussion of a nonexistent romance.

Evidently sensing his resolve, Paulette released Dan's shoulder and switched subjects. "The man you seek, he has Martine's book?"

"I think so."

"You said it can cause war. But you did not say how. What is in this book?"

"Old religious stuff." And a ticking bomb with a huge blast radius.

Chapter 22

Visions of the strangler robbed Bernard Leroux of any sleep, at all. Lying on the hard floor in Dominic's office didn't help, but it was the visions that kept him awake. For hours now, they'd slithered through his head in increasingly vicious panoramas of carnage that made him cringe like a sinner on Judgment Day.

God's wrath, manifest.

If only Martine had not brought him that book, that fruit from the Tree of Knowledge.

He rolled onto his side again, trying to ignore the pain shooting through his bursitis-ridden hip.

The Sixth Book of Moses was genuine, and as sacred as the whole known library of Dead Sea Scrolls. He had no right to possess it. It should reside in the Holy Land where scholars wiser than he could debate its implications, not under an edge of the threadbare carpet on Dominic's floor.

He'd been a fool to say the strangler had stolen it, even more of a fool to imagine she couldn't find him. She was Mashchith, God's

Angel of Death. He saw that now. She had spared him once, but when she discovered she had the wrong book, she would not spare him again.

If he could only sleep, he might wake with a solution that didn't involve returning the book to Martine and admitting his deception. She was the only person who looked up to him. Losing her respect would leave a void as unbearable as losing a daughter.

He couldn't pretend that he had simply mislaid it in his office, either. She would see right through that lie. And he couldn't hide it somewhere in the museum without the constant fear that another employee might find it.

He curled into a fetal position. But it didn't relieve the aching in his hip. *This damned floor.*

With considerable effort and creaking of joints, he pushed himself upright just enough to move over and plop down in Dominic's chair. He crossed his arms on the desk to cushion his head. "Come, Hypnos, lull me to sleep."

The ancient Greek spirit did not visit him.

Instead came more visions of the Last Judgment. Blood, fire, pain. Excruciating pain. Hot irons applied to his most tender spots, the skin stripped slowly from his body. The robed Inquisitor fixing him with merciless eyes, urging in a pseudo-sympathetic tone, "Confess, Bernardo. Repent your sins."

#

After three hours of sleep, Dan had showered, shaved, and dressed in under fifteen minutes. He now stood in Paulette's kitchen waiting to plunge the coffee press. At the sound of bare feet behind him, he turned to see Martine looking puffy-eyed in jeans and a misbuttoned white blouse.

"Sorry," he said, "I didn't mean to wake you."

"I smelled coffee." She pulled two mugs out of a cupboard and set them on the counter. "You look ready to go … somewhere."

"I think I know where Geoff is staying. I want to check it out." He plunged the press, filled both cups, and handed her one. "If it's the place I think, there'll be surveillance cameras. So I want to get there while it's dark."

"Cameras in the Louvre can record in infrared. Darkness doesn't matter."

"But usually the resolution in infrared isn't as good as in normal lighting."

"You can't count on that."

"I know." He smiled inwardly. Despite looking sleep-deprived and pleasantly disheveled, she was right on top of things. "I'm going to keep my head down and stagger like a drunk after an all-night binge."

"I'm coming with you."

He'd planned on going alone. But with cameras trained on the sidewalk, especially if they recorded for later viewing, a woman hanging around might raise fewer alarms than a man would. "Okay. Then drink that quickly and finish getting dressed. It'll be hard to find a cab at this hour."

"I'll call us one now."

While she was upstairs, Dan found the Magic Tape he'd noticed on the bench that held Paulette's paints, brushes, and artist's miscellanea. He tore off a two-inch strip and affixed it over the LED flash on his phone. Using one of her smallest brushes, he covered the part of the tape directly over the flash with blue paint. After blowing on the paint to speed its drying, he covered the first piece of tape with a second and painted this one purple. His cellphone was now a UV light.

But he wasn't yet done. In Paulette's laundry room, he rummaged through her cleaning supplies and found a small spray bottle that contained a clear liquid with the odor of isopropyl alcohol. He poured it out, rinsed the bottle, then added two inches of water and a dash of dishwashing detergent. Shaking the mixture gave him a dilute solution that would fluoresce under UV. A crude but effective way to identify which keys on a combination pad were most frequently pressed.

Martine came down with a lively step and an eager expression. "The cab should be here."

"You have toothpaste on the corner of your mouth."

"Picky, picky." She wiped it away.

Their taxi, a shiny white Peugeot, idled at curbside. When Dan gave the address in English, the driver said, "French, please. Or …" He made a writing gesture with his hand. Martine asked Dan then gave it in French.

As the taxi pulled away, Dan said, "Look out for that dog."

The driver didn't react.

Craning her neck, Martine asked, "What dog?"

"Just testing how openly we can speak." Still, Dan kept his voice low as he explained his logic about a woman drawing less attention than a man. "Our first goal is to get into the building. There's bound to be a keypad at the street entrance, like the one into Paulette's complex. If we're lucky, the combination keys will be more worn than the others. If you can't tell, give the keypad a light spray of this." He handed her the bottle of soap solution.

"What is it?"

"A dilute detergent. It'll stick to unused keys better than to those with fingerprints." He gave her his phone. "Switch on the flashlight app and look at the screen. The buttons on the keypad that do *not* glow are the ones we want."

"But that doesn't give us the combination."

"It narrows the possibilities."

She rolled her eyes. "I think it's a long shot."

The rolling-eye thing again. Man, he was getting tired of that. "Do you have a better idea?"

"We'll see."

Just before the nearest intersection to the safe house, he told the driver, *"Arrêtez."* Stop. To Martine, he said, "Ask him to wait here, please."

Dan's watch showed 5:52. The sky was black, the temperature arctic. Their exhalations showed beneath the streetlight where they got out of the car. No sounds, no signs of life. Perfect. "Two doors up. On your right."

Martine batted her eyes. "Should I try to look like a frozen hooker?"

"In jeans and boots? If you want to play hooker, you should have worn a miniskirt and five-inch heels."

"Sounds like the voice of experience."

Their verbal sparring might have been fun under different circumstances, but now was not the time. It was already six o'clock. Then a pang of guilt bit him. *Do not send an amateur into a potentially dangerous situation.* "Look, never mind. I'll do it."

"Don't trust me?"

"No. It's just—"

She turned and strode away.

Damn. "Keep your face down."

She flipped him the bird over her shoulder.

Racked with second thoughts, Dan braced to act if something went wrong. Maybe they should have gone together, a tipsy couple in a loving mood. Or maybe abort and just find a place to watch the building and catch Geoff coming out. There was still time.

From the entrance, Martine waved for him to come.

Uh-oh. He gripped his pistol and dashed down the sidewalk, only to find her with one foot propping open the door. *Already?* "What did you do?"

"I buzzed a random ground-floor flat. If your Geoff is so security conscious, he won't be staying on the ground floor."

Dan couldn't suppress a grin.

"Should I take that smirk as approval?"

"In spades." He followed her into a small, dimly lit lobby where a staircase of dark wood wrapped around the walls and rose to three stories above them. On this level, he counted four doors. The nearer one on their left was partly open, revealing an elderly woman in a yellow housecoat who peered at them disapprovingly.

Martine spoke to her in French and received a glare before the door slammed. "I apologized and told her the person we wanted was on the next floor."

"Well done." He really should remember that the simplest ways were often the best. "Now we're looking for a door with a high-security lock. Could be another combination pad or a lock that takes either a three-sided key or a circular one like in vending machines. I'll check the front apartments. You check the rear."

On the top floor, Dan found it. And his hopes sank. The lock was a Schlage touchscreen deadbolt. With programmable codes up to eight digits long, it was essentially uncrackable. Even if he identified all the correct numerals with soap and UV, the number of possible combinations and sequences was astronomical.

He then saw something that froze him in place—a pinhole lens embedded in the upper left corner of the doorjamb and probably activated by a motion sensor. Why hadn't he anticipated that? He could at least have blinded it with his flashlight.

Quickly stepping to the side, he held up his hand to prevent Martine from coming any closer.

"What's wrong?" she asked.

He pointed. "If it records, I've been made."

"We have to get out of here, now." She headed toward the stairs.

He hurried after her, mentally bashing himself in the head. Once outside again and walking toward the street corner, he opened his jacket to let the freezing air cool his adrenaline-charged body. "Man, I sure screwed that up."

"So you're human, after all."

"Barely." If he weren't champing at the bit to nail Geoff, he wouldn't have made this kind of mistake.

"At least we know where he's staying." She stopped. "But if he realizes we've found him, he'll move somewhere else."

"I doubt it. He'd be giving up a fortified location with computing power as well as firepower. Our big problem now is we don't know how soon he intends to sell the book. It could be today."

"You're sure he plans to sell it?"

"With Geoff, it's always about glory or money." Dan's failure to admit it sooner still threatened to bring bile to his throat. "I don't see any glory in this for him."

"What about the cellphones and card keys I took out of Jade's pockets? They might help."

"We're thinking along the same lines. I have them with me. We can check them out over breakfast."

"At this hour," she said, "the only places open would be McDonald's or a fancy hotel."

"Let's splurge." He was in no mood for an Egg McMuffin.

"Your treat?"

"Your mother's."

Thankfully, their cab hadn't budged. When they'd climbed in, she told the driver, *"L'hôtel George Cinq."*

"Ouch." The George Cinq was one of the *grande dames* among Parisian hotels, an ultra-luxury establishment now owned by a Saudi prince. "I said your mother's treat, not punish her."

"She owes us. After all we've been through, I'd like to be waited on like royalty and served something unforgettable."

"Fine with me." They were hardly dressed for it, but staff in top-flight hotels would never mention such a thing. For all they knew, he and Martine could be rock stars or some other breed of eccentric rich.

A brief ride through light traffic brought them to the hotel's triple-arched entrance. They walked into a tennis court-sized lobby of polished stone, crystal chandeliers, and huge glass vases bursting with pink roses that infused the air with a florist-shop fragrance.

A woman at reception apologized that breakfast service would not begin until seven o'clock, ten minutes from now. But if they cared to wait in one of the seating areas, she would have coffee brought to them.

They'd barely shed their jackets and sat down when a liveried waiter arrived with a silver platter bearing coffee and an assortment of teas.

When he left, Martine poured heavy cream into her coffee. "Don't you love this place?"

"A lot more than McDonald's." But what he really liked was her dazzling smile, a welcome if temporary antidote to his dismal failure at Geoff's place.

"Why are you staring?"

"You're nice to look at."

For a second, she seemed taken aback. Then she brushed it off with, "You've seen more of me than this."

On that beach in the Caymans, yes. "Still ..." he said and let the word hang there.

"Still?"

Dan was about to say something like he barely knew her back then, when his peripheral vision caught a man in a tuxedo approaching them.

Two feet away, the man stopped and bowed slightly. "Madame, monsieur, your table is ready. May I escort you?"

As they followed him, Martine took Dan's hand in hers.

It felt warm, encouraging.

The guy in the tuxedo stopped at a table for two and pulled out an upholstered armchair. "Madame?"

As soon as they were seated, Dan said to him, "Before you go, we found a wallet and want to return it to its owner. These were in it." He held out Jade's two cardkeys, one with a large red "A," the other with a silver fleur-de-lis on a dark blue background. "Can you tell which hotels these come from?"

"Our manager might be able to help you. If you will permit me?"

"Sure. Just bring them back."

When the man had left, Martine said, "Smooth."

"Hey, I can be smooth."

"Uh-huh."

He tugged at an imaginary tie. "I don't get no respect."

"But you're going to get food," she said as a waitress approached them with menus.

Dan decided on the American breakfast—American only in the sense that it included fresh orange juice and two eggs. Martine ordered à la carte. A lobster omelet, Iberian cured ham, crepes with lemon juice and sugar, an assortment of red berries, and a selection of French cheeses. Plus cappuccino and freshly squeezed papaya juice.

Dan gaped at her.

"What?" she said, as if she didn't know. "I'm hungry, and I've never had a lobster omelet."

How she was going to stuff all that into her slim body, he had no idea. If he was lucky, she'd give him a few bites. In the meantime, they had work to do.

He laid Jade's cellphones on the table. "You want the iPhone or the burner?"

"The burner."

He slid it across to her, then activated the iPhone. As he'd feared, the screen waited for touch ID. Not possible, unless he could return to the hospital and place Jade's thumb on it while she was unconscious.

"Not locked," Martine exclaimed.

"Let me see."

"Wait." Her fingers danced over the screen. "Good Lord, I think this phone belonged to the man who tried to kill her."

"Which man? Two men tried to kill her."

"The first one. There's a message stream here, and I think it's between Jade and your friend, Geoff."

Dan thrust out his hand. "Give me the phone, will you?"

Martine ignored his request. "I'm starting to like Jade. She's using her attacker's phone to taunt Geoff. No. To ... jack with him. Is that the expression?"

Dan reached to grab the phone, but Martine pulled it to her chest.

Leaning back out of reach, she read from the screen. "The first line says, 'She killed me.' He says, 'Explain yourself,'" and she replies, 'I died in an alley near her hotel.' When he asks who this is, she says, 'Your worst nightmare, asshole.'"

That did sound like Jade. "Would you give it to me, please?"

"Patience. This is interesting. She says the book will now cost him an extra million dollars, plus the second half of her fee." Martine flicked her finger up the screen. "Some back-and-forth about the money, then they agree to meet."

"Where?"

"It says she'll tell him tomorrow. That would be today."

"But Geoff somehow tracked her down and shot her." How he'd done that, Dan didn't know. The bastard's tradecraft was mediocre at best.

At last, Martine handed over the phone.

As Dan took it, two waiters wheeled up a trolley of covered plates. After laying out the plates, the waiters paused a moment, then removed the covers with a flourish. For him, *ta da,* two eggs over easy—plus a glass of juice and a bowl of fresh fruit. For Martine, a fantastic-smelling feast that took up two-thirds of their table.

While she gleefully sampled every dish, he read the message stream she had just summarized, then scrolled up for other messages. Nothing except an address, apparently sent by Geoff. "We have a place to start."

"Great." She turned her attention in earnest to the omelet and Iberian ham. "Delicious. No, better than delicious. Sublime. You want a bite?"

"Sure." He sampled both and thought, if he were ever on Death Row, this was what he would order for his last meal. Fat chance he'd get it.

Martine had just pushed across her plate of crepes when the man in the tuxedo returned with an envelope.

After thanking him, Dan opened the envelope and dug out Jade's card keys plus a folded piece of thick paper. On the paper, a feminine hand had written two addresses in European penmanship using a fountain pen. He homed in on the second one. "Got it."

"Got what?" Martine asked, a spoonful of berries halfway to her mouth.

"The keys are for different hotels on the same street. One is the same address I just saw on the burner phone."

"I saw an address, but the texts below were more interesting. You don't want a crepe? They're very good." She drew the plate back and dug in.

"Are you listening to me?"

"Of course, I am. For some reason, Jade had rooms in two hotels, and Geoff knew one of them."

As Martine alternated spoonfuls of berries with bites of cheese, Dan explained why Jade would have two rooms, finishing with, "She was laying a trap."

"But somehow it backfired." Martine dabbed her lips with a crisp linen napkin. "You're not eating."

"You want it?" He held out his plate.

With an admonishing frown, she said, "Not after cheese. Besides, your eggs will be cold by now."

She was right. But it didn't matter. He downed the eggs, savoring their rich buttery flavor, then wiped the remaining yolk from his plate with a croissant whose crispy crust shattered like a Christmas tree ornament with each bite he took.

Unfortunately, they were no closer to recovering the book. They knew where Jade had been staying and where she was now. They knew where the book was, or at least who had it. Dan felt certain Geoff had lined up a buyer, probably several potential buyers. That made sense. Play them against each other to raise the price. So an auction. But where? A physical location or on the internet? The internet, of course, at a site no doubt buried somewhere inside the Dark Web. Geoff, for all his near-disastrous screw-ups with the field agents he was supposed to support, excelled at everything related to computers.

Dan's shoulders slumped. His chances of finding the auction site and intervening were roughly zero. Not only that. Geoff could conduct an online sale without ever leaving the safe house. "Shit."

Reaching across the table, Martine laid a hand on his. "Don't tell me we're screwed again. Come on, Jardani. You're full of ideas. We have to get that book."

"Hang on a second." Geoff might conduct an auction from the safe house, but he couldn't deliver the book without either leaving the place or having the successful bidder meet him there. That was the weak link, the point at which the book would be out in the open.

Snatching it would be dangerous as hell. Geoff would surely be armed. He always was. The buyer might be, also. No problem for me, Dan thought. But he needed Martine to help him, and it could definitely be a problem for her.

Silently he mouthed an old Gypsy prayer, *Te n'avel man pascotia ando drom.* May no misfortune happen to me on the road. "Or to this lovely lady with me," he whispered.

"What did you say?"

"Nothing. It's just an old invocation."

"What about the book?"

He summarized his thoughts on grabbing it at the handoff. "To do that, we have to set up surveillance at the safe house."

"We don't even know when the sale will take place, let alone when the book will change hands. It could be days from now. Just watching?"

"Yes, I'm afraid. Unless you can think of something else."

After paying a breakfast bill of nearly two hundred euros— three hundred dollars— Dan walked her outside, declined the doorman's offer of a cab, and strode with her to the nearest corner to hail a taxi.

They had a lot left to do, none of it pleasant.

Chapter 23

The confessional felt like an upright coffin. Beyond the grate, a balding priest with a hooked nose stared straight ahead, his wrinkled face more stern than compassionate. When Leroux reluctantly admitted his last confession had been twenty years ago, the man's dour expression deepened into a scowl, as though he knew it had been much longer. Had God whispered "lie" in the man's ear? No. The tipoff must have come from the quavering in Leroux's voice.

Clutching his hands together, he assured himself, *Everyone lies in the confessional. No one reveals all his sins.* Priests surely knew that and used it to their advantage. Yet they did possess the authority to absolve.

Leroux sat up straighter and took a fortifying breath. "I have stolen a book."

The priest eyed him as if to ask, *Is that your great sin?*

"It's a very old book," Leroux explained. "Very important." Without mentioning its religious significance or the fact that its existence had been kept secret for centuries, he said, "There are people who are willing to kill for it."

That caught the priest's attention. The man turned to face him through the grate. "What is the nature of this book?"

"It deals with a highly inflammatory subject. One that impacts the deeply held beliefs of many people. More than that I cannot say."

"Cannot or will not?"

"For your own safety, Father, I will not."

"God protects me."

"As He protects us all." *I hope.* "Still, I must remain silent about the book's contents."

After a long pause, the priest replied, "You stole this book where? From whom?"

"A woman brought it to me. She acquired it from an old collection." Despite being circumspect, Leroux felt relieved that he was telling the truth. Maybe he should come to confession more often.

"Why," the priest asked, "do you think some people would kill to obtain this book?"

"One person has already tried to kill *me*." Memory of the strangler sent a shiver up his back. "I cannot bear to go through that again. Please, what must I do?"

The priest resumed his stoical gaze forward. "Obviously, you must return the book to its rightful owner. Either to this woman you mentioned or to the original collection."

Leroux rolled his lips in. He'd been afraid the priest would say that. Could he in good conscience burden Martine with the yoke he had hung around his own neck? Absolutely not.

Unless he warned her of the danger. He could let *her* decide. She did have Jardani to help her.

"Say five Our Fathers and ten Hail Marys," the priest instructed him. "Then do what is right."

Somewhat comforted, Leroux left the confessional. On a folding wooden chair facing the church's main altar, he sat and bowed his head. But instead of begging mercy from God or the Virgin, he pulled out his phone. He needed to send a message to Martine, arrange a safe place to hand over the book. What if the strangler could somehow monitor his calls or see his messages? *Damn.* All he wanted was to resume the life he'd had before she and Jardani showed up. The quiet life of a scholar content to tease meaning out of obscure texts.

Obscure texts. That was it. He would send a message only Martine could decode.

Then he'd be free.

#

Headed toward the safe house in the cab they'd hailed after breakfast, Dan was searching his memory for vantage points where they could stake out Geoff's building, when Martine said, "What if we approach this a different way?"

He turned to face her. "Meaning?"

"Impersonate Jade." A devilish smile lit Martine's face. "Play mind games with him the way she did, using the same phone she used."

"Interesting. Go on."

"Pretend she was wearing a flak jacket, or whatever. Now she's coming for him."

"That'd keep him inside and on guard."

"Okay, she knows where he's staying, and she's going to bomb it."

"Better." He loved a fertile mind, especially when it spurred his own. "So, he has to get out."

"And take the book with him. He'd never leave it there."

"But she won't mention the book," Dan said, expanding on Martine's scenario. "All she cares about is her fee and the extra million. Either he meets her with the money, or she blows his ass to smithereens."

"That's good."

"Of course, he doesn't have a million bucks." Dan doubted Geoff ever did. "But he'll interrupt whatever he's doing to finish the job of killing her and saving his neck."

"So where do they meet?"

"Not in town." Dan pointed outside the taxi's windows, where Parisian life was returning to normal after Christmas Day— shops opening, pedestrians scurrying, traffic crawling. "We need some place out of the way. A park, for instance."

"If he thinks meeting her means she won't bomb his apartment, then he won't bring the book."

But Dan was ready for that. "I'll surprise him, take him down. If he doesn't have the book, I'll wrench the safe house combination out of him."

"Then what? You can't just kill him."

The cab halted, trapped in gridlock caused by a fender bender several cars ahead.

"This is a problem," Martine said.

"Want to walk? It's only about a mile from here."

"I don't mean a problem now. I mean a problem if you … 'subdue' Geoff in a remote place like, say, the Bois de Boulogne. If he tells us the safe house combination, we won't know if it's the truth. But we can't take him back there to make sure we get in, because we could get snarled in traffic just like this. If he's bloody or gagged or—"

"—otherwise in obvious distress, I get it. That's why you and I have to work together on this." When she eyed him questioningly, Dan hastened to add, "I'll keep him under control in the Bois de

Boulogne or wherever, while you go to the safe house. When you have the book, call me, and I'll meet you at Paulette's."

"That could work. But what about Geoff? Afterwards? No, don't tell me."

Dan wasn't sure himself about the details. But one thing was certain. The only way Geoff would leave Paris was in a body bag.

"Oh, damn. Speaking of calls …" Martine pulled out her phone and turned it on. "I need to tell my mother we're okay."

"Now?"

She ran her finger up the screen. "Good Lord. Six new messages from her. The last one says she'll arrive here at nine-forty this morning."

"We don't have time to deal with her yet."

As their taxi finally worked its way around the fender bender, Martine's eyes widened. "Wait a second. There's also a message from Leroux, sent ten minutes ago. It says, 'I must see you immediately. What you seek is where the right elbow meets the left knee.'"

"What does that mean?" Had the guy had gone off his rocker?

Her lips curved into a grin. "It means he has something for us and wants to meet us at the Rodin Museum."

"I still don't get it. And please turn off your phone before Geoff spots it." When she had, he asked, "What does Leroux have, and how do you conclude the Rodin Museum?"

Suddenly her face lit up brighter than a 500-watt bulb. "This could be a miracle."

"Dammit, Martine."

She told the driver to pull over, then beamed at Dan like a lottery winner. "What do we seek?"

"Besides happiness and world peace?"

"Stop being sarcastic. This is big."

"Okay, what?"

"The book!"

Had Leroux's craziness infected her? "He doesn't have the book. Geoff does."

"As you're fond of saying, that's what we *think*. We think Jade snatched it from Leroux, and Geoff shot her to get it. But what if we're wrong?"

"That's one hell of a long shot."

"Maybe, but we can't afford to not check it out."

"By going all the way to the Rodin Museum? And what even makes you think that's the place?"

"You know his statue, The Thinker?"

"Of course"

"Show me The Thinker's pose."

Gnashing his teeth, Dan figured the sooner they got this over with, the sooner they could get down to the real business of finding a surveillance spot near the safe house. He leaned forward, put his elbow on his knee, and curled his hand under his chin.

"Wrong," she exclaimed. "You placed your right elbow on your right knee. The Thinker's right elbow is on his left knee."

Dan tried it. "That's awkward."

"That's Rodin. Leroux and I used to joke about the poor model having to hold that pose for hours." She grasped Dan's hand. "If Leroux has the book, we have to meet him."

Dan wrestled with their options. If they wasted time on some hare-brained idea of Leroux's, Geoff could auction off the book before they got to him. On the other hand, he still had to deliver it. Which gave them a little leeway. "Make it fast."

"Musée Rodin," she said to the driver. *"Rapidement."*

"Oui, madame." The man lurched back into traffic, honking at other drivers as he rounded several turns. His smiling face in the rearview mirror told Dan he was happy for the extra fare and anticipated a big tip for how skillfully he was capitalizing on the tiniest spaces between other vehicles.

Dan might have appreciated the man's skill more if there weren't something else bothering him. Two disruptions in as many minutes. First, Astrid arriving at a time that was inconvenient, to say the least. Then Leroux's cryptic message and request to meet immediately. Dan's experience of "coincidences" was that they were always linked, and never in a good way.

As their driver made a quick turn off Rue de Rivoli and negotiated the Place de la Concorde, with its beautiful Egyptian obelisk and ugly Ferris wheel, Dan twisted in his seat to memorize the vehicles following them. There were too many. Trucks, vans, private cars, other taxis. Plus two motorcycles ridden by leather-clad drivers in helmets with dark faceplates. He zeroed in on the motorcyclists until they peeled off at a turn and continued along the Seine toward the Louvre, while their own driver crossed over a bridge to the Left Bank.

A swerving right onto the Quai d'Orsay and a subsequent left separated them from the few remaining vehicles Dan had memorized. Still, as they approached Les Invalides, he said, "Ask the driver to stop here."

"Why? The museum is over there."

"*Arrêtez ici,*" he told the guy before he could make the last turn.

Martine narrowed her eyes. "Now you're angry with me?"

"I'm not angry." When the driver had let them off, Dan hustled her across the divided boulevard to the street that fronted Rodin's former house. "I want time to think."

"Think about The Thinker?" She smiled at her own quip then checked her watch. "The museum doesn't even open for twenty minutes. Which means, by the way, my mother has just landed."

"She can wait." He drew Martine to the front of a nutrition shop with a good view of all the tourists queued up to enter the modern building that served as the museum's entrance. "Leroux said 'immediately' in his message. But he's not in that line."

Martine looked across the street. "Maybe he's already inside. Louvre employees have special privileges at other museums. Hey, I have my ID."

Hoping she was right about Leroux, Dan followed her to the front of the line, where she presented her Louvre ID to the armed guard at the entrance.

Inside the building, which housed offices, ticket counters, and a souvenir shop, Martine submitted her ID to two more inspections before she and Dan were admitted onto the grounds of the large estate Rodin had once called home.

Straight ahead lay the mansion, in the left front corner of which Dan had once spent half an hour admiring his all-time favorite sculpture, *Young Girl in a Flowered Hat*. No way he would see it today.

Their objective lay out here on the grounds, where bright sunlight warmed the morning. To their left rose the artist's monumental *La Porte de l'Enfer*, a bronze depiction of the Gates of Hell. On a stone pedestal to their right stood *Le Penseur*, The Thinker.

Glad to be ahead of the crowd, Dan walked with Martine toward the larger-than-lifesize bronze figure of a naked man with his right elbow on his left knee. It stood at the center of a patio ringed by eight trees that had been pruned into cones.

Leroux stepped out from behind the statue. The old scholar looked frazzled, his eyes sunken, his clothing wrinkled, his reddish-gray hair stringy as though unwashed for several days.

But Dan zeroed in on the worn canvas satchel clutched to Leroux's chest. In other circumstances, the satchel and the man's anxious demeanor would have screamed, "Bomb!" With Leroux, however, anxiety on his face gave way to a look of relief as Martine rushed up and threw her arms around him.

After a long hug, she stood back. "Monsieur, are you okay? You do not look well."

He ran a hand through his hair, with no discernable effect, then said in a faltering voice, "I have sinned terribly."

That did not sound like the intellectual who studied all religions but embraced none. What had happened to him?

"Jardani, I am so happy to see you."

"Monsieur," Dan said neutrally, coming forward to shake hands. Leroux's was moist.

"You must forgive me." Glancing around apprehensively, Leroux fumbled with the straps to his satchel. "I deceived you."

"How?" Martine asked in a warm but guarded tone.

From his satchel Leroux sheepishly withdrew a book.

The book. Dan recognized the binding and the scars on its leather cover, telltale signs he'd forgotten about when preparing to meet Jade. His heart rate launched into overdrive.

Leroux held it out to Martine. "Please take it."

"Monsieur, I—"

"Take it," Dan said. "Four people are headed right for us." As she concealed it under her jacket, Dan turned to face the new arrivals, ready to disable all of them if necessary.

To his relief, there was no need. The tourists, two pairs speaking German, snapped photos of The Thinker, walked around it taking more photos, and hurried off. But another pair was coming.

Keeping an eye on them, Dan said, "Let's go back outside. There's a café across the street."

Leroux clutched Dan's elbow. "Jardani, you forgive me, don't you?"

Not in this lifetime. "Walk."

Once on the street, Dan pointed to the café. Inside, he selected a table in the far corner and ordered coffee for them all. "Now," he said to Leroux, "tell us everything."

A torrent of words poured out of the man. Most revealing was that the "strangler" had stolen the wrong book from his office and would no doubt come back to kill him when she discovered her mistake.

Martine tried to console him with, "Don't worry about that."

But Dan couldn't help twisting the knife. "Because of you, she's in a hospital, with two bullet holes in her."

Leroux's jaw dropped.

Martine shot Dan a venomous scowl. "That's not his fault."

Okay, okay. She was right. Geoff would have gunned down Jade regardless of what book she had. Even if she'd had no book at all. What drove Geoff was that he *thought* she had the book.

"I'm so sorry," Leroux blubbered, not at all the man who'd taken charge of their first meeting.

"I forgive you," Martine said.

But Dan was now thinking beyond sorrow and forgiveness. Geoff did not have the book.

This was a whole new ballgame.

Chapter 24

To show Adar who was boss, Geoff waited nearly half an hour after their ten o'clock appointment time before passing through the rotating front door of Le Meurice.

The lobby could have been lifted straight out of some sheik's palace. Everything was white or gold. White marble columns ringed by gold wreaths were crowned with multi-armed, gold-colored lamps resembling chandeliers. White vases seven feet high burst with white flowers. The couches and chairs were white leather trimmed with gold. If you were rich and liked gaudy, this was the place for you.

And there, primly enthroned at one of the seating groups, was a smallish man who had to be Adar. Dark suit, maroon tie, neatly trimmed beard. Sipping coffee, pinky-up as if he was civilized. A second cup and saucer sat on the table before him.

After a quick scan for any heavyweights Adar might have brought, Geoff strode up to him.

The man rose to shake hands. "May I offer you coffee?"

"Business first." Arab, Iranian, whatever the guy was, they all liked to wait until the end of pleasantries before conducting business. Well, screw that. They'd do this the American way. Geoff took the seat opposite and withdrew the book from his attaché case. "I believe you're interested in this."

With a barely perceptible frown, Adar drew the book to his side of the table and opened it. After a minute or so, he started turning pages, then groups of pages. His frown deepened. "What is this?"

"What do you think it is?"

Adar pushed it back. "This is nothing but a Zionist commentary on their so-called Talmud. It is *not* the book you advertised."

"Bullshit."

"Sir." Adar leaned forward, his dark eyes unblinking. "Do not waste my time with games."

"You trying to haggle with me? It ain't gonna work."

Adar's gaze hardened. "Where is the book you offered to sell?"

"In front of you."

A long moment of silence. The guy was cratering. Geoff could see the indecision in his face.

Finally, Adar sat up straighter. "If you believe that, then regrettably there is no business between us." He rose from his chair.

"Hey, wait a minute."

"Good day, sir."

Dumbstruck, Geoff stared at the man's back as a million bucks walked away.

#

Descending to the Louvre's lobby, Astrid checked her phone again. No messages, no missed calls.

From the instant her plane touched down at Charles de Gaulle, she'd been calling Martine's cell, her flat, her office, Dan's cell, even her own house in Rueil-Malmaison in case Martine was there. No response anywhere. Worried sick about Martine's safety, she'd finally taken an airport cab to the museum in hopes that her daughter was just temporarily out of the office.

Please, God, protect my little girl. That was supposed to be Dan's job, but he wasn't answering, either. She should never have sent them on this mission. Powerful forces would not hesitate to kill for that book.

With cold fingers, Astrid pocketed her phone. At the bottom of the stairs, she placed her handbag on the x-ray machine's conveyor belt. Since she planned to stay at her house, she had brought no luggage.

Once past security, she smoothed the jacket of her business suit and headed for the Information counter. She felt grungy after the long flight, unwashed, unkempt. Fortunately, a quick comb-out during the taxi ride had made her short hair presentable.

"I'm here to see Martine Desmarais," she told a woman behind the counter. "She's an employee."

"Do you have an appointment?"

"I'm her mother. I have something urgent to tell her."

The woman, who could have passed for a freshly minted schoolteacher, eyed her uncertainly then said, "Your name please?"

Astrid produced her World Bank identity pass.

A minute later, having consulted a directory, punched buttons on her desktop phone, and listened, the woman hung up and shook her head. "No answer."

"Then I want to see her office."

"I'm sorry, Madame. Employees' offices are off-limits."

Astrid struggled to remain calm. Arguing with a functionary who had no authority to bend a rule never worked. "Let me speak to your supervisor. No. A director."

With a glance skyward, the woman left.

She returned in the wake of another woman, this one more matronly, in her fifties, wearing a skirt and blouse that were both a size too small. The new arrival inspected Astrid's ID, then placed it back on the counter. "I'm sure you can appreciate that parts of the Louvre are restricted."

"I'm a vice president at the World Bank. Not a thief or terrorist."

"Still—"

"I need to see my daughter!" Instantly regretting her outburst, Astrid reined in her tone and lowered her voice. "There's a family emergency."

"I'm informed she is not here."

"No. You were informed that she's not answering her phone. That doesn't mean she's not in the museum somewhere."

A slow shake of the head, as if to ask, *"Why does this happen to me?"* then the woman led her back to a glass-paneled office within a warren of similar offices. "Your daughter's name?"

Astrid told her.

The woman typed on her keyboard. "She is not here. Her last time was twenty-fifth December." She looked up at Astrid. "Your daughter must be dedicated to work on Christmas."

So, Martine was in Paris. Thank goodness. "Was she alone?"

"Impossible to tell. Employees are not supposed to allow others to enter with them. But sometimes …" She shrugged.

"What about CCTV?"

"Do you have a judge's order?" the woman said sarcastically.

Do you have a gram of compassion? "Please, I'm desperate. She could be in danger. Can we go to her office? I might see something to tell me where she is."

"As I told you, that's a restricted area." The woman got up from her chair. "I have done all I can."

"All you've done is—"

"Madame! It is time for you to leave. Shall I call a guard to escort you?"

Seething, Astrid stomped back toward the public area, the woman's imperious presence close behind every step of the way.

People milled around the lobby, snailed forward in lines to purchase tickets and in other lines to enter the various exhibits. Astrid headed for a pillar. With her back to it, she scrolled through a mental list of potentially helpful contacts in the government. One immediately stood out. Christophe. Ex-lover, occasional dinner partner since then, source of her initial information on the Sixth Book of Moses, and a high-ranking member of French foreign intelligence. If anyone could breach the Louvre's bureaucracy, he could.

She called his private number.

"*Ma chérie!* You are in town? I found a wonderful new place to take you for dinner."

"I would love to join you," she said. "First, though, I need your help."

"Of course. Anything." But as she explained her problem, the tone of his responses became wary, then concerned. Then it brightened again. "I will be there in twenty minutes."

It took him thirty. And when he arrived, he had two other men with him, one a thin fellow in a grey suit, the other a ham-fisted bruiser in a brown leather jacket.

After kissing Astrid on both cheeks and giving her hand a squeeze, Christophe flashed his ID at the Information counter. "I want to see your supervisor. Immediately."

With a horrified expression, as if there might be a bomb threat, the woman rushed away and quickly returned with the same matronly supervisor as before.

Christophe thrust out his ID like a priest brandishing a cross at the devil. "Your office. Now. And summon *your* supervisor."

Astrid smiled inwardly at the way he instantly took command. Do this, now. Do that, now. He'd preferred *her* to take charge when they were lovers. But this was no time for fond reminiscence. She had to find Martine, make sure she was safe. No, she *was* safe. Astrid refused to believe otherwise. Still, she needed to embrace her, apologize for placing her in peril—such peril that even Dan might not be able to shield her.

The next quarter-hour flew by in a gratifying whirl, Christophe scolding, citing "national security," then softening his tone as the supervisor's supervisor, a dour woman named Madame Allard, led them all back into the bowels of the museum.

They stopped at a heavy oak door, which Madame Allard seemed surprised to find unlocked.

Astrid had never been here before, in her daughter's office. The thought saddened her. She should have shown more interest. Still, the room looked like Martine—organized, clean, nothing amiss so far as Astrid could tell. And no damned clue as to why she hadn't replied to countless messages or where she might be now. Unless … "Can you check her computer?"

"Constance?" Madame Allard said to the woman in the too-tight blouse.

Looking miffed at being told what to do in front of outsiders, "Constance" tugged at the sides of her skirt, then sat and typed on Martine's keyboard. "It's locked." She turned to Astrid. "Her birthdate?"

Astrid told her.

The woman typed and shook her head. "Any pets?"

"No."

One of Christophe's colleagues, the thin man in the gray suit, said, "Let me try." After a few moments of rapid-fire typing, he leaned closer as the monitor came to life. A minute later, he rose from the chair. "No recent emails, but here are her searches."

Charged with hope, Astrid replaced him at the computer and saw a long list of web pages Martine had visited in the past few days. Pages about Muslims, Jews, Christians, Israeli law, extremist groups of all stripes. Clearly, she had figured out how important the Moses book was, and how dangerous.

But what was this? Holding her finger on the last search in the list, Astrid said, "Who is Bernard Leroux?"

Madame Allard shrugged.

"He's an employee." Constance, now apparently willing to cooperate with a "national security" investigation, waved Astrid out of the chair and took her place. She pulled up a new window, typed in a code that appeared as dots, and scrolled down the resulting page. "Yes. He's a specialist here in ancient languages."

Why search for him if he's here in the museum? Did Martine suspect him of something, want to consult with him privately? The man's specialty suggested the latter. Examining the page, Astrid memorized Leroux's home address, then said, "Where is his office?"

Constance checked the screen she'd pulled up, then led them downstairs to another oak door, this one locked.

Shouldering her aside, Madame Allard produced a key, apparently a passkey, that opened the door.

Astrid was beginning to like this woman. No nonsense, get the job done.

With a nod of appreciation to her, Astrid pushed open the door and walked into an office the size of Martine's but otherwise totally different. Books everywhere. Jammed into the shelves, piled on the floor, stacked on the desk. The smell of cannabis hung in the air. A coffee mug on the desk contained some brownish liquid that looked too thin to be coffee. Astrid sniffed it. Armagnac.

Madame Allard, evidently recognizing the scent of cannabis, turned to Christophe. "This is highly irregular. Our regulations forbid—"

Astrid tuned her out. There, in a neat stack on the floor, stood the four Louvre volumes. Admittedly they'd been her secondary objective when she recruited Dan, but the goal of returning looted treasures to their rightful owners remained. Anxious that Madame Allard not notice them and start asking questions, Astrid said, "I'm finished here."

Once upstairs again, she thanked the two supervisors.

Christophe, plainly preserving his advantage, told the women he might have to return. On the escalator leading to street level, he took Astrid's hand. "What did we accomplish?"

"We know Martine is in danger."

Disbelief knitted his brow. "You just saw her office. It's undisturbed. Nothing suspicious on her computer. Granted, that man's office is a pigsty and he smokes pot, but so what? What does he have to do with anything? And where's the danger?"

"We need to speak to him."

"Why?"

They reached the top of the escalator and walked out into a cold but sunny day. "Can your men come with us?"

"No." He stopped and faced her. "Neither can I, unless you tell me what this is all about."

Christophe would scoff. She knew he would. But she needed his help to find Martine before something terrible happened.

"Astrid," he said—not *ma chérie*—"there are disturbing developments in the Middle East. Senior officials from Hamas and Hezbollah are meeting in Damascus with the intelligence chiefs of Syria and Iran. This could be bad for Israel and the whole region." He checked his watch. "I need to stay on top of it."

A chill more frigid than the air around them swept through Astrid's body. Had the book already fallen into the wrong hands? Had the disaster she feared already started?

"Christophe, one cup of coffee. Afterwards, you can return to your office, if you think your work there is more important than what I'm going to tell you."

He eyed her guardedly, then looked around and pointed to a place called Café Marly, a hundred meters across the courtyard from where they stood. Once inside, he gestured for his two men to take a separate table. When coffees arrived, he stirred sugar into his and said, "Well?"

Astrid started at the beginning, the transcript he had given her of an interview with a Vatican librarian and the librarian's statement that a sixth Book of Moses, purportedly authentic but not included in the Bible, allegedly denied all Jewish claims to the Holy Land.

Christophe clanked down his cup on its saucer. "Is this about that stupid book?"

"It's not stupid. It could be the basis of those developments you mentioned."

He shook his head in a pitying way. "Who cares about some nonsense in an old book? And what does it have to do with your daughter?"

To shock him off his high horse, Astrid said outright, "She stole the book."

"What?"

"From that monastery in Prague the librarian mentioned."

Christophe glanced aside, blew out a breath, and looked back at her. "Why on earth did she do that? No, that's not the question. The question is, what does it have to do with the fact that you can't find her?"

A waiter asked if they wanted more coffee. Having barely touched hers, Astrid declined. When the man had topped off Christophe's cup, she leaned forward across the table. "As you mentioned when you gave me the transcript, only religious fanatics would care about the book. Martine has it"—*or had it*—"and French security has now detected a meeting among Israel's worst enemies."

"Ma chérie." He placed a hand on one of hers. "You're connecting unrelated dots."

"How can you say that?" she blustered. "My daughter is missing. The book is missing. Do you have any idea what could happen if the Middle East exploded in an all-out war? Because of that book?"

"Ma chérie —"

"Stop saying that, dammit. Think of the superpowers allied with each side, especially America's love affair with Israel. If not that, think of Israel's own nuclear weapons. Their so-called Iron Dome. Think of the lives lost. Thousands, millions." She shook her head. "At a minimum, think of the global economic collapse that could result if the wealth of Saudi Arabia and Kuwait and the Emirates were destroyed. Not just the oil, but everything they own around the world, including large chunks of the national debt of all countries whose economies are denominated in dollars or euros."

"Because of a book?"

"Yes!" She lowered her voice. "That book justifies the annihilation of Jews in Israel. Which is only the first domino to fall."

Sitting back, Christophe rubbed his chin, a contemplative frown on his face. "You think we could stop all this by finding your daughter?"

"Yes. Especially if she still has the book."

"And if she doesn't?"

At least I'll have Martine. "If she doesn't, she'll know where it is. The key to finding her is Bernard Leroux, the man with the messy office. He was the last search on Martine's computer. The page she pulled up included his home address. That's where we have to go."

Chapter 25

Geoff parked the big Mercedes taxi in the underground garage and tramped up the stairs to the safe-house apartment. Fucking Adar, acting all suave and debonair. What did *he* know? The book was real. Jade had shepherded it all the way from Prague to Paris. Once it was here, she'd grabbed it. It had to be real.

Didn't it?

Of course it was.

But if Adar blurted out his accusation on the auction website, the whole thing could fall through. Needing to think, Geoff poured himself a glass of Johnny Walker Black and took a healthy swig. Never mind that it was not quite noon. This was serious.

He should have followed the prissy dick up to his room and blown his damn brains out.

Geoff plopped onto the couch. Damage control. He was good at that. He wouldn't mention Adar, unless the asshole inserted himself into the auction. Then he'd brand the guy as an illiterate imbecile or a two-bit haggler trying to keep the price down.

And he would prove the book's authenticity by posting photos of its first few pages. He'd been planning to, anyway, since other potential buyers had demanded photos before they would bid. This was the perfect time.

Up yours, Adar.

#

"I'm glad she's not home," Dan said as he surveyed Paulette's living room. "It gives us a chance to conceal the book."

"What difference does it make if she's here or not?" Martine's eyes narrowed. "Or don't you trust her?"

"Of course, I trust her. She's been a savior for us." He walked to the tall bookcase near the kitchen entrance. "But if someone comes looking for it, I'd rather she be truly ignorant."

"Your paranoia is showing again. Who would come looking for it? No one even knows we're here."

"Geoff might figure it out. There were two jackets on the sidewalk when he shot Jade. And he saw the open door. That's why he shot at it."

Dan turned his attention to Paulette's books. They ranged from coffee-table volumes about the works of Chagall, Rothko, Picasso and so on, to novels by the likes of Hemingway and Steinbeck and poetry by Allen Ginsberg. But one thing seemed strange. "Why does a blind woman keep a couple hundred books, none of them in braille?"

"I don't know. Ask her."

"Maybe when this is over. In the meantime, one in a hundred is pretty good odds. Can you give it to me?"

"If you're worried Geoff will come looking for it, shouldn't you also be concerned that he'll wonder the same thing—about no braille books—and search for it there?"

"Can you think of a better place?"

With an eye roll, she handed over the book. "I'm going to get some wine."

While she was gone, Dan found a thin volume on cave paintings in southern France, wrapped its dust jacket around the Moses book, and slid that into the place where the cave-painting volume had been. He made space for the latter on the next shelf up. Satisfied that nothing looked amiss, he walked out to the deck and lay back on one of the two chaise longues. The midday sun felt so good on his face that he pulled off his jacket and sweater, shut his eyes, and let the rays warm him through his T-shirt.

It had been an exceptionally good day, so far. They'd recovered the book, found out where Geoff was staying, found out where Jade had been staying—which might come in handy—enjoyed a millionaire's breakfast at the George Cinq, and formulated the rudiments of a plan to draw Geoff out of the safe house.

The patio door behind him rolled open. "A little chilly for sunbathing," Martine said.

"You should try it. With no wind, it feels great."

"Uh-huh." She came up beside him. "You want some wine?"

He opened his eyes to see her holding two glasses and a bottle of Chablis. "Actually, yes. I'm feeling pretty happy about what we've accomplished in the past six hours."

She half-filled both glasses and handed him one before setting the bottle on the deck and reclining on the lounge next to his. "I feel sorry for Leroux. All he wanted was his moment in the spotlight."

"Look on the bright side. What he has instead is peace of mind."

"Always the pragmatist."

"Versus what? Romanticist? There's nothing romantic about a book that could launch an invasion of Israel." Where God only knew how many relatives he had.

"That's not what I meant. I was speaking of Leroux." As if to show they were on the same page, Martine took off her jacket and lay back. "Hmm. The sun does feel good."

Dan allowed himself a moment of gazing at her. But there were still plans to be made. "You mentioned the Bois de Boulogne. I've never been there."

"We're onto Geoff again?" she said, her eyes now closed.

"Unfinished business."

"You could just drop it, you know. We have what we want. He has nothing." Turning toward him, she opened her eyes. "You won."

"Not yet."

She took a sip of her Chablis. "It's a male thing, isn't it?"

"It's a justice thing."

She cocked her head as though maybe he was right. "The Bois de Boulogne is a forest on the western edge of Paris. Much of it is still pleasant, but at night it's a place for sex workers to pick up customers. Straight, gay, whatever." She paused. "Is Geoff gay?"

"Not that I know of." Although Geoff was married, that didn't necessarily mean he wasn't a closet gay or bisexual. Nor did the fact that he boasted of female conquests. Still, Dan had never detected any hints on that score.

"Too bad. That might have been a way to lure him."

"We already have a way."

"Just thinking." Then she sat up straight. "I almost forgot. There's a Gypsy camp in the forest."

Surprised, Dan sat up also. "Tell me about it."

"Sorry. Should I have said Roma?"

"Either is okay. Tell me about the camp."

"Last year." She looked down, as if trying to recall, then at him again. "Yes, they had a … shanty town, I think you call it. Built along an abandoned railway track that used to circle Paris. La Petite

Ceinture. After a few years, neighbors complained about the noise. The police came and tore down the shacks. There were photos in the newspapers. Children crying, food and toys and mattresses left behind. After that, they moved to Bois de Boulogne."

The never-ending story. Outsiders who only want to be left alone instead find themselves persecuted. Or worse. Gypsies, Jews, refugee Muslims, Africans from "not-our-tribe." Where in this world could the dispossessed find acceptance?

"Then forget the Bois de Boulogne," he said. "The last thing those people need is a crime anywhere near them. Especially one that could involve bloodshed."

"But I thought they might be able—"

"No!" His muscles tightened as a light breeze blew away the sun's warmth. "Remember what happened at Lom's house. Gunfire, Molotov cocktails. We cannot ask the Roma here to endure more suffering, just so I can settle a score."

"Where, then? If you insist on doing it."

"I don't know yet."

"Well, let's figure it out inside. It's getting chilly out here." She picked up her jacket. "Can you bring the wine?"

Dan followed her through the sliding door and closed it behind him.

While he set the bottle on Paulette's coffee table and took a seat on the leather couch, Martine walked to the bookcase. "I don't see it here."

"Bottom shelf, the cave-painting book."

"Wait." She spun around to face him. "Why leave it here at all? We're supposed to leave it at my mother's house. A taxi can take us there in thirty minutes."

Uh-oh. Crunch time. With what he had learned from Leroux about the book's importance, Dan was no longer willing to just hand it over to Astrid. It was a bombshell, but also a treasure. What would she do with it? She obviously knew something about it, or she wouldn't have asked them to steal it. But she'd acted as though taking this book were an afterthought. A ploy to downplay its significance? The way Astrid's eyes had bored into his, he was inclined, even more than before, to think so.

In any case, if they gave it to her, there were only three things she could do. Hide it. In which case why not leave it in the monastery? Destroy it, which Martine had suspected and which made sense considering Astrid's position in the World Bank and the catastrophic consequences the book's revelation could have on global financial markets. Or give it to someone else, a "definite maybe" that gained credence when he tied it to the facts that she had recruited him by contacting Geoff and that Geoff was desperate to acquire and sell the book.

Beyond the sickening possibility that Astrid and Geoff might be in this together, there was the uncertainty of what Martine would do when her mother's real objectives came to light. Gears within gears.

It all added up to one thing. Since his and Martine's unforeseen recovery of the book this morning, he hadn't thought through the "what now?"

But there was a way to stall. "Speaking of your mother, shouldn't you call her?"

"Oh, my God, I keep forgetting. I'm sure she's worried about me." Martine lifted her jacket off the back of the couch and dug out her phone.

"No. You should use a burner, but I'm out of them. Can you wait a few minutes while I go buy some more?" *And buy myself more time?*

"I shouldn't. She landed three hours ago and is probably frantic by this point." Phone in hand, Martine paced. "In her head, she knows I can take care of myself. But in her heart, I'm still her little girl. It annoys the hell out of me, but it's my own fault." Martine touched the place on her upper arm where Dan had seen a four-inch scar when they were in the Caymans. "I sealed my fate when I told her I'd been cut by a would-be rapist in New Haven."

"Okay," Dan conceded, "but make it quick. Longer than about two minutes will allow Geoff to home in on our location. Just tell your mother you're okay and you'll explain later."

Martine stopped pacing and thumbed a number. *"Maman! C'est moi."*

The rest of what she said was so rapid-fire that Dan only caught a few words. They included his name and *très bien* and *Nous l'avon*, We have it. He made a slicing motion with his fingers across his throat. When she appeared not to notice, he got up, stood in front of her, and repeated the gesture.

A few more words, then Martine finally ended the call. "I'm sorry," she told him with an exasperated shake of her head. "I couldn't get rid of her."

Dan hoped to hell Geoff hadn't monitored the transmission. If he had—

"But I solved our main problem." Martine picked up her wineglass from the coffee table and took a long sip. "We're meeting my mother in one hour, at her house. We'll give her the book and be done with it."

No way. Digging his nails into his palms, Dan scrambled for plausible reasons to postpone the meeting. "We can't meet with her today. We have to concentrate on Geoff."

"What? We've fought like hell to get this book. Now—"

"Not just this book. The Louvre books also."

"Which are now safely in Leroux's office."

"I'm not sure how safe they are."

She threw up her hands. "What's gotten into you? Give my mother this book, and you're free to concentrate on Geoff."

"Geoff comes first." *Why? Come on, man, think of a reason.* He felt guilty deceiving her, but it had to be done. His gaze fell on the bookcase. "For Paulette's safety. You talked a long time on the phone. Long enough to give Geoff a very good fix on our location. If he comes here, whether the book's here or not, Paulette will be in lethal danger."

Martine's face clouded. "Is that really possible?"

"Yes." *Play it up.* "Until we eliminate him from the picture, we're all in danger. We need to do what you said about impersonating Jade. Draw him out to some place that's *like* the Bois de Boulogne but not the Bois de Boulogne. When I've finished with him, we can give the book to your mother."

With a look of disappointment, Martine walked to the leather armchair and sat heavily. "She's going to be angry."

"So what?" Sensing an opportunity to find out why Martine seemed so anxious to please her mother, he leaned toward her. "You're a grown woman, perfectly capable of making your own decisions. She may think you're her 'little girl,' but you took all the risk. Big-time risks. More than anyone else, you have the right to choose what should be done and when."

She shut her eyes a moment. "Okay, I'll call her back."

"Let me go buy some phones first." He stood from the couch.

"Hurry. I want to get this over with."

#

Jade blinked open her eyes. *What the hell?* With an effort, she pushed herself up against the pillow behind her. Wires taped to her chest, an IV tube in the back of her hand, monitors beeping softly. A hospital room. *Shit.*

Slowly it started coming back. She and Lovel facing off on a sidewalk, on the verge of making the exchange when gunfire broke out. A dark Mercedes taxi, glimpsed as she went down. Burning pain in her chest and side.

She touched the two spots, then gingerly pressed the bandages covering them. Only dull pain, probably due to local anesthetic. They'd hurt more later. But, thank her luck, neither seemed to be life-threatening. The bullet that hit her below the left collarbone had apparently missed her lung. The one that got her in the side might be only a flesh wound. In fact—she reached behind her and felt another bandage—the bullet had gone right through her, evidently without damaging any internal organs.

Although she had no memory of it, someone obviously had brought her here. Lovel? If so, she owed him. But he also still owed *her* the identity of her Control.

Control. That limpdick bastard was almost certainly the shooter. Fortunately for her, he was a crappy shot. Unfortunately for him, she wasn't.

Wait. How could Control possibly know where she would be? She'd called him from one hotel, switched off the assailant's phone, and gone to her other hotel. No tracks. No trace.

Christ, maybe it wasn't Control.

She coughed and winced at the pain in her chest—like someone had jammed a thumb into the wound. On top of that, her mouth felt parched. She tried to swallow but couldn't. Ah, a clear plastic cup of water stood on the table beside her. She sucked down half of it through the straw, then set the cup back down.

If not Control, there was only one other possibility. Lovel. He knew exactly where she would be. Lovel was behind the door when the shooting happened, but he could have *hired* the gunman. And he could have been using the door to protect himself from stray bullets.

Would Lovel really double-cross her? He seemed more … honorable than that. Besides, if he wanted her dead, he could have finished her off right there on the sidewalk.

The sidewalk. She did have other memories. Collapsing in a sprawl, knowing she'd been shot, searching for help in that second between hitting the ground and losing consciousness. And glimpsing Lovel's face behind the door. A face in shock.

No way would he be shocked if he'd planned the whole thing. She shut her eyes in relief. Despite their wary relationship, she'd come to think of him as someone she could trust.

She sat up, felt immediately woozy, and lay back again on the pillow. *Take it slow.* The main thing was getting out of here. Which meant finding something to wear besides this ugly smock with the stupid floral pattern. Maybe knock out a nurse and put on her uniform?

Then she noticed there was a narrow closet in one corner of the room. If this place was like an American hospital, her clothes would be there. No need for a nurse's uniform.

She sat up slowly this time, giving her blood flow a chance to adjust. When she was fully upright, she peeled the tape off the back of her hand and extracted the IV needle. A drop of blood formed where it had been. One drop only. A good sign.

Finally, she swung her legs over the edge and stood, steadying herself until her vision cleared. *Okay, think.* Once she pulled off the monitor wires, alarms would sound. Nurses would come to check on her. She had to move fast.

To increase her circulation, she took deep breaths and, keeping a hand on the edge of the bed, did calf raises on the cold floor. Lifting, lowering. Lifting, lowering. That was better.

More confident now, she took a step toward the closet and felt the monitor wires tug. *Now or never.* She untied the smock's bow and, in one sweeping motion, tore off both smock and wires.

Three halting steps brought her to the closet. *Yes!* Her clothes were there. She snatched them out and, still a little shaky, hastened back to the bed. Jeans first, then socks and boots. Ignoring her bra and blood-soaked T-shirt, she slipped on the less-bloody sweater and picked up her jacket.

A nurse barged in, stopped short, then rushed up to her, cackling something Jade couldn't understand but could readily imagine—What are you doing? You can't do that, blah, blah, blah.

Jade put on her jacket.

"Madame, s'il vous plaît," the nurse pleaded, grasping her elbow.

Jade pushed her away. Thanks to adrenaline, she was beginning to feel normal again. She made her way out of the room and scanned the corridor. There. An illuminated sign with up-down arrows for an elevator. Tracing her fingers along the wall to steady herself, she walked to the elevator doors. As she punched "down," another nurse came at her, cackling like the first one. Jade fixed her with a back-off glare.

The bell dinged. The doors opened. A few minutes later, she was on the street, hailing a taxi.

From memory, she gave the address of her second hotel. Only when the cab had settled into traffic did she search her pockets for the cardkey. *Crap.* No cardkey for either hotel. And no cellphones. Someone—it had to be Lovel—had cleaned her out.

To make matters worse, she felt moisture at the sites of her two wounds. They were oozing. "Stop at a pharmacy," she told the driver.

Gauze, tape, antiseptic ointment, a large bottle of ibuprofen, all paid for with cash Lovel had apparently decided to leave in her jeans pocket. Her luck held at the hotel, also, where the man behind the desk remembered her and issued a new cardkey.

Upstairs in her room, after checking to be sure her passports and credit cards were still there and nothing had been disturbed, she stripped to the waist. The dressings, although slightly bloodstained, looked fresh, probably changed this morning. Speaking of which, what morning was this? Her watch would have told her, but she must have left it in the hospital. She called downstairs and learned today was December 26. Good. Only one night in the hospital.

No. Not good. Besides no watch, she had neither Lovel's dossier nor the book. If they'd been in her hospital room or that closet, she would have noticed them. Which meant Lovel must have grabbed them after she was shot. Her leverage was gone.

Along with her energy.

Giving in to mounting fatigue, she stretched out on the bed.

She'd screwed up big-time. No way should a gunman have been able to approach her from behind. Or from any direction. She'd been too focused on Lovel. A mistake then, but not now. Lovel owed her. She'd kept her part of the bargain, and he'd damn-well better keep his. The book for Control's name.

Not rested but close enough, Jade eased off the bed, wheeled her roller bag out of the closet, and opened it on the floor. Beneath a few changes of clothing lay her disassembled rifle and the viciously curved Karambit knife. That's what she would use on Control, the knife. Close up and personal. Carve out the eyes and shove them into his mouth, before slicing off his dick and watching him bleed to death.

She thumbed the razor-sharp blade.

But as she stood, a whoosh of dizziness swamped her like a giant wave. She staggered toward the bed on rubbery legs, couldn't make it, and quickly sat on the floor to keep from falling. Through hazy vision she saw fresh blood spreading under the bandage on her side. The one on her chest …

Darkness fell.

Chapter 26

Geoff hurled his glass at the wall. "God *damn* that stupid bitch!" He kicked the wooden coffee table, threw the cushions off the couch, and started to kick the table again but stopped. His toes hurt from the first time. If he hadn't already killed Jade, he'd rip her throat out right now. She stole the wrong damn book.

Turning back to one of his computer screens, he reread the messages. "Not what you said." "What is this?" "Scammer!!!" All these in response to the photos he'd posted to prove the book's validity.

He looked around for his drink, then remembered throwing it against the wall. Its remains lay on the floor in a glittering fan of glass shards and bourbon splatters. *Lord, please let me kill her again.*

After filling another glass, he picked up a seat cushion and back cushion, replaced them on the couch, and sank down to think. Dan had originally stolen the book. No way would he make a mistake, not if Astrid described it correctly. That was one thing you could count on with Dan—no mistakes.

He'd brought the book to Paris and, presumably on Astrid's instructions, had given it to a person in the Louvre. Jade had stolen it from that person, or thought she had. But clearly she'd blown it. Which meant the book was still somewhere in the museum. Somewhere within God-only-knew how many thousands of square feet. Unless.

Unless Dan had only *shown* it to someone in the Louvre, to confirm its authenticity or for some other reason, and had since sent it to Astrid. If that was the case, Astrid had it. Or soon would.

Geoff took a swallow of bourbon. He could catch the first flight back to Washington, call her, and arrange a meeting. *Hang on.* Why not call her from here? Confirm first that she had the book—the right book—*then* set up a meeting. That was better.

And Astrid would be much easier to neutralize than Jade.

#

It took all the skills she had honed over years of dealing with Third World officials for Astrid to suppress the anger boiling inside her. *Start with the positive and work from there.* "At least Martine is safe," she said to Christophe. "And so is the book."

"Then we're finished?" In the backseat of the car, as one of his men drove, Christophe placed a hand on hers. "No war or financial crisis in the Middle East?"

"Not so long as Martine has the book." She dropped the phone back in her purse. "But it's so frustrating not to know why I can't meet her now." Maddening was more like it. Sitting on pins and needles all this time, only to receive a call from her daughter saying, "Don't worry," but refusing to explain where she and Dan were or why they couldn't hand over the book "just yet."

And Dan wouldn't answer his phone, either. What was going on?

She glanced at the heads of the two men in front—the big one who had picked the lock to Leroux's apartment and searched the place thoroughly, and the smaller one who'd hacked into Leroux's computer and found nothing useful. She felt grateful for their efforts, and to Christophe for trying to help. But now the only thing she could do was wait. She hated it.

Her phone chirped. *Martine?*

"Astrid, this is Geoff."

"Who?"

"Geoff Fairchild," he said. "We had lunch in Washington when you asked me to contact Dan Lovel for you."

"Oh, Geoff. Yes, of course." The smooth talker with a zealous appetite for champagne and a rather handsy way of escorting her out to her car. She glanced ceilingward to let Christophe know she didn't want this call but had to take it.

After some useless chitchat, Geoff asked about the books she'd mentioned, whether Dan had managed to acquire them for her.

"Yes, he and Martine recovered them. They're here in Paris."

"You're in Paris?" He paused. "What a coincidence. So am I. Let's get together. I'd love to see the book. I mean, the books. And you."

Despite being thankful for Geoff's assistance, meeting him any time soon ranked just below getting a hip replacement. "I'm not sure."

"Who's Martine?" His words sounded a little slurred, as though he'd recently consumed a bottle of his beloved champagne.

"My daughter. Didn't I tell you?"

"I don't think so. But I'd like to meet her, as well."

"Can I call you back? I'm in the middle of something."

"Sure." He gave her his number. "I'll treat you both to a meal at the Tour d'Argent. And please bring the Bible book. I really would like to see it."

The Bible book? Why that one, when the Louvre books would be far more interesting to most people? And why leave Dan out of the dinner invitation? A creepy feeling slid up her back. "I'll call you."

When she'd pressed the End icon, Christophe asked, "Who is Geoff?"

"An official with the American Diplomatic Security Service. He put me in touch with the agent who saved my life, Dan Lovel. I told you about that. Dan is the one who's been accompanying Martine."

"Your white knight," Christophe said with a hint of envy. "And this Geoff fellow, what does he want?"

"I'm not really sure." She told him about the conversation, then added, "Does it strike you as strange? Aside from you and me, he is the only person who has seen the transcript of that interview with the Vatican librarian. He knows, or could figure out, how explosive the Moses book is. He calls it the Bible book. And now that it's in Paris, he just happens to be here also, *and* wants me to show him that specific book?" Something she had no intention of doing. "Plus, he didn't include Dan in his offer of dinner. That could have been an oversight, but he and Dan are supposedly friends."

"*Ma chérie*, I think you're imagining intrigue where there is none." Christophe gave her a patronizing smile, damn him. "But I'll be happy to place your mind at ease." He tapped a number on his phone and spoke with authority. "Give me everything we have on Geoff Fairchild, an official with the American DSS. Plus a former DSS agent named …" He turned to her. "Spell Dan's surname."

"Christophe, Dan is not an issue." But when he insisted, she spelled it. "And Geoff is with a G."

After conveying the information, he finished his call with, "Both of them Priority One. This number."

"You're wasting your time with Dan," she said. "But thank you with Geoff."

"It is best to know with whom we are dealing."

"*You* are not dealing with either of them."

He wrapped his hand around hers. "If you are, then I most certainly am."

Men. Such egos. So needful of appearing valorous. It was demeaning in a way, but sometimes useful. "If you want to help, I'm desperate for a shower and change of clothes. Could you take me to my house?"

He used his phone again and asked, "Any news from the Middle East?" After listening a moment, "If things escalate even a little, call me immediately." He re-pocketed his phone, told Astrid, "No change," and relayed her address to the burly fellow in the driver's seat.

Half an hour later, they crunched down her gravel driveway and stopped. Home. A three-story, nineteenth-century house surrounded by linden trees and horse chestnuts and with a back garden that sloped down to the Seine. The place was far too big for one person, but she loved it. Just being here relaxed her.

"Wait," Christophe said when she started to get out of the car. "Give me your key. I would like my men to check inside first."

"Christophe! I don't need—"

"You've been dealing with foreign agents, one of whom you don't trust and the other you can't reach."

"Didn't you just say I was seeing intrigue where there is none?"

"Humor me. It will only take five minutes."

She clamped her jaw. There was a boundary between valor and overprotectiveness. But exhaustion siphoned off her resistance.

After more like fifteen minutes, Christophe ushered her through her own front door like a welcoming butler.

The main reception room, with its Italian-modern furniture surrounded by original oak paneling, smelled stuffy from several months of disuse. She crossed to the far curtains and drew them aside to reveal the view that had sold her on this house, a sweeping panorama down the back lawn to where the Seine divided around île de Chatou, an island much loved by the Impressionists. Opening a pair of doors that led onto the patio and its stone balustrade, she breathed in the woody fragrances of nature on a winter afternoon. *My sanctuary.*

Finally, she turned back to Christophe. "I'm going up to shower."

"I could scrub your back," he offered.

Tempting but no, especially not with his two men in the house. "Another time, perhaps."

Upstairs, she treated herself to a long hot soak under the spray, then blow-dried her hair, brushed it out, and dressed in slacks and a cashmere sweater.

Returning to the main reception room, she found Christophe sitting on one of the white leather couches, his face pensive. "You've learned something?"

"Several things." He patted the cushion beside his and waited for her to sit. "Dan Lovel went off the grid six years ago. We have no information about him after that."

"Which tells you …?"

"He does not want to be found, which could mean he's doing things he shouldn't."

Extrapolating from nothing. "As I understand it, he now works for private clients, recovering stolen art and destroying counterfeits. His last job I know of, before this one, was blowing up counterfeit wine that a Sicilian mafioso was making. So it's not surprising he keeps a low profile. I expect there are powerful people who want him dead."

Christophe arched his eyebrows. "Would you like a job with the DGSE? We had nothing about his current activities."

"There's no reason they should interest you." *And I told you so.* "As for being 'off the grid,' that's why I had to contact him through his former boss, Geoff Fairchild."

"Ah, Mister Fairchild. He's a different story. Passed over for promotion twice before becoming a deputy director. Then four days ago, he arrives in Paris on a passport in one of his two known aliases." Christophe paused dramatically. "Neither of those aliases, nor anyone using his real name, has checked into a hotel."

"That's strange." Butterflies rose in her stomach.

"Yes and no. DSS has a safe house on Rue du Temple. That's probably where he's staying. The reason he's here, the ostensible reason, is that he's inspecting DSS facilities in several European countries."

The butterflies settled until it occurred to her, "Why do you say ostensible?"

"Because four days is a long time to conduct a routine examination of a two-bedroom apartment."

In an effort to keep the butterflies grounded, she asked, "Could he be using Paris as a base for visiting places like Belgium and Switzerland?"

"DSS does not have a safe house in Belgium, and there is no record of his having crossed into Switzerland or any other EU country."

"How would you know? Our borders are open."

"Believe me," he said, "we know who enters and leaves our country. I think Mister Fairchild is here for more than just an inspection."

Astrid bit the inside of her cheek. "I don't like it."

#

The Jardin des Plantes, France's national botanical garden, felt to Dan like a piece of paradise, a welcome refuge from the bustle and noise of Paris. It would also be an excellent place to take down Geoff. One spot in particular seemed ideal, a gazebo called the

Gloriette de Bufon, located within a shrub-lined labyrinth near the western end of the seventy-odd acres.

"The problem," he said as he and Martine left the garden through a pair of big iron gates, "is that the whole place closes at five-thirty."

"Did you imagine he would come here after dark? I doubt it."

"You're probably right. We'll set up a meeting for tomorrow morning."

They crossed a main street and walked back toward Paulette's house, twenty minutes away. When they reached the small plaza called Place de la Contrescarpe, Martine stopped. "The smells of these restaurants are making my mouth water."

His, too. With little effort, he picked out aromas of cassoulet, escargot, and roasting lamb. Hunching his shoulders against the cold breeze, he said, "Let's bring Paulette back here for dinner."

"Or maybe down Rue Mouffetard." She pointed at the street on the other side of the plaza. "Hemingway lived at the bottom of that road. Paulette loves his writing. And they have even better restaurants than here."

"Deal. But first, we need to call Geoff. Or rather, Jade needs to send him a text."

They had climbed steadily uphill since the Jardin des Plantes and continued climbing now, along narrow streets flanked by shops, apartment buildings, a school, and a few more restaurants. Just before Rue Saint-Jacques they descended toward Paulette's house along a slippery cobblestone sidewalk, Dan thankful that he and Martine were wearing good boots.

They found Paulette standing before a large blank canvas, a glass of white wine in her hand. While Martine apologized for disturbing her and Paulette shrugged it off, Dan wondered what it must be like for a blind artist to contemplate a work she hadn't yet started and would never see.

Paulette poured glasses for Martine and himself, then accepted their offer of dinner. After they'd all chatted about Hemingway and which restaurants he might have frequented as a starving writer, Dan said, "I want to replenish some of the wine you've given us."

"No, no. You brought a lovely one last night."

"I insist. Martine would you help me choose?"

Paulette protested again but finally turned up her hands.

At the wine shop, Dan purchased two bottles of a better-than-average Saint-Émilion. Carrying the bottles in a plastic bag, he waited for a break in traffic, then hustled Martine across Rue Saint-Jacques to the forecourt of the Panthéon, where the stink of diesel exhaust and the honking of horns were a little more distant.

"Can you take this?" he asked, holding out the bag to Martine. "I'll need both thumbs."

"I want to see what you write before you send it. Jade had a distinctive style."

He knew that and had been composing as they walked. Using the burner phone Martine had found in Jade's pocket, the one that wasn't Jade's, he typed,

You fucked up, asshole. I was wearing a vest.
If you want your book, deposit my $ and meet me tomorrow 0900.
Gloriette de bufon in jardin des plantes

"Take out the commas and the final period," Martine said. "Jade doesn't punctuate."

"Good catch." When he'd done it, Martine nodded her approval, and he sent the text.

Three minutes passed before they received,

Who is this?

-

Your nightmare. Remember

Whoever you are, you have nothing I want.

Dan turned to Martine. "At this point, Jade would call his bluff."

"What's her ace in the hole?"

He typed,

Then I burn your book

"That's good," she said, and he touched Send.

\#

It couldn't be Jade. Jade was dead.

Unless she *had* been wearing a vest. Geoff slammed his palm on the desktop. "Son of a bitch!"

He booted the program that monitored cell phone locations. Colin's phone was flashing in front of the Panthéon. Jade had used that phone before. But no way could she have the book. Astrid's daughter, Martine, had it. He typed,

Go ahead.

It was then he noticed a call made four hours previously. Martine's phone, which had been dead for days. The call came from a building on Rue Saint-Jacques. *Rue Saint-Jacques?* He peered more closely at the screen, willing his vision to sharpen. Yes. The sidewalk in front of that building was exactly where he'd shot Jade. *And* it was just a few hundred yards from where Jade, or someone impersonating her, now texted,

Last chance

Were Jade and Martine in this together? Maybe this so-called "Jade" *was* Martine. Or Dan. If Martine was holed-up in that building, which looked like an apartment building on the screen, Dan was probably there with her. If Jade was still alive, Dan could be with both of them. If, if, if.

Geoff sat heavily on the desk chair, wishing now that he hadn't polished off half a bottle of bourbon. But even a sheet or two to the wind, he could outmaneuver Dan—and certainly Jade if she was working alone.

So ... one target or three?

Plan for three. The pieces fit. Martine had used her phone in that building. The door to the building had been slightly open when he shot Jade. And Dan could have been the dark figure cowering behind it.

Another text flashed on the screen. Geoff stared at it in shock.

The safe house's address.

He rushed to the blinds and drew them closed. Jade, according to her reputation, was an expert marksman, and if she knew where he was, she probably knew also that the windows weren't bulletproof. How in the world did she— Never mind. This changed things.

Man, he could use another drink. But not yet.

Think it through. Jade might have the advantage but— No. In fact, she didn't. She would never shoot him, because a dead man couldn't deposit the money she demanded.

Stalemate.

Then it struck him. Not a stalemate, either. The advantage was actually his. He knew, or was pretty sure, where Jade was, also. All he had to do was agree to her meeting, then stake out that big wooden door in front of the apartment building. When she or Dan came out, follow them to some convenient spot and kill them. If they had the book, take it. If they didn't, go back to the door, wait for someone else to open it, and slip inside. A few questions to other residents would disclose which apartment Martine had been staying in. Pick the lock, find the book, and he was home free.

The problem was, he didn't know what Martine looked like. He wouldn't need to know if Dan or Jade came out with the book. But if neither of them had it, he'd have to describe Martine to other residents to find her apartment. Maybe: "Recently arrived French woman, possibly with an American man." Could work. In the meantime, he'd do an internet search on Astrid's daughter.

You are the man. Adapt to change and capitalize on it.

Plus, there was still the chance that Astrid would accept his invitation to the Tour d'Argent and bring the book, with or without Martine. That would be the easiest solution of all. In any event, he had all bases covered.

Grinning, he typed,

OK. Tomorrow at 0900.

Chapter 27

Dan shut off the phone he and Martine had been using. "This won't work."

"Why not?" she asked. "He took a long time before agreeing to meet. I think he weighed his choices and decided this was the best."

"Geoff is impetuous. He makes snap decisions, often the wrong ones." Dan turned up his collar. Darkness had fallen, along with the temperature. He smelled snow in the offing. "But he's also shrewd. Taking that long to answer tells me he was working on a trap."

"I don't see how he could trap us if we get to the Jardin the minute it opens."

"He could pick us off at the entrance."

"That doesn't make sense." Turning up her own collar, she started back toward Rue Saint-Jacques. "He's expecting Jade, not us."

"But if he sees *me*—"

"There are several entrances to the garden. He can't watch all of them."

"My brain agrees with you. The odds are in our favor. But my gut says don't do it." They paused at the curb. "It was a bad idea. I apologize."

Instead of taking a jab at him for admitting another failure, Martine nudged his shoulder with hers in a "pals" sort of way. "I bet we scared the crap out of him with the address of the safe house. That has to be worth something."

Dan grinned at the memory, then jogged across with her through a break in traffic. "If nothing else, it's worth that." On the other hand, it would definitely make Geoff more cautious, which did them no good.

As they walked along the street, Dan noticed the chocolate shop and stopped. "Does Paulette like chocolates?"

"Who doesn't?"

"Let's buy her some."

Martine helped him choose four kinds of truffles—grenache, hazelnut, clotted cream, and one spiced with hot pepper. Outside, she looped her arm through his.

Nudging his shoulder had been one thing, her arm through his seemed like something more. But she had flirted briefly on other occasions, then turned it off as quickly as she'd turned it on. He chalked it up to bouts of playfulness. Nothing else.

By the time they reached Paulette's door, snow was falling. They found her ready to brave the elements in jeans, a thick sweater, and calf-high boots.

"I hope you like Saint-Émilion," Martine said as Dan carried the bottles into the kitchen.

"Very much."

"And chocolates?" She placed the gold-colored box in Paulette's hand.

"*Absolument.* Especially with red wine."

They ate one of each kind between sips from their glasses.

"They are all delicious," Paulette said. "But my favorite is the one with hot pepper. It is new for me."

Dan liked it best, also. "I believe it originates in South America."

"Vive l'Amérique du Sud."

Saving the rest of the chocolates and the remainder of that bottle for later, they set out for the restaurant. He held Paulette's hand as her white cane clacked back and forth over the uneven stone sidewalks now wet from snow. Martine walked a few paces ahead, alerting Paulette to potential stumbling points.

"I do not need help," Paulette insisted several times. But she kept hold of Dan's hand.

Finally, they turned onto Rue Mouffetard, where they made their way past closed shops and fast-food joints to the place Paulette had chosen, a bistro Hemingway had supposedly frequented. Through the windows it looked like a working-class establishment, with brick walls, straight-backed wooden chairs, and no tablecloths. Patrons occupied about two-thirds of the seats, a good sign on a frigid night when most people would stay home.

The warm air inside greeted them with mouthwatering aromas of roast pork, sautéed onions, fresh bread, and sausages. Having eaten nothing since his and Martine's "millionaire breakfast" this morning, Dan couldn't wait to dig in.

Like a lot of older restaurants, this one was long and narrow, with a row of tables along each wall and a third row down the center. A waiter parked them at a table midway back against one wall, where Dan took a seat facing the door and opposite Martine and Paulette. Black-and-white photos dotted the walls, portraying people and local street scenes from the pre-war twentieth century. He searched in vain for a picture of Hemingway.

From the surprisingly extensive wine list, Dan chose a Cahors. Called "black wine" in medieval times, it was essentially a Malbec and should go well with hearty food. When the waiter opened the bottle and poured him the obligatory sample, he wasn't disappointed. The women liked it, also.

"*Mes dames, monsieur.*" Their waiter handed out menus.

"Shall I read for you?" Dan asked Paulette.

Martine shook her head silently, indicating Paulette could fend for herself.

"There is no need," Paulette said. "If they do not have what I want, they will suggest … *alternatives?* I think it is the same word in English."

In the end, she asked for chicken livers in a mustard-cream sauce, which, despite not being on the menu, the waiter declared an excellent choice. Martine selected mushrooms topped with melted Gruyere cheese, followed by duck breast in a green peppercorn sauce. Dan chose escargot to start, then a burgundy-braised pork shank over orzo.

Settling back, he was glad he and Martine had already given Paulette a sanitized version of their activities today. That left them all free to simply enjoy a good meal together.

He was about to toast Papa Hemingway when the door opened and— *What the hell?*

Geoff Fairchild?

Dan gripped the Glock in his jacket pocket. Without taking his eyes off Geoff, he mentally reviewed the "playing field." Not good. There was one public door and probably a second door in the back for employees. The wooden tables could provide cover if overturned. But the place was crowded. On entering he'd noted twenty-five people, counting waiters. All were potential witnesses— or potential victims.

Martine and Paulette made it even worse. He'd do anything necessary to protect them, which put him at a disadvantage.

He had to play this smoothly.

"What's the matter?" Martine asked, evidently seeing a change in Dan's expression.

"We have company. No, don't turn around. It's Geoff. Listen to me closely. You do *not* know who he is. Neither do you, Paulette. I know him but did not know he was in Paris. Have we got that straight? Just stay calm."

Martine leaned closer to Paulette. *"Ce Geoff, il est très dangereux."*

Dan switched his gaze from Martine's concern and Paulette's shock to Geoff's phony surprise as he spotted them.

He was stylishly decked out in the same wool-and-cashmere overcoat he'd worn at the zoo in Washington. But his trousers were uncharacteristically wrinkled, as if he'd slept in them. Stress? If so, that was definitely bad. Geoff under stress often did rash things, some of which shed blood.

Well, not tonight, pal.

Ready for anything, Dan raised his hand in a beckoning gesture. At the same time, he released his hold on the Glock. Gunfire in a crowded restaurant was far too risky. In the event of violence, he'd have to handle it some other way.

Unfortunately, he had taken the chair by the wall, a routine precaution against someone coming up behind him. That choice was now a handicap. Geoff, who'd obviously planned this encounter, would take the one vacant chair at their table. Which boxed in Dan against the wall. And it was too late to change seats without looking suspicious.

As much for himself as for Martine and Paulette, he repeated, "Stay calm."

When Geoff, grinning like a lottery winner, fronted up to their table, Dan rose and said, "What a surprise. I had no idea you were in Paris. What brings you here?"

"Business." He glanced at Martine and Paulette before lowering his voice. "Checking on facilities."

By which he could only mean the safe house, where he evidently wasn't getting much rest. The corners of his eyes were bloodshot. His face sprouted at least a day's worth of dark stubble. His speech wasn't slurred, but his breath stank of bourbon. Despite putting up a cheerful front, the creep was frazzled. Which made him even more unpredictable than usual.

"Well, it's a happy coincidence," Dan said, "that we both picked the same restaurant. Let me introduce two friends of mine, Paulette and Martine. Care to join us?"

"I'd love to." He extended a hand toward Paulette. "I'm Geoff Fairchild. Dan and I used to work together."

It took a moment before she apparently realized Geoff was speaking to her. She held out her hand. *"Enchanté, monsieur."*

After shaking hands with both women, he shed his overcoat and took the empty seat at Dan's left.

The waiter brought a fourth glass, poured from the wine bottle on their table, and handed Geoff a menu. He then said something in French.

"He will hang your coat for you," Martine translated.

"No need." Geoff draped it over the back of his chair, a transparent sign that the tailored pockets held one or more weapons the guy wanted to keep close. After knocking back a slug of wine, he pinched the sleeve of Dan's leather jacket. "Are you cold? It seems warm in here to me."

The fool was trying to get him to take off his jacket, the same neutralizing tactic Dan had used with Jade last night. But in this case, the comment also provided an opportunity for Dan to throw him off his game.

"I always wear a jacket. It's where I keep my Skorpion."

Geoff froze, his mouth slightly open. Clearly, he understood Skorpion to mean a Czech vz.61, the pistol-sized sub-machinegun once favored by East Bloc operatives.

Having set the hook, Dan gave him a good-humored smile to let out some slack.

Geoff broke into a nervous grin. "You almost had me there."

Tug a little. "Wanna see it?" For three full seconds, he enjoyed the uncertainty clouding Geoff's face. Then he played out more line. "Just joking. What are you going to have? We've already ordered."

After a moment of hesitation, Geoff picked up the menu and perused it between oblique glances at Dan. The guy's hands were steady, a credit to him, but the whiteness in his thumbnails showed how tightly he held the menu and how tightly he remained wound.

As Geoff read, Martine whispered something in Paulette's ear. Paulette nodded and silently unfolded her cane. Dan wondered if they were going to leave, until Martine slipped her knife off the table and into her lap. *Oh, hell no.* Both women were preparing for a fight. He scowled and shook his head.

Top priority was concluding this evening without incident. As Sun Tzu wrote twenty-five hundred years ago, "A battle avoided cannot be lost."

As a last resort, if things did go sideways, he'd crush Geoff's trachea and claim the guy was choking on his food.

When their waiter reappeared, Geoff ordered the house pâté and entrecôte, then slipped again into charming mode with a big smile at Martine. "Are you, by any chance, Astrid Desmarais' daughter?"

Her eyes widened. "How did you know?"

"She mentioned her daughter's name is Martine."

"You've spoken with her?"

"I'm the one who put her in touch with Dan. She told me just today that you two had obtained the books she was … concerned about. Congratulations."

Whoa. Geoff and Astrid—today? Dan logged that revelation with a sinking feeling. For the second time in twenty-four hours, he wondered if those two were in this together. Probing for clarification, he said, "I didn't know you and Astrid were still in contact."

Aside from a quick smirk, Geoff ignored him and returned to Martine. "She's really looking forward to receiving them. The books. But I gather you still have them."

That was big news. It confirmed not only that Geoff knew he had the wrong book, but also that his agreement to meet "Jade" at the botanical garden was, indeed, a trap. Most important, since he was focusing on Martine, it meant that *she* was now Geoff's target.

The bastard knew too much. On top of that, he was much more on-the-ball than Dan's nasal Breathalyzer suggested he should be. The Skorpion ruse would gain little in this situation. Dan needed something else.

"The books are being analyzed," Martine said.

"Analyzed?" Geoff squinted at her.

"By an expert at the Louvre."

Yes. Martine, whose innocent expression revealed nothing, had come to the rescue.

Although Geoff's face darkened, he kept a casual tone. "How long will that take?"

"Hard to say," Dan interjected. "You know how scholars are." Nothing like vague timing to muddy up plans.

Arrival of their appetizers paused the conversation. Geoff, who probably hadn't bothered with food between glasses of whiskey, sampled his pâté, then devoured it like a famished animal. When his plate was clean, he switched again to charming mode. "Nothing for you, Paulette? The pâté is delicious."

"She's a model," Dan lied, loathe to disclose anything personal about her. "Girlish figure and all that."

"How interesting." Geoff cast her a reappraising eye. "High fashion?"

She smiled sweetly. "I pose nude for artists."

Dan almost choked. What a pixie.

Geoff gaped but quickly recovered, his gaze running over her anew. "I don't think I've ever met a nude model before."

"Take an art class," she murmured as sweetly as she had smiled.

Geoff finally tore his stare from Paulette's chest and fixed it again on Martine. "We were talking about the books you and Dan acquired. Your mother said they were old and very important. I'd love to see them. I'm interested in old books."

About as much you're interested in how to conjugate Latin verbs. Dan forked in his last escargot. "They're just an inventory of the Louvre's collections in the eighteen hundreds."

"Oh?" Geoff swung his head around to face him. "I thought there was also a book from the Bible."

"That one," Dan said, "was probably a waste of time. The expert in the Louvre thinks it's phony."

"What?" Geoff frowned. "Why would he think that?"

"Something about the linguistics," Martine said.

Perfect. Dan followed her lead with exaggerations of Leroux's early comments. "Seems a lot of the words and phrases don't fit the book's supposed age. The expert thinks it might have been written by some crackpot hundreds of years later. Like I said, a waste of our effort."

The waiter returned with their main courses and asked whether they wanted another bottle of wine.

"Oui," Dan told him in hopes that more alcohol would blunt Geoff's acumen. So far, the bastard was managing to stay sharp. His sour expression testified to that.

For a while, they ate in silence. Paulette seemed as pleased with her chicken livers as Martine did with her duck breast. Between bites of pork shank, Dan kept his eyes on Geoff's hands, one of which now clutched a sharply pointed steak knife. There was really no reason for him to use it —if there ever had been. But Geoff was harder to read when he wasn't speaking.

To reboot some semblance of a convivial conversation, Dan asked him, "How long are you in Paris?"

"I'll be in and out, off and on." He took a sip of wine. "You?"

"Depends on the man at the Louvre."

"Then you're giving the book to Astrid, right?"

"Books, plural."

"That's what I meant." Geoff cut off another bite of his entrecôte. "Where will you meet her? I'd like to join you."

"I don't know where. It'll be up to her."

Expanding on Dan's intentional ambiguity, Martine offered, "She may want us to give them to her back in Washington, or come see them in the Louvre, or who knows? My mother is always changing her mind."

Although Geoff had swallowed his most recent bite of steak, his jaw muscles kept working. From Dan's perspective, they looked like writhing larvae under his stubbled cheek. Gratifying in one way, but mounting frustration in a man like Geoff had to be stopped.

To change subjects, Dan said, "Paulette, are you still interested in learning how to ski? I've read there are some resorts in the French Alps that have great beginners' slopes. Martine and I could take you there."

"I would love that. But you must hold my hand."

"I'd be happy to." Dan leaned closer to Geoff. "She's blind, in case you hadn't noticed."

"I noticed."

"Do you ski?" Dan asked him.

"Black slopes." The words came out as a challenge.

"That's way better than me." And clearly his attempt to defuse Geoff's frustration wasn't working. Best to just call it quits. "Does anyone want dessert? I don't have room for it."

"Neither do I," Martine said. "Not even coffee."

Paulette shook her head.

"Geoff?" Dan pointedly laid his napkin on the table.

"I guess not."

"Well, it was great seeing you." Dan pushed his chair back. "I'll pay the check."

With no move to get up, Geoff said, "Where are you staying?"

"A hotel near the Sorbonne. Why?"

"Just wondering."

Their waiter rushed up. *"Dessert, monsieur? Café?"*

Paulette spoke with him in French that Dan couldn't understand except for *l'addition s'il vous plaît.* The bill, please.

When it came, Dan laid two hundred euros on top of it.

Martine and Paulette rose from their chairs.

Geoff didn't move. Instead, he glared at Dan. "You know, I got you this job. I'd think you would be grateful enough to show me the fruits of your labors."

Uh-oh. The guilt thing was sometimes a desperate person's last effort before getting violent. With one eye on Geoff's trachea, Dan said, "The books? I'd gladly show you, but I don't have them. My best advice is to stay in touch with Astrid. Now, if you can let me past, I need to take the ladies home."

Geoff rose and stepped back from the table. "Let's grab a taxi together."

No way. What Dan really wanted was to put the women in a cab, hang back out of sight, and disable this son of a bitch the moment he came out.

Suddenly Martine bent over, clutching her stomach.

"What's wrong?" Dan rushed around to her. "Martine?" Had Geoff somehow poisoned her?

She gulped air. "I think I'm going to throw up."

"We need to get her to a doctor."

Paulette called for their waiter and spoke rapidly. "Five minutes," she told them as the waiter rushed away, no doubt horrified that other patrons might think Martine's distress came from the restaurant's food.

If Martine had been poisoned, five minutes might be too long. He'd have to force her to vomit with a modified Heimlich.

"Oh, God, here it comes." She made gurgling sounds.

As the three of them rushed out of the restaurant, Dan looked back to see Geoff still standing by their table. *If you did this, I'll rip your fucking heart out with my bare hands.*

On the sidewalk, Martine still held her stomach but looked less distressed. Maybe the cold air helped.

Dan kept his arm around her, ready to perform the Heimlich if her legs weakened or she showed any other sign of a worsening condition.

When their cab arrived, after only two minutes, he eased Martine into the back seat and slid in after her while Paulette climbed in the front and said something to the driver.

In seconds, they were jouncing down the cobblestone street.

Martine sat upright and peered out the rear window. "We made it."

Huh? Dan stared at her. "You're feeling better?"

"*Tu étais excellent.*" Paulette said.

"*Merci.*" To Dan, Martine explained, "I figured Geoff wouldn't want to sit next to a person about to throw up."

Dan slumped with relief at the belated realization that she'd faked the whole thing. *Jesus, girl, don't do that to me again.* As their cab slowed to round a corner, he looked back out the window.

"Still not following us?" Martine asked.

"Not yet."

In the front passenger's seat, Paulette turned to them. "It will be difficult for him. I said to the waiter ..." She switched to French.

"Bravo," Martine exclaimed. "She told our waiter that, if Geoff asks for a taxi, to say yes but not to call one."

More like brilliant. Thanking his lucky stars for two colleagues who could pull off a con like that without his even noticing, he reached forward and squeezed Paulette's shoulder. "Bravo, indeed."

She smiled, then frowned. "He is the man who shot that woman last night?"

"Yes," Dan said.

"How did he find us?"

That was a very good question. "All I can imagine is that he followed us from your building."

Paulette's eyebrows shot up above her black glasses. "How can he know where I live?"

"I'm not sure." But he *was* sure that Paulette now was also in danger. Which made his palms sweat. He looked at the talented blonde Parisian who'd become his friend. Even more than before, he had to protect her. But he couldn't be with her all the time. And if Geoff could take down a professional like Jade, what chance did a blind woman stand?

Chapter 28

Given any choice, Jade would never have eaten at an Indian restaurant. The pungent stink of curry almost made her throat seize. But she needed food, and this place had a clear view of the spot where she'd been shot last night and of the apartment building where Lovel and his girlfriend were staying.

Seated by the front window, she picked at her plate of plain rice, alternating every few bites with a spoonful of yogurt. The waiter, a thin guy with a pockmarked face that she attributed to childhood smallpox in the "old country," had put on a hangdog expression when that was all she ordered. But they were the only two items on the menu she thought she could keep down.

At 9:30, he returned to tell her they would close soon. *Screw them.* They could wait until she'd finished. Or until Lovel came out of that door or approached it to go in.

If the restaurant did close on her, she'd have to come back tomorrow morning and lurk somewhere. A crappy prospect, given the snow now falling in earnest. Even crappier was the waning effectiveness of the six ibuprofens she'd taken in her hotel room and her failure to bring more with her. Despite having wrapped her wounds in pressure bandages, they hurt with each breath she took.

She was about to force down another mouthful of rice when a taxi pulled up across the street. As she zeroed in on it, Lovel and his girlfriend climbed out, along with a second woman who'd been sitting in front.

Jade slapped ten euros on the table and dashed outside.

"Lovel!" she called as she hurried across the street. "I need to talk to you."

His mouth literally fell open. "Jade?"

Chugging up to him, she saw that the woman from the front seat carried a white cane and wore black glasses. Interesting, but as irrelevant as Lovel's girlfriend. "You owe me. I'm here to collect."

"What the hell are you doing out of the hospital?"

"Tell me Control's name and where he is."

As the cab drove off, Lovel glanced around anxiously. "Come inside."

"Blow me. We made a deal. I want a name and address. Now!"

"You need more information than that, and out here is not the place. He could be coming any minute. And he's armed."

"Don't try to play me." Drawing her knife, she stepped behind the girlfriend.

Lovel pulled her pistol from his pocket and aimed it between her eyes. "You're not faster than a bullet."

"You willing to gamble on that?" Gripping the girlfriend's chin, Jade pressed her blade to the exposed throat. "I don't have all night."

"You sure don't." He took the blind woman's hand, drew her to the big wooden door, and punched the code panel at the side. "Martine, come with us. She won't hurt you."

"Wanna bet?" Jade spat.

"Listen to me. We just left the guy you want. He's pissed off and probably heading here as we speak. You want to get shot again?"

"He's not kidding," the girlfriend, Martine, said with a level of calm that took bigger ovaries than Jade had expected.

Without releasing her, Jade scanned the street. A couple walking in the distance but no traffic. Across the road, someone in the Indian restaurant flipped the sign in the window to *Fermé*/Closed.

"Get in here, dammit," Lovel called from his building's open door.

Fuck. Lowering her knife, she pushed Martine toward him.

The moment they were all inside, Lovel poked his head back out, turned it left, right, left, and shut the door. Then he whirled on her. "Why aren't you in the hospital? They spent hours working on you. You're lucky to be alive."

She'd wondered before but now felt certain. "You took me there?"

"An ambulance did."

"But Dan and I were in the hospital with you," Martine said. "Until almost midnight."

"We should go in my house." The blind woman spoke in a soft French accent, seemingly unperturbed by all the talk of gunshots and hospitals. She turned her jet-black glasses toward Jade. "It is freezing out here, and you must be tired."

Don't remind me. Only adrenaline kept her going, and her wounds now hurt like hell. Plus, she was clearly off her game if neither Lovel nor Martine had been intimidated by her knife. She closed it and put it back in her pocket.

Still, she was in no mood to sit by a fire and do the tea-and-crumpets thing. "You got your book. So just give me the bastard's name and location, and I'll be out of your lives."

"If you mean the book you had when he shot you, you're wrong. It wasn't the book he wanted, and he knows it. At least now he does."

"Bullshit."

Lovel shook his head slowly. "Sorry to say, you got shot for nothing."

Was he trying to renege on their deal? "Do not screw with me. You *owe* me a name."

"She's right." Martine turned to Lovel. "Either you tell her, or I will."

"Would you let me handle this?" Lovel's strained tone betrayed rising frustration.

"I agree with Martine," the blind woman said.

Lovel visibly ground his teeth.

Good. He was losing and knew it. *So let's get this over with.* Snow flurries swirled down in the courtyard, and she was starting to shiver.

Martine turned to face her. "His name is Geoff Fairchild."

"God dammit!" Lovel growled.

Ignoring his outburst, Martine said, "He's staying at a U.S. government safe house on Rue du Temple in the Third Arrondissement," and gave the address and apartment number.

Lovel shouldered her aside. "Jade, don't do it."

"He means be careful," Martine said. "There are surveillance cameras at the street entrance and on his door."

"Listen to me!" With fire in his eyes, Lovel planted himself so close that Jade could smell the wine on his breath. "The place is a fortress. There's no way to get in. You need to let me do this."

Jade stepped around him and faced Martine. "If you ever need heavyweight help, just search LinkedIn for Alternative Conflict Resolution." With that, she shot Lovel a scowl and left.

#

Still fuming that he'd had to tramp half an hour through four inches of snow, Geoff finally reached the Mercedes he'd parked a block from the apartment building where he had spotted Dan exiting with two women. Trailing them unseen to the restaurant had been a piece of cake. He was a pro at that sort of thing, a damn-sight better than Dan ever was. But slogging back was a bone-chilling pain in the ass.

Someone had stuck a piece of paper under one of his windshield wipers. A parking ticket? *It's nighttime. No one needs a loading zone at night.* He tossed it on the ground, climbed in, and fired up the engine to get the heater going.

What a wasted evening. All he'd learned, aside from the fact that Dan no longer trusted him—big deal—was that the book was somewhere in the Louvre. Even that could be bullshit, like Dan's Skorpion probably was.

He hoped Martine had barfed her guts out all over him.

As the car's blower began delivering warm air, Geoff cheered himself with the one confirmation he'd heard. The book ultimately, maybe soon, would be given to Astrid. All he had to do was get close to her and stay close until she received it. When that happened, he'd restart the auction and post photos of the book. No. He'd restart the auction tonight, with a money-back guarantee that the book proved God had disallowed all Jewish claims to the Holy Land. That's what Astrid had told him, and she had no reason to lie. In fact— *Wait.*

He rubbed his eyes. Was that possible? He turned on his windshield wipers to clear the view. It *was* her. Jade was alive and coming out of the same apartment building where he'd started tracking Dan and his two bitches. All of them were in this together.

He withdrew the .45 caliber Springfield pistol from his coat pocket. But uncertainty stopped him from putting the car in gear. He had failed to kill her in his drive-by attempt last night, and that was with an Uzi. If he failed in a second drive-by, he might never get another chance. Besides that, his vision was a little hazy. As Jade turned the corner up ahead, he laid the pistol on the seat beside him and rubbed his eyes again. Too much wine. He should stick to bourbon.

Better to drive to her hotel and wait for her inside. He had another pistol in the trunk, with a silencer. Two shots to the chest, two to the head when she was down, and he'd be out the door before a desk clerk realized what was happening. Clean and sweet.

With a smile, he re-pocketed the Springfield and put the car in gear.

At Jade's hotel, the one she'd come out of, he found the lobby empty and told the girl behind the counter he was waiting for a guest. Before she could respond, he walked to one of the armchairs and angled it toward a window that gave a reflected view of the entrance.

Unlike a lot of hotel chairs, this one was actually comfortable. Very comfortable.

#

Dan made no progress in his attempt to sway Martine and Paulette. Both of them steadfastly maintained that letting Jade handle Geoff was the right thing to do.

As he watched them climb the stairs, Martine's parting shot reverberated in his ears. "Let her do the dirty work. Our job is to deliver the book to my mother."

Not that he had a choice anymore. Jade knew where Geoff was staying. She had a sniper rifle. The guy was as good as dead.

Wishing he had a cigar, Dan walked out onto Paulette's deck, now blanketed in five inches of snow with more falling. Did it really make a difference who pulled the trigger? Maybe not, so long as it happened before Geoff shot anyone else in his determination to possess that book.

Dan turned up his face to the falling flakes. The night air was still. Most of the windows around him were dark, the untroubled snug in their beds. He envied them. They'd never had to accustom themselves to killing other people. Sure, they saw it in movies and cheered when the good guy won. What they didn't see was that, despite the morality of the act, the good guy suffered also. A piece of his soul died with the villain.

So let Jade do it. After his years in the DSS, Dan's soul had been whittled away enough.

His job now, besides protecting Martine and Paulette, was making sure that book did not fall into the wrong hands. Even in the "right" hands, it could have tragic consequences. Just look at how it had affected Leroux, reducing the scholar to a blubbering husk of his former self.

It was almost like a curse.

Dan kicked the snow in front of him. If he'd somehow been able to foresee all this, he would have left the damned thing in that monastery, locked up among the other "forbidden" books.

Maybe that was the answer—not chancing another visit to the monastery, but reburying the book. Or more precisely, drowning it. The Seine lay just down the hill from where he stood. If the book vanished, its curse would vanish with it. Or almost. Jade would still hunt down Geoff. But there'd be no deaths after that. No more violence. It was the nearest thing he could do to rolling the clock back two weeks.

Dan went into the house, retrieved the book, and left. Clutching it in one hand, he made his way down the snow-slickened sidewalk, past darkened shops, past the Panthéon and Sorbonne, to the bridge that crossed over to Notre Dame.

The lit-up cathedral soared majestically skyward through flurries of snow, a beacon for the faithful much grander than the monastery in Prague. Although not religious, he felt it somehow appropriate that the book, once removed from a place of God, should return to the elements before another place of God.

He brushed snow off a foot-wide section of the balustrade, put the book in its place, and eased it forward until it teetered on the edge. Half an inch more and it would be gone.

But an unnerving sense of trespassing on forbidden ground stayed his hand. Did he have the right to do this? Cursed or not, holy or not, the book was a unique source of knowledge, priceless knowledge according to Leroux. Dan shut his eyes. The very idea of destroying knowledge grated like a rasp on his conscience.

An arctic gust struck him. The book wobbled. He slapped his hand on top of it.

"Shit."

He drew the book back. He wasn't sure what he would do with it, but it was not going in the river.

#

After spending more time than she should have, checking out the address Martine had given her, Jade decided the rooftop across from Fairchild's building offered the best vantage point for a shot through his windows. It would be her fallback. Her first choice remained the knife, if she could find any way to use it.

Although successful, her recon had drained her. Suck it up, she told herself. Some sleep and a mouthful of pain killers would put her right. But it was late now, the streets deserted. She searched in vain for a cab and finally slogged back through ankle-deep snow toward her hotel. The bullet holes in her hurt so bad she almost couldn't stand it. Twice she scooped up handfuls of snow to numb them. The relief was temporary at best.

At last in her hotel lobby, she instantly noticed a man snoring—or rather the back of his head—in an armchair angled away from the door. She glanced at the desk clerk, who shrugged. With a shrug of her own, she headed for the elevator.

Upstairs in her room, she popped open the bottle of ibuprofen she'd left on the bathroom sink and downed eight tablets. While waiting for them to work, she turned on the faucets in the tub, then stripped and examined her bandages. No visible blood, until she peeled off the tape. The rolls of gauze she'd used to put pressure on each wound were stained with yellow, as well as red. From Ranger training, she was pretty sure that was okay.

Relieved, she slipped gingerly into the hot bath. Her wounds screamed, but she slowly submerged herself up to the neck.

A shot through Geoff Fairchild's window wouldn't be half as gratifying as taking him down with the knife. Could she lure him out of his fortress? Maybe. Unfortunately, she didn't have a good idea of what he looked like. She'd only glimpsed him from afar, that morning at the zoo in Washington. Tall, slender build, medium-brown hair graying at the temples. All good if you wanted to blend in, but not much help to her.

On the other hand, like Lovel, he had constantly checked his surroundings as he approached the gorilla house. That behavior was typical of people in the business of covert operations. No effort at subtlety could completely hide it. If he did come out, it would confirm his identity.

Shutting her eyes, she played out their encounter. She would walk up from behind and plunge her knife into his kidney. Support him as he fell. Let him down gently while she sawed through his spine, leaned close, and whispered, "You fucked with the wrong chick."

Chapter 29

Images of pandemonium on the floor of the New York Stock Exchange woke Astrid with a jolt.

Just a nightmare, she realized as she lay there breathing heavily. Still, she couldn't shake off the scene. Stock symbols turning from green to red at lightning speed, share prices plummeting, traders clutching their heads like the man in Munch's *The Scream*. All happening before the computers could halt trading.

Which was impossible, of course. The computers *would* halt trading. They were designed specifically to prevent panic sell-offs. But the NYSE was only one of sixty major exchanges around the world. On most of the others, prices would drop through the floor. Trillions of dollars would be wiped off the books, companies would collapse, countries would go bankrupt.

Not to mention the human consequences. Food and medicines running out because there was no money to replenish supplies. Riots in the streets. The hollow eyes and fly-covered faces of the starving. Always it was the powerless who suffered worst.

Her heart pounded so hard it hurt.

"Are you okay?" Christophe asked, rolling over to face her.

The spell broke. As her anxiety settled, she wondered if she had blown things out of proportion. No. They had all happened before, on a much smaller scale.

"A bad dream," she told him, supremely grateful to be in her own bed.

"Not about me, I hope."

"No." She brushed a shock of hair from his face. "Would you like coffee?"

"I'd prefer more of you."

"You'll have to settle for coffee." She slipped out from under the covers, pulled a robe from her armoire, and padded downstairs to start the kettle boiling. She probably shouldn't have let him stay last night. It conveyed the erroneous impression that she wanted to restart their affair. But he *was* good. And he knew exactly what pleased her most.

Thankful for that, she poured boiling water over the ground coffee in her press and set the plunger. She found an unopened carton of grapefruit juice in her refrigerator and a bag of croissants in the freezer. She unsealed the juice carton, smelled it, and winced. If Christophe wanted breakfast, then microwaved croissants would have to do.

He deserved a more substantial meal for all the help he'd given her yesterday and especially for having banished, at least for one night, her anxieties about Martine and that godforsaken book.

Outside the kitchen windows, pre-dawn light from an overcast sky revealed a landscape muted by heavy snow. Flowerpots and bushes were mere bumps in a carpet of white. Tree branches bowed under the weight, and snow was still falling. It would all be gorgeous if she weren't facing a day of such uncertainty.

The clock on her oven read 7:56. Christophe's men would pick him up in an hour. Then she'd be here alone, with nothing to do but bite her nails and wait for Martine to call.

Astrid plunged the coffee and filled two mugs. In the bedroom, she found Christophe sitting back against a pillow, his muscular chest accentuated by oblique light from the table lamp at his side. He smiled as she came around to hand him his mug. But instead of taking it, he undid the belt of her robe and traced his fingertips along the undersides of her breasts.

She shut her eyes a moment as a tingle ran through her. They still had an hour.

#

Christophe's men arrived fifteen minutes late, excusing themselves with news that the road was buried in heavy snow.

"How bad is it?" Astrid asked them.

Christophe squeezed her hand. "Don't worry. We'll get someone to clear it." In a lowered voice, he asked, "Dinner tonight?"

"Call me first."

After he and his men had left, Astrid poured herself another cup of coffee and opened her patio doors to a sweeping vista of absolute beauty. From here to the Seine, the entire landscape was white and pure and utterly quiet. A Zen garden could not have been more calming.

It would be even more calming once the burden of that book was lifted. "Please," she prayed to no one in particular, "let Martine call today. Let her bring the book here. And let it perish in my fireplace. Until then—"

Her lights went out.

Thinking it must be a circuit breaker, she checked the breaker box. Everything looked okay. She climbed the stairs to her bedroom. None of the lamps worked.

Had heavy snow brought down a power line? *Damn.* Her whole house ran on electricity. She called the local office of Électricité de France, but the number returned a busy signal. Probably other people in her neighborhood were calling with complaints. If the utility lived up to its reputation, it could be days before power was restored. They'd all freeze by then.

Thankfully, she had stockpiled a load of firewood. After brushing snow off the neat stack on her patio, she brought in an armload, positioned three of the logs in her fireplace, and set them alight. She could handle this.

#

During a nearly sleepless night, Dan had finally made his decision about the book. Convinced it was the best solution, he showered, shaved, and walked into the kitchen to make coffee. He was on his second cup and peering out the windows at what had to be a record snowfall, when voices drew his attention to the upstairs landing.

"Coffee's ready," he announced as the two women came down.

"I smelled it." Paulette, who wasn't wearing her dark glasses, reached the bottom of the stairs and turned toward the kitchen.

"I'll bring it. You two have a seat."

"You sound cheerful," Martine said.

Dan carried in two mugs of coffee, handed them out, and settled on the couch beside her. "I've been thinking about the Moses book. The best thing we can do is persuade Leroux to take it back."

"What?" Martine gaped at him. "We're giving it to my mother. End of story. She's the whole reason we got it."

Having played out all sorts of scenarios in his head, Dan was ready for this one, whether Martine liked it or not. "I hate to say it, but I don't trust her."

"Where does that come from? You said you respected her. So what don't you trust?"

"I think she wants to destroy it."

"Why would she do that?" Paulette asked, her gaze aimed a foot above his head.

"We know the book could generate violence in the Middle East, maybe even war. War can devastate the economies of smaller countries, and Astrid's specialty is bolstering the economic health of those countries."

"Bolster?" Paulette asked.

"Reinforce." Martine turned to Dan. "I know I said that before, but maybe she just wants to hide it."

"Then she could have left it in the monastery. No one knew it was there, or even knew it existed, except her somehow. In fact, she kept it a secret from me when she asked me to help you. Possibly because I'm half-Jewish, I don't know. But instead of leaving it there, in total obscurity, she went to a lot of trouble to acquire it. Hell, she went so far as to send her only child."

"Now you're sounding like the Bible. 'His only begotten son?'"

"This isn't a joke. If I put myself in her place, I'd want to burn it to ashes. Problem solved."

"Perhaps he is right," Paulette said.

"I don't care. It's going to my mother, and I'm giving it to her today."

Dan struggled to stay civil. "It belongs in the hands of scholars."

"Like Leroux? Did you see how he looked when he gave it to us? He wants nothing to do with it."

"But he knows people who can give it the attention it deserves. People who would analyze it thoroughly, debate the pros and cons of one interpretation versus another. We already know they trickle out their findings. So, there'd be no bombshells to ignite international conflict."

In the unyielding tone of a judge passing sentence, Martine said, "She gave us a job. We accepted it. I find the book, you provide muscle. It's not your job to second-guess her. She's getting it. And what she does with it afterwards is up to her."

He ground his teeth. Martine wasn't driven by what was right or wrong. She was driven by some deep-seated need to please Astrid, regardless of the consequences. "Why are you so anxious to kowtow to your mother?"

"I'm not kowtowing."

"It sure looks like you are. Like you'll do anything to satisfy her, even if it's the wrong thing."

"Go fuck yourself." She smacked down her mug on the coffee table. "You don't know anything about us." Glaring, she sprang off the couch and stomped upstairs.

Well, that sure worked.

Paulette, who'd prudently stayed out of the row, turned to him with a look of sympathetic sadness. "Why were you cruel?"

"I just wanted her to examine her motives. What we do with that book is extremely important. Emotional baggage should not influence our judgment."

"Are you certain your judgment is best?"

"What would you do?"

Paulette leaned forward, resting her forearms on her knees. "I would think about the future. About you and Martine. You are meant to be together. But you make it difficult."

"I don't know what will happen in the future." If this morning were any measure, he and Martine would part ways under conditions as glacial as the weather outside.

"Dan, I like you very much. But you think with your brain and not with your heart. In the end, which is more important?"

This was not the end. The end, at least for him, would come when the book was in safekeeping. Only then would he feel comfortable washing his hands of this whole business.

But he'd never feel comfortable without Martine's consent. They'd stolen the book—the books—together. They'd dodged irate monks in Prague, gunfire and Molotov cocktails in Usti. They'd crossed borders illegally. She'd been there with him when Jade was shot, and later in the hospital. Just last night she'd dug him out of a hole with Geoff at the restaurant. Hell, it was thanks to her they had a safe place to stay with Paulette.

"I'll talk to her again," he conceded.

He took the stairs slowly. What if she wouldn't budge? If his most reasonable arguments hadn't swayed her, what could he say now? An appeal to do it for *him*? Fat chance. He needed a compromise of some sort. But how did you compromise between doing something and not? It was binary—on or off.

Or was it? Swallowing hard, he knocked on her door. When he received no answer, he opened it to see her sitting on the bed, her cheeks moist.

"Get out," she snapped.

"I'm sorry." He stepped inside. "Maybe I acted like an ass."

"Maybe?"

"Look, I was—"

"Just go away."

He took a settling breath, held it, then let it out slowly. "How about we call your mother and ask what she plans to do with it? No, something more neutral. Talk to her about what *she* thinks should happen to it."

"I promised her."

There it was again, a need to prove she had fulfilled her mission. Fine. But what happened to the book afterwards was far more important. "Look, we're the ones who fought to get it here. We've learned how important it is, how valuable to some people. Geoff Fairchild was willing to kill to get his hands on it, and he could have shot one of us. After all of that, don't you think we deserve a say in this, also?"

She wiped her cheeks. "And *our* say would be to give it to Leroux? She would never go for that. She doesn't even know the man."

"We could tell her about him. She might even like the idea of consigning the book to academics. You know, the whole thing about taking ages to analyze it and releasing their findings slowly?"

Martine straightened her shoulders. "And what if she says no, she wants it?"

That wasn't going to happen. But he needed more time to figure out how to handle the various situations that could arise. Much as he hated to lie to Martine, he stalled with, "Then we give it to her."

She looked at him guardedly. "You would agree to that?"

"Only if you're satisfied that what she plans to do with it is the right thing."

Her eyes bored into his. "She has to at least see it."

The fierceness in her voice made him wonder if Martine had an axe to grind with her mother. If so, that was their business. "I have no problem with showing it to her."

"Good. Because that's what's going to happen." Martine pulled out her phone. "I'll call her now."

Dan held up his hand. "Let me go down and get you a burner."

"Oh, come on. We're almost finished with this whole business."

Almost, but not quite. "Who inexplicably showed up at the restaurant last night? After you used your own phone once before?"

"Okay, okay."

When he reached the bottom of the stairs, Paulette said, "Your footsteps sound *résolu*."

"We came to an agreement."

"*Très bien.* And …?"

"She won."

Paulette smiled. "You will be happy for that."

Dan wasn't so sure. But he was determined to win the inevitable battle with Astrid, not just because the idea of willfully wiping out ancient knowledge turned his stomach, but increasingly because that knowledge pertained to his own ancestors. He couldn't help feeling that a text in which God specifically repudiated Jewish claims to the Holy Land would deal a huge blow to millions of people. Possibly an incendiary blow within Israel itself, pitting the ultra-orthodox right against the secular left. Jews killing Jews over a book that should have stayed hidden.

How Martine would react to his confrontation with her mother was uncertain. He suspected she would be more occupied with a confrontation of her own. In any case, this day was unlikely to end on a pleasant note.

"We'll see," he said to Paulette.

After retrieving one of the two pre-paid phones in his jacket pocket, he took it to Martine and listened to her end of a conversation that began, "*Maman.*" He caught very little of the rest but could read her face, which went from triumphant to crestfallen to determined before Martine disconnected.

"She's snowed in, and she has no electricity. Snowplows are supposed to clear her road, but she hasn't seen them yet."

"So we're postponing?" he asked hopefully.

"No. I'm going to call for a taxi and tell them we need a four-wheel drive."

#

Seated on the broad stone hearth of her fireplace, Astrid wished she had somehow retrofitted the stone house with good insulation.

Despite the crackling fire, her reception room seemed colder by the minute.

Never mind. Martine was on her way, in a four-wheel drive that was probably Dan's idea. If there was still no power when they'd finished incinerating the book, Martine and Dan could take her back to Paris. She would show her gratitude by—

Her phone pinged. *Martine again?*

But it was Christophe. "Dinner may be off," he said. "We have an emergency. The Israelis have gone on full alert."

#

Checking on the auction he'd restarted last night, Geoff punched the air triumphantly. Three inquiries already, two asking how soon they could see photos. His fingers itched to type, "Today," but he'd been stung once already, when Adar informed him he had the wrong book. If that happened again, he would lose all credibility, as well as any chance of retiring to a Mediterranean island.

The inquiries would have to go unanswered until he had the real thing.

In the meantime, he needed more aspirin. He never should have drunk that wine last night. Red wine especially gave him headaches. But he'd had to appear congenial.

After downing four tablets, he searched the kitchen for something to counteract their corrosive effect on his stomach. He had barely set foot in here since arriving, and all he found now was stuff left over from previous agents who'd used the place. The cupboards held some canned fruit, four cartons of French crackers, and a box of cornflakes. He filled a bowl with cornflakes, only to discover there was no milk in the fridge. Screw it. He carried the bowl into his living room and ate cereal with his fingers while pondering his next move.

Jade needed to die. He'd missed a chance at her last night when that damned wine made him doze off in the lobby of her hotel. But he was sober now. He could find her again, blow her brains out, and watch her blood freeze solid on the snow-covered ground as he spat in her dying face.

But she'd have to wait. The book came first. Jade's most recent texts, claiming she would give it to him in the botanical garden, were bullshit, a ploy to draw him out. He knew from Astrid that her daughter had it. She was the target. And he knew where she was staying.

His next move would be staking out that apartment building. If Dan was with her, he was a target also. Geoff pictured the arrogant bastard going down in a hail of gunfire. Frosting on the cake.

He dumped the last of the cornflakes into his mouth. *You've got the plan, buddy.* Plus, if they somehow eluded him, there was the fallback of grabbing the book from Astrid. In fact, he should call her now, set her up with a reminder of his interest in the book and renew his offer of dinner at one of the best restaurants in town.

Leaving the empty bowl on the coffee table, he picked up his phone from the desk and punched in her number. It rang twice before she answered. "Astrid," he said as if she were a long-lost sister, "this is Geoff Fairchild."

"Oh. Hello," she replied with less enthusiasm than he'd hoped for.

After a few sentences of polite conversation, he broached the subject of the book, ending with, "I'm leaving Paris soon and would really like to see it before I go."

"I'm not sure if … when that will be possible."

Uh-oh. "What's wrong?"

"Martine and Dan are supposed to bring me the book today, but there's a lot of snow on the roads."

Today. Fantastic. "Bring it where?"

"My house."

"May I join you?"

"My power is out. And there's all this snow, and it's still coming down."

Careful not to push too hard, he sidestepped the power issue and said, "If Dan and Martine can get through, so can I. When are they coming?"

"This morning, if they can make it."

"Where do you live?"

She hesitated.

"Is there a problem?" he asked, then laid on the guilt trip. "I hope not. After all, I'm the one who put you in touch with Dan." When Astrid didn't respond, he slathered it on thicker. "Plus, I love old books, and I'm fascinated with what you told me about this one. It would be a huge treat for me."

After an audible exhalation, she finally told him her address, in a place called Rueil-Malmaison about ten miles outside Paris.

Geoff thanked her profusely and ended the call.

Manipulating Astrid had been touch-and-go there for a minute, but his powers of persuasion were as sharp as ever. Now he didn't have to waste time staking out that apartment building. With luck, he might even get to Astrid's before Dan and Martine did.

Once he secured the book, he'd watch Dan breathe his last. "So long, Danny boy. I hope you enjoyed the ride 'cause this is where you get off."

And after Dan, it would be good-bye, Jade. Man, when it rained, it poured. Pennies from heaven. Tons of them, because tonight—tomorrow at the latest—he'd be a millionaire.

Gleefully, he unlocked the weapons cabinet. "Hello, my sweets. Which ones of you should I choose?"

Chapter 30

After waking every three hours to down more ibuprofen, Jade finally got up when honking horns signaled the beginning of morning traffic. The overcast sky hung gray and cheerless. Half a foot of snow topped her windowsill and the visible rooftops. It would be a great day to crawl back into bed, if there weren't someone she needed to kill.

She called down to room service for ham and eggs and a pot of coffee—protein to build up her strength and caffeine to keep her alert. While waiting, she re-dressed her wounds with pressure bandages, put on her warmest clothing, and packed her disassembled sniper rifle into a shoulder bag.

Her weapon of choice, the Karambit knife, went into a side pocket of the bag, where it most likely would stay without ever tasting Fairchild's blood. Overnight, as she'd lain awake waiting for fresh doses of the painkiller to kick in, she had failed to come up with any way to lure him outside. A rifle shot through his window, from the rooftop across the street, would have to suffice. Instant death was too good for the bastard but, realistically, she had to play the hand fate dealt her.

It might be her only chance, and she needed this kill more than she'd ever needed anything else in her whole damn life. If for some reason she failed, her self-respect would—

"Stop doubting yourself."

She was good, maybe the best in the business. Only a fleeting lapse of concentration had allowed Fairchild to get the drop on her. There was no way in hell that would happen again.

Someone knocked on her door and called out, "*Service d'étage.* Room service."

After checking through the peephole, Jade let the woman wheel in her cart, then signed the receipt and sat down to breakfast. It smelled great. Her ham and buttery eggs came with an assortment of warm, yeasty breads, two little bottles of jam, and even a dish of pineapple. She ate it all, grateful for real food after the yogurt and rice of last night.

But she drank only two cups of coffee. When you were sighted in and waiting for the target, nothing was worse than an urgent need to pee. For Fairchild though, she'd go in her pants, if necessary, to take the shot.

Downstairs, after asking the man at the front desk to call her a cab, she walked outside to wait. At street level, the winter landscape bore no resemblance to the view of snowy rooftops and balconies visible from her room. Tires and pedestrians had crushed the snow to gray slush, except in the gutters.

The taxi arrived in under five minutes. When they reached her destination, she had the driver circle Fairchild's block before dropping her around the corner from his building.

Christ, it was cold. Waiting on a frozen rooftop for the prick to appear in one of his windows would take every shivering ounce of her strength. Only one thing would make the effort worthwhile—

watching Fairchild's head explode in a burst of bone and brain.

Warmed by that image, she tied her black scarf over her head, hunched her shoulders forward like an old woman, and joined the flow of people moving along the sidewalk across from Fairchild's place. Staying close to the building fronts, she shuffled at an elderly pace until she reached the doorway that faced his. There she stopped and pretended to search for something in her shoulder bag.

After several long minutes, a middle-aged man came out of the door next to her. Before it could close, she slipped inside but stopped as a clacking sound, like that of a metal roll-up door, came to her through the traffic noise. Looking back, she watched the grate guarding the underground garage of Fairchild's building clatter slowly upward.

From the basement parking area, a black Mercedes taxi inched its way to the top of the ramp. When Fairchild shot her, he'd been in a dark Mercedes. She had only glimpsed it, and him, before passing out. But she remembered the make from its grille. And the guy driving this one *could* be a match for the asshole himself.

Damn. There was no time to assemble her rifle and too much traffic to risk a shot straight across the street. She'd have to flag down a cab to follow him—*if* she could even find one in this crush of cars.

As though to slap her in the face, a break in traffic opened up on Fairchild's side of the street. In seconds he'd be gone.

But the Mercedes stayed put. Then it reversed back down the ramp.

She didn't know why, and it didn't matter. Fairchild or not, this was her chance to get into his building. Dashing outside, she threaded her way as fast as she could between the vehicles. Drivers hit their brakes and leaned on their horns, but the grate was coming down again. It was barely three feet above the ground when she slid under, dragging her shoulder bag behind her.

Pain shot from her wounds, bursting through her side and shoulder like exploding firecrackers. She curled up, but that hurt more. Still on the ground, she rolled over to the wall of the ramp where it was relatively dark. Just breathing was torture. But she was inside.

Gritting her teeth, she rose slowly to a crouch and surveyed the garage. Beneath a ceiling lamp, a man was punching a number pad beside the basement door. It was the same guy she'd seen several weeks ago on that equally cold morning at the Washington zoo—Geoffrey Fucking Fairchild.

He disappeared into the building. But he'd soon be back. That much was evident from the way he'd parked his Mercedes in front of two cars that were still in their spaces. She'd get him when he came out again and, thank her luck, she could now use the knife.

Unfortunately, the door he had gone through was in the middle of a long concrete wall that afforded no cover at all. She could press her back to the wall and nail him the moment he emerged—unless some other resident came out behind him.

Too risky.

Better to catch him in his car. She'd seen it on TV and in movies, the assassin hides in the back seat and strangles or knifes the driver just before he starts the engine. But movies were full of unrealistic crap. Would it work in real life? She'd never tried it.

On the plus side, the light in here was dim. She was only five-foot-five and clothed in black. The Mercedes was big and also black. Although she always checked the rear seat before entering a car, Fairchild in a hurry might not.

On the negative side, if he did check … what a cock-up that would be. Could she possibly scramble out fast enough to run him down? Would he yank open the back door on his side and trap her with a pistol? She'd be a sitting duck. Damn Lovel for taking her Glock.

All her nerves seemed to fire simultaneously. Maybe she should just assemble her rifle, hide behind another car, and pop him when he came out. After all, shooting him from afar had been her previous plan. On any other job, that's exactly what she would do.

But this wasn't any other job. This was *her* job. She could not let the opportunity pass. She was too close to feeling her blade slice through his throat, to whispering sweet good-byes in his ear as he bled out behind the steering wheel.

Charged with anticipation, she dashed around to the far side of his car. He'd left it unlocked, another sign he would be back soon. After retrieving her knife from the bag, she opened the rear door, stowed the bag behind his seat, then huddled on the floor behind the passenger's seat and pulled the door closed.

#

Damned glad he'd remembered his bidders before heading out, Geoff descended the stairs with a lightness in his step. He'd played it well. To their question this morning of when they could see photos of the book, he had now typed, "Posting them today. Auction tonight." It was a simple, straightforward response that confirmed *he* was running this show.

Next stop, Astrid's house.

At the bottom of the stairwell, as he pushed open the door to the garage, his phone chirped. A text from ... Adar? "Ring me immediately at the following number," it read. Geoff pictured their previous encounter—the lobby of the George Cinq—the prick telling him it was the wrong book and walking away like some snotty-nosed potentate. Well, screw him.

Or, maybe play him. What could it hurt? Walking toward his car, Geoff thumbed the number in Adar's text. It picked up on the second ring. "What's so important?" Geoff said.

"Are you still trying to sell the worthless book you showed me?"

"I was testing you. I'm only interested in serious buyers. But you walked away."

"You brought—"

"The real one goes on sale tonight." Geoff opened the door of his car. "If you doubt me, you can look at the photos." *Set the bait.* "And bid with the others."

"If you are telling the truth this time, I want it."

"Oh, yeah?" Sliding into the driver's seat, Geoff grinned. "So do several other people."

"I said I want it."

Geoff shut his door. He had the guy. *Now up the ante.* "In case you've forgotten, Adar, you disrespected me last time. So if you want it outside the auction, the price is three million. Euros, not dollars, in used bills."

"I still need to see it first. Bring it to where we met previously. Ring me when you are here."

Spoken with no hesitation. Geoff wondered if he should have demanded five million. Don't push it, he told himself. "Fine. I'll be there tonight. The book for the money."

"If the book is genuine."

"It's genuine, all right. And tonight is your last chance. Three million in cash or it's going up for grabs."

"I heard you." Then Adar's voice dropped to an ominous tone. "This is also *your* last chance."

#

Three million euros? This was almost too good to believe. That much money would set her up for life. All she had to do was stay low and remain hidden back here until Fairchild made his exchange with this Adar character.

But did she dare gamble on not being spotted before then? Fairchild started the car.

Decision time. She could slit his throat right now, before the car started moving. Or she could trust her own abilities—wait for the exchange, then have her way with the bastard *and* pocket a hefty grand prize. She gnawed her lip.

Trust yourself.

As he put the car in gear, Jade relaxed her grip on the knife.

#

According to the car's GPS, it was nearly a straight shot to Astrid's house. Estimated time was forty minutes. For ten miles? Probably the snow. Wimpy Parisians couldn't handle it. He'd show them how.

Geoff pulled up to the sensor that opened the security grate. He paused briefly at the top of the ramp, then burned rubber to snatch a space in morning traffic. The driver he'd cut off laid into his horn. Geoff flipped him the bird, then switched on his windshield wipers to clean off the falling snow.

At Rue de Rivoli, he made a right and settled into the flow that would take him past the Louvre, around the Arc de Triomphe, and out to La Defense, whose modern rectangular "arch" was meant to mimic the Triomphe. He'd seen them all before and might have enjoyed seeing them again. But all he could think about was Adar's implied threat.

Geoff placed his driving on mental autopilot while he reexamined his meeting with the arrogant dick. There was no way the guy had been armed. Geoff would have detected that, just as readily as he would have noticed any bodyguards lurking in the background of the hotel lobby. There were, however, side rooms off the lobby.

Okay, assume Adar had muscle at his disposal. It didn't matter. Geoff would deliver the real book this time. Adar would confirm it, then hand over a briefcase which Geoff would check. Done deal, as promised. No need for anyone to get hinky.

But what if Adar planned to double-cross him after the exchange?

Let him try. Geoff would be carrying the same pistol and an Uzi he had now, and he would put on a bulletproof vest before the meeting. They might tail him back to the safe house. But the place was impregnable. Except for the windows. DSS hadn't got around yet to installing bullet-proof glass. Never mind. All he had to do was draw the curtains, and nobody would know when or where to shoot.

"So fuck you," he said out loud, "and the camel you rode in on."

Glancing around, Geoff realized he had already passed the Arc de Triomphe. Ahead, through blowing snow, lay the Seine and La Defense. And Astrid's house. *And* the book.

All that money for some old gobbledygook from the Bible. Either Adar was a rich fanatic or, more likely, he was acting on behalf of an extremist government. Either way, Geoff wasn't about to complain. Whatever drove those assholes made no difference. Produce the book, get instantly rich. Plain and simple.

Except he couldn't quite shake a nagging suspicion that Adar might somehow be dealing from a stacked deck.

#

To Dan, this looked like the end of the trail. They'd had relatively smooth sailing all the way to Rueil-Malmaison, the highways merely wet from tire-melted slush. But the road from there lay buried under snow, initially a few inconsequential inches of it, then abruptly two feet or more.

His best guess about the sudden change was that a snowplow had given up or been called to some other area. Their way ahead was marked by only a slight depression in the snow and a break in the forest canopy overhead.

"Can our driver get through this?" he asked Martine, silently hoping he could not. Despite having planned for several contingencies with Astrid, Dan still believed the best outcome for today would be postponing their meeting, allowing him more time to convince Martine they should take the book to Leroux.

Martine spoke to the twenty-something driver of their Toyota Land Cruiser, who said, *"Bien sûr."* With a smile, he pressed some buttons, turned a knob, and pulled the stick into four-wheel drive.

They crunched forward for about a quarter of a mile, snow scraping the undercarriage, before a thud stopped them.

"Merde." Their driver climbed out. When he got back in, he shook his head and spoke to Martine in a dejected voice.

"We ran into a log," she translated. "He can't go over it."

More than just a log, Dan thought. In front of them to the right, a ragged tree stump suggested an entire trunk had fallen across the road, probably an old tree that couldn't handle the added weight of all this snow. "How much farther to your mother's house?"

"About a kilometer, I think. Maybe less."

Seeing another opportunity to delay meeting Astrid, he offered a lopsided choice. "We can return to Paris and try again tomorrow. Or we can chance plodding through knee-deep snow and pray we don't freeze to death."

She had a brief, urgent-sounding conversation with the driver.

When they finished, the guy began backing up.

"What's happening?" Dan asked, afraid he knew.

"Give him a minute," she said.

After about forty feet, the driver stopped, got out again, and trudged into the woods.

Clearly, he was searching for a way around the fallen trunk. But if one tree was down, others might be, also. And finding a way through could be near-impossible. Dan hoped so.

Fifteen minutes later, the guy reappeared in front of them, striding along their tire ruts with a victorious grin that scuttled Dan's hopes. *"On peut le faire."*

Martine beamed. "He says we can do it."

The route he'd found tested both man and machine. In low gear, the Land Cruiser jounced over buried obstacles, lurched side-to-side over uneven terrain, and tossed its passengers in all directions as the driver spun the wheel left and right. Bracing himself, Dan felt like he was riding one of those mechanical bulls. Small branches scraped their windows or simply snapped off.

Finally they reached the road again and reverted to the relatively smooth job of bulldozing through snow. A short rise followed by a gradual descent brought them to a point where Martine shouted, *"Ici."*

Although disappointed, Dan had to admire the driver's fortitude. It had been a Herculean effort, apparently undertaken for no better reason than to please the lady. At the bottom of the driveway, Dan gave him a hundred euros over the price on the meter and asked him to wait.

"Avec joie."

Outside the vehicle lay an idyllic scene straight off a Christmas card—trees and ground covered in pristine snow, a lone house beneath a dark gray sky that suggested supper would soon be on the table. The house was built of stone, probably in the nineteenth century, and rose three stories, the third marked by ornate dormer windows in a steeply pitched roof. Unlike on a Christmas card, no lights shone in any of the windows. And it was still mid-morning, so there'd be no supper. But a wisp of smoke rising from one of the chimneys confirmed Astrid was home.

Squaring her shoulders, Martine stomped to a front door of iron-studded oak that looked strong enough to withstand a battering ram. She rapped a brass knocker in the shape of a dolphin. They waited.

She was about to knock again when the door opened.

"Martine!" Astrid threw her arms around her daughter, who pointedly did not reciprocate. "I'm so happy you're safe. And Dan. Come in, come in."

Inside felt almost as cold as outside. Dan followed as Astrid, in a thick wool sweater, drew Martine into a large, wood-paneled reception room where logs blazed in a fireplace and a blanket on the stone hearth indicated Astrid had been huddling there.

"Is that your only warmth?" he asked.

"I had a power failure. They're supposed to fix it soon."

With a tree lying across the road, Dan doubted "soon" would be today. They would probably end up having to take Astrid back with them to Paris, which negated their advantage of being able to walk away if things became too ugly.

"I can't serve you coffee or tea," she said, "but I can offer you cognac."

It was a bit early for alcohol. But at least cognac would warm the insides. "Yes, please. Martine?"

"No," she said firmly and went to sit by the fire.

Astrid left and returned with a single snifter of amber liquid, which she handed to him. "I'm glad the snowplow got through."

"It didn't," Martine told her in a surprisingly severe tone. "The road is blocked. We had to fight our way through the forest to get here. Just like we had to fight our way across half of Europe to bring you your book."

Whoa. After all the signs this morning, Dan had expected Martine to make sure her mother knew the job was grueling. But not so soon. Not before even a few familial pleasantries.

Astrid, no doubt accustomed to coping with antagonistic finance ministers, replied diplomatically, "I'm sorry you had difficulties."

"Difficulties?" Martine's face reddened with anger. "You call wading across rivers in the middle of the night, freezing our asses off in a blizzard 'difficulties?' What about gunfire, people chasing us every inch of the way? I can't count how many times we barely escaped getting killed. Are those 'difficulties,' also?"

Uh-oh. While Martine might have a need to prove herself, her flaring temper threatened to derail this into a train wreck. He butted in with, "It was tough, but thanks to Martine—"

"Shut up," she spat, her eyes still fixed on her mother. "All to do your dirty work."

"Darling, please." Astrid took a step toward her.

"Don't!" After a hostile pause, Martine picked up the blanket from the hearth and wrapped it around herself. "How do you think it feels to be a disappointment all your life? You wouldn't know, would you? You, in your lofty tower of global finance. While your daughter, who had all the advantages of your precious genes *and* the best schools, somehow ended up in a dusty old museum, translating ancient texts that nobody cares about. Plus, couldn't keep a husband, which I also inherited from you."

"Martine, stop it!" Astrid's eyes glistened with unshed tears. "I have always loved you."

"Oooh. That gives me such a warm feeling."

Astrid snarled something in French, then tramped into the kitchen.

Moving quickly, Dan seated himself on the opposite side of the fire from Martine. "You've made your point. Please don't push it too far."

"Don't tell me what to do. You haven't spent a lifetime trying to live up to the impossible expectations of the only parent who ever mattered. Well, this time I have. And she's damn-well going to know it."

At the potential risk of forever alienating the one woman you wanted to please.

Astrid returned, carrying a snifter filled to the brim with cognac. She wiped her lips with her thumb knuckle, a suggestion that she'd just downed one glass and this was her second. Looking more resentful than Dan had ever seen her, she took another swallow. "I gave you everything."

"And I squandered it, didn't I? Ungrateful bitch that I am." Martine threw off the blanket and stood. "Speaking of ungrateful bitches, did it ever occur to you to say thanks?"

This had to stop. "Astrid, here's your book." From inside his jacket, he withdrew the slim volume, wrapped in a white plastic grocery bag he had found at Paulette's house.

Slowly she tore her gaze from Martine and advanced toward him, her hand outstretched. "Give it to me."

At last they'd reached a situation he had planned for. He held up the book, then lowered it to his side. "Not yet."

Chapter 31

When Fairchild stopped, growled "Shit," and threw the car in reverse, Jade silently mouthed her own curse. During the long ride out here, wherever "here" was, she'd concluded that he must be on his way to get the book he wanted—versus the one she had stolen for him. If he already had the "right" book, there would be no reason to put off this Adar person until tonight. Now something had gone wrong.

Plus, her legs were numb from the cramped position she'd been coiled in for the past thirty or forty minutes. They'd be useless if he spotted her.

The car stopped again.

Jade raised her knife.

But Fairchild shifted to a forward gear, and the car rocked left as it climbed some sort of embankment, his tires crunching into deeper snow. Several bounces later, he stopped yet again. "God dammit!"

His door opened then slammed shut.

After nearly a minute of waiting for it to open again, she risked raising her head to see what he was doing. There he was, forty feet ahead, plodding along a tire rut in the snow.

Jade struggled onto the rear seat to flex her legs and restore circulation. The car's interior was still warm. Outside, with tree branches bent under snowpack, it looked even colder than in the city. She could stay here in the warmth, which would soon fade, or follow him and find out what was going on.

Like that was a real choice. This close to her quarry, there was no chance she'd let him out of her sight. She eased open her door.

Hang on. Following him would be no problem, but she would have to return to the car before he did, to conceal herself until he exchanged the book for the money. And she had to do it without leaving an extra set of footprints in the snow.

She eased her door closed and climbed over the console into the front, pulling her bag behind her. Ahead the coast was clear. Fairchild must have angled back to a road of some sort. She exited through the driver's door and carefully placed her feet in the depressions he'd left. After six steps, she reached the front of the car and the compacted tire tracks left by someone who had come this way before them. From there, it was easy.

#

In spite of his overcoat, Geoff shivered. It was a long damn slog, getting back to the road then trudging along tire tracks for what must have been half a mile so far. And while the silenced pistol rode easily in his coat pocket, the Uzi shoved into the back of his waistband transmitted cold like a frozen hand.

On the plus side, the tracks were fresh, almost certainly made by a four-wheel drive Dan had hired. Who else would bash his way through a forest on a day like this?

Geoff halted at the smell of wood smoke. Beyond a turn in the distance rose a stone building. As he approached, he caught sight of a vehicle, a Land Cruiser. It had to be Dan's, which meant this had to be Astrid's house. At last.

The driver's door opened. But the man who got out wasn't Dan. Younger and several inches shorter, he was probably Dan's driver. Definitely he was a complication Geoff didn't need.

As the hapless schmuck lit a cigarette, Geoff withdrew the silenced pistol and strode forward, holding the gun behind his leg. *"Bonjour."*

The fellow started. *"Bonjour, monsieur."*

"You speak English?"

"A little." His eyes shifted to beyond Geoff, most likely searching for the vehicle Geoff had arrived in. Not seeing it, of course, he asked, "You are a ... *voisin?*"

Geoff's French wasn't great, but he knew the word for neighbor. "Yes, *voisin*. You bring a man here?"

"A man and woman."

Whatever he said next, Geoff didn't catch. Nor did he care. With the confirmation he needed, Geoff raised his pistol and blew a hole in the guy's forehead.

For a satisfying moment, he watched steaming red blood spread over the white snow. The driver's cigarette, beside his hand, emitted pale gray smoke that would never be inhaled.

Geoff ground out the cigarette. "Bad for your health."

#

In the chill of Astrid's reception room, Dan gnawed his lip and wondered if he should just concede.

Astrid, after confirming her intention to destroy the book, had not budged an inch. And Martine was no help. She sat brooding on the hearth beside the big open fireplace, her foul mood clearly a result of his diverting Astrid's attention before Martine could finish venting.

He had prepared for Plan C, tossing the book in the fire, and was about to implement it when a hard rap on Astrid's door stopped him. "Are you expecting someone else?"

"No." Astrid's eyes narrowed, then brightened. "Unless it is Christophe."

"Who's that?"

"A friend." She grabbed a mohair blanket off one of the couches, wrapped it around her shoulders, and headed for the door.

Dan turned to Martine. "Christophe?"

She shrugged.

Almost inaudibly at this distance, Astrid said, "Mister Fairchild. I forgot you were coming."

Dan's stomach tightened. He had *not* planned for this. Quickly he chambered a round in the Glock and pushed the pistol into his left back pocket. Geoff would be less suspicious of his left hand moving and might not remember that Dan was equally proficient with either hand.

"What's wrong?" Martine asked, apparently jolted out of her sulk.

"Geoff's here."

With a look of shock, she rose from the hearth. "He wants the book."

"And most likely me. Move closer to the kitchen door, would you? If I have trouble controlling this, I don't want you in the line of fire."

She cast off the blanket. "I can take care of myself."

"Not against bullets." As she halfheartedly stepped toward the kitchen, he shoved the plastic-wrapped book behind a cushion of the nearest couch.

"Geoffrey Fairchild," Astrid announced, leading him into the reception room. "I believe you all know each other?" When the men locked eyes and neither moved to shake hands, her pasted-on smile turned into a frown of apprehension.

Good. It was beginning to dawn on her that this turn of events might not have a pleasant ending. Geoff, on the other hand, seemed to think it would. In the flickering firelight, his smirk said as much. His expensive overcoat, with the pockets custom-tailored to conceal pistols, couldn't mask the added length of a silencer. Dampness around the coat's hem and a clot of ice adhering to one shoe showed he had walked through snow to get here, which in turn suggested he'd left the safe-house car at that tree trunk in the road. Geoff wasn't one for discomfort. He wouldn't have trekked all this way just to pay a social visit.

Stalling until he could get him alone, Dan asked, "What brings you here?"

"Astrid invited me. To see the book."

"What book?"

"Oh, aren't we coy. The Bible book, dickhead. The one we talked about at the restaurant last night." Geoff's hand slipped into his coat pocket. "Remember now?"

This was happening too fast. He needed to unclutter the playing field ASAP. "Astrid, could I have a refill on the cognac? Maybe Geoff would like one, also."

Martine beckoned her mother. "Come, *Maman*, I'll help you. Cognacs all around sounds great. It's freezing in here."

"No, stay," Geoff said politely but firmly. He withdrew the silenced pistol and held it at his thigh, out of everyone's sight except Dan's. "Let's see the book first."

"*Maman*, I can't carry all the glasses myself."

When Astrid started to move, Geoff wrapped his free arm around her shoulder. "Cognac can wait."

"Take your hands off her," Martine snapped.

"Relax, honey." Geoff brought the pistol around to the front of his thigh, in plain view for Martine. "Let's all be sure we understand who's in charge here."

Dan's pulse raced. With Astrid effectively hostage, he would only get one shot. Turning slightly to the left to hide his hand, he pulled the Glock from his hip pocket. As he did, he caught a glimpse of a now-familiar figure moving outside the window. Jade.

What the hell was *she* doing here?

#

Jade stopped in her tracks. Although it was as dark as sundown out here and she was dressed in black, Lovel had somehow spotted her. His brief look of recognition showed it.

The good news was, he stayed cool. The bad news was that he had just withdrawn the Glock, no doubt to take down Fairchild who must be off to the side somewhere. She couldn't see Fairchild from this angle, but she had seen the mess he made of that unarmed guy beside the Land Cruiser. A chickenshit execution for probably no better reason than the poor bastard was just there.

Fairchild definitely needed to die.

She moved closer through the snow and peered inside. In the shifting shadows of light from a fireplace, the cocksucker held a pistol, also. Worse, he had his arm around some gray-haired woman who looked scared to death. On the other side of the room, Lovel's girlfriend looked poised to strike but equally frightened.

What a clusterfuck. Lovel would never get out of this, not without collateral damage and maybe not at all.

In any case, she could not let him try. Fairchild was hers. If it cost her three million euros to take him down now, so be it. Stepping back, she unslung her shoulder bag and felt that old sense of calm, the calm that embraced her when her target was almost in her crosshairs.

#

At light speed, Dan reassessed the situation. He knew Jade was there. Geoff did not. Despite the dim light in here, she could surely see the pistol in his own left hand and the one in Geoff's right. She knew there'd be gunfire but didn't know which of them was the better shot. With that uncertainty, she might try to take matters into her own hands. Dan couldn't allow that. There was too much at stake.

In an effort to stand her down, he gave a barely perceptible shake of his head.

She retreated from view.

Grateful that she seemed willing to leave this to him, Dan kept the Glock hidden behind his hip and said to Geoff, "Sorry to disappoint you, but we didn't bring the Bible book."

"I think you did."

"We told you last night it's bogus."

Geoff stepped behind Astrid, threw his forearm around her neck, and placed the silencer at her temple. "Give it to me. Now!"

Astrid looked terrified, her eyes wide, her mouth open. She gripped Geoff's arm to no avail.

Martine advanced on them.

"Don't," Dan told her. To Geoff, he said, "There's no need for violence." As he spoke, Dan searched for even the slightest opportunity.

But Geoff's finger was on the trigger, his hand steady. His head, now barely visible behind Astrid's, was a tough shot, and the coward knew it. Even if Dan succeeded, Geoff's death-throe reflexes could contract the muscles in his trigger finger.

Astrid trembled in his grip. Martine inched into the kitchen doorway, maybe to grab a knife or some other weapon.

"One more step," Geoff snarled, "and your mother dies."

Martine stopped.

Geoff switched his stare back to Dan. "Show me both hands. Then take off your jacket and turn around slowly."

Unwilling to risk either woman's life for a book—any book—Dan placed the Glock on a nearby end table and did as instructed. He felt naked, almost powerless. All he had left was the possibility of capitalizing on Geoff's self-confidence. "Satisfied?"

Grinning, Geoff said, "You forgot who trained you. I know all your little quirks, including that look you get when you think you have the upper hand."

Geoff had not been one of his trainers. But Dan wasn't about to point that out. With no other options, he resorted to Plan C. "Okay, you win."

"I always win."

Hold that thought. Dan moved to the couch where he'd concealed the book. "It's here. Behind this cushion."

Geoff, three feet behind the couch, shifted his pistol from Astrid to Dan. "Do not try to fuck with me."

"Want your book?"

"Bring it out very slowly."

Playing to Geoff's ego, Dan replied, "I will. But don't shoot anyone, okay? Please don't shoot."

"Oh, say it again." Geoff's lips twisted into a sadistic grin. "I knew you were a pussy."

It was working. The pistol lowered slightly, a sign that Geoff was relaxing as his vanity and sense of omnipotence grew. "Please don't hurt us," Dan said and withdrew the book in the white plastic bag.

"Show it to me."

Unwrapping it slowly, Dan backed three steps toward the open fireplace. "I put it in a modern book cover to keep it hidden."

"Such a clever boy. Take off the cover."

Praying Geoff would panic and push Astrid aside, Dan said, "Or *you* could," and tossed the book on the fire.

It landed in a burst of sparks.

"No!" With horror on his face, Geoff dashed to the fireplace and snatched up an iron poker. "Back off," he shouted at Dan. "Move and I'll kill you." He jabbed the poker into the flames, then bent to get a better angle. "Bastard!"

Dan launched himself, driving Geoff forward. He threw his weight onto Geoff's back to pin him there and jammed the guy's face into the fire.

Geoff howled. His legs kicked as he tried to push himself up. His arms flailed like a drowning swimmer's. But he kept hold of both the poker and the pistol. His hair started sizzling.

Searing pain scorched Dan's hands. Unable to hold him like this any longer, he switched to using a forearm on the back of Geoff's neck.

Suddenly the silenced pistol went off. Bullets ricocheted off the back of the fireplace.

Martine cried out.

Dan whipped around and, in that moment, knew he'd made a mistake.

Somehow still fighting, Geoff twisted and swung the iron poker. It slammed into the side of Dan's head.

#

From her new vantage point on the patio outside a pair of French doors, Jade now had a clear view of everything. The gray-haired woman was down, victim of a stray bullet that had grazed her forehead. Lovel's girlfriend knelt beside her. Lovel was down but struggling to his hands and knees. Fairchild staggered. His face looked like a charred brisket with one open eye and a blood-red mouth. *Well done, Lovel. Until you let yourself be distracted.*

Now, as Fairchild dropped the poker and aimed his pistol, Lovel was staring at certain death.

#

Dan tried to focus through a blinding, ear-throbbing headache. Dress shoes, trouser legs, the hem of a coat. Fairchild's overcoat. Damn, the prick was standing over him. How was that possible?

Dan raised his eyes further, to the dark hole in the middle of a silencer. Above it, the blackened remains of Geoff's face glowered. A cheekbone showed, and part of Geoff's jaw. For some reason, the exposed bones and teeth captured Dan's attention more than his own impending death.

If only … wait a second. Martine! She'd cried out. Dan peered behind him but couldn't see her.

Geoff's voice, weirdly gurgling and raspy at the same time, uttered, "I've wanted to do this for a long time."

Dan looked back at him and at the silencer inching closer. He didn't fear dying, but having to go this way both saddened him and pissed him off. *Think, man. Don't let this just happen.* "The book! You're letting it burn."

A glint came to Geoff's one eye. Something resembling a sneer twisted what was left of his mouth. "Pulled it out. I win." His finger tightened on the trigger. "You lose."

In a last-ditch effort, Dan rolled onto his back and drew up his knees. He was about to kick at Geoff's shins in an attempt to knock him over, when the guy's throat exploded in a spray of blood.

#

As Dan watched in disbelief, Geoff crumpled to the floor, face-down on his knees and chest like a toddler sleeping on its stomach. But despite being burned *and* shot, the son of a bitch miraculously still lived. Hoarse gasps rattled in the carnage of his throat. Jade—it had to be her—must have purposely taken a neck shot instead of a head shot. Why?

Of course. To temporarily spare Geoff's life so she could watch him bleed out.

A rush of arctic air yanked Dan's eyes to the patio doors. Sure enough, there she stood, with an M110 sniper rifle. For a second, he saw her in a western, entering through saloon doors.

The sound of running feet behind him shattered that vision. Dan spun around, with the excruciating consequence of an even-more-splitting headache, now accompanied by a threat of nausea.

Martine dashed into the kitchen and returned with a wet dishtowel. "Help me! *Maman* has been shot."

Dan had feared it was Martine. But his relief quickly vanished. "How bad?"

As he fought vertigo to stand upright, Jade said calmly, "Nothing serious. She'll be fine."

"How the hell do *you* know?" Martine lowered herself behind the couch.

Dan's apprehension eased. He accepted Jade's opinion. She was a pro and not emotionally invested in Astrid's welfare the way Martine was.

Jade shut the French doors and walked into the room. To Dan, she said, "That was quite a whack you took. Are you nauseous?"

"Yeah. But I'll be okay."

"You have a—"

"Concussion. It's not the first time."

"Take half a dozen ibuprofen and eat some ginger."

With that, she kicked Geoff onto his side and knelt by his head. "Wanna know why you're dying? It's because you double-crossed me." She leaned closer to the charcoal stub that had once been an ear, and to the puddle of blood spreading from Geoff's carotid arteries. "All you had to do was honor our contract. But no. You hired a goon to kill me. And when that didn't work, you tried it yourself." She glanced up at Dan as if to thank him for saving her, then turned back to Geoff. "Well, asshole, this is your reward. I hope you enjoy Hell."

A moment later, blood stopped pumping from Geoff's neck.

Chapter 32

Dan frisked Geoff's body, removing an Uzi, two cellphones, and his wallet, keys, and watch. At the same time, Jade used kitchen towels to wipe up the blood on the floor and the broken glass beneath the bullet hole she'd put through one of the panes in the patio doors.

He envied her. Cleaning up blood and glass was pretty impersonal. Having to handle Geoff's remains—and endure close-up the stench of his burned flesh, the horrific sight of his blistered and blackened face, the ragged hole that had once been his throat—nearly brought up the contents of Dan's stomach.

Not to mention that the corpse, or rather the man it had been, was once his best friend. Yes, Geoff had tried to kill Jade and would have killed everyone in this room if Jade hadn't acted. But it shouldn't have happened this way. A simple bullet through the heart would have sufficed.

"Earth to Lovel," Jade said.

Dan snapped out of it. "Give me a second."

What was done was done. Shoving aside his useless regrets, he stood and stretched.

Astrid now sat on a couch, letting Martine clean her forehead wound and tape a row of Band-Aids butterfly-style across it. The animosity between them seemed to have abated as Martine took charge of her mother's welfare, a role reversal that Dan felt certain was not lost on either woman. He hoped it was a first step toward reconciliation. If so, then at least *something* good would come from this mess.

Meanwhile, there was a lot of work to do. To Jade he said, "Grab that blanket from the hearth."

"You forgot the wedding ring."

Her comment brought to mind an image of Geoff's wife, Ruth. Having met her on several social occasions, Dan suspected their marriage had become loveless. She might be happier in the long run without her husband, but news of his death, when she finally received it, would probably break her heart.

"It won't come off," Dan said of the ring.

"Take the finger." Jade pulled out a vicious-looking knife.

No way. There'd be no more mutilation of the only colleague he'd ever felt comfortable confiding in, traitor though Geoff was.

"Don't bother," Dan said. "The cops will eventually identify him, anyway." Dental x-rays, what remained of his fingerprints, maybe DNA if it was on record anywhere outside the U.S. government. "We just need to slow the process."

Jade shrugged, pocketed her knife, and brought the blanket.

He helped her spread it out and roll Geoff's body onto it.

"I wish it hadn't come to this," Martine said. Having finished tending to Astrid, she now sat beside her, looking worn out.

"Same here." Dan laid the soiled kitchen towels on top of Geoff's body. "But he was going to kill us."

"He threatened to. But if we'd given him the book—"

"He killed your driver outside," Jade said.

Oh, no. Dan had forgotten about the driver—how he'd pulled out all the stops to get here, how proud he'd been when they finally arrived. Poor innocent bastard.

Martine shut her eyes. "That's horrible."

"Mon Dieu." Astrid, evidently returning to full awareness, gaped at Geoff's body. "Is that Mister Fairchild?"

"What's left of him," Jade told her, tying together two of the blanket's corners to secure Geoff's feet.

Astrid peered at her. "Who are *you?*"

"She saved our lives." Dan tied the corners at his end of the blanket. "Ready?"

He and Jade hoisted the bundle.

Astrid pushed herself upright on the couch. "What are you doing?"

"Martine can fill you in."

Together, Dan and Jade lugged Geoff's body—like a hammock between them—out the patio doors, across Astrid's terrace, and down the long sweep of her snow-covered lawn to the Seine.

As they did, Dan scanned their surroundings for any possibility that they might be observed. There was only parkland at this end of the narrow island facing them in the river. On Astrid's side, snow-packed trees screened her property from her neighbors.

"We're clear," Jade said, evidently having conducted her own visual survey.

On three, they swung Geoff's body into the river. It hit with a splash too loud for Dan's comfort. "Quiet," he whispered, listening for voices or the crunch of footsteps in the snow.

When no sounds came, he looked back at the bundle. It floated in a weak current, then stopped, possibly caught on a shallow snag. Dan steeled himself to wade in and dislodge it. But the flow slowly rotated it and carried it on. A minute or so later, it sank out of sight.

Dan finally relaxed. It would take a long time for Geoff to surface. The waterlogged weight of his overcoat and the blanket should hold him under for days, if not weeks. Plus, the frigid water would inhibit decomposition and the accompanying formation of bodily gases that could refloat him.

Jade broke into his thoughts with, "What about the hardware?"

Hardware? Oh. She meant the stuff he had taken off Geoff's body. "You want his Uzi?"

"No. No weapons. I'm flying out of here at the first opportunity."

Smart move. In her line of work, hit and run was the wisest course. "Then I'll get rid of it and the rest of his things on the way back to Paris."

And Geoff Fairchild would be no more than a memory. Dan swallowed hard, then straightened his shoulders. *Damn you, Geoff. It was your own fucking fault.*

But as Dan peered again at the spot where the body had disappeared, he realized that Geoff *would* be more than a memory to DSS. When Geoff failed to return to the office or respond to attempts at contacting him, he'd become a Code Black emergency. DSS would mount an urgent search. There'd be messages to US embassies and growing panic as analysts pored over his official files in search of compromising information that interrogators might wring out of him.

All that fruitless scurrying until Geoff's body was found and identified, at which point panic would give way to confusion.

"So we're done," Jade said.

"Not quite." He glanced at Astrid's house. "We have to finish cleaning up."

"We?"

"Yes, we." Heading toward the house, he pulled out Geoff's keys and jangled them. "Unless you want to walk back to Paris."

She caught up and trudged next to him. "You really are a prick, aren't you?"

"A grateful prick. Sorry for not saying so before, but thank you for taking that shot."

"Don't get all gushy on me. I didn't do it for you."

"Oh, I remember now. You had some misguided notion that Geoff was yours."

"Misguided?" Jade punched him in the shoulder, then stopped and pulled up her sweatshirt to reveal the adhesive tape and gauze covering the wound in her side. "You got a bullet hole in you?" She raised her sweatshirt higher, exposing her bra and the bandage between her breast and collarbone. "I've got two."

Dan recognized their exchange as what the Service had called "post-traumatic banter," the sarcastic jousting agents engaged in to regain some semblance of normalcy after a life-threatening experience. In truth, it helped. "Okay, he was yours."

"Men," she huffed, pulling the sweatshirt down. "It's all about you."

"Hey, I conceded, didn't I?"

She narrowed her eyes, then cocked her head slightly from one side to the other, as though accepting that might be true. "Maybe you're not such a prick, after all."

Faint praise, but he'd take it.

As they continued toward Astrid's house, Jade pointed at their shin-deep footprints in the snow. "You better pray for a thaw. Even a blizzard won't hide these."

She was dead-right about that. Once the body was found, the cops would immediately search the banks for where it went in. Fortunately, it would take a while for Geoff to surface. Or so he hoped.

As for a thaw, one might be coming. The overcast had thinned. Afternoon sun shone dimly, like a flashlight through multiple layers of tissue paper. Although it was still freezing out here, seeing a hint of sunlight encouraged him.

On top of that, his nausea was gone. His head still hurt but had not noticeably bled since he'd wiped it with his sleeve before frisking Geoff's body.

When they reentered the house, Dan stopped. Astrid sat glowering, next to the fire. Martine, presumably the one who had beefed up the flames with new logs, stood next to her. Between them, the charred book lay open on the hearth.

"Where is the real one?" Astrid demanded.

Martine stared at him with a poker face, her eyes penetrating but revealing nothing about whether she approved or disapproved of his deception.

Jade walked over and looked down at two full-page photos of cave paintings. For the first time since he'd known her, she laughed out loud. "Lovel, you're a better bluffer than I thought."

"The real one's safe," he said. "If I'd brought it, it would be ashes by now." The book's pages, cut from an ancient scroll and crinkled with age, would have caught on fire much more readily than the glossy, flat-lying pages of that picture book. "I couldn't take the risk."

"It *should* be ashes," Astrid declared for the fourth or fifth time since their initial argument began.

"We've been through all that. I disagree, and you know it."

Martine angled her head toward the kitchen. "We should talk." When he'd followed her in, she said, "Maybe my mother is right."

"What?"

"Shh." She glanced over his shoulder, then drew him to the farthest corner of the room. "This Christophe she mentioned? It turns out he's an ex-lover who works in French intelligence. After he left here this morning, he called her to say that Israel had just gone on 'full alert,' his words." She bit her lip. "War could break out any minute. I think we have to destroy the book. And *prove* its destruction for all parties involved. Post photos on YouTube or Instagram, or wherever."

It was the worst of the scenarios they had considered—that one or more Muslim nations would become aware of the book and what it said, and consider it justification for obliterating Jewish "usurpers" in the Holy Land.

As to how they had become aware, it was almost certainly as Dan had suspected. Geoff had offered it for sale, probably with pumped up promises of what it said—and with no care in the world for the consequences. People would die. Thousands, if not more. Geoff didn't give a damn, so long as he could retire to some tropical paradise and thumb his nose at the bureaucracy that had twice passed him over for advancement.

He had paid for his greed but left behind the genuine threat of a second Holocaust if the conflict went nuclear.

Martine's belief that "publicly" destroying the book would remove the justification and avert conflict might well be the only viable solution. The thought revolted him.

"The book," Martine said, "is it still at Paulette's?"

"Yes." Then a possible work-around struck him. "Does your mother have any old books? We could burn one of them, instead."

Martine shook her head. "French classics, some modern novels, and a few treatises on economic theory." She paused. "But what about Leroux? He has lots of old books."

"Excellent!" Dan grasped her hands. "We'll go to his office as soon as—"

Her phone chirped.

After a brief exchange with the caller, she held the phone to her chest and told Dan, "It's Christophe. *Maman* used my phone to call him." Following a rapid conversation in French, she disconnected. "He says he'll be here in half an hour."

"Shit." This was disastrous. Or wait a minute. Maybe not. Dan shut his eyes and breathed slowly as ideas spun through his head, spiraling around like stars coalescing into a galaxy with Christophe at its center.

"Are you okay?" she asked.

"There may be a way out of this. But we'll need your mother's cooperation. And we have to get rid of Jade." Dan walked Martine through his plan, flimsy as a bridge made of spider webs, but the best he could come up with until Martine started adding improvements.

Reasonably satisfied, they returned to the big reception room. The patio doors stood wide-open. The fire roared, and Jade was tossing on another log.

"To air out the stink of burned flesh," she said.

Astrid had moved back to a couch, probably because it was too hot on the hearth. Apparently, she was willing to let Jade do the "housework." She peered at Dan. "Well?"

"We'll take care of the book," Martine said.

"Where is it?"

"At a friend's house."

Astrid leapt from the couch, her face crimson with a fury Dan had never seen before. "Do you have any idea what you have done? You lied to me about bringing the book, and now precious hours will be lost while the Middle East prepares for all-out war."

Dan wanted to say there would *be* no crisis if Astrid had simply said nothing about the book and let it stay in the monastery. But he held his tongue. They needed her on their side.

"*Maman*, Christophe is on his way."

Astrid's face lit up. "He'll straighten this out."

"Who's Christophe?" Jade asked.

"French intelligence." Dan pointed to her rifle. "You better get packed. We have less than thirty minutes."

Methodically, with no hint of fluster, she disassembled her rifle and zipped it into her shoulder bag. "What about the other body?"

"Another body?" Astrid gaped at her. Evidently, she'd still been dazed during that part of the earlier conversation.

"Their driver outside," Jade told her. "Fairchild shot him through the head."

"Oh, no."

"See if you can find a dark blanket," Dan said to Martine. As she headed for the stairs, he led Jade out the front door. They heaved the driver's frozen body into the back of the Land Cruiser. Throwing him in the river would have been quicker, but his destination probably was on record, and the vehicle's GPS undoubtedly could be interrogated. There was no choice but to drive the poor guy back to Paris and leave him and his Land Cruiser in a parking lot. At least he wouldn't have "disappeared." His family, distraught though they might be, would have some degree of closure.

When Martine arrived with the blanket, Dan draped it over the body, hoping like hell Christophe wouldn't notice. He handed Geoff's keys to Jade. "Good luck and thanks again."

She shook his hand, then nodded good-bye to Martine.

"By the way," Dan asked, "where are you off to?"

Jade cast him a look that said, *Really? You expect me to tell you?*

As she set off through the snow, Dan and Martine hustled back inside. They had fifteen minutes to convince Astrid that their plan would work.

"Let me do the talking," Martine said. "She's still mad at you."

They found Astrid pacing with a half-full snifter of cognac in her hand. She had closed the patio doors.

"*Maman*, we have a solution that will satisfy everyone."

Astrid eyed her disdainfully. "It will satisfy me to see that book—"

"*Maman!* Please listen."

With a glance at her watch, Astrid said, "Christophe will be here any minute. Then you'll see what—"

"Stop!"

Tense silence filled the room, broken only by the crackling of the fire.

Dan took a seat on one of the couches. Although mother and daughter faced each other like boxers waiting for the bell, Astrid had finally shut up. And there was still time.

Martine explained that Geoff *thought* he had the book and had offered it for sale. When he realized he had the wrong book, he came here to get the real one. He had buyers who were willing to pay a lot of money for an Old Testament text denying Jewish rights to Israel.

"How could Mr. Fairchild possibly know what is in that book?" Astrid demanded.

Dan answered, "I think he learned it from you."

"He did not!"

"Geoff told me you contacted him about how to get in touch with me. He never gives something for nothing. He would have wanted to know why."

For a long moment, Astrid stared at him. Then she lowered her head and covered her face with her hands.

"Never mind," Dan said. "There's no way you could have known how conniving he was. The main thing now is that someone influential, probably in Iran, believed Geoff's claim and initiated preparations for war. Which is why, as you said earlier, Israel went onto alert." He paused to let Astrid absorb that. "The good news, I *think*, is that nothing will happen until that person actually acquires the book and can use it to rally support for an attack on Israel."

Astrid jutted out her chin. "Which is why it must be destroyed."

"No, *Maman*. It's why we need to prove that there never *was* such a book. The book Fairchild claimed to have was something totally different."

"He couldn't read ancient Hebrew," Dan added. "So how would he know?"

Astrid sank down on the couch opposite him, her eyes doubtful but with a slight glimmer of hope.

Martine sat next to her. "Only three people have ever seen the real book. Dan, myself, and a scholar at the Louvre who won't dare say a word. We'll produce a different book and say that is the one Fairchild had."

"Ultimately," Dan said, "we'll tell the media, show the phony book, and not mention Fairchild by name."

"How can you do that?" Astrid asked.

Dan checked his watch. It was almost time. "That's where Christophe comes in."

Chapter 33

When the knock came, twenty minutes later than expected, Astrid rushed to her front door. Dan heard her say, *"Mon chéri,"* then *"Ce n'est rien,"* It's nothing.

A moment later she returned on the arm of a tall, trim man in his middle fifties. Obviously, it was Christophe, her supposed ex-lover, although Dan suspected "once-and-current" was closer to the mark, considering Christophe had left here this morning.

He had longish salt-and-pepper hair, a day's growth of beard, and intense blue eyes that looked capable of skewering a stubborn informant.

Astrid spoke to him in French, then switched to English. "This is my daughter, Martine, and her friend, Dan Lovel."

"Dan Lovel?" Christophe stared at him as if sizing up a cobra.

Surprised the guy seemed to know of him, Dan stepped forward to shake hands.

Christophe granted him a strong but perfunctory shake, then bestowed air kisses on Martine's cheeks and turned back to Astrid.

"We were delayed because the road crew I called is still cutting up that fallen tree. We had to wait for them to make a path around it for us. The electricity company will repair your line as soon as the road is open."

"Thank you so much. Would you like a cognac? We have something to discuss."

"I assumed you wanted me to take you to Paris. My men are waiting outside."

While Dan logged that last comment, Astrid said, "It's about the Moses book."

Christophe narrowed his eyes. "I thought that was settled."

"Not quite." Astrid drew him to the couch where she'd been sitting. In mixed French and English, she began relating everything, from Geoff's appearance at her door, to his burned body being carried out by Dan and a woman named Jade, to Dan and Martine's plan for defusing a Middle East war.

Christophe pointed at her forehead. "Is that how you received this injury? During the fight?"

"As I told you, it's nothing."

"She's being brave," Martine said. "It came from a stray bullet."

"*Ma chérie!*" He took hold of Astrid's hand. A few words in French passed between them, then Christophe drilled his eyes into Dan's. "Are you responsible for this?"

"Geoff is," Dan said, well aware that most people in the intelligence business preferred short, straight answers. "He fired a wild shot. It bounced off the back of the fireplace."

"That's exactly what happened," Martine confirmed. "I saw it all."

After a glance at the fireplace, Christophe turned back to Dan. "Then you killed him?"

"No. A woman he shot two days ago took her revenge."

"This Jade?"

"Yes." Dan seated himself on the facing couch, where Martine joined him. "If she hadn't, the three of us would be dead."

Christophe looked dubious.

"If you don't believe me, ask Astrid." When she nodded, Dan cut to the chase. "In any event, Jade's gone now. What's important is that we need your help."

"*I* will determine what is important. Where is Mr. Fairchild's body?"

"At the bottom of the river, somewhere downstream. It probably won't surface for several weeks."

"What makes you so sure?"

"He's pretty heavily weighted down."

After seeming to accept that, Christophe asked, "Does your DSS know he is dead?"

"No. And when he's found, forensic identification will be difficult. So, there's plenty of time before DSS needs to be notified."

"Why difficult?"

"You'll see when you retrieve him." In fact, it might be best not to tell DSS. Avoid an inquiry. Just consign the body to an anonymous grave. But Christophe probably wouldn't go that far.

Although Dan appreciated that the man wanted complete a picture of the events, he was growing frustrated with the incessant questions.

Thankfully, Martine picked up the ball. "Christophe, all we're asking you to do is announce that you have found a man's body and a book he had with him."

Christophe shot Dan a scowl. "You said his body will not surface for—"

"You won't have a body," Dan told him. "You'll just *say* you do. Found somewhere in Paris. Nowhere near this house."

"But you will have a book," Martine said. "Not the real one, but one we'll get for you."

Christophe looked at Astrid.

She clasped his hand. "Please do it. I believe it is the only way to avoid a major catastrophe in the Middle East. Perhaps even a worldwide economic collapse."

"Why a worldwide collapse?"

"Christophe! We talked about this before." She paused, as though to compose herself. "Who has all the money? The Gulf states. Western markets, whole western economies, have become dependent on their investments. And it's all based on oil. If their production were destroyed ... well, you can imagine. And even worse would be a conflict involving nuclear weapons."

Christophe appeared to ponder that a moment, his face betraying a mixture of doubt and unease. He turned back to Martine. "So, no body and a false book. Continue."

"We're asking you show the book on television," she said, "opened to the first page. Say you believe it's a clue to the dead man's identity and possibly to his murderer. Then appeal to viewers for their help. The nation or nations preparing for war with Israel will see the broadcast and realize that what they thought was their justification is nothing of the sort. The Middle East will go back to its normal stand-off."

Well aware that intelligence services never made public announcements, let alone public appeals, Dan said, "Of course a reporter should make the announcement and attribute everything to the police. And the police will have to agree."

"I assumed that," Christophe replied as if insulted. "What is difficult for me is why you think that seeing this wrong book will make any difference?"

Dan answered, "You know as well as I do that no individual country in the Middle East could win a war with Israel. Look at what happened to Egypt in nineteen sixty-six. But the Moses book is so explosive that whoever acquired it could use it to inflame other

Muslim nations. Incite mass demonstrations in the streets. Rally support for a full-blown holy war to 'cleanse' the region of all Jews."

"That is a very large assumption."

"No," Astrid replied. "It is not."

To Christophe, Martine said, "You told *Maman* that Israel is on full alert. Dan and I think that's because Geoff Fairchild offered the Moses book for sale in an online auction. One or more buyers reported this to their governments, who reacted by preparing to capitalize on this so-called biblical proof that Jews have no claim to the Holy Land."

"But Fairchild couldn't clench the deal," Dan added, "until he could actually demonstrate that he had such a book. So, showing the book he *supposedly* had—a different one entirely—should defuse the situation by removing the whole excuse for a multi-national attack based on God's word."

"It's a good strategy," Astrid said, clutching Christophe's arm.

Christophe spoke with her in French, then let out an audible breath. "I will have that cognac now."

Dan wanted to shout, "Yes!" The man was coming around to acceptance, or at least seriously considering their plan.

When Astrid went into the kitchen, Christophe asked Martine, "Where is the real book?"

"Safe."

He glanced ceilingward. "And the false book?"

"We'll get it for you."

"When?"

She looked at Dan.

"Give us a few hours," he said. "We'll get it to you in time for the evening news tonight."

Astrid returned with a snifter of cognac and handed it to Christophe. "*Mon cher*, have you agreed?"

With a look of resignation, he muttered, "*Merde alors.*"

#

Having already burned the contents of Geoff's wallet and given Jade the guy's keys, Dan disposed of the cellphones and watch at three different places outside Rueil-Malmaison. Where their road to Paris crossed the Seine, he stopped the Land Cruiser, got out as if checking his tires, and hurled the Uzi and Geoff's pistol into the river. *Sayonara, you back-stabbing shit.*

"What about the driver?" Martine asked as they continued toward Paris.

"He'll have to stay back there until we ditch the car."

"We drive around with a corpse?"

"Unless you have a better idea."

"If I do, I'll tell you. In the meantime, what do you think we should do with the real book?"

"I'd still like to give it to scholars in Israel."

She rolled her lips in. "You assume it will take them a long time to release their analyses. But do you really want to rely on what we *think* they'll do?" She paused. "The more people who know about it, the more chance there is of a leak."

"I doubt that will happen."

"But we can't be sure. And even if you're right, when their findings eventually *are* made public, what's to stop the kind of conflagration we're trying to head off right now? We might just be delaying it."

Dan's grip tightened around the steering wheel. Why hadn't he thought of those things? Because he'd broken one of his cardinal rules. He had focused on the goal but failed miserably to consider alternative consequences. "What do *you* think we should do?"

"I'm not sure. But I do know that, if we give it to someone else, we lose control of it."

"Are you suggesting we hide it again?"

"I'm not suggesting anything. But I guess I'm wondering how important it is that *anyone* analyze the book. The world has gotten along for centuries, millennia, without even knowing about it."

"You do want to hide it. Or destroy it."

"Dammit, Dan, stop jumping to conclusions. I'm just thinking out loud. The way you did when you tried to convince me we were being followed from Usti to Paris."

"I was right about that," he said and immediately regretted his words.

Frosty silence filled the car. The winter air outside was probably warmer. As they passed La Defense and continued toward Paris, Dan replayed everything Martine had said. She was right about all of it. Maybe the best thing to do was put the book in a safe deposit box in some Parisian bank.

At last he negotiated the bend around the Arc de Triomphe and could broach an uncontentious subject. "Can you help me find a place to dump this car? The street's no good, because the driver is in back." And probably thawing by now. "How about a commercial car park?"

"There are lots of underground garages. But they all have security cameras."

That figured. Paris was one of the most surveilled cities in the world. And of course neither he nor Martine wore a hoodie or a hat that would hide their faces. "I'm wide open to other ideas."

She seemed to ponder that, then shook her head. "I don't have any." After consulting her phone, she directed him to an underground garage near Les Invalides.

Dan found a space in one corner and backed in part way. "Get out while I wipe down all the surfaces." Once he'd finished, he continued backing until the rear bumper touched the wall, which made spotting the body almost impossible.

They walked up to street level, their heads lowered to avoid facial capture by the cameras, and emerged into early evening lights and a clearing sky. At the first intersection, Martine flagged down a taxi and told the driver, *"Le Louvre, s'il vous plaît. Porte des Lions."*

#

Approaching Charles de Gaulle airport, Jade switched off the navigation system. It had served her well, allowing her to choose a circuitous route that avoided central Paris. Now her goal was in sight.

And her shoulder bag was empty. Immediately after crossing the Seine, she had turned off the highway and circled back to the river, where she found a quiet place between two barges moored to the bank. She dropped her knife in the water, then walked fifty yards tossing in each part of her rifle, separately, along the way. There was no reason for anyone to search the bottom here, and if they did, it would take divers. The space between the barges and bank was much too narrow to be dragged by a police boat.

Not that it mattered. Only an ingrained compulsion to cover her tracks had driven her to take those measures. There was no bullet in Fairchild to compare with her rifle—it had gone straight through his neck and into the wall next to a door jamb, where she'd dug it out with her knife. So, no bullet and no way to connect the rifle's parts to her.

Besides, in a few hours, she'd be gone.

She pulled into long-term parking. After carefully cleaning every surface she had touched or might have touched, she crushed the car's key fob with her foot and dropped the pieces into two separate trash bins.

On the Departures board inside, she found an Air France flight to New York, boarding now and leaving in just under an hour. She rushed to the nearest Air France desk. With one of her fake credit cards, she bought a first-class ticket, a time-tested way to ensure she got on.

An attractive flight attendant with a bob haircut led her to a huge sleeper seat in the second row. It faced what looked like a settee, but a quick mental calculation told Jade it was for her feet when the seat was laid flat. *Cool.*

She declined the flight attendant's offer to hang her jacket but said, "Yes, please," to champagne. After several drinks and a meal, she planned to sleep the whole way. For now, she settled back in her seat.

When her champagne arrived, Jade took a grateful swallow. What a waste of time this had been. The assignment was simple—make sure a book got to Paris, then steal it. Yeah, sure. Simple until the client decided to kill you. She clamped her jaw.

Well, the client was dead and gone. Along with the second half of her fee *and* the three million euros she had planned to take off Fairchild after he made the exchange.

Other than the first half of her fee, she had gained nothing, except two bullet holes she didn't need and a working acquaintance with Dan Lovel. She took another sip of champagne.

Lovel was good. And pretty good-looking. Closing her eyes, she pictured him. Maybe they *would* work together at some future time. He was not worth the three million euros she'd lost. But if their paths ever did cross again, he might be worth …

Forget it.

#

The smell of stale marijuana smoke hung in Leroux's office, soured by the rancid stink of male perspiration. The latter suggested their venerable scholar might still be fretting over the possibility that

Jade would revisit him. To ease the man's mind, Dan went to the desk and wrote on a pad of paper:

She's gone.
Jardani

That settled, he glanced around. Predictably, the four Louvre volumes remained stacked on the floor. Dan pointed at them. "Your mother lied to me about those. She used the Nazi murders of my grandparents to recruit me, but she never really gave a damn about returning stolen artworks to their countries of origin. Did you?"

"Of course, I did." Martine looked offended, as though he'd impugned her honor—which unfortunately he had. "I still do. And I think she does, also."

Pleased to hear it, Dan turned to the bookcases. "Okay, then let's get started. We need something slim, written in Hebrew."

"Not so fast. You don't trust me?"

Uh-oh. She was referring to his "Did you" question. "I've trusted you ever since Prague. It's just that the original purpose of our mission, the whole reason I agreed, seems to have been lost." When she didn't reply, he said, "Believe me, I'm glad it's still important to you." *And that you weren't part of your mother's scheme.*

Possibly mollified—he couldn't be sure—she shifted her attention to the bookshelves lining one side of Leroux's office.

"Hey," he said in an attempt at levity, "I'm paranoid. You've told me so a dozen times."

"It's not your most appealing trait."

Hoping the storm had blown over, at least for now, Dan scanned the bookshelves on the other side of the office.

They searched for a quarter of an hour before Martine exclaimed, "Here!"

The book she held open was slightly larger and a little thicker than the Moses book but otherwise very close. "Good job. Now what about the Louvre books? I wouldn't leave them out like this."

She looked around, then stashed them under Leroux's desk. "I'll give them to my mother when this all blows over."

"Then we're done here."

"Wait. We need to find out where Christophe is and where he wants us to deliver this." She thumbed her phone, said, "*Maman*," and launched into a rapid conversation in French. When she finished, she told Dan, "DGSE headquarters. In the Twentieth Arrondissement. We'll need another cab."

#

Security at the Direction Générale de la Sécurité Extérieure, was as tight as in any US intelligence facility—magnetometers, full-body scans, x-ray imaging of all carried items, cameras no doubt tied to facial-recognition software. Despite the fact that Christophe—a supposed big shot at the agency—stood waiting for them on the other side, Dan and Martine were spared none of it.

When they'd passed, Christophe led them to a small conference room where a blonde woman whose face had benefited from plastic surgery was already seated at the table.

A veteran newscaster, Dan figured, one who had probably established a reputation for scooping the competition and breaking big stories.

The conversation took place in French, most of which Dan couldn't catch.

Eventually, Martine said to him, "Give her the book."

"First, let me say a couple of things. You understand English?"

"Of course," the woman replied.

"It will help if you mention that the man appears to be in his middle fifties. He is well-dressed, and his clothing suggests he is American."

The reporter glanced at Christophe, who nodded.

"Also, he was wearing a gold Rolex watch." If Geoff had met a potential buyer, the buyer might have noticed that. Never mind that the watch was counterfeit, purchased in Indonesia a decade ago. And never mind that Dan had thrown it into a pond on the outskirts of Rueil-Malmaison.

"Anything else?" she asked.

"It's extremely important that the camera zooms in on the text of the book. At least the first page and preferably the following two, also."

"I already told her," Christophe said.

"Then I guess that's it." Mentally crossing his fingers, Dan slid over the book.

The woman paged through it, inclined her head toward Christophe, and left.

When she was gone, Dan asked, "Where's Astrid? I expected her to be here."

Christophe stood. "I do not want her in this building. It could damage her credibility with foreign governments."

Martine thanked him for his help.

"I did not do it for you."

#

An hour later, Dan and Martine sat on Paulette's couch, sipping a robust Pommard and listening to the evening news on a radio Paulette had brought down from her bedroom.

Dan chided himself for expecting to watch the broadcast on television. But Paulette was so perceptive he'd half-forgotten she couldn't see. In any case, according to her, the radio station played a simultaneous broadcast of the top TV channel in Paris.

"Here it is," Martine said, obviously referring to the story Christophe had planted with his compliant reporter.

"Translate for me. Please."

"Breaking news. A man's body has been found by police in the Bois de Vincennes. He was in his middle fifties. Well-dressed, probably American."

"What's the Bois de Vincennes?"

"A large park on the eastern side of Paris."

Okay, that worked.

"No identification, but he wore a gold Rolex and had an old book in ancient Hebrew." Martine paused. "I think she's showing it now."

This was the most important part. Dan held his breath, hoping the camera lingered and wishing he had a TV to confirm it. After about ten seconds, he heard a page turn. Another ten seconds passed before the reporter's voice resumed.

"Police," Martine translated, "believe this book is an important clue to the man's killer. They say there is evidence the dead man was planning to sell it. She doesn't say what evidence."

Because there *was* no real evidence. Only Dan's gut feeling.

"They say that identifying the book will help to identify the body. And possibly the murderer. They request the public's assistance. If you have any information about the man or the book, please call blah, blah, blah."

Dan finally relaxed. The newscaster was definitely a pro. She had run the story as an exclusive, covered all the points, and placed heavy emphasis on the book. They couldn't have asked for more.

Reaching for the wine bottle to top up their glasses, he said, "Now we wait."

#

In a small bistro fifteen minutes from DGSE headquarters, Astrid clinked her glass against Christophe's. "I hope this works."

"You say that as if you don't believe it will."

"I'm just nervous. When will we know if tensions have settled down?"

He glanced around the half-full restaurant and lowered his voice. "There are situation boards at headquarters. Earlier this evening, the Middle East board was lit up with red lights and two purple. Red means preparations in progress for conventional war. Purple signifies nuclear powers set to launch."

"Oh, God." Although she had never seen this board, Astrid pictured a big video display mounted on a wall with one light per country. "Are the purple ones Israel and Iran?"

"Yes. When they go back to red, or preferably yellow..." He held up his hand and crossed his fingers ... "then we're safe. I'll be informed immediately."

"Yellow is ..."

"The closest we get in the Middle East to a normal state of militarily readiness. It's basically what the Americans call DEFCON Four or, in Israel's case, DEFCON three."

"I pray," she said, "for yellow."

Chapter 34

Panting hard, Dan trudged up to Paulette's house just before six in the morning. He'd spent the last half hour running wind sprints through the empty streets of the Latin Quarter. It helped that he wore hiking boots. They made the dashes tougher, the burn in his legs and lungs more intense. The pain of his frustration more bearable.

But no less real.

Martine was gone. The book was gone. Sometime during the night, she had disappeared from Paulette's house and taken the Moses book with her. Where she had gone was anyone's guess. Her ability to enter the Louvre at any hour made it an obvious choice, but she could be counting on that to fool him. She also had an apartment of her own and probably other friends besides Paulette. Not to mention that she could have left Paris for somewhere else. Too many options.

He knocked on the glass door, then pressed the code that let him in.

Paulette emerged from the kitchen. She wore black slacks and a white shirt, rather than the thick robe she'd had on earlier. "Do you feel better?" she asked.

"Yes, thanks." Much better than an hour ago when he'd first discovered Martine and the book were missing. Now, instead of outraged, he felt deeply embarrassed at how he'd ransacked Martine's room and grilled Paulette as though she were an accomplice in Martine's betrayal.

Finding Martine's phone under her mattress had only interrupted his interrogation. On it, a text from Astrid read, "The plan worked. Catastrophe averted. Where is the book?" Like a kid having a tantrum, he'd thrown the phone against a wall.

What a bullying, self-centered ass he'd been. Embarrassment didn't begin to describe his regret. "Paulette, I am truly ashamed of my behavior this morning. You did not deserve it. I apologize sincerely."

"There is no harm," she replied. "You were angry."

"That's not an excuse." Especially since he prided himself on separating emotions from his actions. "You've been very kind to us, to *me*. I'm really, really sorry."

With a smile he couldn't quite read, she said, *"J'accepte."* Then she pointed toward the kitchen. "I made coffee. Would you like some?"

That was it? After everything he'd put her through and all his agonizing since, she had simply accepted his apology and dismissed the subject?

Feeling more relieved than he deserved, he said, "I'd love some," and plopped onto the couch.

She went into the kitchen and soon returned with two mugs. After placing one on the glass coffee table in front of him, she sat in her chair and cradled the other mug in both hands. "Are you still angry?"

"Just disappointed."

"You think Martine does not trust you."

"I thought we were a team. We worked well together."

Leaning forward, Paulette set her mug on the table. "After my accident, I was very angry. I asked, 'Why me? I have been a good person, a faithful wife.' Then my husband left." She paused as though gathering strength. "I thought of *suicide*. You understand?"

"Yes." Although she pronounced it the French way, it was the same word in English.

"But my *psychiatre* helped me to accept my blindness. And divorce. Now I am … content? I think that is the word." She sat back. "Of course, I hope to love again one day. If it happens, I will be happy, instead of only content. If it does not happen, content is still much better than angry."

Clearly, what he was supposed to learn from Paulette's experience came from something like the Serenity Prayer. Accept what he could not change, move on, and hope for the best. Hoping for a positive outcome was not part of his operational psyche. He relied on plans and backup plans. But in this case, he had no choice. In fact, with Martine's concern yesterday about the book eventually coming to light, he should have anticipated what she would do—destroy it or hide it where no one could find it.

In either case, the heartrending truth was that she did not trust him. Maybe he deserved that after implying in Leroux's office last night that he didn't trust *her*, or at least her motives.

No wonder his girlfriends had rarely lasted more than a year—he was his own worst enemy.

As to moving on, he again had no choice. This had been his toughest job ever, with its myriad uncertainties and Geoff's death. But there would be other jobs. And in a practical sense, averting war in the Middle East was the most successful outcome he could have asked for. It was time to let go.

Happy? That was a different matter. Given his personality and the life he had chosen, contentment was probably the best he could expect.

"You are very quiet," Paulette said.

Refocusing, he admitted, "I was thinking about what you told me. And thank you, by the way, for being so candid."

"I believe there is nothing you can do about Martine and the book. But I also believe she will come back to you."

The former was absolutely true. The latter he doubted.

#

Ninety percent of the Louvre's possessions were never exhibited. There wasn't enough space or public interest, or the pieces simply didn't measure up to finer examples. Instead, they were crammed into row after row of basement storerooms where few, if any, would ever again see the light of day.

Near the back of this particular storeroom stood a dusty old map case full of minor medieval sketches and individual leaves from illuminated manuscripts. Martine placed the book behind a stack of loose vellum pages in the second drawer down.

The case was identified by a yellowed label affixed to its upper left corner. On it, some curator had written "3602" in penmanship typical of the early 1900s.

Half a dozen other cases and numerous wooden crates crowded the rest of the room. All bore similar labels, coded inscriptions on the headstones of pieces permanently consigned to Dead Storage.

#

Although it was barely sunset, Dan's cab driver would take him no deeper into the Bois de Boulogne than an intersection of two roads near a place called the Pavillon Royal. From there, Dan trekked a hundred yards into the forest before catching his first whiff of outdoor cooking. Fried bread, pork, and onions. The fried bread smelled like his mother's, a mouthwatering aroma that said, "You are home."

Of course, he wasn't home. But he was close to the encampment of the Romani who had recently been evicted by French police from a disused railroad right-of-way in central Paris.

These people wouldn't know him from Adam. Like Lom, the leader of the Roma community in Usti, they'd be suspicious at first—justifiably suspicious and probably hostile to outsiders. This time, however, Dan had brought a bottle of Slivovitz in hopes of paving his way to a traditional meal and an evening among kindred souls who expected nothing of him beyond a few shots of the fiery liquor and perhaps a good tale.

He soon glimpsed firelight. Almost certainly, open fires were illegal in the forest. But French authorities made concessions when it suited them.

Twenty feet away from the clearing, he coughed to announce his presence.

Two women rose from beside the fire. Three nearby men pulled knives.

Dan paused to give them a good look at him. Then he took a deep breath and approached slowly, his arms out, one hand holding the bottle.

"I am Jardani, of the Camlo people."

About the Author

John Oehler has spent much of his life overseas, beginning in 1966 with two years as a Peace Corps Volunteer in Nepal. His time in the Himalayan kingdom immersed him in a culture of Hindu gods and Buddhist monks, gave him breathtaking opportunities to trek into the high mountains, reduced him to a scrawny 150 pounds, and ignited his passion for foreign lands.

He subsequently earned a Ph.D. in Geology at UCLA and spent the next three years working in Australia where he travelled extensively through the harsh beauty of the Outback. Upon returning to the United States, he went to work for a major oil company, first in research, then in international exploration. The latter took him to about fifty countries and fueled his writing with quirky characters, exotic settings, and cultural contrasts.

All of John's novels have originated from personal experience. While living in London, he became interested in the business and culture of perfumes, an interest that blossomed during later visits to the renowned perfume school in Versailles and led to his novel APHRODESIA. While working in Egypt, he spotted a potential way to break into the Egyptian Museum in Cairo. Combining that with a longstanding attraction to Egyptology gave rise to his novel PAPURUS. His work in Venezuela, combined with his vacations there in the jungles and highlands, inspired his novel TEPUI. During a Christmas vacation in Prague, he spent an afternoon at a monastery where he learned about their collection of "forbidden books." His imagination took over and created his latest (2019) novel EX LIBRIS.

John has an abiding love of animals, strong interests in art, history, and science, and a hunger for challenging experiences. Writing gives him a chance to combine all of these into page-turners that keep readers thinking long after they finish the final chapter.

Also by John Oehler

Tepui

In 1559, forty-nine Spaniards exploring a tributary of the Orinoco River reached a sheer-sided, cloud-capped mountain called Tepui Zupay. When they tried to climb it, all but six of them were slaughtered by Amazons. Or so claimed Friar Sylvestre, the expedition's chronicler. But Sylvestre made many bizarre claims: rivers of blood, plants that lead to gold.

Jerry Pace, a burn-scarred botanist struggling for tenure at UCLA, thinks the friar was high on mushrooms. Jerry's best friend, the historian who just acquired Sylvestre's journal, disagrees. He plans to retrace the expedition's footsteps and wants Jerry to come with him. Jerry refuses, until he spots a stain between the journal's pages—a stain that could only have been left by a plant that died out with the dinosaurs. Now he has to find that plant.

But the Venezuelan wilderness does not forgive intruders. Battered and broken, they reach a remote Catholic orphanage where the old prioress warns of death awaiting any who would venture farther. But an exotic Indian girl leads them on, through piranha-infested rivers and jungles teaming with poisonous plants, to Tepui Zupay—the forbidden mountain no outsider has set eyes on since the Spaniards met their doom.

> "This is the kind of book you are always hoping to find and read. Exciting and grabs you right from the start and carries you along on a great adventure, mystery with historical insight, characters you can relate to and become emotionally involved with and just a little love interest.".
>
> "Sumptuous reading. Definitely one of my new favorite authors of historical adventure. Intelligent and smooth prose--a really delightful read!"
>
> "If You Want to Go on a Great Adventure - This is it! I loved the story and ...it is obvious why this novel won an award".
>
> "Could not put it down! Very exciting story. The setting was realistic, the plot pulled you along (relentlessly!) and you really cared what happened to the characters."

Papyrus

Rika Teferi, a former soldier in Eritrea's war for independence, is working on her doctorate in the Cairo Museum when an accidental tea spill uncovers hidden writing on a papyrus written by Queen Tiye to her youngest son, Tutankhamun. Horrified at the spill but aching to read the entire secret text, Rika reluctantly agrees to let a visiting remote-sensing expert, David Chamberlain, smuggle the priceless papyrus out of the museum and scan it with instruments on his specialized aircraft. The results are stunning.

"*Torrent of a plot that has action and tension on every page.*"

"*I literally held my breath.*"

"*It's rare I find a thriller that takes me for a ride all the way to the last page.*"

"*It kept me up well past my bedtime.*"

"*A fantastic read and amazing work of art.*"

"*A truly incredible adventure into ancient Egypt and modern technology.*"

"*...thinking about the people and the events long after I turned the final page.*"

Aphrodesia

Great perfumes have always had one purpose—to seduce. Today, as in the past, a true aphrodisiac is the Holy Grail of the perfumer's art.

Eric Foster, a student at the world's top perfume school, creates a scent based on the fragrance the Queen of Sheba wore to seduce King Solomon. The result is an aphrodisiac of astonishing potency. But when his creation is tied to an outbreak of passion-driven homicides, Eric becomes the NYPD's prime suspect, facing a charge of serial murder.

"*I've never read anything like it, and highly doubt I'll ever find or read anything like it again. It's truly unique.*"

"*A really kick-ass story, and you'll get the bonus of some truly masterful writing.*"

"I had not read and finished a book in over 10 years. Yet, I started this one and couldn't put it down until I was done."

"You will never again look at perfume in the same way."

"What a page-turner. Although I had never thought much about perfume, I found the story of the industry fascinating, especially when the perfume in question was an aphrodisiac! On top of all that, the sex scenes were extremely erotic!"

"A delicious story."

Manufactured by Amazon.ca
Bolton, ON